Ryder Stephens

Veronica L Ventura

For Singapore Book Club.

CONTENTS

Gracias a la vida que me ha dado tanto
Me ha dado la risa y me ha dado el llanto
Asi yo distingo dicha de quebranto
los dos materiales que forman mi canto

Thank you to life, which has given me so much.
It gave me laughter, and it gave me tears.
With them, I distinguish happiness from pain,
the two elements that make up my song.

-Violeta Parra

PART ONE

CHAPTER ONE

Social service replaced the police, who replaced the ambulance, who had replaced my mom, and nobody came to take her place. My father never showed. Gone was the life we were meant to begin, and in came these people: officers, social workers, funeral clerks, more and different, and foreign and confusing. They crowded my life and crammed my thoughts, and nothing stopped me from seeing my mother's face.

And then she came, that woman with the same face, but wrinkled, a woman who took me by her arms only to hold me at their length. She nodded as if my presence now confirmed my existence. And then she barked orders to the funeral home, instructions to the movers. She authorized social services to take me away.

The funeral ruined everyone's Christmas, I heard them say. *Thank God, they got it done by Christmas Eve. Did you get the flight back? I still haven't wrapped the presents.* One by one, people I didn't know strolled out the synagogue's doors, chatting and laughing as if Samantha Stephen's life had only been a show.

"It'll be okay," a voice whispered in my ear.

It was Katherine's, the young and quiet social worker assigned to my case. Only she had the guts to stay by my side, to walk me away from the woman in the box, to hold my hand as she diverted my eyes.

I sat rod-straight in her car as it merged into the San Francisco traffic. Clenching my stomach when it lurched forward, then stopped, the need to vomit harder and harder to hold. We moved on, slowly picking up speed as we crossed the bridge to Oakland, the tires pulsing with each rivet they passed. Da-duh, da-duh, on repeat. A punishing thud. I covered my ears and focused ahead, watching the shipping cranes stretch their necks as if there was something worthy in life to see. A bird dove towards the water; a boat zoomed further away. Nobody wanted to be close to me.

Katherine steered away from it all, snaking into postal codes only meant for TV. I saw parks with weeds and graffiti on walls. Boys in baggy shorts crowded around a couch. "It'll be okay," she mumbled, repeating the only phrase she seemed to know. "We're here."

No. I clutched my hands between my knees, refusing to grab the handle that would toss me into this world. I wouldn't walk around the plastic toys littering the yard, wouldn't hear the screams of too many children circling the house.

Katherine inched up their walk, her measured steps contradicting her reassuring words. A door flew open.

"Get back here!" Shouted a woman in pursuit of a toddler. He was naked and filthy, with little streams running from his nose. I followed them into the streets, then whipped my attention to the old man coughing as he walked from around the side. His eyebrows were bushy and pants too loose; he wore suspenders that belonged to a farm or a rodeo or anyplace else besides a home.

He held out his hand, and Katherine's shoulders collapsed. "Mr. Smyth?" He nodded and then she sighed, grateful to finally unburden her load. She relinquished control, passing a sturdy binder to this tall and skinny foe.

"We'll hold onto that there violin, too" the old man said as if it were natural to break off a piece of someone's soul. "There's a time and a place for music. We prefer the music of the gospel. Do you know any Christian songs?" He asked, pointing to the portrait of Jesus hanging on the wall.

Katherine left, abandoning me in the middle of the afternoon with nothing but fear to guide me into the night.

Lonely, scared, and responsible, the burden of fault hit hard. It stole my grief and replaced it with guilt. For all the times I rolled my eyes and turned up the TV. For when I didn't thank her for picking me up, dropping me off, for making me dinner, I supposed I earned my penance tossing around this unfamiliar bed.

4

Unable to sleep, I inched towards the master bedroom, letting their spastic snores cover the sounds of my search. I slid open the closet, peaked into their bathroom. Making little headway, I hopped over a dog bed, and there it was. My violin thrown aside as if it were worth no more than an animal's toy. Cruel. Uncivilized.

I felt my way into the kitchen, tiptoeing over the laminate flooring that was old from wear and weathered from time. The sight of that binder sealing a decision I had already made. I filled one pocket with pink and white cookies, the other with a wad of cash. Both found in jars, both mine now.

Outside, I inhaled a breath of freedom then choked back the heartache of pursuing it alone. I ran. Pounding my feet hard against the pavement, I thought of the friends I missed, the life I needed. My chest heaved to catch up with the breaths that came from the sprint, from the sobs, from the confusion that pushed me down this nameless street. I clenched my eyes, and still, I saw their faces. My friends. Their looks changing from elation to confusion to question, wondering why, how. I couldn't go back to Seattle.

I needed to see my dad.

Rumbling and noisy, a means arrived, and I chased it down that dark and deserted street until risking more, I thrust my hand between its closing doors. "I need to go to another state."

Gruff, annoyed to be working this early the day after Christ was born, the bus driver flicked two fingers in the air before the doors converged.

"Two. I take the number two?" A nod, I think, and I waited because I didn't know what else there was to do.

The darkness around me was an unexpected calm, the approaching headlights a sudden worry. I pulled my hands out from under my arms and picked up my violin. Ready. "Can you tell me when we get to the main bus station?"

"You mean the Greyhound terminal?" Kinder, this bus driver waited for me to find a seat before putting the bus in gear.

I sat in the front row passenger side nervous about missing my stop, of not missing it. "I'm going to see my father in Las Vegas."

The signal light flashed left.

A child alone, boarding a bus at the break of dawn on the day after Christmas, who clutched a violin and shouldered a backpack. She was heading to the Greyhound bus terminal to buy a ticket to take her to the city of sin, and all he could say was, "Good for you."

Too involved in their own lives, all of them, the entire world. This bus driver had one duty to fulfill, to drive in circles and pick up people who needed to be someplace else. Katherine was tasked to do the same: drop off the girl orphaned by death. She was ordered to settle yet another kid rejected by their father.

"Temporary," Katherine said. "Until we can find a more permanent placement. We'll find you a familiar home."

No. I had a permanent home, already familiar, with my father. Katherine, you didn't understand. He was just sick or injured or caught up in work. I knew my father. He might not be a man who cheered on the sidelines or sat through his daughter's concerts, but he was a man who cared about his family, about his wife, about his *only* child. Somebody just didn't tell him the facts. That was all!

"He's at the Bellagio again. They comped him a room," the memory of mother's voice rang loud in my head. She had sat me down the night he didn't show, explained why he was in Vegas instead of San Francisco, how he would come later, why there was nothing to worry about. Calm and soothing, when she wandered over to the desk to do whatever it was that she needed to do, I let her be. Only now could I see all that I missed, all that she hid.

Driven by panic, once that bus arrived in Las Vegas, I shoved my way through the crowd, zeroing in on the fountains and colors of the Bellagio's show. I flung open the door. People everywhere laughed, doubling over, an entire world unburdened by grief. I swiveled my head from side to side, searching for my father, for the security, for an end to this nightmare that wouldn't stop. Nothing.

I stepped towards the slot machines. No, he liked card games, my mother's uninvited voice reminding me. I spun, heading for the rows of tables. Futile. How did I think I could walk into a room crowded with hundreds, in a city jammed with thousands, and find the man who gave me life?

A hand gripped my shoulder. "Sorry, kid, you need to be twenty-one to be on the floor."

I swallowed, my day traveling in silence making it hard to speak. "Um, I'm not going to gamble." I shifted my feet, which only revealed my innocent ways. "I just need to find my father. His phone's turned off."

The guard sighed, a tell-tale sign to indicate how many times he had done this before. "What does he like to play?"

"Blackjack." Another pearl from a woman who was no more. I followed his finger, which pointed left. "I'll walk with you and let you have a look."

But he need not bother. Up ahead was a man who stood tall because he knew the way to succeed, who raised his fist in the air because he knew how to win. From behind, I smothered him in a hug.

"What the…"

A stranger's face mocked mine, his hands shoving me away. A vulgar mouth poured insults into my open wound.

Heat rushed to my head. "Sorry, sorry." And I crashed into the security guard, dropping my violin case with an unforgiving bang. "Sorry, sorry." I anchored my foot, ready to bolt.

"Hold on there, young buck." The guard's teeth clenched into a brazen grin. "Why don't I just help you to call your mom?" My heart shattered into a million pieces, tumbling to my feet faster than I could run for the door.

Outside, a Santa Clause crossed my path, his dinging bell out of sync with time and reason. Christmas had passed, along with my chance. My stomach growled; my hands shook. With my senses overpowered, I lost control.

"What the fuck are you doing here?"

Horns and chimes, and cheers and drunkenness—too much to process. I caught my breath; surely, I heard that wrong. I worked my way back through the revolving door, following the familiar voice. "Dad?" The button-down was rumpled, but the colors I knew: sea-blue stripes, sea-blue eyes. "Dad?" Closing in, I tripped on his heels.

That same security guard slipped between me and the man who would never break my heart.

My father thrust his chest forward, commanding the authority I knew he had. "You're supposed to be inahome." They hung there, the words that slurred together. He swayed, then braced himself against the guard. His hand slipped, falling inside the guard's collar, which lassoed his neck, which forced a gag. Snickers, people laughing at my dad. The guard pushed him off. He fell. "I said watthehell you doin' here?" Drool collected beneath his lip.

I buckled, crumpling against this hardened guard.

My father's vacant face slowly wilted. "Go!" And then he climbed back to his feet, which pointed wrong. "Go." The repeat command was weak, muffled by the unforgivable distance growing between this reckless parent and his orphaned child.

He gave up his kid for drugs. Willingly, and without remorse or sympathy or—I looked again over my shoulder to see a different ending. Laughter and bells and no, the agony of betrayal slammed into the torment of grief. Bastard!

Too hurt to cry, I ran. Never stopping. By the time I reached that filthy, smelly blob of a building they called a bus terminal, the only thing I knew as fact was how far I needed to get away. I called the long shot. And with all of seconds behind my decision, I mimicked my father and tossed bills at the agent. I would travel twenty-five hundred miles in fifty-nine hours. I could go no further than New York.

CHAPTER TWO

The city of dreams would replace that city of sin. What would happen, how I should dress, where I should buy my food, perhaps something I should have considered before boarding that bus. But if I kept my eyes pointed earth-bound, and raised my voice no louder than a mouse, maybe even I wouldn't notice my trembling hands.

Maybe.

Because each time courage came, when I opened my eye a sliver, curious bystanders judged. From where, they asked. Alone? Your parents are where? I could barely squeeze together the lies to make them stop.

A grey-haired woman walking down the aisle flicked the hood of my raincoat, it's thin plastic shell dimpling from her touch. "You're going to NYC at this time of year in *that?*" I got spooked, then stammered, and came within seconds of giving myself away.

"She's with me." A teenage girl leaned across the aisle. "Yep, sorry, we just thought we'd get lucky with a free seat between us." Dumping herself into the empty seat, she started talking without knowing how to stop. Her finger pointed as if lecturing from a pulpit. It tapped on a spiral notebook cradled in her lap. Educating and inspiring, her answers to the few questions I asked were long, and I hung my mouth as she spoke, taking in the coolness of her vibe.

Her name was Rubi, and she navigated the minefield of life on the run with the ease of an experienced pro. She had ripped jeans, with blond hair streaked pink in front and purple underneath; such confidence toyed with mine. "You're free now, Ryder. No more adults tramplin' your dreams. You made the right choice to run, for sure."

I'd told her nothing about why I was sitting next to her on a Greyhound bus, or why I was alone; nothing about how I had no clue what to do when I got to New York. But she put words in my mouth, creating nicely packaged lies. I rehearsed them as she spoke, and I spoke them when she stopped.

"Yes, Rubi, my parents sent me to live with my grandmother when I didn't want to." A lie. "Yes, Rubi, they do drugs too, just like yours." Yes, yes, more lies, yes. I repackaged her story into a future past life.

A bulleted list came next. "Gyms. Ryder, they're open twenty-four-hours, seven days a week. Get yourself a membership and voila! You have a shower, soap—they even have lockers."

I glued my eyes to the page torn from her notebook, to the shadowed boxes running down the margin: stay in well-lit areas, never walk alone, *buses*, underlined and emboldened.

"They run around the clock." Her pink pencil moved back to the top of her list. "But gyms: stay clean, use their Wi-Fi, and if you stay there, you're much less likely to wake up with a knife in your side or your wallet gone."

I suspect now I should have seen the difference between her and me, that her four extra years were lessons from failure, that when she talked of metal detectors in her schools, and police walking its halls, that she was nothing like me. But I didn't want to wake up with a knife in my side, and I needed the wallet stuffed into my pocket. So, I asked more and nodded nervously because I didn't even know that these were the answers to the questions I didn't ask.

And all of that helped me how?

Standing on the puddled pavement of this New York City street, watching that bus with its warm interior crawl away, I clutched my arms. An icy blast penetrated my jacket as if it were paper, and I cursed that wretched know-it-all for chucking me into this arctic blast. It was her fault that I was curled into a ball, tucked under an awning.

"I killed it by hawking sketches on the street, Ryder," she had bragged, brazenly plucking my violin cradled protectively in my arms. "You have that violin, do something with it beside Googling pictures of that New York Music Group. If you think you're that good, then just unload on the streets. Pop the case, and watch the bills fly!"

Watch what bills fly? From who? The storm that had frozen my thoughts drained these streets and only the howling wind stayed to take part in my misery. What did she know about the harsh reality of New York City's life-terminating winter or its earth-shattering prices? Rubi, the wronged! "Life is better on the streets, you'll see." Yeah, right.

***

Having lived in this city for four days now, what hadn't worked out burned out, and everything withdrew its welcome. The NY subways that had allowed for three nights of sheltered sleep, the coffee shops offering a warm place to hide. Those that had a place to go grew wise to the habits of those that didn't. Off. Go. Out.

Forget about the gyms, no membership offered without a credit card. And *buses*, they dropped you off in shadowy streets where creepy old men stood too close.

I walked, following the specks of gum littering the pavement, searching for a recognizable shape. A paw print, maybe, or an arrow; no, a gun. I moved my right shoe from one black stain to another, and when no clear pattern emerged, I knew it. I failed again.

"Stand under the awning, for Christ's sake. It's pouring out," a stranger's voice shouted at me from afar.

I ignored it because I deserved to shiver and freeze, to inflict discomfort as punishment for all my mistakes. I needed the rain to trickle down my face and hide my tears. Nervous and compulsive, I crisscrossed my Converse All-Stars so fast muddy water oozed through the metal-rimmed holes. One foot landed on the loose lace of the other and yanked it free.

Tie it right, Ryder.

I jammed my hands against my ears to block the memory of her voice. No, Mom! I won't tie it at all.

"Are you stupid or something?" The man shouted louder to penetrate my muffled ears. "You're bleeding. Come here!"

The wind tossed a bucket of rain into my side, and I willed my feet to move, to make the misery stop, to reach for the protection this man had found, but I just shuffled: one foot crushing the other.

"Stop doing that."

Authority had taken over his request, and being an obedient child, I separated my feet, planting them shoulder's width apart.

"Not that, stop picking at your hand and come stand under the shelter."

I was doing it again. "It's okay."

"You're peeling your skin off. It's not okay."

It was. And if picking at scabs on my palms granted my mind a moment's rest, then I should be allowed to do it. I was not his problem. I wasn't anybody's problem.

"Here comes the number seven. What bus are you waiting for?"

The one that made you warm. Stupid question. And I would ride it until it stopped at any door that didn't lock, in front of a place without a guard. I would stay there until I heard that dreaded alarm: *Hey, kid.*

The wind echoed again, reverberating against the bus stop barrier this loudmouthed man had slid behind. Yet another adult who feigned compassion only to drop from sight when the effort proved too much.

The bus arrived and I leaped in front of him, showing that I, too, at the age of thirteen, had mastered arrogance.

"Move it," he yelled as we boarded, forgetting he just pretended to be my friend. "You should buy a MetroCard. It's faster. I'm getting soaked out here. Move onto the bus!"

"I don't have enough money for a MetroCard!"

The bus driver looked down from her perch to lend me the sympathy I desperately needed. "Girlfriend, it's okay, take your time." Dimpled and plump, this woman's smile connected me to a time when life wasn't so cruel. "Honey, you just count out the coins and find a dry seat on the bus." She winked, waiting patiently for me to pick up the rain-soaked coins that had slid between my beet-red fingers.

"Jesus," the man barked as the doors closed on him and his impatient ways, the driver holding the lever that would free him only on her command. He pushed and shoved, and she lowered her other hand to pass me the coins I had just passed to her.

"Thank you," I said no louder than that mouse trapped under a bucket. Too weak to express my gratitude properly, I barely lifted my limp hand away from my side. One dollar was all it would take for the deposit on a new MetroCard, and I couldn't spare it, my rumbling stomach reminding me why.

A shove from the hostile man pushed me deeper into the bus, past the soot-stained windows complicating the kaleidoscope of colors flashing behind. A kid rubbed a circle to expose a party. Confetti and lights, banners declaring *Auld Lang Syne*. Two days had passed since the year turned over, and while the rest of the world reinvented their resolutions, all I wanted was to stay alive.

The bus lurched forward, sending me unexpectedly down the aisle. My backpack swung wide, hitting an old lady settling into her seat. The violin slipped, my wet hands no match for the shifting gears. "I'm sorry. I'm sorry." And nobody cared.

I missed her.

She would have told me where to sit on this unrecognizable bus in this unfamiliar city, told me to not think about the noxious smell, or better yet, made fun of it. She would have prodded me to guess what this dirt-stained bus reminded me of, and I would have offered a movie, one that I could picture in my mind, but couldn't quite remember. I would have struggled, and brooded over who was in it, what it was titled, or whether I even liked it. She would have known which one I meant.

A flash, an image. I hated her.

And the weight of that conflict pushed on me as if it were the ocean. Still, I was diligent and industrious and wronged and angry, and when my life just up and vanished; when nobody I trusted stepped up to the plate; when caring for me became an inconvenient choice, what choice did I have?

A paper cone with a plastic whistle was wedged between two open seats, its multi-colored streamers spread out evenly from side to side. Such symmetry calmed my raging nerves.

"Are you gonna sit or what?" The cone squashed beneath my violin. "Move that," the cruel man blared.

He chucked my violin into my lap, forcing the backpack between my knees. Pressed tight against the window, I distanced myself from his scent by scrubbing a hole and watching those city lights rush past in streams. A city too crazy to comprehend, yellow merged to orange, red to white.

The man grasped the handle in front of us, pulling my focus away from the hysteria outside. Ratty and overused, his hand wore a silver ring with a large gold nugget at its core. It was the shape of an animal—two lions, maybe. I tipped towards it to get a better view.

"Mind your own fucking business," he growled.

I supposed I knew what would come next, that the thing I

desired would turn against me, that because I had sought out warmth, now the heat would suffocate. No room to shed my jacket, I squirmed.

"Jesus Christ. What the fuck is wrong with you?"

The bus driver adjusted the rearview mirror so that the reflection captured her concern, and I saw my eyebrows tent. Darting from view, I picked yet another scab, ripping it from its base. Blood oozed freely.

Ryder, treat your hands with respect.

I wiped the blood onto my only pair of jeans. Do not tell me what to do! No longer would my mother give me advice. She lost the right. The bus driver offered more than *that* woman ever could.

Hyperventilating from the anger of that memory, the fear from this heartless man, of the asphyxiating heat. The battling lions loomed closer. I stood.

"What the fuck now?"

"I missed my stop."

He swung his legs into the aisle, giving me too little room to squeeze past. I stumbled over my backpack and fell into his lap.

"Oh, so that's how you want to play it."

Panicked, I shot upright. Then, against all rational thought, I reached over him to grab my violin.

"What's in this thing?"

"It's mine." No. It was me. This violin created the person suddenly commanding courage. "Leave me alone."

The rearview still pointed wrong, and a knowing nod told me this bus driver had reached her verdict. When the bus door opened, I leaped headfirst into the unforgiving rain. Nobody could consider me lost.

The bus crept beside me, refusing to accelerate. The front door swiveled, and blasphemous shouts came from the passengers begging to keep warm. "You get home now and put something warm in your belly, you hear?" Her voice was light and upbeat as if we were strolling in Central Park on a sunny afternoon. "It's too cold to be outside without a hat." An undeniable fact reinforced by the icy vortex swirling around. "Your mama—"

Spinning 180 degrees, I braced myself for nature's assault and refused this kind but curious woman the space to speak. The wind punished me for my sins and shoved me into a wall.

Huddled under a doorway, I pulled out my phone and stared at the black screen. Nobody had texted, not a soul called. Not even Katherine. Did she even have my number? My thumb triggered the sensor, which opened the last App searched: Google Maps. A blue dot pulsed, telling me where I was. And close but a million miles away, the red teardrop tapered to the place I wanted to be. I scoffed. A location set four days ago on the day I arrived. Carnegie Hall. Who was I to think I could just stroll in and ask for an audition?

Yet, the pull was strong, a dream planted by my mother, who held onto it as her own. Her passion permeated my childhood, which riddled me with guilt. I pinched open the map, and the landmarks crystallized, the building's name sharpened: *Carnegie Hall, World-renowned classical music hall,* it read. The illustrious home of the Itzhak Perlman stage. My hero.

I chewed at the wounds on my hands, my teeth gnawing at the scab so recently formed. The more I thought about doing this alone, the harder I bit; the harder I bit, the more I suppressed. The blood trickled down my palm.

"Go to the hospital." The voice was deep, a man; his shoes were new. "Go to the hospital and pretend yous sick." *Yous:* my breathing grew shallow, restricting all movement. "If ya do it right, tonight, ya got youself a bed."

Bed. I rolled my eyes up to his hands, which were casually pocketed in his jeans.

"Just give 'em a bogus phone number for your toads, and then vomit. They'd be whiskin' you in, givin' you a bed, an IV, and drugs that will make ya forget who'd be in the White House." His bright smile contrasted sharply against his dark-toned skin. "When ya wake up, just aks for a bathroom and bolt before they can aks ya for i-den-ti-fi-ca-tion." He enunciated it like he invented the word.

Shaggy, but kempt, he smelled like Dove. The man sitting next to me on the bus reeked of cigarettes, and I pressed myself against the window to create a space. This man smelled like soap, and I rose to my feet to quiz him for answers. "How do I make myself vomit?"

"You serious?" His laugh—whose did it sound like? "That be street-life 101."

"What's 101?"

"What's 101?" Arching his back, he threw his face over his shoulder. "Ooohhhh, girl."

15

Donkey, in Shrek. That was who.

"What grade are ya in?"

Should I lie?

"Don't lie now."

The way he tilted his head and scrunched his long bushy eyebrows made me grin from the similarity. Seven of my fingers waved in the air, which he pointed to individually and then counted. Out loud.

"Seven. Seventh grade, huh?" His eyes rolled upward and to the left. *Left rollers are truth-tellers: right rollers are liars*: my mother's method.

"Yeah, maybe I didn't know what 101 was until I started ditching those classes in high school. Ya got youself a reprieve, but you gonna have to step up your game if you're gonna make it on the streets."

"I don't live on the streets."

Never let people know you're weak. Rubi's reasoning rang in my head.

"The hell you don't. *Par-don* my French." His satchel opened, and rummaging occurred, too long to worry whether he was searching for a gun. A small package of tissues came forth, of which he handed me one and pulled another for himself. "Relax."

Trust your gut, but also trust people who know the streets. They've been there.

"First things first, this cover ain't no good. How much money you got?"

My pulse surged; Rubi's reassurance vanished. I dove my hand into my front pocket, guarding the one hundred and two dollars I had left to my name.

"Look, ya have no reason to trust me. I get it. I'm homeless too."

Backing away, raising my hands like Wonder Woman before a fight, I spoke with a calm I neither possessed nor expressed. "You don't look homeless."

"Steady, kid. Look, I'll back away too. Truth be told, you kind of stink, and I'm afraid of people who stink."

What? I ground to a halt. Tucking my nose into my jacket, I inhaled and gagged. "Jesus." More annoyed than embarrassed that this homeless, degenerate of a man presented himself to the world in a more pleasing way than me, it affronted my sense of order.

"Why don't *you* stink? I mean, if you're homeless and all, like you say, where are you taking a shower?"

"The Bowery." Deadpan look. "Kid, listen, it's a place that gives clothes and showers to the homeless." His glistening white shoes did a little dance. "Nice, huh? And theys totally comfy."

"You don't talk homeless." Complimenting him on false pretenses seemed like something Wonder Woman would do.

"Nice stereotyping. Ya know what that is?"

Please. Third-grade curriculum. I knew pre-algebra, all the constitutional amendments, the fifty state capitals in alphabetical order. I knew that Anne Frank hid in an attic and that Harriot Beecher Stowe wrote Uncle Tom's Cabin.

He squatted to double knot his sparkling white sneaker.

And none of it helped. I bent to meet his eye, Google map's red teardrop forefront in my mind. *Carnegie Hall, World-renowned.* "Um, how can I get a shower? You see, I have this *really* important audition tomorrow, and I can't look or smell like this."

"Oh, I see. So, yous come to the Big Apple to be a star."

I scrunched my lips into a contemptuous line—my Draco Malfoy stare.

"Ah." His hands exploded in a poof above his head. "I see it now, your name in lights. Kid, go home. Ain't nobody gonna make you a star."

Lasers shot from my eyes. Birdbrain. I didn't need Rubi's confidence to stare down this man. I was already a star, already won first place in the Concerto Competition at Interlochen, already sat second-chair, first-violin in the Seattle Youth Symphony. I had a drawer full of frickin' medals.

Still raised high in the air, his hands arrogantly clapped. "I'll give you this, kid, ya have a look of confidence that might get ya in a door. But after that, and after all them others follow ya through that same revolving door, you be toast. Go home, my friend."

With my hands locked on my hips, I took back the two steps I lost when he only made me scared. "Assumptions make an 'ass' of 'u' and 'me.' Do you get that? A-S-S-U-M-E."

"Kid, do you want a shower or not?"

Oh, yeah, I stepped closer.

"Second thing," he lectured, relaxing his voice. "Don't trust me. Don't trust nobody. You was gonna to split with me to a place ya knew nothin' about, to ful-fill the possibility of somethin' I know ya needed." His head shook as if to erase my error from his thoughts. "Promise me that ya won't do that again."

The wind picked up, and I tucked my face into my jacket, something I immediately regretted. "So, no shower then."

I followed his finger down the street, which drew my attention to a light flickering in front of a school.

"Walk right past it and turn left at the next light."

"They'll just let me in?"

"No, they probably turn ya over to the authorities, unless yous come up with something good to say and quick."

The ocean smell from his recent bath complicated my judgment. "You're my father."

"Whoa." Giving back the two steps I reclaimed, he retreated too fast and crossed over the point of protection. "Damn, it's wet out here. Move closer to the building, so I have me some space under this pathetic excuse for a cover." The wind rushed through in a whirlwind of destruction, and we crouched close to block its brutal force. "Listen here," he said, jamming my chest with his finger, "I ain't nobody's father."

"For one day, one night. Just tell them I'm your kid."

"I was just there. Think they might get suspicious, especially, ya know, with me black and yous white. We'd need documentation."

And from my oversized pack came the unexpected treasure— the binder I snagged off the counter before I ran, the one I adorned with Rubi's pink pencil. I accurately labeled it *My life*.

"You ran away with documentation?"

Bewildered by this man's ignorance, I shook my head. Of course, I ran away with documentation. Page one: my birth certificate; page two: my school report cards; three: my vaccination records; four through ten: my awards and certificates from all the violin achievements, and finally, page eleven: her death certificate.

His widening eyes smoothed out those little lines that had crested across his brow. "What kind of kid are you? I don't even have that stuff, and I'm thirty-six."

Perhaps the reason why he was homeless. I continued to feign competence in the ways of resurrecting a life until his eyes softened, confirming the hoax a success. If I had actually put this packet together, I would have scrapped the last page and shifted my awards front and center, followed, no doubt, by my perfect grades. But I didn't, Katherine the social worker did.

"Looks like ya have everything in there to start school. You plannin' on goin' to school, aren't ya?" He poked me in the chest again, hard enough this time to hear the thud.

I felt terrible about leaving Katherine. She was the only one who never asked the hard questions, never rushed her words, never pretended what happened wouldn't stay with me forever.

"Hey," he said, poking me again, but this time with enough warning that I mastered the dodge. "Focus: I was aksin' if you was goin' to school?" With my inch-thick binder buried in his lap, he carelessly tossed the pages back and forth. "Ah, wait, ya got a problem." He stopped, his raised eyebrows indicating that he, too, could be suspicious of ignorance. "No proof of address." The binder now received a thump from that same ungloved hand. "Won't let ya into school without no proof of address."

I pulled it close and began the fastidious task of ironing out the creases now desecrating my past. I had thought about school, tangentially, but what was more important? Carnegie Hall or school?

"Hey, you a drifter, aren't ya? Stay the course. Ya know what ya need to do?"

Of course, I didn't, but I pinned my shoulders back anyway.

"Right—" not buying it— "so, here's the deal. Let say ya want to go to that school right there."

"Is it a good one? I only want to go to a good school."

"Jesus, kid, yous something else. Look at youself, tucked into a crevice with a thirty-six-year-old homeless man beggin' him to pretend to be your father so you can score a shower in a shelter. Take the ego down a notch, alright, then take stock of what your life has become."

That mouse jumped back under the bucket, and his ear, red as his running nose, moved closer to my lips. "Can you help me?" I asked.

"Where yous stayin' tonight?" The streetlights flickered, casting a menacing shadow over his cryptic words. "Look, kid." His hands raised in surrender. "I mean ya no harm. I know a guy who will rent a cot in the corner of a four-story walk-up for fifty bucks a week. You got that?"

I traced over the thin stack of bills crumpled in my pocket. "Is it safe?"

"No, nothin's safe. I told you that." No poke, just an extended finger. "*You* stay there, *you* watch your back. *You* don't leave your po-ssessions, nothin', especially that sure to be valuable violin ya got. *You* hear me?" By the end of his sermon, four fingers waved an inch from my face.

"Why are you helping me?"

"Because our kind helps each other. It's all we got."

Our kind.

How did I become *this* kind? I was normal, a kid from a good home, who went to a great school, with friends. A kid who worried about boys and gossip, not showers and rent. But my mother undid that when she left me alone in San Francisco. My father destroyed that when he rejected me in Las Vegas. And Katherine didn't try to change it when she whisked me from the funeral home to abandon me at the door of that foster family. That horrible day I began my slide into *this* kind.

Katherine told me to stay. "I know it's Christmas Day, and this is hard," she said. "But it's only been a few days since your mother died. Promise me you'll give it a chance." She asked for patience. I gave her none.

Those foster people were not *my* kind. I knew that the moment I unwrapped my only present and stared into the face of the Bible. "This is all you need to get you through such a terrible time," they said. "Let us pray."

No.

"It's on the other side of town. Follow me onto this bus."

"Huh?"

"Jesus, kid, yous obviously distracted. I get that, but I'm freezin' my ass off out here. So, *yous* either focus and let me help or yous on your own."

Trust left me long before this man reminded me not to, and no amount of tugging at my arm would move my feet.

"There are thirty other people on the bus. How much damage could I do?"

In India, people got raped on crowded buses. A quick spin to take in my surroundings was meant to push that thought aside. It didn't. Still, I found myself sitting next to a man whose name I never learned. My only friend in New York.

CHAPTER THREE

It was a different bus, but the same bus, the smell was sour. And still, I couldn't remember the name of the movie it was meant to remind me of. I looked at my new friend, at his old stained jacket mismatched against his bright white shoes, and I missed her all over again.

"Yous got a smartphone?" this homeless man asked.

A cracked Blackberry was clutched in the hands of the man to our left. An old Motorola was two seats ahead.

"One with internet?"

I saw a cheap iPod nano, a paperback, crumpled newspapers, and he wanted me to dig out the latest model of the most expensive iPhone. His snapping fingers hastened a foolish decision.

"Nice!"

When he flipped it over, I casually pushed my mother's iPad Pro deeper into my bag. Katherine had handed it to me at the funeral, maybe thinking it was mine. I didn't ask her where she got it or why. I just punched in the six-digit passcode I wasn't supposed to know and hid.

"This thing got money on it?"

Huh?

"Jesus, snap out of it. Does your phone have credit?"

The phone worked. Was that what he meant? Death did not extend to living plastic. My mother's credit card was as useful as it was active. Tied to iTunes, contracted with AT&T, if she only had set up the Apple Pay.

"You have a pop?"

He wanted a soda?

"The guy listed on that birth certificate in that binder of yours, that Max Stephens. He still alive?"

My next breath came as a gasp.

"I'll take that as a yes. "Google his name and find out if there be somebody else with the same name in Manhattan." I had yet to unlock the phone. "Kid, do—what's your name anyway?"

"My name is Ryder, Ryder Stephens." It was on my birth certificate, report cards, on all my awards. He noticed my dad's name, but not mine.

His sexist finger jabbed the home button. "Type."

Doing as told, my thumbs danced across the keypad as delicately as my fingertips marched up the neck of my violin. The act brought a moment's pleasure. Typing duped my mind into pretending I was flattening a string to create that magical sound. If I just could figure out how to audition, everything would be okay. I could play. I would forget. Life would be better again. "I need a shower."

"Kid, Ryder, what you need to do is concentrate. Hit Search." And there it was: not one but three Max Stephens right here in Manhattan.

"Why do I care about this?"

"Because you need to steal his mail."

What?

Never discount the lessons learned from rethinking a stereotype. This nameless man taught me more on that bus ride across mid-town than any teacher in school ever could. Kudos to him and his teaching style for the practical and relevant payoff. Either that or credit to my parents for keeping me out of situations where I needed this education.

Street cred, 101. Lying was crucial because nobody wanted to hear your story. Stories were excuses for those who had enough to survive, and excuses were curses for all of us trying to make a comeback.

"Yous at the bottom of a hole looking up, ain't nobody gonna come down to get ya. *You* have to convince them it's worth their time to throw a rope. Got it?"

Got it, and once I had that rope, I was to hold tight, climb to the surface, and then steal that very rope that rescued me from uncertainty.

"Once yous on a level playing field, everyone will walk away. Got it?"

Got it, equity was not equality. The short man could not see over the same fence as the tall man. Sometimes, one must acquire a box to have the same visual.

"Got it?"

Got it. If nobody gave you a box, 'acquire' it. Subsidize equality to make equity. Lesson learned.

We exited the bus and walked six miserable blocks through a freezing wind that turned the rain into a weapon. And when we arrived at his destination, I stepped over the broken glass sprinkling the sidewalk and tried to ignore the garbage rotting outside the door.

"Trust me," my escort urged.

I didn't, but still, somehow, he persuaded me to hand over half my remaining assets to my new, twenty-eight-year-old landlord, Levi. Fifty dollars paid on Monday, January 2nd, guaranteed a disgusting but dry place to call home until Monday, January 9th.

Feeling cheated, I stole three pieces of chocolate off his bed.

"Don't do that again!" Contradicting himself, my nameless friend lectured again. "You steal from him; bad things will happen. Got it?"

Got it. I never stole again, from him.

"That cot's yours." Levi kicked a green cot like they had in army movies, which jammed it further into its corner, its polyester purple sheet slipping onto the floor. There was no pillow. "I'd wash those sheets before you sleep on 'em."

I swung my head to his voice and then back to my designated spot. Grocery store baskets—the type used for oranges—were stacked tenuously one on top of each other. A single chemistry jar with a slender tube rising from the top and a tinier one jutting from its side sat on the middle shelf. I reached. A slap hit hard.

"Unless you have the means to pay for the privilege, no handlin' the hookah." A clueless nod probably gave me away.

"Alrighty there, young lass, yous in good hands."

"You're leaving?"

"Gots my own crib to crawl back to tonight. Tuck into yours so yous ready for your big day tomorrow." An eye roll between the two men ended in laughter. "Au-di-tion." Their hands met mid-air. "If you can make it here, go home, kid." And as he sauntered out, his finger flipped the switch, sending the room into total darkness.

"Sweet dreams, boy and girl."

Hardly possible.

"You better not snore, kid," Levi groaned.

I crawled fully clothed onto the cot, on top of the sheet that needed to be washed. Curled into a ball, with my arms pulled tight to my chest, I smelled chocolate, a residue left from my first mistake. *You steal from him, bad things happen.* I licked my palm until the sweetness turned to salt and spooned my backpack until my arms turned numb from its weight.

A distant bedspring creaked.

Darling, come here. I needed her now. *We should take in the sights before your school starts in the New Year.* A paralyzing comfort; no, a craved regret. I forced her voice away and then yearned to hear it ten-times louder. *Let's go here. It's a must-see in San Francisco.* Heartless, why was I so cruel? *No, Mom, you always want to do boring things, gloomy things. Nobody visits a prison on purpose!* Hurt crisscrossed her face, and still, I walked away from her endless anxiety, her restlessness, from her suffocating needs.

Alcatraz Island, where the lonely got lonelier, where they locked our tour up in solitary confinement. Where I couldn't see my hand, couldn't find my mom—where I panicked. *I'm right behind you, sweetheart. I'm not going anywhere.* She lied. Two days we had lived in that city; two days later, she would be dead.

A lighter flashed, bubbles gurgled, and a noxious scent filled this haunted room. A cough, then silence. It filled the night only because sleep could not. Each time my lids sealed, my nameless friend threw them wide open. *Take the ego down a notch. Take stock in what your life has become.* Perhaps I drifted off between the racing worries. Probably not. All I knew was that once that sun peeked around the edge of the curtain, I could see my hand—a fraction of what was needed to gain control.

Punching in the address of my father's clone, another blue dot led my way. Grateful that each step took me farther away from Levi, nothing could separate me from the odor that followed. *Gyms, Ryder, free showers.* No, Rubi, not free. I opened the door to the place with the Golden Arch.

Rough paper towels, city water, and cheap liquid soap were all that were needed to staunch the stench steaming from under my arms. Maybe, because by the time they made it to my body in a single unit, all that remained were congealed balls of tissue not worthy of the job. I splashed water over my naked body, even contemplated using the toilet bowl as an easier means to the end. Not there *yet*, I went back to the sink and the paper towels and the fruitless effort this was all becoming.

"Hey, kid!" A knock, the call to arms.

I slipped a too-thin dress out of my bag and yanked it over my too-thin body. Tomorrow maybe, I would look for the courage to use the shower in my new—for lack of a better word—home.

I checked my hair in the first window I passed, my clothes in the second. By the end of the street, I knew I could play the part. All mail people were the same, I told myself. Just like in Seattle— the only home I really knew. The person carrying the mail was tired, burdened, and eager to relieve themselves of their load.

"Can I help you?" So, how come it was that I couldn't find the words? "You okay, hun'?" I hung my mouth with the lie that refused to exit. "Are you waiting for a late Christmas present?" Nothing. "Which house is yours?" I pointed to where the internet told me to go. "Maximillian Stephens?" I nodded. "Here, ya go."

Complicit by way of ignorance, she handed me a stack of mail: a Christmas card, an electric bill, an advertisement for housing, something from T-Mobile, more. I rounded the corner, wedging myself between a dumpster and a fence, and silently ripped them open. "Please, God, let this be the beginning of a perfect day."

Proof of residency on multiple fronts, I closed my eyes and slowed my breathing. Justice. And when I opened them, the fattest raindrop I'd ever seen landed right in the middle of the page.

***

"The gaps in your application need to be addressed."

What was I thinking? Elated from my luck stealing the mail, driven by the mocking from that homeless man, I confidently punched wrongful facts into the online application for the NY youth symphony. Then, with everything to lose, I swaggered into the building where the red teardrop landed.

"You're almost there, but unfortunately, section A needs to be completed before we can proceed." This receptionist was kind, too welcoming, too much of a grown-up for the child in me to process.

I froze, and my Fitbit changed its instructions to *exhale*. But I didn't do that. No. I ran away fast, hiding in the first alley I saw. Defeated by my own conscience, I crouched under yet another awning and bit my nail, then finger, eventually working my anxiety out on my palm.

I rose to my feet even though my legs still shook. Feeling

lightheaded from falling so suddenly from heights too tall, I bumped into person after person, into people who had other people. The subway stairs headed down; a bus stopped at the corner; my stomach grumbled. By foot or transport? I took the stairs, squeezing my violin tight against my back, my pack growing heavier with each step down. A man opened the emergency exit for a woman carrying too many boxes. A free ride came next.

I reached my sanctuary without spending a dime. This hovel, dark and grimy as it was, welcomed me into its warm and paid for arms. Glad to be alone, I inhaled a less than cleansing breath, then choked back a more than noxious gag. Somebody had left the bathroom door ajar. Fifty dollars I paid to live in such squalor. How could I live here when I belonged there, at Carnegie Hall?

Suddenly, a force tossed me forward, pushing me further into the empty room. "What up with her?"

The voice accented, an odor swallowing me whole, I tensed before clenching my fists tight. The man moved towards me, a chain somewhere on his body rattling fiercely with each step he took. He grabbed my shoulder and spun me around. A boy. Just a rootless child pretending just like me.

His arm swung behind, and a clump of bills dropped from his tattooed fingers. Levi caught it mid-air, deftly refilling the boy's palm with something wrong.

"Got me a new weekly renter." Levi flicked my chin. "Money up in five days, my love."

"If I could spare it, I'd loan out my services." That slimy boy grabbed himself in a gesture I only somewhat understood, one that they did in music videos where kissing came before rubbing, which came before—I stumbled into the hall. Shadows spoke; I darted back towards the room, then out.

"Leave her alone." Levi tossed the wad of cash onto his futon, then stepped between me and this beast of a boy.

"Ah, I'm just dickin' with you, hot stuff. My name's Miguel." Playfully elbowing Levi aside, he held out that grime-covered hand, pimples filled the spaces where his wispy beard could not. "What, too good to slip some skin?" Levi shoved him through the open door. But he returned too quick, with more of his groin filling his hand. "Anytime, Sweetheart, just name the place."

No longer did I fight his meaning. He left, but not before my heart beat through my ears.

"Look." I jumped. "Chill. Yeah, I get it. You don't have the fifty bucks." Levi smoothed out Miguel's wrinkled cash, rolling it into a tube, and arrogantly snapping a rubber band around its core. "There are ways to get it." I grabbed the doorjamb, bracing myself. "Come here."

I stiffened, Miguel's gesture replaying ominously in my head. "Whatever." Kneeling on his tattered futon, his slouching shoulders were just as indifferent as his empty eyes. He rammed his finger against the glass. "Her."

All I saw was a kid sitting in a café slurping something definitely delicious from a plastic cup.

"She's about your age, and white, which is hard to come by in these parts."

It looked chocolatey, with a cone of whipped cream spiraled on top.

"Her bag! See it?"

Oh, and chocolate chips, too! A little puddle of saliva pooled inside my lip. "I don't like it. Not my style."

"Oh, my God! It's not the bag you're after, numbnuts, it's the contents: her ID, her money, whatever else you can pawn across town."

Shocked. No.

"The more time you spend shaking your head, the less time you have sleeping on my cot. Go!" A command so forceful, it took only his glare to wear down my fragile veneer and expose the frightened child clinging to its core.

The jingling bells announced my imminent crime, and the girl's eyes bounced up, fleetingly darting to the source. A fork stalled near her lips, and chocolate dripped shamelessly from its edge. Laughing, she flicked her finger rapidly against her phone, stopping then laughing, her chosen images shared with her friends. With her bag in her blind spot, they all giggled loud.

Soundlessly, I slid into the table behind, my palms as damp as dew. One stretch of my foot, I missed the strap; a second go, my pulse was in my throat. Further, I strained, and the bag was between my legs. I felt filthy, the dishonor of the act smearing its residue across my soul. Her straw moved gratingly against its plastic hole, its squeak a punishment for my crime. I darted outside.

"You brought it here?" Levi scolded. "The purse gets dumped. Rule one!" Plunging into it, he held the ID to my face, which

27

brought on a stream of murmurs about glasses, a haircut, about changing who I was to match the kid with the squeaky straw. Levi opened the wallet and expertly counted the cash: fifty went into his pocket, five went into mine. "Congratulations. you have until Monday, January 16th."

I flipped over the five, staring at the face of a president lucky enough to be shot in the head. I wondered again how Rubi survived.

CHAPTER FOUR

With absolutely nothing in my calendar, my days were without a purpose, something that left my obsessive compulsion in an unacceptable state. I had a timetable for everything, a little script that marked the moments of my orderly day. It varied depending on the time of year, or season, and holidays messed with it quite a bit; but overall, I adhered to a structured march around a predictable clock.

But ever since this new life was forced on me, that routine was shot. And today, on Thursday the 5th of January, one week since I arrived in this city, I fared no better than the 4th or the 3rd or probably the 6th or the 7th.

3:30 every day, that was when I used to practice, back when my clock ticked on time. Today, where did I need to be? Nowhere. And certainly not Carnegie Hall. How could I have blown it that bad? Running into an alley like a scared little girl.

I needed to practice, but... I didn't have enough fingers to count the reasons. *But* Levi scared me, *but* his building crawled with boys in cloaked hoodies with worrisome tattoos. *But* it was too cold outside, too dark in alleys. The library was too quiet, the subway too loud.

The still of the basement beckoned. Tiptoeing down, the steps creaked before the shadows loomed. I walked headfirst into a spider's web, freaked, and escaped back up the stairs.

Go home, kid. Ain't nobody gonna make you a star.

No. Not true. I had dreams and goals, and confidence and—I rummaged through my pocket—a *phone*. Lighting my way with its flashlight, I found every switch and hastily threw them on, transforming this haunted dungeon into a well-lit stage. I took a deep breath, which did nothing to steady my nerves and propped the sheet music against my case.

Muting the strings to silence my presence, I laid ten pennies across the table: all evenly spaced, each one head-side up. Ready. I nestled my violin against my chin and glided my bow effortlessly across the string. Perfect. I stacked the first coin on top of the second. Eight more waited. I played it again. My finger slipped and fell flat, and the two coins separated. A third pass was pure, a fourth flawed. I stacked the coins. I divided the coins—every passage must be clean. Concentrating, focusing, I played it again and again; each time it was perfect and better, and softer and elegant. The pile grew: five pennies, six, seven pennies tall. Then, wrong, a minor third came out as a major fourth, and the tower tumbled. It didn't matter where I was, or how trivial the mistake, if I messed up, all the pennies fell. Ten times perfect. It had to be, and when that happened—and only then—would I allow myself a pass to proceed.

Crash! Giggles. Bang. "Shhh."

Two haggard-looking souls toppled into the basement, and I snaked behind a bookshelf, a rusted tricycle nestled into the space preventing me from a full conceal. Youngish, their skin was wax paper, their hair string cheese. And when they crossed my path, the smell, my God. I choked to hold back the gag.

"There's somebody here."

"No, there's not. Where's the spoon?"

It was as if they swam in a sewer and forgot to shower.

A Bic lighter flicked, then swayed, and an acidic smell overrode the stench. Vinegar? No, urine.

"Get the needle. Quick."

A rubber band snapped, plastic percussed, and then a nightmare prodded to life. One minute, two, ten minutes gone, when was long enough?

I scooched forward, holding my breath, stretching my neck without making a sound. A crumpled mass had congealed on the floor. Two human beings slumped together in what could have been a peaceful pose if it weren't for their look of death. I tiptoed around them, my breath rapid, who knew a heart could beat that quick?

They never stirred.

Outside, I walked fast because the rhythm paced my thoughts, because the fresh air replaced the misery I just inhaled. Through courtyards, down the avenues, and across the parks: I hiked, I observed, I looked at my watch. 11:12 a.m. Two kids ran past, their giggles echoing off the walls. One picked up a snowball and chucked it with all his might. It landed a foot in front of his shoe. Playful laughter came next, and the harmony of it calmed me more. I walked.

A teenage boy flicked a cigarette over the chain-link fence, and I followed the little bits of orange as they floated into the air. 11:18, I climbed onto a playground swing and rocked it slowly, my pendulum curving to the beat of the emptiness I felt inside. I pushed against the ground. The swing responded. I kicked again, stronger with nerve, angrier with spite. It stalled, the links of the chain crumpling together into a weightless suspension. Was I free?

No. How could you be free if you have nowhere to go?

We're moving to San Francisco. My own voice caged me in. *The third week in December, we're leaving Seattle.* My friend had grabbed the chain as I swung backward, jerking me from its seat, tumbling me to the ground. *My mom says I can come back to visit.*

I dragged my boots against the slushy New York snow, and I took in where I stopped: at a tired-looking school, with an insufficient park. I spotted a lonely bird who had forgotten her path, who wandered over to the stairs to peck for scraps, no one around to tend to its needs.

I twisted the swing in circles, tightening the chain around its supports so tight that when it could go no further, I pulled my feet up and stood on the icy seat. Slipping, I held the chain firm, swinging erratically until I regained my footing. My hair flew out at ninety-degrees, my arms extended. The moment was filled with nausea and fun, and still, I couldn't keep the voices away.

It's because of her, isn't it? My mother didn't want to move—not at all. *No, for Christ's sake, Samantha, I've told you that a thousand times.* But my father decided what we were going to do. *Ryder, go outside and play with your friends.* My dad, a man of few words, who demanded compliance, pointed his finger towards our door. I left because it was safer to ask my friend to come to the park than to hear them together.

That swing jerked and swung back the other way, a tire screeched somewhere off in the distance, and next to me, a sign came into focus. **Winter Break! December 22nd—January 8th.** I looked at my Fitbit: January 5th, just over two months since my father left, nineteen days since my mother and I moved to San Francisco, fifteen since she died. **Office re-opened January**

31

2nd—January 6th.

A different voice spoke, one of direction and know-how, one that understood what it was like to fend for yourself, to make your mark. My kind. *Yous going to school, aren't ya?*

An image flashed: wasted human lives rotting on the basement floor, tattooed fingers passing money behind a back. I shuddered. Miguel. The rat-faced boy who smelled like a skunk, who spent his days in some drug-induced haze facilitated by my dear roommate Levi. He had maybe two or three years on me, max. I needed school if for nothing else than to not become him.

Walk right past the school and turn left at the next light. I followed my homeless friend's voice until a brick building stopped my path. I stared at it confused, trying to make sense of the graffiti that had swallowed its walls, of the line of souls holding it up.

So many of them, all as different as a box of chocolate, as immovable as a mountain's silhouette. I zeroed in on the only woman I saw. Her blankets heaped high above her head; a canvas bag bulged between her legs.

I cataloged the contents of my life. So much promise the day I ran, so much junk it was in truth. I needed a cup; I had a beany baby hanging from a keychain. I would die for a knife; I had an old Teddy Bear named Billy my best friend gave me when I was eight.

That plump woman turned and spoke to a disinterested man, and her blanket slid to the ground. The man looked ancient, with crisscrossed wrinkles marking his face. He kicked the base of his shopping cart hard as if the force would align the wheel, which would mend his life. He never said a word. All of them the same, and all of them different. Sunken and broken, these men and women, whoever they were, wherever they were from, sat behind that fence and waited patiently. They stood in that line to beg for a box.

I spoke to the only man that smiled.

"What's his name?" said the chosen man who waited in line for soup, for clothes, for a shower, or maybe just to wait. "Don't know? Kid, that's definitely a problem. You're looking for a thirty-six-year-old black man in a homeless shelter." His laughter rippled down the line. "Next, you off to find a Nigger leading a KKK meeting?"

"Don't be givin' my girl a hard time, now."

Familiarity did breed content. I wrote that once in a paper, and my mother laughed. *Contempt, Ryder.* No, Mom, nothing about this man was wrong. He found me a bed, in a warm room, with a man who—so far—had done no harm. Yes, my familiarity with this man made me content. I trapped him in a hug.

"Whoa!" The Dove had flown off, and a rank and sour odor had taken its place. My next breath came from my mouth. Still, it stuck to my tongue. "You have to take a shower."

"Ahh. So that's how you greet an old friend?" He chuckled. "I tell ya, Wes, this kid's somethin' else. Ooohwee. She has this 'life binder,' got herself *aaallll* sorted out. Mm, mm, mm."

"Yeah, well," I said, guilty for passing judgment on a man who chose not to lay crumpled on a basement floor. "Not exactly sorted. I need somebody to present it to the school. Ya know, a kid my age doesn't just walk in and register herself." A glance around made the request all that more urgent. No way would I end up in this line, uh, uh, uh. "You *need* to shower and come with me. It starts *Monday!* If we mess up today, we still have tomorrow to fix it." I tugged at his sleeve, pushing him to the front of the line.

"Kid, slow down there. Let's refresh: I'm black, you white, remember?" More laughter; heads bobbed out at angles down the line.

"Yeah, just tell 'em yous adopted me." When in Rome, talk the talk. A line full of comedians, they mimicked me mimicking them. "What?"

"What, she say? What, is that black people don't adopt no white kids. White folk adopt black kids. That just how it work." He spoke more homeless in front of his friends.

"I'll do it," said a barely audible voice at the end of the block. "Yeah, I'll do it if y'all let me kick to the front."

I forced my way free from Wes and my nameless friend, thinking it odd how I knew the name of his friend, but not his, and examined this man's perfect white face. Young, but not too much. Good-looking, but not cocky. He had brown hair, a match, blue eyes, a bonus. If he only had my freckles.

"Go take a shower," I ordered, and the line parted so quickly it was as if Moses had waved his staff.

And after the man who would become my father walked into the shelter to groom for his role, I pulled my nameless friend closer. "You're coming with me," I said. "I don't trust him."

"Wes, she trusts the black man more than the white." He

33

ruffled my hair. "Smart kid."

This man, Wes, did all the talking. "Listen, your name is Max Stephens, okay? You lost your wallet yesterday, okay? But your kid here has her birth certificate, her mother's death certificate, and proof of residency. The school's not one of them fancy ones, kind of for working-class folks, so there should be a spot. If you stand tall and tell the lie with conviction, nobody will question you. Got it?"

"Yeah, I got it."

"Don't fuck it up. This kid's too smart not to be in school."

What I loved most about my new friends was their desire to help without the need to question. Wes, my provisional brother/free-wheeling uncle, brought up my mother's death as a matter of fact, not a situation to solve—much respect my friend. If I wanted to tell you the details, I would. What I didn't know about my new friends was that, as deceitful and wrong as our acts were to society, the triumph of our plan filled these men with a sense of purpose, a deed worthy of pride.

Public school 101. Class started on Monday, January 9th, but my lessons began that very day. "School Rules!" Wes tore it in half as soon as we were outside the school gates. "Fuck that, Ryder. You want to get ahead, you listen to me: glare, don't let nobody push you around, meet every man in the eye. Got it."

Got it. No longer did success come from a rigid posture or perfect prose. No. Swearing was encouraged, slouching a must: own the turf and play the part.

A part, for sure, because at no point in his lecture did any of this feel like the life I was born to live.

CHAPTER FIVE

Two days later, I continued with the life I was *forced* to live.

Saturday used to be a day spent perched on the edge of my chair, with a bow in one hand and the violin in the other. I couldn't recall a time when that day wasn't filled with music and structure, and friends and orchestra.

But today, as I pulled the purple sheet over my face, hoping then praying it would block the frigid air from attacking my core, where did I have to go?

The door opened, which drew the draft briskly across the room. My toes curled to find a morsel of warmth.

"Rent's due, my love."

"No, it's not, Levi, and don't call me that. Today is the seventh. I paid you until the sixteenth."

"It's better to plan ahead than fail to plan."

"What are you, a poet?"

"That's what the ladies say," he said, seductively unbuttoning his shirt, exposing the threads of hair as if that defined him as a man. A little bit of vomit rose in my mouth.

But if I were honest, in the five days holed up on this wretched cot, Levi had pitched some pretty practical advice. From stealing tips left on restaurant tables to understanding the value of the convenience store penny dish, nothing was wrong because we had all been screwed.

"The fifteenth is closer than you think. Go find yourself another purse." He picked up his pipe. "Or better yet, get a job."

"The *sixteenth*, Levi!" Bastard trying to shortchange me a day. "And I'm thirteen. Nobody's going to hire me."

He waited until after he inhaled before rolling his eyes. "Jesus, do I have to teach you everything?" Air passed reluctantly through his pursed lips, which, once complete, brought on a gut-splitting cough. "Yes, I do. What did you steal last week?" A wet burp followed.

"A purse."

Clapping like the Queen of England, his theatrics grated. "Now, love." I cringed. "What was in that purse?"

I flared my nostrils to show him that *I* knew that *he* knew damn well what was in that purse. "Money. That you took from me and left me with hardly enough to eat." I picked up his pipe, ready to do what with it I didn't know. His slap hit hard.

"What else?" He said, his voice transforming into a contrasting calm, a consequence no doubt from his recent inhale.

I reached into my back pocket, timidly unsure if the next move would upset or please.

"Bingo, yes, the driver's license. Now go get yourself a job." The lighter flicked again and then went dead. "Pass me that other lighter."

"What, you want me to drive there?"

"I can't take this. Jesus, you're hopeless. Pass me the fucking lighter."

A little bit scared, a touch curious, I grabbed the second lighter off the window ledge, and my nerves dropped it two inches short of his hand.

"Fuckin' hopeless."

"Ohhhh." The lightbulb clicked; good grades only got you so far. They certainly didn't take me down these dark alleys of criminal intent. I scooped up the lighter, and looking for praise, pointed the flame towards the hole in his pipe. "I use it to apply for a job?"

Again, with the mockery, his hands slowly slapped together. "Genius, you are. Now, go."

"Where?"

"How the fuck should I know, just get out of here and get me my fifty bucks."

***

"You're back."

When I left Levi's, there was only one red teardrop on my mind. No need for Google to show me where. I knew the way by heart.

"Well, welcome again to Carnegie. My name is Ms. Ng." The same woman I ran from on Thursday reached for my hand as if she forgot I acted like a fool. "You know, I've reviewed the portions of your application from the other day." She winked and then offered a threatening smile. "And I think I understand why you may have scurried off so quickly."

My nerves lassoed my tongue, and I leaned on my heels, making sure the path to the exit was clear.

"Just follow me to the back, and we'll get this sorted."

I stepped closer to the front just as she disappeared behind the back. Free from making yet another mistake, I spun on my soles only to run into a wall of a man.

"Well, hello there," he beamed, his inviting crow's feet sprouting from his chocolate-colored eyes. He rattled the leather bracelets running up his wrists, then swooped a grey-streaked ponytail over his shoulder.

Ms. Ng interrupted the pleasure. "There you are. Ryder, I thought you followed me through the door. Please come back to my office."

The man leaned closer, and a complex spice filled the space. "She has mint meltaways in her top drawer. I'd go with her if I were you." He winked. "Grab one for me too." And he sauntered away, owning the moment as much as he owned the room.

She waited until he cleared the lobby before she whispered, explaining that the man that passed was the man that mattered: Mr. Schroeder, the conductor of the Youth Symphony Orchestra.

That was the Maestro. I had studied everything needed to impress that man. I knew how he liked kids with courage because he said so in the New York Magazine, that he demanded a personality to come through music because he told the BBC. I knew he loved zebras and opera and hot chocolate and teamwork. I hated opera, was apathetic about zebras, but everything else…oh God, please tell me I didn't look scared.

"Come, Ryder." She tugged at my sleeve, and I stumbled behind. Still in a state of awe, I expected more. I thought she'd drag me into an awe-inspiring academy. One with minimalist paintings paired to ornate sculptures, a place so lavish, you drew your breath to adjust your status. But no, this place was dark and shadowy, and cold and fearful. The halls cruelly closed me in.

"Please, have a seat." Ms. Ng swept her hand over a benched crowded with books and folders, and a mug and a fork. I stood erect.

"Oh, let me get that for you."

And as she moved one pile of clutter on top of another, a pink teddy-bear perched on her desk judged me as I judged her. It had one leg tucked beneath its torso, the other dangled off the edge. I reached for the wrong to make it right.

"Okay, now," she said, clicking open a folder. "Your application says that you played in the Seattle Youth Symphony, but the last permanent address was in San Francisco."

Stunned. I froze my hand mid-air, halfway to the bear. I hadn't mastered that part of the lie. Steady. Look calm. Acquire. The homeless man's lesson used and applied. I told the truth. "Um, my father was transferred to San Francisco just after Halloween, but we, my mother and I, stayed in Seattle to finish the semester. We arrived in San Francisco the week before Christmas, on December seventeenth."

Her head bounced, readily accepting these words as fact.

"Um, but something happened to his company where they needed him in New York, and since the school year hadn't begun, they transferred him again." I fought the urge to fidget, to bite my lower lip and dig into my wounds.

She nodded: I exhaled. "So, we may contact…" she paused as she scrolled through my file. "Yes, here, Roman Moretti, your Seattle conductor?"

Mr. Moretti knew nothing that happened after we arrived in San Francisco. I signaled yes and waited for her serve because I knew where I belonged.

"Okay, moving on then. The registration fee is $575. Of course, that's just after you've placed. The audition fee is only $95. Just have your parents—"

I bulged my eyes, giving away what I didn't have to give.

"Yes, that's what I thought, especially given the blanks in the application. Not to worry. We have waivers, financial aid, work-study opportunities for those who find it hard to—" She stopped, scooching her chair closer to mine. "Don't worry, sweetheart, where there is a will, there's a way."

My nerves shot me upright, and my arm tangled in hers. The 'life binder' in my hand crashed to the floor.

"I'll get that." She scrambled, hurriedly picking up the loose papers that spread across the room. "Oh, Ryder, pardon my intrusion, but it does appear that this is a part of the information you will need to apply for financial aid."

She held up one of the stolen letters, and words stamped in red meant nothing to me, but everything to her: IMPORTANT TAX DOCUMENTS ENCLOSED – W2. A complicated surprise settled into her brow. "Why do you have your father's tax documents?"

I swallowed.

"Well," she said, protectively patting my knee. "I guess it is that time of year. The important thing here is that your father's income falls below the threshold. Far below." She rolled a pen over her ear while rambling indecipherably under her breath. "Why don't I just help him by filling out parts of the form, okay?" Her pen scratched the paper. "You don't need to tell him I saw this, alright?"

Was $32,853.92 low? It sure seemed like a hell of a lot of money to me. I pulled the bear into my arms, realizing only then that the leg was not tucked but missing. A one-legged pink bear propped on her shelf for all to see and love.

"Just have them fill in the gross earnings." She pointed to a box in the grid. "And sign here."

Flipping that one pink leg up and down, I watched her lips convert from concern to comfort.

"Her name is Daisy." She stroked the bear as if it were a child. "I've had her for over twenty years. Can't seem to throw her away."

This woman would never check.

"The audition is two weeks from today, on Saturday, the twenty-first." She spoke with a monotoned inflection, but her body language more than readable. "Can you be ready for that?" It leaned, full of trust and compassion, of a benevolence that had nothing to do with this audition.

"Yes, Ms. Ng," I answered, riddled with guilt for lying to such a caring soul. I placed my sweaty hand on hers. "Thank you." I would skip school, practice in lobbies, train stations, cafés whether or not the owners allowed. Anything not to disappoint this woman cheated from the truth.

I left with a rim of sheet music tucked under my arm, and a panic carved deep into my core. Still, it was a victory, if only just. I was not the person who woke up on a smelly cot in a freezing cold coffin, who held lighters out for drugged-out landlords. I was a person who landed an audition for the world's most renowned youth orchestras, a person who could carry a lie, who would survive.

My mind reached over to the people walking by. And they looked back and told me the truth: they didn't know me, love me. They didn't care. Nobody cared. What did it matter if I got an audition if there was nobody to tell?

I looked at the musical score in my hand.

Oh. The excerpt was advanced, much harder than what I played in Seattle. I ducked into the subway and found a corner, and the train screeched to a halt. A bell chimed. Loudspeakers announced a delay. Moans. Profanity. Ugliness. I couldn't master this piece here in the cacophony of the commuter's dungeon.

Out on the street again, I focused on the calming symmetry of the zebra crossing instead of the conspicuous black gum stains littering the sidewalk. Playing with a full orchestra took focus and devotion; it meant playing more and thinking less and surviving still. I looked ahead. The sky was blue.

But when I reached my hovel, it took all of seconds for clouds to hover. "Did you get a job, my love? Tick-tock, tick-tock. That cement sidewalk is going to feel pretty-pretty cold."

"You know, Levi? You're an A-hole."

"On the contrary, love, I do believe I'm quite generous. $200 a month for a roof over your head in a city like this is a steal."

I spun one hundred eighty degrees only to face a wall with its bottom half missing. I kicked it, sending a piece of sheetrock straight to the ground. "Fuck you." I stomped the debris, and a plume of dust swelled into the air. With nobody around to scold me, I said it again, only louder and with a bit of my newly acquired New York drawl. "Fuck yuuu."

"That's the spirit, my love." Jumping from his futon, he clasped his hands against my shoulders. "That's my girl!"

I shuddered from the unexpected honor.

CHAPTER SIX

Two days later, I had seven days left to come up with rent, an impossible task that distracted me from the worry directly at my feet. Middle School, Number 21, the less than inspiring name of the more than foreboding building.

My first day of school, and as I walked towards its doors, raucous screams pierced the air. I focused on the slushy footprints scattering the stairs. A pair of boots stepped into view, and I rolled my eyes up to meet a boy with my father's cruelty in his eyes.

I stiffened.

Larger than the average seventh-grader, whiter than the majority-minority, his blue Aryan eyes and golden blond hair should have made him a target. It didn't. He stepped too close. "You new?"

No more committed than a shark swimming into minnows, he lost interest in my muted response, choosing instead to lunge at a crowd of six-graders playing tic-tac-toe with a stick. He threw his lasso around these boys of lesser wills, and dirt kicked up in puffed pillows as other kids jostled to get a better view. He spun on his heel, arms wide, chest out—the universal posture of an insecure boy.

He stopped. "You again. Whatsthefuck's amatter with you?" His words blended together into a plaster of hate. He shoved me. This boy, with his pointless power, lurched forward then back. I flinched then stumbled, my feet tripping me to the ground, my pale knuckles clenching my violin. The crowd shifted, forming a different circle, mercilessly placing me at its core.

"Well?"

The bell, a shrill fit more to signal a fire than to announce the beginning of school, cut his lasso slack. And like ants scurrying in a storm, the schoolyard emptied. I sat there alone, the soil that had absorbed my shock running between my fingers. So far from the grandeur of even an average suburban school, who could plan for a welcoming like this?

"Get in here," said the teacher, who finally arrived. "You think you're special?"

No, sir, not anymore.

He led me through the doors, and the mildewed pine punished me more. A janitor pushed debris below a cracked window. Green paint peeled off the wall. Too rough and displaced, I chipped it off, and little flakes of color wedged under my nail.

"Alright now. Bell rang. Late to class."

The clock read 5:02. I glanced at my Fitbit, 7:45. I looked back to the clock, to my watch, to the clock, repeat. I walked to the room handwritten on my schedule, where an old Mac computer sat next to an unloved plant. Papers spilled over scattered pens, which surrounded a collection of dirty mugs. I couldn't pull my eyes away from the mess.

"Please, everybody quiet!" shouted the woman in front, waving her hands as if to signal a cab. "Everyone, now, to your seats." Her shirt pulled away from her skirt, exposing the three baby elephants trekking across her back. Her hands lowered; the tattoo disappeared. I supposed I should have been smart enough to know what to do. "Ah, you must be Ryder. Come, have a seat." But I needed to be told.

San Francisco to Las Vegas to New York City: all by myself. A cot, an audition, a homeless friend. I could handle this school. I pulled my chair closer to the table and felt the telltale lump stuck beneath its surface.

"Everyone, this is Ryder. Say hello to—"

A nerf football flew across the room, and a high-five converged over my desk. Something was said in a slang I had never heard, with an accent as if it were spoken in tongue. I bounced my head and grinned and laughed—*San Francisco to Las Vegas to New York City*—and somehow, I survived.

A petite girl distributed papers. She wore Coke-bottle glasses and parted her hair with a ruler. One landed on my desk, bringing with it a whisper. "I like your earrings." Odd to hear such humanity when nothing else around me felt remotely real.

"Okay, class, listen to the instructions carefully. I want you to circle the subject, underline the verb, and place a box around the predicate. You'll want to use a pencil."

I jerked my head around the room looking for somebody else who thought this was a joke, anyone who would say *seriously* and mean it. Coke-bottle buried her head inches from the page, the high-fivers scratched their heads. And as the nerf football bounced back and forth in the teacher's hand, I picked at the green paint under my nail.

"Ryder." She walked down the aisle. "Are you having trouble? You haven't started the assignment."

The boy from behind me leaned over to see, the slurping of his gathering breath a mere inch from my ear. He blew. The green paint picked from my nails sprinkled like confetti over the page.

"Gabriel, keep your unsanitary habits to yourself." The bully from the playground had a name.

I picked up my pencil and circled then underlined then boxed and handed her the form. She looked suspicious, making me doubt myself when I knew I shouldn't. She smiled. Gabriel sneered. If only I could hear a bell.

But I had to endure six more classes before the last one rang. The hall clock read 5:02. I stopped and stared again. The second hand frozen, time refusing to move.

Outside, kids arched wide, a purposeful barrier buffering them against the need to care. Not a soul spoke to me, not even Gabriel. Cars pulled up, accepted their cargo, and pulled away. Nobody noticed I just stood there watching, longing, remembering what it was like to wait for my mother, not ever realizing what it would feel like if she never came. "No." I didn't want to see her face again. "Stop," I said it soft, so that nobody would hear, but said it out loud so that it would shake me free.

I boarded a bus because by now I had learned—buses take you away.

And this one lumbered like all the others. Through its windows, I watched a police officer walking with his stick, and a homeless man cuddling next to his dog. The officer crouched, scratched the dog's ears, and then this man in charge of the wellbeing of others straightened up and strolled away.

The traffic gridlocked, I stood by the doors, ready, the low price tag hardly the only reason to take this city by foot. Hopping off, the crowded streets swallowed the dog and the man and the officer that didn't care. I pushed through them all, landing at the base of a building, with lions guarding its entrance, tiers of stairs running up to its doors. Demanding respect, this building mocked my school. As grand as a palace, as inviting as an auditorium, I clutched my violin and pretended. The beginnings of a smile took hold.

A little girl rushed past me, perilously taking the stairs two at a time, her innocent struggle only widening my grin. "Mommy, wait for me." She slipped on some ice, bringing on a wail. Her mother rushed to her side. And that was all it took to bring me down.

"It's just a library," I said out loud. Talking to myself helped. It forced me to take control, to focus on these stairs, this building, on the present. "Walk through those doors and become better," I commanded. Because once inside those walls, I would find perspective. I could forget I missed my school, that I mourned my life.

Believing this was crucial.

I counted the steps as I wandered up. Losing track halfway, I ran back and started again. Double-checking, I repeated it again, skipping a step and multiplying it by two. I walked up five and ran down three. Leaping over two, I totally screwed up the math. What a strange and magnificent place.

The inside was as marvelous as its facade. I coughed, and a cavernous echo answered back twice. Stairs shot off on either side and climbing to the top didn't bring me any closer to the arching stone windows towering above. An American Hogwarts— I waited for the steps to shift around the hall.

"Go ahead."

A British accent spoke. It was so calm and cultured. Out of the corner of my eye, I twirled to make sure it didn't come from the portrait hanging on the wall.

"Hun, over here? Would you like to come in and study?"

The librarian's red and white striped turtleneck clashed comically with her pastel-flowered sweater, but her eyes matched her voice, so I smiled from her kindness. "Are you talking to me?"

"Yes." Her front tooth sat crookedly against the next. It matched her voice.

"I can come in?"

She brought her finger to her lips as I was sure she had done a thousand times before. "If you're quiet and intend only to read."

I flipped open my mother's iPad, and nervously tapped the icons.

"Ah, yes, one of my favorites: *To Kill a Mockingbird.* It makes me think of my father. Atticus Finch, who wouldn't love to have him as a dad?"

My shoulders hung.

But she recovered quickly, floundering to rebuild my fallen face with tangents about books and characters and authors and series.

"My mother gave it to me." Cutting her attempts in half, she let my catharsis restore her awkward ramble. "She said Jem, Scout's brother, reminded her of me. That I'm of the age where life starts to look different, just like he was." Maybe she said that. Maybe not. I had lied so many times now; I couldn't always be sure of what was real.

"Well, Jem was a brave and righteous boy who loved his family dearly. Your mother must be a lucky woman to have you around."

"I'll tell her you said so." Fantasy turned into truth. No longer did I bite my palms to will away the wrong. I just burrowed into my imagination and played with those friends to recreate the past I should have lived.

"Well, come on in and finish your book. This is a reading room, the Rose Reading Room. It's a special place in the main branch of the New York Public Library. It was just restored." I listened intently, the honesty of the distraction a welcome surprise. "The library is over a hundred years old. It opened in 1911. Under this building," she said, her finger tapping against her desk. "Burrowed far beneath Bryant Park—" and that finger swung towards the park I just trudged across—"lies a storage compartment filled with over four million books."

"Whoa."

For the thousand and oneth time, her finger raised to her lips. I giggled. She went on, describing how the building had deteriorated, how the fumes from the exhaust caused more damage than the harshness of the weather. Then, after her lesson was complete, she threw gold straight into my heart. "And you are welcome here anytime."

Anytime! Anytime meant everything. When it was cold, when it rained, when I was lonely and scared and needed a woman in a red and white striped turtleneck with a pastel-flowered sweater to flash a crooked smile.

I stayed until the light left those windows, and the chandeliers lit up the exit. And I pledged my return without any reason to doubt my plan.

But that was Monday.

On Tuesday, the chandeliers weren't needed because the library closed at five. I stood outside, missing my new fashion-challenged friend and loathing the lions for reminding me of my mother. "No," I blurted loudly, blocking her image from toying with my mind.

"Excuse me?" A man's voice cut through the dozens circling around. I ignored it, choosing instead to judge the men in expensive black overcoats, the teens in baggy jeans with ski caps pulled low over their ears. The mothers with strollers, mothers dragging wrestling toddlers, mothers chatting with their daughters. And suddenly, all I saw were mothers.

"No!"

"Excuse me, are you talking to me?

Not a mistake. A tall man, a wealthy man, a *gentleman* so much different from Levi, from Wes, from my nameless friend, he kept enough distance to respect my space but showed enough concern to challenge my guard.

"You said, no." His eyebrows straightened, merging before he spoke again. "Were you talking to me?"

A rush of red flushed across my cheeks. "I'm sorry, mister, I didn't mean to speak out loud." Embarrassed, I took a few steps back, and he didn't follow. He waited, keeping his hands casually in his pockets, nodding knowingly the way a father would when calming a child. I moved forward a fraction of a step.

"Hey now, talking to yourself is good practice. Nobody's around to give you a hard time. You should do it more often. Stand in front of a bathroom mirror and let yourself have it."

He looked like he should be wearing a tie. Like he belonged in that business district where sophisticated men wore designer suits and had Bluetooth devices hanging from their ear. He should be glancing at his watch, waving his hand in the air, cursing the taxi that didn't stop instead of talking to a thirteen-year-old girl who spoke to herself.

"Well, sir, you heard me." I kicked the step.

"Yes, a rookie-move on your part." His hands didn't wave. No shocking expletives split the air. He smiled. "Are you studying here at the library?"

"Yeah."

"Yes. A young lady like you who studies in a place like this should use proper English."

Fatherly advice, caring guidance, an Atticus Finch. My spine stretched long to be worthy of his praise.

"Well—"

"I'm reading *To Kill a Mockingbird*." Cut off, and unprepared for such a flight of idea, he stayed silent, and my face grew hotter as I continued to embarrass myself in front of this important-looking man.

His smile was slow to come, but not because he wasn't amused. "Well, there's a lot of courage in that book. You look like you have some courage yourself."

"Yeah, sorry, yes, thank you, I think I do."

"All right then, good. Well, I would love to talk with you about it, but I'm wanted back at work. You take care." His nod came as an approval, and I should know by now not to let my mind wander. Not to think of him that way, with children who ran to his side when he returned from work—not to dream of a better father like I always had.

At the corner, before jumping into a taxi to go someplace where he was needed—where his absence would be noted if he spent one more moment on the steps with me—he waved. It was a knife that sliced my heart in two. Why couldn't my father have asked me about my courage, about how much it took to run away to be by his side?

I pressed the little round button on my phone and saw the ocean spilling onto a sandy shore, the default image on an iPhone screen. Resetting that took courage. Never let anyone say that crisscrossing this country alone on a bus was hard. It wasn't. It was the boredom that came after the fury from loss. I couldn't move, couldn't run up steps, or under awnings, or through the rain. I lived in a mourner's gallows, my last moments with her on repeat in my head.

My mother said goodbye; she waved, her head tilted, her mouth stayed parted. I responded, yes? No. Did I wave back? Repeat. She said goodbye. Click. iPhoto: she looked happy. Click. Instagram: she was laughing. Click. Swipe. Scroll. No. I deleted that one, and the next, and then I opened them all and placed a tick mark next to each. Then with more courage than it took to run to my father, or across this country, or into the home of a drug dealer, I clicked the trash bin and my old life was gone.

Survival of the mind.

CHAPTER SEVEN

Surviving reality was quite a different story. So desperate, I even contemplated going to church, although for all the wrong reasons. If I sat on the end, maybe all the way at the back, then when the collection plate landed in my—

A fist slammed against the bathroom door. It belonged to another one of Levi's never-ending "clients" replenishing their stock. "How much time do you need to take a wiz?"

None of your business, you fucking druggie. I had done well in street-lingo 101. Not only did I say it in times of need, I thought it all the time.

I pulled my t-shirt over my nose. This bathroom stunk. Least of all because somebody left a rotting carton of General Tso's Chicken on the edge of the sink. Breathing through my mouth, I went back to counting my cash.

The fist banged again, so loud I thought the door might come off its hinge. "Fuckin' A, Ryder!"

Great. He knew my name.

Ready to make sure he knew to keep his distance, when I raised my fist to bang back, I sent the General's meal flying. Sticky clumps of breaded chicken wedged between the missing pieces of tile.

Undeterred, I finished stuffing the eleven ones into my pocket and stacked the coins where the meal had been: one quarter, two nickels, three dimes, and a penny. My net worth, $11.66, $38.34 shy of what I needed to pay the rent, which was due tomorrow. I thought again about the best place to sit in church.

"Levi!" The shrieking voice outside the door ushered in the master of the house. "Who'd you rent to, Kim Kardashian?" The key clinked beside the lock.

I thrust the coins inside my jeans with such fury, the penny missed and rolled into the slime. Down on my knees, I crawled through the muck to pursue that one one-hundredth of a dollar. Vanished. The penny disappeared into the same black hole that swallowed my life. I looked around for somebody to throw me a rope.

A fortune cookie lay beside my knee. Not the rescue I had hope for, but advice was advice. And food was food. I picked it up, forgetting to dust off the crud. Then—abandoning all reason—I opened my mouth.

Bang. The door shook hard, which rattled my nerves, which restored my sanity. I dropped the cookie, wiping the filth onto the wall, which only served to make the whole thing worse. "Fuck!" I crushed the cookie beneath my foot, shattering it into a hundred different pieces.

You will die alone and poorly dressed; the fortune cookie's message hardly reassuring.

The bathroom door flew open. "What the hell are you doing in here?"

"Seven dollars and fourteen cents per day, Levi! I'll pay you each night." Hands on hips, lips pursed; I slapped seven ones into his hands. "Take it or leave it."

"Leave it!"

Huh? Having lost the authority I never had, I stomped my foot. "It's a good deal, Levi!"

Mimicking me, he added a childish whimper. "It's a good deal, Levi! Grow up, Ryder! You've had a week to come up with the cash. Tomorrow's the sixteenth. Payment expected in full."

My breathing couldn't catch up to my anger. I sneered one last time at the unfinished meal wasting away on the bathroom floor, then grabbed my violin before pushing through Levi en route to an escape.

Taking the stairs two and three at a time, free from his cruelty, it started to rain. A vagrant pushed her bulging cart in front of me, and the meaning of the message rang loud and clear. *I would die alone and poorly dressed*, just like her.

No. That woman *deserved* her prophecy, damn it! I had talents and skills, a real opportunity. I would crush that audition. In less than a block, the idea of playing at Carnegie wiped the slate and falsely upgraded my confidence. I wouldn't go back to California. I didn't care how horrible that school was, that I had no place to sleep, or that come tomorrow I would be flat broke, hungry, and

desperate. I was going to play at Carnegie Hall. Period.
I had courage!

I forged on, rushing past the bakery whose scent always twisted my stomach into knots, and around the rusted shopping cart somebody carelessly left behind. Yes, I had lots of courage. I could face the harsh reality of living on the streets, and I would prove it. With the smell of freshly baked bread drifting away in my rear, I eyed the 7-Eleven ahead. And with reckless audacity—and not a bit of guilt—I grabbed the prettiest umbrella from the display and carried on down the street. No 'hey, kid.' Nothing. Not bothering to glance back, I popped it open and strolled ahead. Fear be gone. Within a block, I stole an orange off a fruit stand, and a bottled juice from a hotdog cart. I'd show you fair, Levi. The key to buying fairness was now more evident than ever: steal it in stride. Fair was fair!

Think confident; be confident. Body language matters. If you feel small, you are small; stand tall, and be strong. Always these little pep talks my mother had at the ready. More when I was younger, when playing in front of all those strangers scared me half to death. But still more recently, when she was unpacking the boxes...

I dropped the umbrella, and the rain ran across my face, the image hurdling towards me stealing my air. *Honey, open that box, I think they must be in there.* We laughed; she laughed because they weren't there, or in the next box or the next. *The Christmas tree will have to go unlit this year.* But I begged, said that a tree needed lights, that this was our first Christmas in San Francisco, that it had to be perfect. I pressed, but she said she was too tired. I pleaded and whined and acted in complete disregard to her wishes. I got my way. I always got my way. *I'm right behind you, sweetheart. I'm not going anywhere.* You LIED.

No, stop, no, not now: not ever. I backed away from the memory and smothered it into a pile of smoldering ash. She would not spoil this. I had an orange, an umbrella, and a juice. I swung the violin case off my back and cradled it in my arms.

If I nailed the audition. If. There would be no *if* unless I practiced, and no place to practice, *if* I had nowhere to live, and no place to live *if* I didn't find a job. I crumpled under a covered archway, tucking in my feet as if I were three.

I opened the case, and the air filled with the smell of ancient wood. Such a beautiful instrument. I ran my hand over the grain, cresting the bridge, the white, chalky resin dusting my fingers. Pluck. The A string echoed. I pulled the string harder with force. The resonance swelled, the acoustics of my chosen spot manipulating my mood. I tightened the bow. The clashing harmonies of tuning an instrument came next, and a passerby slowed.

Just unload on the streets, Ryder. Pop the case, and watch the bills fly!

Placing my only quarter square inside the case, I let my violin deliver a show. Nothing happened. With reservation, the quarter became a dollar, exchanging it for one of my remaining ten. I played harder, never taking my eye off that bill. Nobody noticed. I changed course, switched up the tempo, forgot about the dollar, and wore my heart on my sleeve. Still, they walked by.

All my mother's practical advice, all those pep talks, they failed me now, just as she failed me then.

The roar of the traffic replaced the serenity of my ballad, and nobody blinked when I swapped that dollar with my violin and packed away my only chance to survive.

"Hey kid, where you going?" At my back, came a thundering voice. "You were good for business, keep playing."

Standing on the spot where I just failed was a man with a gut as large as a house. And almost as protuberant as his gut was his mustache, which was the same as that guy from that show my dad used to watch.

"Get back here!" His greasy hands wiped an apron tied somewhere beneath a fold.

A Dunlop. Get it, Ryder? Just like the tire. His belly gone and Dunlopped right over his belt. My father's voice now, too? Stop. Both of you stop.

Scowling, I refused to yield to the shouts of a man who forced me to hear the voice of my father. "Your business. I wasn't exactly making a killing," I seethed.

Swinging a chair over a rail to the dry sidewalk under the awning, he tapped it gently. A charade. No way did this boisterous bulk have a sensitive side. "Keep playing anyway, it's good practice for you."

"Sir, no offense, but I don't need practice, I need a job."

A little puff of air parted his lips.

"No, I'm sixteen."

And a pudgy little finger perched under them to force a frown.

"No, really. I just had a birthday." I dug into my pocket to retrieve my crime. "See?"

Flipping the ID back and forth as if that would make the photo match. Finally, he mimicked Levi and held it square to my jaw, the plastic edge scratching against my frost-burned skin. Just confiscate it, I thought. Add more salt to my wounds.

"You know how to clean tables?"

Clean tables. I focused on his Dunlop, which all too quickly resurrected my father's voice. *Since when is it my job to do the dishes, Samantha? I put money on this table for us to eat, not for me to clean!*

"Is that a no? Because our help hasn't shown in over two days, and I'm busting my balls here." The chair swung back over to the balcony. "If you can play the violin like that, you must have a smidge of discipline. What I can —"

"I do. I will. Whatever you want. I won't disappoint you. Promise." I almost saluted.

"Every day from six to ten pm, sometimes later on the weekends. Okay with your parents or whoever's building you?" Mumbling followed, something about Socialists and the fucked-up world.

The door flew open, overtaking his ramblings with the high-pitched chimes of cutlery on china, the monotonous murmurs of a collective crowd: a sudden laugh. "So, get in here." The walls were brick, painted black; the floors were wood. They clicked under his heel. A large mirror hung against the wall. "And kid, cash under the table, alright?" I nodded, the unmistakable aroma of garlic roasting stealing my attention away.

The digital clock on the receptionist's stand read three-thirty. "Sir, should I go put my things away and come back at six?"

"Kid, don't call me, sir, and no, just stash them in the back."

It seemed odd that he spoke of six in one sentence and three-thirty in another, but I neither had the confidence nor courage to ask for clarification. Nor did I have the wherewithal to ask for any specifics. How much would be passed under whatever table remained as unclear as my math. If I had taken the time to count backward from ten to six, then I would have landed on the number four, times that by seven and figured out that was almost what I knew to be a full-time job. I think.

But I didn't do that. No, I wiped the counters, then folded the tablecloths. I rolled napkins and swept the floor. My legs began their burn three hours into the shift, and my stomach revolted an hour after that. Too scared to ask for a break, I pilfered bread from unemptied baskets, inhaling some in the toilet, and slipping others into my violin case. If I were caught, I was sure that would be my end, but I didn't, so I took four more.

"Lucky break, kid. You can go home early." A peek at my phone left me questioning his math. Ten thirty and my eyes barely fought off gravity. "Go ahead, go. Here, take one of our take-out menus. Spread the word. See you tomorrow, and don't be late."

"Um, sir." I gently bounced my foot off a stool to buy him time.

"Hey, what'd I tell you about that?"

I stopped. "Sir?"

"Marco! I told you to call me Marco. And what? Don't tell me you have no place to go? Fucking Democrats."

I clasped my hands behind my back, triangulating my eyes to the napkin I dropped earlier and was too tired to retrieve. "Oh, yeah, Marco, um, were you going to pay me?" I could hardly hear my words.

"Pay you, yeah, of course, at the end of the week." Then he did what they all did. He disappeared, callously leaving me cashless.

My muscles twitched, undecided if they should keep my post or follow his steps into the kitchen. I rarely chose well in these situations, nor did I know which one was right, in part because of my age, in full because of his size. He chose for me.

"What are you still doing here?" A sauce covered meatball was squished between his thick fingers, and when he took a bite, little chunks of tomato burrowed to the fur overtaking his lip. "You cannot be that hard off."

I traced the back of my teeth with my tongue, and said a prayer: *Please God, I won't ever think about stealing from your collection baskets again.*

"Okay, here, for today. I'll pay out your shift, but the rest will come next Sunday. Deal?"

"Deal." Now the proud owner of a ticket to another week of survival, I bolted from the door, skipping, eager to show off my success to Levi, the loathsome landlord.

CHAPTER EIGHT

A man burst out of one alley and ran into another. I froze: scared to look from where he came, too smart to follow him to where he was going. A horn blared. That skip became a sprint. New York City nights scared the living shit out of me. Too few people roaming the streets, too many sounds terrorizing my nerves. Ominous shadows, the pungent smell of urine, no one behind me, not a soul in front, I took refuge in the only store open.

Not yet feeling completely safe, I calmed myself by reading the trashy magazines on display. Brad Pitt had nobody to date. Who cared? So old. Somebody I didn't recognize may or may not be pregnant, a new computer could now detect when your dog needed a bone.

I moved deeper into the core, past the woman at the counter who looked as bored as she was tired. Toothpaste and hairbrushes, deodorant and nail clippers, I reached. I pulled back. The security camera followed my every move.

"Um, excuse me, do you sell Metro Cards?" I asked.

The clerk's head neither bobbed nor shook, it just wobbled in a pattern for me to puzzle.

"How much for the hot dog?"

A finger pointed to a sign. A mute, an idiot, or something in between, I continued my monologue until I walked from that store with a metro card topped up to eight dollars and a cheese-drenched hotdog pushed halfway through my mouth. Ten dollars gone. So, what? I was a working girl now: financially secure. I relished the moment, then decide. The woman on the magazine's cover was pregnant, for sure.

It wasn't until after I got home; when my full belly robbed me of all common sense that I pulled out my cash and counted it on my cot. "I've been robbed!"

A woman with porcelain eyes shot up from Levi's bed.

Startled by her presence, but too angry to care, I demanded answers from this stranger occupying my space.

"I worked all day today, and he paid me, but all I have is $25."

"Fuck!" She yanked the blanket down to her waist, exposing the empty bed beside her, Levi strangely absent. "How many hours did you work? And where?"

"At an Italian restaurant, and like *seven* full hours."

"Well, that's what you get for schlepping in a restaurant that works off tips."

Tips?

"Welcome to the year 2017. The minimum wage for tipped food service workers is $5.00, so..." She stopped, stumped by the challenge of this fourth-grade math.

"Yeah, that's $35!" A nauseating punch hit its mark. "Wait, what, $5.00—five dollars for each hour?" I got $11.50 for babysitting, ten for raking my neighbor's leaves. "You're not serious."

Rolling over, her shirt slid up revealing a tattooed dragon with deep yellow eyes, wings spread as wide as her shoulders, and a curvaceous tongue licking her hip. Ghetto. Just like my teacher. Where do these people develop this drive to deface?

"Put a cork in it. I have to work tomorrow too."

"Where do you work?"

"Fuck. You're about as sharp as a marble, ya know? You don't understand what put a cork in it means. You don't understand tipping. You're way overpaying Levi for sleeping on that cot," she said with a smirk, clearly enjoying the speed at which my mouth dropped to the floor. "Yeah, smarten up, it's a tough life all around."

"So, where do you work?"

"Fuckin' Marble. McDonald's, $9.35 an hour, good-night!"

Nine-thirty-five times seven equals: carry the three, carry the two. Wow! If I worked there, I would have $65.45.

"Minus taxes," she mumbled.

Huh?

If I hadn't bought that MetroCard, I'd have — no, I pulled out the take-out menu Marco gave me and scribbled on the back. Twenty-five plus the eleven I already had was thirty-six. If I didn't spend the ten for the MetroCard and the food I should have stolen, I—damn it—I'd still be four dollars shy. I sunk into my cot.

Something had to give.

And come Monday morning, I decided that would be Levi. As soon as daylight broke, I marched to Levi's futon with the fortitude of somebody who has everything to lose. "Here." I woke him up by sprinkling thirty-six dollars over his chest.

He bolted upright, reflexively counting as if he were a banker in a booth. I saw a smirk, and with the lassitude of someone without a heart, his hand waved goodbye.

"No, Levi, please, I'll get you the last fourteen." I grabbed his fist mid-wave. "I have a job now, and I'm scheduled to work from six until ten tonight."

"Harsh," he said, swinging his feet off the bed to sink the cash into his pocket. "Dude, easier just to steal women's purses, don't ya think?"

No kidding. Only my second day on the job and I was already dreading busting my ass for four hours straight. "He paid me cash yesterday, but I miscalculated and bought a MetroCard. The guy said he would only pay me per day for yesterday; after that, it was weekly."

Levi's arms cradled his head, his feet propping up on a chair in an I-told-you-so move. "See, nobody does daily."

Nothing followed: no pity, no compassion, just a smug look from a boy who enjoyed holding all the cards. And all my cash. I offered my hand, waiting for the thirty-six dollars to return.

"You plannin' on keeping your stuff here today while you're at school?"

I tugged at the straps securing my violin to my back. "I'd never leave you with my violin."

"Oh, no, God forbid anything should separate you from that useless piece of wood." He picked up my t-shirt and crumpled it into a ball. The hairbrush came next. Toothbrush, socks, my spare pair of shoes, all of them he swept into the trash.

"What are you doing? Stop it!"

His hand patted the pocket where my money had gone. "Storage fee, non-refundable," he said as his fingers cracked, preparing for another attack. He took a step closer, and his meanness grew. "But, if you deliver the rent in full by tonight, I *may* not charge you interest." His breath was rancid, his unkempt beard threatening. Every part of my body tensed as he shoved me out the door.

Click. The lock set.

Out in the hall, I panicked before I fumed because nothing I could do would change him into a decent man. Did I just forfeit thirty-six dollars? And did he just say I needed to come up with fifty?

The doorknob wouldn't budge. I knocked frantically, my violin bouncing against my back. "Levi, come on, please. Levi, I need that money."

A one-dollar bill slid under the door. "Spend it wisely, my child. And when you come back, knock three times if you have the money. Then, I'll give you back your things."

Fucking asshole. The entire way to school, my hand stayed in my pocket, protecting my only assets left: one dollar and sixty-six cents? Wait, sixty-five.

I never found that penny that rolled off into the slime.

***

When I exited the subway, I paused. *Check your balance here.* I knew my balance, eight dollars minus the $2.50 for the one-way trip, equaled... Wait, what? I wasted how much on a stupid train when I could have walked for free? $2.50! That was thirty minutes' worth of work!

I arrived at school pissed, hungry, and scheming because—fuming over Levi's heartlessness—I forgot to palm the penny dish at *Chuck's Tobacco and Stationery* on the corner of 6th and Park. It was manned by a girl who spent her life on the phone, a kid who wouldn't let a second pass without replying to a text. Robbing her was easier than stealing cookies from the deli on 2nd and Bond, where I also forgot to go.

Why was I even sitting in class, pretending to pay attention to this teacher blah blahing about World War I, when I could be stealing and eating, and... a pool of saliva filled inside my mouth. I went to my happy place, to that refrigerator in my dreams. I licked my lips at the sight of the roasted chicken, the cooked ears of corn. Today, there was a strawberry resting in the egg tray, and grapes dangling off the shelf.

I shot my hand in the air. "Um, Ms. Wollard, can I go to the bathroom?"

"Ryder, class started ten minutes ago. Please plan accordingly."

I bit my lip and squirmed for effect.

"Fine, but please hurry back."

How many people would be in the cafeteria now? Too many to pocket a crime. The front office had that jar full of mints. No. Too risky. Mr. Meyers, the music teacher? Ooohhh, maybe. He was a man who preferred silence, who asked little. A man who also had packages of ramen noodles on the second shelf, inside the wooden bowl, beside the mug that read *Musicians duet better.*

I raced to his room and stared at him from the door. All music teachers' offices were the same in my experience. They had sheet music piled haphazardly on chairs, instruments perched against the wall. There was always a wrinkled jacket, a collection of mugs, and the owner of it all slumped over their desk tapping.

This man used a pencil, and it stopped for a beat before darting to the top of a page to circle a stanza. He tilted his head, then erased the circle. He underlined the title.

"Oh, Ryder, how can I help you?"

I knew that title. I stepped forward. "Are we playing *The Four Seasons*? I played that piece last year in the Seattle Youth Symphony Orchestra."

"Oh, no. This is for the High School Orchestra," he said, breaking off a piece of a humongous blueberry muffin I somehow missed. The aroma of sugar and berries suddenly present with every breath I took. "You know that you're too advanced for this middle school orchestra, right?" Wasteful crumbs stacked in mounds on top of his desk. "There are spots in the high school for select middle school students." he said, shamelessly brushing them into the bin.

I swallowed.

"You should look into the New York Youth Symphony. They're playing *The Four Seasons* for the spring concert. Might even be a solo in it for you, if you work at it."

I pivoted towards the door; my mission a failure.

"Ryder."

I paused just for a moment, but long enough to see a column of Ritz Crackers roll across his desk. It landed in my hand before toppling over the edge.

Gasping instead of thanking, I rammed two crackers into my mouth before crossing his threshold, my satisfied stomach restoring reason. Did he say solo? I twisted around the door. "Uh,

Mr. Meyers, can I practice in here at lunch?" Little bits of cracker tumbled over my lip.

His head bounced once.

I struggled with the simplicity of that moment. It was the way it used to be: I needed something, I got something. Why did that have to change?

Because my mother did what I asked. *Look Ryder, I bought lights. Now the tree won't go unlit.*

After school, I stewed in a spiraling concoction of resentment and guilt for twenty-two blocks, in twenty-four-degree weather, sneering at every subway entrance, and turning my back to any form of authority. Thoroughly exhausted and insufficiently full from a roll of Ritz, I marched into Marco's two and a half hours early. If he'd let me start early and work until ten-thirty, that would be five dollars times seven hours, which was—for the love of God—still shy of what I owed Levi.

I worked hard, never taking a single break. I said yes, sir, and thank you, and complemented Marco on his clothes. And in return, he yelled.

"I-said-the-end-of-the-week!" It came out smeared, and Marco's body lurched when the words spewed from his mouth. He tossed a dishtowel at my chest. It stunk of mildewed onion. "You forgot the table at the back."

Mildewed onion. That's how I smelled when I knocked three times on Levi's door. "Please, Levi, we need to talk?"

The door cracked an inch. "Let me see the money." But he didn't wait because he knew I couldn't produce. Opening more, out came that garbage can. Tipped over then emptied, one by one, my possessions crashed onto the concrete floor. He opened the door wider only to skid my bag across the hall.

"Consider yourself lucky that I'm giving you back your things. Come back with the full amount tomorrow, and *maybe* you'll get your cot back. It's called tough love, my friend. You *need* me to do this."

The lock clanged together.

Tired and freezing, I slid down the wall, slowly stuffing my things into my bag. A door slammed. Footsteps shuffled on the stairs. I heard the tap on plastic, a rubber band snap. Suddenly terrified of a place I had lived for over two weeks, I gradually rose, placing one shoe down without a sound. The next shoe followed.

A shadow passed ahead. My heart racing fast, my hands shaking, I flew down the four flights of stairs as fast as a sprinter leaping from the block.

The next morning, I woke to the train station's blaring announcements. I let out a sigh, and the cold air crystallized my breath. Uncurling from the ball I wedged myself into, I exited the bathroom stall in which I slept.

I wobbled into the nearest Starbucks, raised the screen covering the cooled drinks and treats, and brazenly lifted a yogurt parfait right off the shelf. Without even a glance at the cashier, or anyone else for that matter, I took another and mindlessly headed for the door.

"Mommy, that lady didn't pay for that."

Fucking kid.

"Hey!"

I broke out into a run, flying down the subway steps and over the turnstile. I slipped through the train door seconds before they closed. Hyperventilating, I tripped over a man whose feet extended beyond his allotted space, and because this was New York, he left them there.

"Goddamnit! I forgot the spoon."

A nun gradually shook her head, the white trim of her black flowing gown, the devout cross that hung across her chest, all of it judging me for who I wasn't. It surprised me that I cared. The doors opened as the nun tsk-tsked, and my bleeding conscience pushed me through the doors.

Unsure of where I landed but seeing spots from hunger, I downed the granola in the little plastic cup and contemplated how to use it as a spoon. Inflexible, it wouldn't extend beyond the opening. If I pinched it—damn—it cracked. A splash of the yogurt spilled across my shirt.

I supposed I deserved this, the punishment for swearing in front of a nun, for skipping school, for believing I had a chance at the orchestra, at becoming an adult.

I dug through my bag, trying to find something to fix this mess—an impossible task after Levi's tough love. There was nothing valuable, but everything needed. I unfolded Marco's menu and attempted to clean the yogurt off my chest.

"Whoa, you might want to watch where you're going there, young lady. These stairs can ice up."

The take-out menu fell through my hands.

The man from the other day, the one that didn't wear a tie even though he looked like he should be wearing a tie.

"So, you're back at the library," he said, bending to retrieve the menu. "Marco's Italian. I've been there. Not too bad, well, my wife likes it."

I was at the library? Fate wasn't cruel. It landed me in front of those majestic stairs, the ones that took me to a better place, to the woman with mismatched clothes, to the friendly face with—

"Hey, why aren't you in school?" His brow furrowed, and as he leaned forward, a lock of hair forebodingly covered an eye, the one left visible refusing to blink.

I pulled back, suddenly hyper-aware of my careless indifference to cutting school.

Three fingers on his right hand spun the ring on his left. It was silver with two hands clutching a heart, and my mind jumped illogically to the man on the bus, the one with the ring where lions battled to the death.

I followed the heart as it vanished under the knuckle, then reappeared, then disappeared. Here one moment, gone the next. Back once more. "It's Valentine's Day," I said, indecipherable nonsense spewing from my lips.

"No, it's not," he scoffed. "And even if it were, that's not a school holiday." His head angled down, which caused his glasses to slide, and an eternity passed before he placed his finger over the bridge to peer over the top. "Well?"

I found myself at a loss, my inexperience negotiating the expectations of old men pairing poorly with the naïve grade-schooler that I was. I kicked at the step between us. "I didn't want to go," I admitted.

Little crow's feet spread from his eyes, and his playful smile allowed me to take a breath. He sat, plopping himself down on the steps like the thirteen-year-old that I was.

"Well," he repeated, his tone changing from stern to serene. "Then I hope you're making use of your time by studying?" He spoke to the air in front of him.

I joined his gaze, taking in Bryant Park as it sprung to life. A yellow cab slowed to a halt, the driver hurriedly exiting to pop the trunk. A folded wheelchair surfaced.

"How old are you?"

"Thirteen."

The taxi driver helped an old woman into the chair.

He kicked my toe, and I found myself staring at his wallet, at a photo in a little plastic sleeve. He flipped it over like a normal person would flick their phone. "That's my son," he said, holding it closer for me to see. "He's nine. You have the same eyes, a translucent blue. My wife's eyes, actually."

My mother's eyes, too. Why was he showing me this?

"Everything okay?"

"Yeah." It came out meek. "Yes, I mean. Everything's fine."

I watched cautiously as this strange, but kind, man patted the space next to him. I saw others sitting too. They had sandwiches and travel mugs and uncovered heads. It was cold, but not terribly so. A woman slurped soup from a paper bowl, an unused spoon wrongfully resting on her knee.

One spot further away than he suggested, I perched on the stair's edge, my feet tucked tight against my thighs.

The weight of his gaze fell into my space. "I have an extra." And an energy bar landed squarely in my lap. "You sure that everything's okay?"

"Yeah, yes," I stammered, flipping the bar over, searching for a place to pry it open. "It's just some boy at school. He owes me money, and I'm not sure how to ask him." Ohhhh, hey. I could dip the energy bar into the yogurt! "Can I eat this now?"

"May you."

Uh-huh. I tugged at the wrapper, and, making no headway, clenched it between my teeth.

"Here, let me help you." And with a deftness to be admired, he sprang the bar free. 'How did you ask him?"

I tried to eat slowly, to show I only needed a snack, to be discrete when slurping the yogurt off the bar.

"You didn't ask him, did you? What are you afraid of, the boy or the question?"

Neither. I was only afraid of ingesting my spoon before I reached the bottom of the cup.

"Why does he owe you money?" He paused, curling that take-out menu into a tube. "Let me offer you some advice. When somebody is speaking with you, you should look them in the eye."

A warmth took over my face. All of me had been consumed by the granola bar, the yogurt, by why this man with photos in plastic covers stopped to talk. I wasn't sure what had left my lips. Did I mention Marco? Miguel? Levi? "I'm sorry. You don't believe me."

He patted my shoulder, then respectfully moved it away—nothing like Levi's clammy grip. "It's okay."

Genuine, concerned, too much a part of the world from which I ran, I wished he would have left it there.

"What's your name?"

"Ryder."

"Ryder." His green-grey eyes stared me down. "I believe you. Listen, whoever is scaring you, don't let him. Never let someone's size or attitude stop you from asking a simple question. And if you don't hear what you want or if he does something that frightens you, just walk away; be the bigger man." He paused, and I waited for another pat that never came. "You okay with that?"

"Yeah…yes."

A pair of shined shoes landed on the step beneath ours. They were expensive, for sure. As were the pants that creased so tight, they buckled four inches above the lace. I followed them up to a belt, the initials GL etched into the gold. His tie was teal.

"You find a friend, Jack?"

What a curious voice.

"Guerin, meet Ryder. She's skipping school today. What do you think about that?"

"I think that you have plenty of people to parent at home and that you should give the kid a break." He winked. "Have a nice day off, kid. Come on, Jack, the meeting's in five."

This man named Jack took one step away before turning around, the rolled-up menu pointing at me as if it were a wand. "Remember, just look 'em in the eye, say your peace, and then walk away." His smile was kind. "Think of Jem."

I missed his kindness before he made it to the bottom step.

***

Focusing was futile.

I sat on those wooden chairs in the spacious Rose Reading Room thinking about food, about this man named Jack. Nobody questioned why a grade-schooler was here in the middle of the day, nobody cared. Jack cared, why?

I watched the clock tick by, setting a plan in motion. I would eat the second yogurt I stole at twelve, leave for work at two. Marco let me start early yesterday, he would do so again today. I could sneak into the storeroom while he was out for a smoke. Cans of tomato sauce were not ideal, but when push came to shove.

Until then, I doodled instead of divided, my math homework unacceptably unfinished before my iPhone buzzed. Its alert reminded me it was time to go to work, to stand and walk across the self-absorbed city, to spend the evening in the company of that foul-tempered man.

"You're early!" A bark, no, a growl worthy of an exclamation point. "Clear that table." An apron landed at my feet.

The rag pushed across the table was a fifty-pound weight, the partially consumed chicken breast an invitation. I circled the plate with my towel and the room with my eyes. A couple argued at a corner table. Their faces were scrunched, her finger pointed, the man's fist balled around his fork. Purposefully, but silently, the dirty rag fell to the floor, and under the table, I inhaled a meal.

Popping up, my face overheating from consuming too much, too fast, I stacked the used dishes into the plastic bin. And all the while, I thought of that man, Jack, wondering about his life, fantasizing about his wife, his kids. What they did, where they went to school, how *they* ate their meals. Diving deep into the fantasy, I let myself float over to *their* table, to help his wife load *their* dishwasher. I cut a chicken breast into bite-sized pieces for his toddler and joked with my nine-year-old brother, who I decided to name Bob.

So distracted by my imagination, I hardly acknowledged the head waiter as he tossed me a soda and popped an entire loaf of garlic bread into my bag. Barely noticed the sign on the door had turned to close. Such a protective and sincere man this waiter was, he offered to walk me to the train.

"Cheapskates tonight," he said as we left. "People just don't understand how much we rely on tips."

Guilt rained down on my head. One bus girl, three waiters, only tonight would this go unchecked. I had started with the change; a five-dollar bill came next. By the night's end—and only because I was desperate—a twenty meant for his pocket landed in mine. Still not enough, the rest I borrowed from the open till.

"Take care, Ryder. Sleep well."

I arrived at Levi's physically exhausted from the shift, mentally drained from deceiving somebody so kind. The honest waiter's wages wrongfully crumpled in Levi's palm; I couldn't look that bastard in the eye.

I sank into my cot utterly defeated, that cathartic fantasy that had allowed my escape gradually transforming into an inescapable trap. I would never have another family. I would always be alone. Before I had a chance to stop it, my sniffling nose competed with my welling eyes. Tears fell fast, and it took everything I had to muffle the sadness spilling into the room.

I cried now? About this father-figure I barely knew and a family he probably didn't even have. I forced out his face, but the tears still came because tomorrow was Wednesday, and the audition was Saturday, and I wasn't ready. Because an hour at lunch would never be enough. Because I would fail. Because I would never succeed in becoming an adult.

I woke early, fatigued from the never-ending worry made possible from my poor decisions. Footsteps landed hard on the floor above, a toilet flushed, a slammed door echoed maliciously in the hall. My sanity withered away.

Guilty from ditching school yesterday, from stealing, from swearing in front of the nun, I thought of Jem. He took his time to think things through. He listened to his father, tried to understand Boo Radley. Jem would never have skipped school.

I got out of bed, the first step to get me through the day. The second involved more theft: pennies palmed at *Chuck's Tobacco*, cookies swiped at the bodega on Bond. I pushed through the school doors and did my best to just exist. But I didn't want to learn about the constitution, or why the square root of sixty-four was eight, I wanted to play. To escape into my music.

When the lunch bell rang, I bolted.

"Pick any practice room you like, Ryder." Mr. Meyers didn't comment on my mood, didn't try to pretend to be my friend.

I nodded once, then chose the farthest from his office, the one hidden behind the drums. It was the first time since *before* that I had a music stand, the only place where I would be able to relish every note. I reached in my pocket for pennies to stack. I found a wad of lint.

Jem.

I slid my bow across the string, and in my head, a penny stacked one on top of another. I played with brilliant vibrato, with fingers slapping, my arpeggios burst in a run over and over again. Spanning two octaves, requiring a painful reach to the tip, so determined to achieve perfection, I fell into a bubble.

Which Mr. Meyers burst. "Okay, wow! But lunch is over," he said, holding the door ajar.

Not yet there, I hadn't perfected the passage to stack the pennies tall. "Mr. Meyers, may I stay after school and practice some more, please?"

A nod.

Will conquering frustration, I practiced from when school let out until I needed to go to work. And when I left that music room, I was better. I was a girl who knew her place and how to get there. At six on the dot, I boldly walked through the restaurant door and right up to my fear. "Marco, I'm sorry to go back on our deal, but may I ask for my pay for the last two days?"

He said nothing—no orders, no barking—just turned his back and walked away.

Walk away, that was what Jack said. But that was advice for me, not Marco. I scrubbed the tables, working out all my anxiety on the tomato sauce burrowed deep inside the grain. All my focus whetted down to that single, solitary spot, and I picked at it fervently. That stain, for now, would be my only burden.

A stack of bills landed on the table, covering up my phony diversion with a grateful reality. "For Monday and Tuesday. Wednesday through Saturday will come Sunday night."

"Thank you." It came out breathy, and I waited for him to leave before I counted my blessings.

"Sixty dollars," I whispered twice.

CHAPTER NINE

Saturday and the audition had finally come. Every reason for my presence in this wretched city was right here, right now.

Most of my muscles relaxed. Most, because I hung onto that necessary bundle of nerves. The ones that made you excited, but also kept you in check, the ones you wished weren't there but would desperately miss if they left. Those nerves ignited the flame.

All I had to do was play.

But Ms. Ng, the curious administrator, stepped between me and my task. As soon as I walked through the doors, I saw her, a coffee cup tipped against her lips masking the telltale signs of a woman decoding a lie. She held it there too long, scrutinizing my rigid form, my stilled chest, analyzing my hands stuffed into my pockets.

"Is your mother here? I sent her an email last week, but she didn't reply," she asked.

I shook my head as if it moved through sludge.

"Well, alright then, come join me in my office." She reached for my hand.

I brought my finger to my lips, finding that hanging cuticle I'd been working all morning. Still, she led me by the elbow.

The pink bear was gone, as were the folders piled high against the bench. Clean and tidy, her room felt more like the principal's office than someplace where you could fake forms to successfully apply for financial aid.

I centered myself in the middle of the room and let my shoulders relax, the order of it all a pleasant surprise. Nice, but slightly off. Books lining the shelves were spiked like the teeth of an alligator's mouth, one tall, the next short. Sloppy and wrong, I got busy correcting the chaos.

"Ahem."

With *Mozart's Favorites* in one hand and a book titled *Watch Me Feed This Squirrel Ambien* in the other, I spun.

"Ryder, are you getting enough to eat?"

The books lowered to cover my core, which only exposed my scrawny arms. "Ummmm." I drew it out, searching for a diversion. The spreadsheet on her computer listed names, which were preceded by addresses and phone numbers, fees paid, fees waived. I saw Stephens sandwiched between Sawyer and Takeo: first name, Ryder, fake home address, real phone number. It was only a matter of time.

"Um, Ms. Ng, which email address did you use for my mother?"

"Samstephens80@bottle.com? What's the bottle stand for?"

I sank into the clutter-free bench. "She liked wine." The words came out tense like they had been crushed between the truth and a lie. "She's been really busy, probably just forgot." Collapsing my hands together, I gnawed again at my cuticle hanging from my nails.

"I can give her a call if—"

"She has another email address that she checks more often," I blurted too fast.

Ms. Ng's body stilled; her eyebrow raised. Finally acquiescing to a logical response, she hovered her fingers an inch above the keys. "Okay, shoot, what is it?"

"Um." A bead of sweat rolled down my brow. "Actually, I have to go to the bathroom." I sprinted out the door, only to turn back halfway down the hall. I popped into the room again. "It's a Gmail address."

How fast can a person create a life? If you're young and savvy, less than it took to complete a flush.

"Ms. Ng, did you get the email? I called her."

"Multi-tasking on the toilet, I see." She didn't laugh, didn't grin. She studied. Shit. She tapped on Outlook and opened the message, and I moved my mouth to the rhythm of the words I wrote.

Dear Ms. Ng,

Ryder mentioned that you had sent an email to my old account. Please use this address for any further questions.

Best regards,
Samantha Stephens

P.S. Thank you for helping Ryder

Leaning back into the chair, with her left hand resting against her mouth, her right dragged a file into her reply. Send.

Bing.

My phone chirped with the telltale alert of an incoming message. Shit.

Loud humming broke the tension. Boots, high and multi-colored, slid sideways, stopping abruptly at the foot of the door. "And who do we have here, Ms. Ng?"

"Mr. Schroeder meet Ms. Stephens. She'll be auditioning for—"

"Violin!" He popped open my case, saddled the violin expertly under his chin, and what I heard next could not be described in words. "A *very* nice instrument., indeed. I must hear it come from somebody with talent." He smothered a laugh.

I forgot to breathe.

"Ryder, don't let him intimidate you. Mr. Schroeder is a teddy bear and a jokester, and on occasion, he's serious."

He motioned me out the door, to the stage that shined at the edge and dulled in the center, to places battered down by years of practice and weathered by decades of sweat. My chair sat on top of a spot no worse from wear.

"So, Ryder, tell me a bit about yourself."

Ms. Ng was right: sometimes a prankster, mostly decisive. Mr. Schroeder teetered his baton between his fingers, beating it gently against my application.

"I need this," I blurted.

"Well, Ryder, that is an *interesting* response." The tapping slowed. "Why do you *need* to be in the New York City Youth Symphony Orchestra?"

My stilted response played poorly as my opening number.

"Don't be nervous. Everybody gets anxious when they sit in this auditorium." His coy smile returned. Passionate, not flaky, I understood. Ahead of me was a person to admire, one who had virtues of what I aspired to become. I balanced my bow as he did with the baton; I failed. It fell to the ground.

"The physics aren't quite right with the bow." He handed me his baton. The—whatever he said—wasn't quite right with the baton either. It joined my bow. "Well, I guessed wrong. You seem quite relaxed."

"Yes, Maestro." I retrieved my bow. "I've been dreaming of Carnegie Hall ever since I was a kid." I took it all in, the ceilings, which were higher than the heavens, the walls, sculpted as a medieval castle. In here, I didn't need bolstered equality. No, in this place, I was that tall man at the fence. "Shall we begin?"

He suppressed a smile. "Okay, then, let's. We'll start first with the excerpts cited in the audition packet, and then move onto your selection where we'll evaluate your technique. Last, we'll review your scales and sight-reading abilities," all said with the seriousness of a man charged with selecting the best.

"What about the Rimsky-Korsakov piece listed in the packet?"

"Those are for either Concertmaster or Principal 2nd violin. If you'd like to try for those, I have the sheet music right—"

"I have it memorized."

His eyes were an owl's, surprised by the sudden burst, impressed by the remark; no, wrong, he was annoyed. I pounced fast to apologize, but he blocked me with his pointed baton. "No need, please, go ahead."

Pinched correctly now, his baton bounced once, then twice, in a rhythm and a sequence. My fingers ran. Across the fingerboard, inching close to the F-holes, my hand leaped over the upper bout and retreated to the neck. In a sinuous movement, I owned the moment.

"Stop, next." More difficult, more arching, more vibrato, less then more. They chose their excerpts wisely. "What is it you chose to play for us?" Stony, unreadable, but not vacant, he was thinking.

"'Meditation from Thais' by Jules Massenet."

"Simple. Go on."

It all melted: the walls, the weight, the worry—blending into a dream. It didn't matter that she died, that my father rejected me. It was okay that my birthright betrayed me. The music paced my emotions, steadied them. I chose when to put the mouse under a bucket and when to lift it. I pushed where I wanted to, and no ocean would block my progress. This moment was mine to control.

"Play the Rimsky-Korsakov piece." No commentary, but more eyes. Curtains parted at the side of the stage where fresh eyes watched the show. I gave them more, twirling around that upbeat piece like a child circling a merry-go-round, unrelenting in my excitement, tireless to their ears.

"Stop." He turned to the parted curtain, caught an eye, and then returned to me. "Ryder, please give me a moment."

One moment, two moments, three, four, he didn't return. To move would be to lose, but the stillness in my body competed poorly with my racing heart. It was as if I had returned to the days when I first arrived in New York. I reached for the hand that fed the fingers that dance on the instrument that resulted in this delay, and I picked. Fervently, I annoyed the wounds that soothed the untold horrors that started three days before Christmas Eve.

Nothing: not even a ruffle of the curtain, and so I sat, picked at my hand, and wiped the blood onto the only dress I owned. I took a deep inhale, surprised by the fresh scent of pine. I was clean and vast, open to opportunity.

"Ryder." A foot parted the curtains. I followed it upwards to a face expressing decision and doubt. "Just give us a few more minutes, please."

Minutes to dwell, seconds to ruminate. The more time they gave, the less time it took for me to deteriorate. Uninvited memories rushed in. Saturday recitals, rows of chairs, my parents sitting upright, proud of the daughter competing with those beyond her years. How come my dad didn't know that I didn't care he lost his job, that he left us alone and moved to Las Vegas? I was not Mom. I would have understood.

No, stop. "Don't think about it," I said out loud. I did well. You felt it when you hit your mark. That room was temporary. Levi was temporary. I was okay. It was okay.

"You okay?" The words came along with a shake. "What happened to your hand?" Mr. Schroeder, this curious conductor who wore leather wristbands as if he were a hippy, who played with his baton as if it were a toy, took my hand in his as if it were a bomb. "You're bleeding."

Stories are excuses, and excuses are curses. "I fell, tripped coming out of the subway, and my hand scraped across the sidewalk. I accidentally picked the scab."

"Well, watch yourself. Protect those hands, they're a gift." He paused long enough to merge those words with an unwanted memory. "You've played Principal 2nd before?"

I nodded. Please, just the verdict. The violin had been my life for a decade now, the orchestra for half that. From the time I held that 1/16th sized violin at the age of three, it was who I was, who my parents made me be.

"We're impressed." My chest that had heaved from the hurtful memories, slowed from his sympathetic smile. "We're just having a hard time deciding where to place you. How well do you sight read?"

I held open my arms, inviting the mystery sheet from which to show off the remainder of my talents.

"How can you play with your hand so torn up?" He asked, but his eyes connected with mine in a way that spoke of truths, of honesty, of knowing that music healed all the things that hurt.

The sheet of music landed on my stand. And I loved that it took all of me to focus on it, to watch the sea of notes ebb and flow, to run up, then down, to be wholly absorbed knowing that no other soul, no other basic need could come between me and the will to play this song.

"We're placing you as Principal 2nd. Congratulations."

Principal 2nd, the leader of the section for second violin. I did it. The hall opened, inviting me into its grandeur. I saw the lights running up the aisles, the glimmer dancing over the carpet. History and provenance going headstrong in my mind. And now I was part of it, part of the future of Carnegie, the future of New York. I *really* did it.

"Tomorrow, Sunday, we've scheduled a make-up practice because of the holiday break. It's at one p.m. I trust that you can make that." The baton clicked slowly against my stand, then pointed at me. "It's important."

CHAPTER TEN

"You're late!"

Three hours had passed since that moment of elation; since I listened to other parents' praise as I aimlessly walked from that music hall with nobody by my side. Not ideal, but far from Levi's sight, I had walked to my school to stash my violin in my outdoor lockers.

I feared everything ahead of me. The lonely Saturday night, the weekend crowd, the anxiety that there would be no diving under tables to devour the scraps, just resignation as I watched the leftovers scraped into the bin.

"Stop the daydreaming, can't you see it's overflowing in here tonight!"

Nobody cared that I got a spot. Marco certainly didn't. Levi, no. Mr. Meyers would, maybe the librarian. He'd care, Jack, the man on the steps, but I'd never see him again, so what did it matter? Why should I even care when there was nobody to tell?

Katherine would, probably. I heard her silent applause as she assembled that binder, sliding each of my awards into their sleeves. "Ryder, this is such an accomplishment. I'd be proud to have you as a daughter," she beamed. Then, why didn't you? Why did you throw me away on Christmas day! To hell with you.

My mother would care. *No, don't go there.* She would pull me into a bear hug and squeeze me until I couldn't breathe. *Ryder, stop!* "You're doing everything I ever wanted for myself," she would have said. *No. She's dead. She doesn't exist anymore!* And then I would have hugged her, reminded her she played better than me, that I would be nothing without her. *STOP.* I couldn't catch my breath.

I pressed the creases into napkins until my thumb was red from abuse; flattened out the table covers from one side and then the other, always making sure a wrinkle still existed so I would have something else to do. A plate passed behind me, the succulent aroma churning my empty stomach. Dysphoria came. A tear fell. Another. I caught myself in the mirror and saw regret: from how I acted, my decision to run, the burden from what was to come. *Think confident; be confident.* No, I wouldn't listen to her anymore. *Body language matters.* But I couldn't help but hear. She was my mom, and I loved her. *If you feel small, you are small.* Her words, not mine, and I would never hear them again. *Stand tall, be strong.* I hated her. More than anything in the world, I hated that woman.

The hatred helped; the anger stopped the tears, and hunger trumped all. I breathed slower, willing myself to hold it together, to accept that I could do this on my own. The mirror spoke, and I saw myself calm, and like footsteps walking away in the snow, the beating in my heart faded to a lull.

The storm was passing, and the restaurant came back to life. I saw smiling friends, furious couples, people that appeared to have too much personality, and those that seemed to have none. Everyone's problems on display, and the chaos of it all restored my place.

With reasoning rebuilt, I worked the nearest napkin into something I learned too long ago to remember when. The ears were bent, and I played with them to make them straight. Better, I moved onto the next table, clearing the dishes and wiping down the chairs. I snuck a roll into my apron. And when nobody saw, I slipped in another.

"Is that a bunny?" A small voice spoke. "I like bunnies, can I see it?"

I hopped the napkin over an imaginary terrain and handed it to a pig-tailed girl. Cute, she had two pink ribbons cascading over her shoulders. Her smile so innocent and pure, you almost missed her see-through eyes.

"Say thank you, Lynzie. That's very nice of—Ryder, is that you?"

A lower voice, an important voice, a voice I had played over and over in my head. A yogurt-covered takeaway menu teetered at the table's edge. I quickly covered my mouth to hide my shock.

"You *work* here?" He waved the menu, then shifted his focus to the other side of the room, to the man who did nothing for the reputation of restaurant owners as a whole. "Is that your father?"

"No." Shaking my head to erase such an awful thought. "God, no!" From the reflection in the mirror, Marco's belly led the way.

"Ah, sorry." I glanced over my shoulder, and the object in the mirror indeed was closer than it appeared. "Really, sorry, but I have to go."

"Ahh, hello there, Mr. Scott, can I help you with anything?" Marco asked.

May I help you, you buffoon.

"Run along Siobhan, I'll take care of the Scotts."

Already ahead of his command, I set my foot to spin.

"Wait, hold up," Jack finally spoke.

I supposed I should have anticipated the firm grip of a man who would only accept the truth. I couldn't meet his eyes, no matter how much of his piece of advice burned into my mind.

"Why did you lie to me?" His voice smaller. "You said your name was Ryder."

Oh, no, please, no. My breathing became a shaky staccato. I just stood there frozen, my lips a quivering mess. No.

"Who's Ryder? Sir, I think you have the wrong girl." Clearly clueless about the fallout to come, Marco bounced the bunny away from this little girl, who Jack called Lynzie and towards the nine-year-old boy, the brother I had named Bob.

"That's Ryder." From the tip of Jack's finger to the button on my shirt could not have been more than a foot. "You hire thirteen-year-olds?"

"Mr. Scott, there's been a misunderstanding. This is Siobhan Schrader, and she's sixteen-years-old."

Low, I could feel the ocean floor erode. "No, Ryder, is that true?" Those green-grey eyes scrunched. "Siobhan?"

"Ryder?"

The little girl's hand reached for my arm. "I really like the way you made the bunny." Her cheeks were frosted pink, the same shade as her dress, and even the lightness of her touch couldn't distract me from Marco's scorn, from Jack's disappointment.

"Okay, right, out back, let's go." Marco's grip replaced Jack's. The charade was over. Cornered in the back room, I could only focus on the gestures that accompanied his cruel but definitive words. The back door flew open, letting in the frigid cold. It was dark outside, the alley a criminal's calling.

"Give me that!" And when he yanked the apron off my body, the bread rolls tumbled to the floor. "Figures. You're out of here!" He pushed my jacket into my chest and shoved me out the door.

Shaking in an alley, the slam brought a lid of a trashcan straight to the ground. I jumped. A cat slithered out from behind. To my left was a dark and foreboding passage; to my right the same; and in front, a second cat leaped from inside the bin, a chicken bone clenched tight between its teeth. I moved towards the stench, to the solution to my hunger. I dipped in, those bags in the bin moving about. I freaked, jumped back: afraid of the dark, terrified of my future, ashamed of what I had become.

I slid down Marco's door and curled into a ball. The latch released, opening it up just enough for the warm air to invite me to stay.

"Mr. Scott, I have this under control. Please return to your seat. This area is for employees only. She's fine." Marco's tone was a fabricated concern.

"She didn't look fine." The man's distress was not. "Where is she?"

"Jack, is this the young girl you told me about, the one from the library?"

"Mrs. Scott, please, Mr. Scott, I'm going to have to insist that you leave the kitchen and return to your children. They're sitting alone at the table."

"Oh, well, that's sweet of you to worry about our children when you don't seem to care about the minor you hired, then fired. Is that right? You fired her? Where is she?"

"Mr. Scott." Marco's voice boomed louder and with more of a threat. "I know you are an important man and are accustomed to getting your way, but this is *my* kitchen in *my* restaurant. How I hire and fire my employees is my concern, not yours. Now, please go tend to your family!"

"Where is she?"

"Sir, don't make me call the police."

Silence, then footsteps, first heavy then light, fading then absent. A door slammed. It all went quiet, leaving me feeling both deserted and relieved. The cycle complete, someone who talked like they cared, could not show that they did. Alone, I rolled tight into a ball and banged my head against my knees. The thud matched my pulse, which swooshed through my ears. A different sound competed. Tap. It interrupted my rhythm, and—tap tap—grew louder, commanding—tap tap—and closer. I banged faster to keep up with its pace. Tap. Tap. Tap.

"What's going on?"

I didn't look up, Jack's presence too near to miss. Little taps coming closer were faster in rhythm. They pitter-patted down the alley until they stopped, no doubt as instructed by their trusted father.

"Hey." He tussled my hair. "You can trust me. What's going on?"

Slowly, giving up, I did as he advised, and raised my head.

"My knees are too old to squat like this." He sat.

I ran. With a sudden burst of adrenaline, I bolted the moment his bum hit the ground. The alley was long, my escape futile. No match was I for a grown man in a foot race, he quickly reached my side.

"Please"—his breathing heavy— "don't do that again. Where do you live? I'm taking you to your home."

I pulled hard and struggled urgently against his grip, too unglued to do the logical thing and scream.

"Jack, stop." A high-pitched voice closed in.

"Yeah, Jack, stop!" No way would this man ever see where I lived.

He hesitated, but not too long, hovering his hand behind my neck. Then, perhaps to test my instincts, and quite possibly his, he moved it away, inviting me to choose my fate.

I turned towards that higher voice. "Jack, stop," she said again, but he already had.

I took one last glance at the end of the alley, at the last chance I had to be done with this man, the last time I could choose to be on my own. My innate instincts resurfaced, and I took a step away from her voice. But before my foot could land on the pavement, his intuition overruled, and I found myself, once again, at the mercy of his grip.

We moved onward towards their car, his family following behind in startled silence.

PART TWO

CHAPTER ELEVEN

Hiss.

Sporadic and disconnected, the static escaping the radio competed with the endless childish banter flooding the car.

"Why aren't you blinking? You don't blink enough. Mom, she's not blinking," his nameless son rambled. "Mom, now she's not opening them. Why aren't you opening them?" Definitely not a Bob, not anywhere close to the brother I wanted.

The station changed, and authority spit from the speakers. Meaningless words strung together: terrorist, Kabul, President, car. The station changed. A woman's cackle screeched, and I tensed from the noxious noise ricocheting off the car's interior. The window came down. Swoosh, another car raced by. A horn shattered my eardrums. Too loud!

"Sarah, please, stop." Jack's voice was clipped but composed, calming me enough to sneak a peek into the rearview mirror, to study the face of the man who, just a week before, had been a fantasy and nothing more. The window glided up. The radio went silent. Peace came.

"You're doing it again. Blink!"

If only for a moment.

"Thomas, enough, keep your opinions to yourself," the woman said.

Thomas, so that was the name of his son. Sarah Scott must be hers. Marco kept calling them Mr. and Mrs. Scott.

"And buckle your seatbelt." The whites of her eyes traveled fast over the three kids wedged tight into the backseat of their car. "And yours too, Ryder."

Stunned, shocked to hear my name flowing from the lips of a woman I didn't know, I clenched my hands between my thighs.

Jack reached for the mirror to measure my obedience, and I hid in the space of the boy who obsessed over if my eyes would close. He shoved me away, squashing me against the girl who giggled when my bunny bounced her way. Her name was Lynzie, so Jack had said.

"Ouch!" She yelped before tossing me back into Thomas.

Jack's hand tilted the rearview mirror more. "Ryder, do as you were told."

The pushing seen at eye level turned into kicks hidden from view—soft enough to know this boy had a heart, hard enough to understand that I didn't have a place in it.

"Finally, we're home. How come we had to leave the restaurant without eating? It was her fault, wasn't it?"

"Thomas, mind your manners."

Diving into an underground garage, when everybody hopped out, Jack stepped squarely in front of his son.

"Sorry, Dad."

Commuting a sentence, this imposing man moved aside, granting the boy entrance into an opulent lift. One after another his family followed—the boy, the girl, the mom.

"Well, come on." Jack's foot blocked the door from closing.

We rode to the top in a disorienting silence, and when the doors opened to a private penthouse, my mouth hung in disbelief. Panels of glass enclosed the space, extending all the way from the cherry wood floor to the domed ceiling many feet above my head. A chandelier spread its tentacles wide.

No comparison to my old life, this entrance was vast. No closed doors sprouted from a narrow hallway; curtains didn't cover tiny windows in dark-stained frames. This entryway didn't just let you in, it invited you into a home.

"Let me get your jacket." Feminine hands swept over my shoulders, removing the physical burden. "Who left the fireplace on?" She added.

"Who turned it on?" A joke, not a fight. Sarah kissed her husband's cheek before flipping a switch, which extinguished the flames. Its sudden stillness sent my attention to the picture above it, to a boat resting peacefully inside a frame. It was modest and quaint, engaging in a way that teased a dream. Not at all how I was welcomed at home. By her—the Mona Lisa. Every day it was the same, those mischievous eyes complicating a smile. My mother chose that. Why couldn't she have chosen a boat?

"Daddy? Can we eat now?" Little Lynzie couldn't have been more than seven. How would she know any difference? A boat, a frowning lady, what did it matter when her mother tied her hair with bows?

"May we." Jack corrected before tossing a leftover pizza box onto the kitchen table. Cardboard quickly dragged against wood as the two children rushed to devour the prize.

One task done, Jack's mouth opened, ready to revive the inquiry, and I scrunched my eyes to brace for another blow.

"No, it's mine!"

But fighting over pizza saved me from revealing too much. That last slice of pepperoni and the dizzying feud that came from it offering a blissful, yet meaningless, reprieve.

"No, Lynzie, let go!"

Losing patience, their father commandeered the wilted slice, and the cold cheese slid, then clung to the end. It just hung there, undecided, as if it wasn't sure how to challenge the laws of nature. Jack gave it a shake, and a brave cat pounced, and for many moments more, we all listened to the jingle of its bell.

It sprang onto Jack's lap, its peaceful purring cutting the mounting tension. A conciliatory meow came next, and Jack replied: softer, quieter, kinder. "Ryder, please look at me and tell me what's going on."

"Will you promise to believe me?"

"You asked me that before, and I did."

Yes, on the library steps when I lied to this man, he believed me.

His hand flowed over the cat's back, running down its tail, and then with nowhere to go, it reached for my hand.

I left it stranded. The room grew cold, a chilling dread replacing the warmth the fire had offered.

"I'm not going to hurt you."

Physically no.

"Sweetheart, we know you're scared. Too many things are frightening in this world, but you are not alone, not in the least."

Sarah said this. Her friendly voice off to my left.

"Mommy, let's make a real one."

I moved with Lynzie to a second fireplace, focusing on her two sticks of kindling thumping together, to old ashes sprinkled too close to the cream-colored tile.

"Not now, honey. We're talking with Ryder," Sarah's voice traveled to her daughter, but her eyes stayed glued to mine, to the strange girl in filthy clothes picking at the scabs on her hands.

Lynzie drummed her sticks against the table, then the couch, then the planter, the steady beat increasing in volume, the pounding deafening. Tap, thud, clank. The speed deteriorating into random chaos. Loud. Frenzied. Painful.

"Make her stop," I yelled.

I deserved that look, the one that took everything Sarah had to hold her temper, the one that if we'd known each other just a while longer would have evolved into a lecture. Her fists curved, creating a ball, the knuckles whitening as her nails drove into her palm. Her eyes darted to her daughter, to that honest smile of her youthful innocence, and the color returned.

Sarah's hand covered mine.

Everything about this woman bothered me: the dimples that sank deep when she smiled, the soft skin, the patience that waited, the attention. "Take all the time you need." Her hand glided back and forth.

Katherine had done this too.

I supposed I should have learned to pull back, to stop the bond before it started, but a woman's touch was comfort. Suddenly, she squeezed my hand tight, and I tried to fight a surge of emotions. I tensed my face, widening my eyes, doing anything to stop the damn from breaking. But when she wrapped her arm around my shoulder, tears squirted from my eyes.

"Ryder?" Sarah whispered. "Do you have a last name?"

I shifted, determined to stop the flow. I found a fly and focused hard. It wanted to escape—I understood. It searched for an exit, panicked that one didn't exist. It circled around the room, gaining momentum, preparing for what it needed to do. At full speed, it crashed into the glass again and again and again.

"Ryder, where do you live?" Jack took over. The tone changed. Lower, sterner, it contrasted with Sarah's faint pleas. "Like I told you in the alley, you can trust us."

Not answering Jack would be a mistake. I opened my mouth to lie, to set a scene that he'd believe, but the first word cracked, then the second, my voice refusing to play along.

Someone's chair leg ground against the tile floor in a punishing scrape. I focused on the tile. It was a soft white. The carpet resting on top was not. That was brown, with patches of beige. The colors matched the sofa, which matched the drapes, which matched the cat.

Sarah's hand squeezed again. "Where do you live?" She asked, repeating Jack's question with a lilt so innocent it could have come from a child. "Okay, let's try this. Where did you sleep last night? Did you sleep on the street?"

I bolted upright, startling the cat who braced his paws wide. "No!"

"Okay, okay," Jack said calmly, patting his hand against the seat. "See, we're getting somewhere." His eyes locked onto mine and lowered me into the chair. "Ryder, remember on the steps of the library, you told me about a boy who owed you money? Coming clean, I never believed you because I knew something else was going on. I just didn't realize it was something like this. How about coming clean now?"

What? The wedge of tissue crumpled under my teeth sprang free. Back on my feet, I pointed my finger an inch from his nose. "You *lied*! You just said you believed me, like three minutes ago. I can't believe anything you say!"

"Ryder. Please." His methodical words infuriated me more. "I'm going to ask that you stay seated and control your temper. You weren't ready to tell me or, for that matter, trust me." This time, his hand sternly lowered me into the chair. "You still don't, and that's fine. But, Ryder, I'm afraid you don't have a choice."

I crossed my arms to defend my attitude, and every part of me grew hot: my mood, my anger, my body. Little beads of sweat collected on my brow. Untangling my arms, choosing instead to take my fury out on the pizza box, I flicked my fingers violently against the cardboard.

Jack yanked it away.

"Well, here we are at a standstill," Jack said as he turned my head by clamping the crown. "Ryder, I would love to promise you whatever it is that you want to hear, but until I know, until you give me just a bit of your trust, I can't help."

"Maybe I should just go then."

"You're smarter than that."

Yes, I was because *when someone throws you a rope, you climb to the top and steal it.* I noticed the worn and tired chair sitting alone in the corner. "Can I sleep here tonight?"

"You're most definitely sleeping here tonight."

A win or an immediate worry, my pent-up breath barely made it past my lips.

"Ryder." Sarah's steady palms pressed flat against the table, her elbows cocking. She leaned until her wrists would bend no more. "We need to see where you live." That easy-going high-pitched voice dropped two octaves. "First."

Sarah's orders unfolded like a captain steering a ship into war. She didn't wait, and no amount of negotiating would change her course. She thrust the jacket into my hands.

"You don't want to bring the children," I instructed.

"We'll decide what we want. Let's get going." An invisible whip ushered me out the door.

***

As we drove away from wealth and into squalor, I saw my choices on full display, something my seat on the subway had hidden far from view. And for the first time, I understood the full extent of my fall. How it looked to others. How as we drove away from the elitist neighborhoods of Tribeca, and around the middle-class of the upper East Side, how, all too suddenly, we fell fast into the filth of Harlem.

"Jack, I'm not taking the kids up there." At odds with the control, which she so recently commanded, her voice became that mouse. "And I'm not sitting in the car with them either."

I told her—if she would have only listened. Even still, from my new perspective, the building looked sinister, much more than it did twelve hours before. Violent even. The screen door hung wrong, dangling at a tilt, and with every gust of wind, it scraped menacingly against the concrete slab.

A teenage boy, with jeans riding low and hair spiked high, stepped onto the porch. He smirked. One pack of smokes rolled out of his pocket, the tap to the back looked cool. A rebel from a high school movie, he ducked his head to light the stick, and a mere second passed before a ring of smoke circled the air.

"Wow! Did you see that, Lynzie?" Thomas awed.

I cracked the door.

"Close it," Jack ordered.

"But this is—"

"I said, close it." Jack held up a finger, only one, and it stayed there for three long breaths.

I inched it closed, barely sounding the latch.

Two other boys joined the one, and a collage of little rings filled the air. Jack's hands gripped the wheel until his veins bulged blue. Waiting for what, he eventually checked my door and then his wife, never stopping to bother with me. "Honey, we'll take the kids to Guerin's."

We headed back up the spiral, back to the safety of wealth and the comfort of a doorman. To where boys wore belts and windows shined—to the building we had just recently left.

"He's on his way down. Evelyn's inside." Sarah's thumbs hovered over her phone, a statue-like posture that formed the moment we pulled away from the curb. "In the elevator."

"Sarah, I don't need the play by play."

Staring at their building, I saw nobody new, just a doorman in uniform, a man with a job. Bored but paid, he traced his shoe over the remnants of gum. I read his mind and wondered if he too would fail.

"He's here."

Where? Confused and tense, the door opposite mine popped open, and that voice I knew filled the car. "Hey, Jack. What's up?" Low, slow, a southern drawl only not from the south. He lived across the street.

"Guerin, you remember, Ryder?"

Puzzled, he didn't remember. I couldn't forget. Creases pressed tight, shoes shined bright, how many men had the initials GL etched meticulously into their belt?

"We won't be long. No more than an hour, I suppose." Jack spoke as if he knew what troubles lay ahead.

The man nodded once like Mr. Meyers would have done, and then with the two kids in tow, the three of them disappeared behind a set of tinted doors.

Moments of silence went unanswered as we idled outside, the digital clock on the dashboard ticking over time. A minute passed.

Another. Too scared to ask why; too nervous not to fidget, I pulled the seatbelt further from my chest, then followed Sarah's gaze. It shot over the building but under the sky. A light flicked on, illuminating the balcony at the top; two children waved, and onward we went.

Not surprised by our return, the boys that had loitered from afar now circled the car up close, and a poorly tattooed hand immediately seized Jack's door.

"Let me get that for you, sir." A hazy blue line etched his skin. It formed a skull, a red one created the crown, and from its skeletal mouth, a thick black smear was a poor excuse for a cigar. "Right this way,"

"Gentlemen." Jack nodded.

Snickers, then mocking, a doo-rag ripped off his head was laid waiter-like over his arm. "Gen-tle-men!" Strutting, chest out, thumbs tucked into imagined lapels. "That's right, my man. We treat you wid respect."

Jack let out a faint chuckle before looping his arm tighter around his wife.

"Get a load of this!" The skinhead ran his pinky down the hood. "Cha-ching!"

Jack's look pivoted first to his wife, reassuring her of her safety, and then to me, telegraphing the caustic conversation soon to come. "Thanks, Tesla knows how to make 'em."

"Whooey. They sure does." The beep from setting the alarm was a call to arms. "What up, man? Where's the trust, brother?"

Jack grabbed my neck, and with a force of a prison guard, shoved me sternly down the shadowy hall. I motioned up, four of my fingers waving through the air. We ascended slowly, inhaling the scent of urine. The second floor smelled like pot. Drawn-out wailing and grunting came from somewhere on the third.

Mumbling to each other and cursing the circumstance that brought them to this place, they stopped at the fourth floor, staring vacantly, bracing themselves for what lay inside.

"Is this it?" Sarah whispered.

I opened the door.

"Yeaahhh, nice ride, totally agree!" Balancing precariously on the window's ledge, Levi had been watching, waiting for us to emerge. "What up, Ryder? I see you made new friends. That's gonna cost you."

Jack glared at Levi, at the stack of used Styrofoam containers, the rolled cash, at the pile of sheetrock trailing from the hole in the wall. He picked up the glass bowl and took a whiff. "Collect your things!" He slammed it against the table.

"Oh, dude, careful, and what kinda greeting is that?"

The fated confrontation between Levi and Jack I did not witness because Sarah intervened: pushing me into the corner, pointing to my bed, asking for confirmation, then not waiting for a reply. She grabbed my foul-smelling bag from under the cot and tossed in everything within her reach. "This yours? And this? Where are all your clothes?" Her actions were a mirror into my all-too-recent past, to when adults rushed in to take control of what they could barely grasp themselves.

I searched the room for more air to breathe.

Jack's words with Levi started off clipped, then swelled to shouts. Demands were made, and Sarah hurried me down the stairs. Jack followed quickly, leaping two stairs for her one, and when he reached her side, he dug spastically through her bag.

"What are you doing?" I yanked the wallet from his grip. Either Levi had lied, or this fiasco made me forget, but I yelled what I thought was fact. "I paid him already." Did I? "Maybe. Only pay him for three—no four—days."

He shuffled through Sarah's wallet and then tunneled into her eyes. "Get her in the car."

Then, she passed the order onto me. "Go!"

CHAPTER TWELVE

Stamina comes from desire, and desire comes from will. The question wasn't whether I was willing to be at the end of their authority, but if I had the stamina to do so. And that answer was burrowed deep within my desire.

Collapsing against the car door, too drained to do anything but stare, those long arms that just packed my bag reached around my chest and clipped the belt. A floral bouquet came and went. We drove back to Guerin's front door and onward to their garage. And because I no longer had the energy to fight against the inevitable, I said nothing. I did nothing. I wanted this to end.

Jack held his words until after our coats found hooks and boots came off, until a chill circled, and nothing but the fireplace could offer hope. I picked up the fireplace remote only for him to snatch it from my hand. Nobody moved. Time stalled then leaped straight into the future, into the one that I no longer controlled.

"Ryder, over there, have a seat." Grave, lacking even a hint of a smile, Jack wore the look of a thousand crusades. "Kids, off to bed."

This nine-year-old boy responded by dutifully taking his younger sister's hand and leading her into the shadows flooding the hall. Siblings. If only I had one.

"Ryder, please sit." Sarah's voice contrasted dramatically with that of her husband's. It was soft and comforting, almost something a scared girl could trust. I resisted her lead but still found myself on the couch, wedged between her and the measures of their life: a child's sketchpad, a well-loved Barbie, a familiar book. Very familiar, too recently significant, I traced my fingers over the title.

"That's a bit too advanced for you." She lifted it from my grip.

"No, I read it." It was a moment that stilled the room, a transition from knowingly dealing with an ignorant runaway to the possibility of something else. "In the sixth grade," I offered as if that would clear her confusion.

"That's not in the middle-school curriculum. Did somebody give it to you to read? Did your mother give it to you?"

Goosebumps came instantly, followed fast by those shallow breaths I tried so hard to hide. The tingling started in my fingers before moving up my hand, and I bounced the tips together to prove they weren't numb.

Sarah showed Jack the title, then tossed the book between her hand, its rapid rhythm no competition for my racing heart.

"It's a good book, *All the Light We Cannot See:* won the Pulitzer Prize, I believe." Jack spoke to Sarah directly, excluding me to serve a purpose. The book stilled in her hands and stranded my eyes.

"The author did a wonderful job with the characters," she said, quickly flipping the pages as if a gust of wind had whooshed through the room.

I seized the book, but it landed wrong, on words my mother had read aloud, on a name, Marie-Laure, the blind abandoned girl. I grabbed an inch and folded it over, and I saw the other name, Werner, the inventive and curious boy. Their world to me back then had been as distant from mine as I was to the moon.

"I think the boy, Werner, grew up in an orphanage." Jack plotted, and then Sarah countered.

"Yes, and the girl had lost her mother, had only a father. He vanished if I remember." She removed the book from my hands. "Where is your father, Ryder?"

That moon closed in and grew larger than my lies. My mother was dead. My father didn't care. And I knew only this: to all the people in this room, in all of New York, any word that came next would be the only truth allowed.

"May I go to bed, please?"

"I'm sorry, sweetheart, no, you can't." Sarah's hair was straight, longer than I remembered in the alley. "Ryder, where is your mother?" It was behind her back then, hidden from view when she jogged down the road. "You are a beautiful, young woman: intelligent." Sarah waved the book in the air as if its presence were needed to defend this fact. "Why were you living in such a place?" Her head swung wide. "And for how long?"

"It wasn't that bad."

"Ryder." Jack rose, moving from that beat-up leather chair to the coffee table opposite me. Removing his glasses, he settled less than a foot away, warming the air around me in a suffocating trap.

I focused on the lonely leather chair in the corner, on its cracks and sags, the scratch that wandered down the side. I pictured an old woman sitting in it with long needles in her hands and a trail of yarn flowing over the arm. She tried to rock, but it wouldn't move. It made me mad, so I focused harder, willing this ridiculous illusion to perform tricks that mattered how.

"It was my mother's," Jack said. "She's no longer with us."

I swallowed.

"Kiddo, evidently, something went wrong in your life. Maybe somebody treated you unjust or scared you, and I empathize with your reasons for keeping quiet."

His hand gripped my knee, and a jolt forced me to scooch away.

"It's okay." His voice was patient, attempting to comfort. "You need to accept the only reason you're sitting here is because we're worried, and because we care."

I brushed his hand away, aware that the closer he got, the more willing I may become.

"Okay," he murmured, reaching for my other hand, tenderly clamping my wrist. "We are strangers to you, and we—" He stopped, abruptly flipping over my hand. "What happened here?" Instinctively, I pulled free. "Tell me."

"I fell."

"Okay," he whispered. "Now, tell me the truth."

My small hand resting in his palm was an egg in a nest— anything could happen, everything could go wrong. He swung himself around to sit beside me on the couch, his eyes examining my wounds.

"It doesn't hurt. I don't know I'm doing it."

No accusation, just attention. Jack leaned and spoke with calm. "Where are your parents?" Closer still, this time with concern. "Maybe they're more worried about you than you think."

"No, they're not. They're dead, both of them." The shock reverberated, pushing their backs upright, pulling their mouths apart. I slid my hand out of Jack's and tucked it under my leg. "December 21st, she died. I never knew my dad."

I wanted this to come out as fact, to coldly state my life's statistics, and then be done, but a tear welled in Sarah's eyes. And when her husband caressed her cheek, a warmth passing between them melted my wall and exposed a longing. I clenched my teeth, stretched open my eyes, trying to hold onto the tear ready to fall.

Sarah stroked my face. "How?"

"I don't remember." Indiscernible, the words barely cleared the air. "I don't know." A flash: a string of red and green lights. I pushed it away, choosing to focus on Jack, to work with a man who was calculating and commanding, who did whatever needed to be done, whenever necessary.

His eyes drooped, pulled down by a complicated sadness, which I had caused. I looked to Sarah, to her face crumpled into a painful scrunch. "You know," she said.

"No." I shook my head hard. "I don't remember anything."

My mind left that couch, wandering over to their elevator. I watched as my shadow pushed the call button once, then twice, pounding against it like bullets spit from a gun. I willed the doors to open. I couldn't have this conversation.

Jack's chest rose and fell against my shoulder. "Try, please." He pleaded.

I closed my eyes, but my mother's deathly blue lips suddenly filled the darkness. I opened them fast. Jack's green-grey eyes locked with mine. Closed again. I searched for a truth I could bear, one from that day, but before the end.

"I just thought there was going to be cake."

They stopped studying me, choosing instead to silently search each other for an interpretation of my cryptic words.

"I looked everywhere."

I had burst through our door, panting by the time I reached the refrigerator. I emptied the entire bottom shelf, searching for the cake I knew she hid. I saw the Tupperware containers piled high on the floor, stacking one on top of the other. Too much clutter; I hated that clutter.

"It wasn't in the car. I didn't know where she put it."

"What happened, Ryder?" Jack asked.

"I met a girl at the park who would be in my class. All I wanted was that cake. I knew she told me to be home by five. I knew it was six. I didn't think it mattered that I forgot to get her something for her birthday. She was the mom. It worked that way."

Sarah's top teeth clamped onto her lower lip, reluctantly committing to my delay. "The car was in the garage?" She finally asked, pulling away until her back arched against the armrest. Her eyes squinted, and a million lines crossed her brow. She reached for my cheek, then stopped, her head tilting as if reconsidering her approach.

"I was just hungry, that's all. I didn't mean to forget." Now dry and serious, I lifted my eyes to meet hers. "Why was I so fixated on that cake?" I cringed reliving how I texted my friends, complaining about how she forgot her own birthday. I laughed at her. I didn't see her.

"If I had come home on time, it wouldn't have happened." More tears followed because when I left for the park, she waved, she said goodbye. I waved back. No, I didn't. But I must have. I did! Bursts of sobs pulsed through their silence.

I squeezed my lids, making the image gone, coercing an alternative truth—one that I could tolerate, that could be said out loud. "She told me she was *too tired* to put up the Christmas lights." Suddenly—senselessly—it clicked, that slide in my mind. It moved forward to the image I could handle, the story I *needed* to create. I burned it deep, building the ladder that toppled, the cord of lights streaming down the stairs, the blood.

"Ryder?"

I described it all, a carnage no child should see, a scene a thousand times better than what I actually saw. "I told her to get up, teased her about her birthday. I didn't see the blood." As I spoke, it all felt real: her body lying on the floor peacefully, as if she was taking a nap. Her lips pink. Her eyes were closed. I didn't see her stare.

But I did. Wide open, hollow, staring through me, making sure I knew it was all my fault. My sobs uncontrolled again, nothing could stop me from seeing her face, or those eyes, or her body contorted. "It's all my fault."

Sarah pulled me tight, burying my head into her chest. "It's not your fault."

But it was. "She didn't wait for me." I burrowed my fingers into

Sarah's arm. "I would have helped." A nausea built, my breaths heaving. "She didn't tell me. Why didn't she tell me?"

The room swallowed my tears.

How my shoes came off, and the sheets turned down. How the blanket covered me, I couldn't say. I lay in a strange bed with a man sitting at my feet and a woman cradling my head, and for the first time in a month, I felt safe.

These two strangers cared. More than my grandmother, who placed me in that foster home. More than my mother's friends who couldn't be bothered. More than everyone else who said they'd be there for me but weren't. None of them cried like Sarah did now, and I would never forget. Ever. And Jack and Sarah knew it, so they held me tight and never let me go.

"It's going to be okay," Sarah said, the last words I remember before sobbing myself to sleep.

CHAPTER THIRTEEN

To forgive and to forget: never in my dreams, never when I was awake. The next morning, I remembered everything: Sarah's tears, Jack's authority, the truth.

Slipping from the sheets, I dangled my feet a foot from the ground, trying to make sense of this room in which I woke. Poles rose like tree trunks from each corner of the bed. A gigantic armoire filled a wall. The comforter matched the couch; the rug matched the footrest; the walls matched it all.

I spun my head towards the laughter. Faint but distinct. I squinted through the crack between the door and its frame. Nothing but mumbling, I cocked my head, moving my ear closer to the voice.

"Do you want me to just tell you what they're talking about?"

Jesus! I jumped so quick I banged my head against the knob.

Thomas had apparated by my side. "You're still not talking to me?" He closed in, his breath the scent of mint. "You didn't say a word to me all last night, and it was kind of rude. I know you have a lot on your mind, but still."

Shocked that such a small frame could exert such poise, I said nothing, did nothing. I just stood there, tending to my wounded ear.

"Well, fine, if you don't want to know. I'll just go back to my room. I was just spying on you anyway."

"Wait!" His arm became my target, pulling me towards him. "No, don't go. What are they saying?"

"They're talking about their lawyer, about what the law says about you."

Instantly, the words from last night began their transformation. My heart leaped, and I winced for setting myself up for such a fall.

"I told them you'd feel that way." His smirk sunk a dimple into his cheek. It was deep and bent as if carved by a knife. "I guess they don't want to get in trouble."

"They're going to turn me in? You have to help me." I yanked my head left, then right, looking for anything that would set me free. The window was a thumb's width open, and I ran towards it, foolishly forgetting we were seven floors up. Frigid air zipped through, the biting chill resurrecting my senses. "I can't go back to California."

"Is *that* where you're from? Wow, that's really far away." Thomas casually leaned against the wall, tapping his foot, as if he were a child in a playground waiting for the bell. "We took a plane there once. I got to sit in *first* class. Ya know, the seats are like *this* big." His hands were spread as wide as he was tall.

I lifted them to dart beneath, frantically searching this too formal room for any trace of my bag.

"I got to meet the president, too. Ya know, he didn't button his suit."

"What?" I just opened the closet and was stunned by how each towel sat symmetrically, one on top of the other. A pillar of ordered colors.

"You know how when you stand, you're supposed to close the top button of your suit, and when you sit down, you open it. The president didn't do that."

"President of what?" I collapsed on the bed, exhausted from my fruitless search.

"The country."

What?

"Ah, you're awake. Let's get some breakfast in you." The woman before me was the mother of the boy who was the son of the man who knew the president. "What's going on with you two?"

"Mom, I was just telling her how you were calling the police."

"Thomas, enough! Sweetheart, we're not calling the police." If her head hadn't tilted towards her son, if her eyes hadn't rolled right, I could have believed her.

More footsteps came, and along with it, an irresistible scent.

From Jack's hand, a crisp slice of bacon swung from side to side. "Do you want this?" The chuckle that followed came from a different man: a guy in worn-out jeans, a father wearing a baseball hat backward with a Yankee's top to match. "Do you?" It tickled as he bounced the bacon off my nose.

Instinctively, I moved my mouth to bite, but by an inch, I missed. Jack brought it closer, and a little pool of saliva crested under my lip. A millisecond too late, he swept it away, the tiny drop of craving splashing onto the floor. "Stop it."

"Well then, come hither, follow me into our kitchen."

Forgetting about Thomas and his harsh words, my rumbling stomach overruled my worries, and I willingly followed Jack down the hall. He spun to face me, teasing me by rocking that strip of heaven back and forth. Then poof! It disappeared into his mouth.

"Whaattt?" I couldn't contain my giggle.

"Take a seat, my friend. I'll whip you up a plate."

I didn't. I trailed him past the refrigerator with its colorful sketches, around the marble-topped island littered with crayons and pencils and stood next to him like a dog waiting for his bone. I salivated at the stove.

"Don't let Sarah see you do this. She's really uptight." He winked, picking up a slice and slowly lowering it into my mouth.

"Oh, my God. That is soooo good."

"Do you want an egg with—"

"Yes, please."

"See, yes, you can be taught." The spatula directed me to the chairs tucked under the kitchen bar.

I followed it further and saw the rest of the family bathed in sunshine as if they were a cat basking in a cone of light. It reflected off the glass in Sarah's hand, off the large plastic jewelry on Lynzie's finger. It made me happy, somehow, to see everything so bright.

"What's that on your neck?" Thomas cut through my moment of peace.

I quickly flipped my collar, but Sarah, folding it down, used her thumb to measure its size.

"It's not a hickey," I said. Once a source of pride, it had now become a telltale sign that my life circled around a dream. "It's an occupational hazard," I explained. "A fiddler's neck, a violin hickey." Nothing but blank looks from them; maybe I misread their standing. "You know when the violin rests against the left side of the neck. It creates friction, and the pressure causes bruising."

"You play the violin? Lynzie bounced in her chair. "My best friend plays the violin!"

"How old is she?

"My age, seven."

"I started when I was three."

"Really." Sarah's eyes moved to Jack's, then to my neck, then back to Jack. "Really."

Seriously? Playing the violin seemed as natural to me as Sunday morning breakfast was to them. And on cue, as if to validate the point, Jack set that sizzlin' plate smack dab in front of my feasting eyes. I picked up my fork, making ready to dive. "Oh, sorry." Rude, I knew, I placed it back down.

"No, go ahead, hun," Sarah urged me on.

"No, I'll wait."

Lynzie squealed. "For what, silly?"

Huh? Wait. Why was nobody rubbing sleep from their eyes? None of them looked like they just rolled out of bed. I shifted to look at the clock on the building across the street. It had all its arms in all the wrong places. "Ohhhh, shit." I grabbed Jack's wrist, triple-tapping his iWatch, stunned to see Mickey's arms pointing to twelve and two. I shot up. "Oh, my God! Shit."

"Hey there, young lady. Language, please," Jack said.

"How could you let me sleep so late?" Irrationally, I pushed the plate frantically away. Then, restoring reason, I rushed it closer to inhale another bite.

Swallowing fast and shoving one more forkful in despite the lack of room, I almost choked as I scolded them again and again. "Why did you do that? Shit." Little bits of egg tumbled over my lip.

"Language!" Jack's voice was sharp.

No more games, Jack rose when I did, but before he could do anything, I bee-lined to the room in which I slept and catapulted through its bathroom door. Horrified by the image looking back at me in the mirror, I wanted to cry. The trauma from last night vandalized my face, bedhead ransacked my hair. I sniffed under my arms and cringed. Along with looking homeless, which I had avoided when I was, I stank. I kicked the door closed.

"Ryder, please tell me what's going on." More forceful, and not the least bit muffled by the barrier, Jack had arrived on the other side of the door.

Why was it always the same question? "I'll tell you when I get back." Clear, concise, and incontestable, I ripped off my clothes and threw on the shower, jumping in before the water warmed.

Finished in two minutes flat, I had refined showering down to an art. Never say I didn't learn anything from living at Levi's. Toweling off, the doorknob rattled, then stopped, then shook again. After a quick sniff, I pulled the same soiled pink t-shirt over my dripping wet hair and tucked it into the well-worn jeans. The door slammed into him when I whipped it open.

"Ah, young lady, you're not going anywhere." Teeth clenched and both arms crossed, I ignored all of it as I ducked and spun like a veteran running-back—all the while reminding him that I would be-back-by-three. Bold, full of confidence, like Thomas, I, too, could morph into a mature adult when push came to shove.

"Let's you and I have a talk." That hand, the one that comforted me last night and teased me this morning, authoritatively grabbed my t-shirt and dragged me across the room.

I hopped, balancing on my left foot while attempting to tug my shoe over the right. "I don't have time."

He lowered me onto the bed, grabbing the desk chair and fixing it four inches from the edge.

"I'm sorry, really Jack, I am, but I need to get to orchestra practice." Slithering under the invisible barrier he placed around me, I ran across the room in search of my other shoe. Finding it under the armoire, I collapsed to the floor, tying the laces into a double knot.

"I think you can miss a week," he said.

Sarah had arrived at the scene. He glanced at her, who, by the look on her face, had already made the leap in logic.

"Wait. What orchestra?" He finally got there.

"Please!" Dread settled. Unequivocally, Mr. Schroeder had made one thing clear: I must be at the studio at one p.m. on Sunday. I latched onto Jack's wrist again, baffled why a grown man, who seemed so much an adult, would choose something as childish as Mickey to display the time.

"It's 12:17!" My breathing took a turn towards hysteria. "We're fucked," I shouted, then reflexively cringed. It took less than a second to remember that this was *not* Levi's, that I need not look far to find somebody to beat me across the head.

"I'm sorry." No response was not good. "I just started saying that, just like in these last few weeks. They all said it, so I—"

"Just thought it would be fine to repeat." His arm cut the air to home in the point, but all I saw was Mickey and his foot tapping the seconds away. Sarah closed in on the conversation, and I grabbed his wrist again to show her the minutes that had passed, the three minutes that felt as if they were twenty.

"Please. Please. Please."

"Jack." The tip of Sarah's finger gently glided across his forearm, and his muscles instantly relaxed. "Let's just talk on the way." Raising her voice, she bellowed over her shoulder. "Kids, go get your coats. Hurry."

***

During the entire trip, from their house to my school—to pick up my violin—to the concert hall, Jack never said a word, and it wasn't because he couldn't get one in.

Always calculating, Sarah cataloged my responses as if she was tasked with writing my biography. "Tell me again. How did you get into the orchestra?"

People audition. How was this such a mystery?

Lynzie wedged her head between the two front seats, announcing to all the cardinal sin of Sarah's rule. "Is my best friend gonna be there? She always goes someplace on the weekend with her violin. Oh, wait, is this Sunday? She goes on Saturday, right Mommy?"

"Sit back, you, and buckle your seatbelt!"

Lynzie—she really didn't look much like a Lynzie—now physically bolted to the backseat, transferred her energy to running her mouth. "What's your favorite cartoon—" random— "do you have a best friend"—immaterial— "do you get to play a solo—" oddly relevant. Caught off guard by the practical question, I had to think.

She poked me in the rib. "Hey, I'm talking to you."

"Ah, no, I don't think so," I murmured, slowly registering Mr. Meyers' comment about the solo, his discarded words that I pushed aside because of my empty stomach. But now it was full, stuffed with eggs and bacon and juice. *The Four Seasons*, that was what Mr. Meyers said they were playing. I peeled away the zipped compartment of my case, pulling out the folder given to me yesterday when I won the spot.

Flick, the pages turned fast. I knew that stanza, and that one, we played the entire movement last year in the Seattle Youth Symphony. And, here, the solo, greeting me like an old, familiar friend. It hadn't been mine to perform, but I pretended as if it were. Standing in front of a mirror, I let myself have it just as Jack had said on the library steps. Because if the call ever came, I would be there to take the helm.

The car clock flipped to 1:09., "You have to drive faster. Mr. Schroeder made me promise that I would be on time."

"Ryder, when we get there, we'll explain why we were late." The rearview mirror tilted, and I saw myself chewing mercilessly at my bottom lip.

"No." The car pa-plumped as he drove over yet another pothole, forcing my "no" to double then echo.

"No, no, what? What'd you tell them that you didn't tell us?"

"Lies."

Sarah took her time to turn, waiting exceptionally long to scan the three children snuggled together in the backseat. Her scarf got tangled in the seat belt, and she tugged at it to get it free. It ripped. "Shit. It's so hot in here."

"Sarah, please, the children. And, no, it's not."

Her face was flushed, the scarf was soaked. I checked the dash, the temperature reading sixty-eight degrees. Not hot, cold, I tucked my fingers under my arms.

Our late entrance went noticed, and I sprinted to the stage, abandoning the entire family at the door. Apologizing profusely to the man with the leather bracelets, I explained in detail the car accident we witnessed pulled to the side of the road.

"It's okay," Mr. Schroeder said, "just glad to see that you brought your family."

Turning my back to that, I removed my violin from its case and kissed the sheet music clenched in my hand, ever so grateful it was a piece I had already mastered.

A slim boy sitting first chair stood for me to pass, the others only twisted. I glanced back to nod my thanks, but his eyes were involved, staring at his stand. Mr. Schroeder's baton tapped, and the boy's head sprung up, his sandy blond hair—meticulously disheveled, yet strikingly tidy—fell in front of his eyes.

The maestro pulsed his fingers, and I wondered why I still watched the boy. Peaceful but serious, his brow bobbed to the soundless beat. That baton lifted high into the air, a collective breath stilled, and only I was not prepared. The downbeat came, and Vivaldi's *Four Seasons* unleashed into the air. I struggled to set my bow.

The music was unrefined but beautiful, and when we reached that solo, Mr. Schroeder lowered his baton. The orchestra hushed, and then he pointed it towards me, asking if I had ever led an orchestra. I said no.

Stepping off his pedestal, he leaned over my stand and, with his stick, pointed to a section of the script where two violins argued for dominance. Back and forth, he said, bickering, until authority broke in and the orchestra resolved the dispute.

"That's what it's like, you understand?"

I nodded. I didn't.

"You're trying to assert your control, but it's not yours to own. These people behind you," he said, waving his hand over the orchestra. "They support your mood, the emotion of the music, and the desire of the audience. You answer to them."

I nodded, yes, because I understood; yes, because my heart galloped. Yes, because I was ready.

He tapped the baton again: pulsing, directing, establishing a rhythm to which the chamber obeyed. Music moved through the auditorium until his hands stopped cold. Silence. He turned towards me, raised the baton, and prodded my argument. I watched him. I matched him. I played.

"Good. Better. Again." And over and anew, we created that dialogue, conversing through music until an hour had passed and reality returned.

"Great work! Violas, focus on the second stanza after the solo. Second violins try to match the intensity at the opening frame. And cellos, well, you know you're my favorite, so keep up the good work." And because we were supposed to, we laughed at his well-worn humor.

"Ryder, come here, please," Mr. Schroeder asked.

I froze, then caught the eye of the boy sitting first chair, who answered my confusion with an indecipherable shrug.

"Ms. Stephens, you are not in trouble. I just want to meet your parents." Still motionless, I glued my eyes to his shoes, but he stepped forward too quick, cruelly leaving me without a crutch.

"Hi. How are you? I'm Sarah Scott."

As if apparating unsuccessfully, in front of me was a smooth white hand with pastel-pink nail polish. It filled the space between myself and the man who—I knew—was about to toss me to the wolves.

"Ryder is staying with us for a while," she explained. "Truly, the symphony sounded lovely. How nice to be surrounded by such talent. I noted the May concert on the calendar outside. Can't wait to hear it."

The rest of her slid by my side, and without a moment's delay, that hand that left Mr. Schroeder's now wrapped itself around my shoulder. She pumped it twice.

"Is she still taking violin lessons from her mother?" he questioned.

Another lie, another regret. My mother and I fought like rancorous dogs when it came to the violin. From the vibrato intensity to the speed of the bow, I flat out refused her the satisfaction of taking pleasure in my music. Too many times, I muted the sound so that she couldn't hear me practice, anything to save myself from another *piece of advice*. Why? Such selfishness.

"Her mother?" Sarah asked. "Ah, yes, there's been a shift. We're making the necessary arrangements. It shouldn't interfere with her preparation for the concert."

Was this true, or was Sarah just a better bullshitter than me?

"Of course, understood." Mr. Schroeder, a man who was as sincere as he was direct, dug into his pocket to retrieve a card that would lead to a call that would clarify the meaning that would end my dream. It passed to Sarah.

I gnawed my lip.

"And Ryder," he said. "There will be an audition for that solo. If you have any questions about how to prepare, talk with Spencer." At the sound of his name, that sandy-haired boy swung around. Impassively interested, he waved his bow.

"Well, thank you, we'll be in touch." Jack shook his hand, as did Thomas. I giggled; what a strange little boy.

"A very polite young man you have here. Ryder, it looks like you're in good hands."

Was I? Stuck between admiring the shrewdness of Sarah's lies and the desire to welcome them as truths, I offered nothing more as we walked as a phony family back to the car. The words *staying with us* playing on repeat in my head.

People weaved through us on the street, forcing us to split apart and then converge. I have no idea why at a crosswalk I stayed behind, letting them move ahead without me, wondering if they'd notice.

There was a hot dog stand parked on the corner with rows of drinks resting on the edge, its salty pretzels dangling from the rail. A large black-leathered hand passed some dollars over the barrier, a weather-worn hand brought a pretzel back. "Here you go, Ryder," Jack said as he ushered me along. "Don't dawdle behind."

Staying with us. It was difficult to fathom given that I had showed up unannounced, forced them deep into Harlem, and now they knew with certainty that somebody, somewhere noticed me gone.

"Okay, in you go, and buckle up," Sarah instructed.

The pretzel was warm, with little chunks of salt on top. I traced them together to form a star. Then sticking my tongue to the northernmost point, I lifted it from the surface. *Staying with us* I shouldn't hope, couldn't.

"Jack, did Levinson call back?" Sarah asked as she tested the strength of the strap.

"No, but he's in Vegas now."

Vegas? I lunged forward only to have the latch catch and strangle my neck.

"He can't do anything until the office opens on Monday, anyway."

Office, what office? I peered out the window and let the first thing I saw pull me away from the conversation I didn't want to hear, a decision I could do nothing about. Eight, nine ten. Ten gothic columns rose so tall the people beneath seemed like ants. A man in a suit dragged a child in a sweatshirt up the towering steps. "What's that building?"

"The courthouse. Give him a call anyhow when we get home," Sarah hinted.

"Who's Levinson?" I asked, then unlatched my seatbelt and leaned over Thomas, wiping away the dew to see the building behind the columns. Closed on a Sunday, the only people loitering its steps were tourists with cameras and homeless with signs. Thomas unlatched his too.

"Who's Levinson?" I asked again, still relying on this distraction to prepare for an answer they might be cruel enough to give.

"Never you mind, Ryder, and put that back on." Her eyes darted to assure herself that the other two had not copied my reckless example. "Thomas!"

"But Ryder did it!"

A look to sink a thousand ships, I slid back into my seat, abandoning the child in the sweatshirt and the man in the suit and the columns sprouting from the stairs. I clicked it together.

Home again, we stepped from the elevator and into the blinding light, ambushing me once more with the memory of the Mona Lisa and her mocking smile. She knew everything: the quiet nature of our family, why people rarely visited. She knew, and she created a myth. With a replica of a masterpiece hanging in our house, who would suspect my family was sad?

Crash.

At least seven boxes tumbled to the floor. Thomas tossed them aside, searching for something. Finding it, an obnoxious game blasted its logo on his Wii U.

"Thomas, turn that down. I have a headache." Sarah ordered as if that was the only reason to stop the noise.

"I'll go get the cards." Lynzie, bouncing from the elevator to the kitchen table to the sofa to the shelves, ended her choreographed routine with a shriek that would have made the Mona Lisa cringe. "Mom! Where are they?"

Jack's phone rang. Keys clinked against a glass bowl. The light grew brighter as the chaos multiplied. Arthur Levinson's name flash across Jack's screen. With the pandemonium seeding the unrest in my mind, Jack's next word didn't stand a chance. Finger outstretched a foot from my nose, he issued a command: "Don't."

Don't what—ask, worry, go?

And in the next instant, Jack and Sarah did just that, secluding themselves behind a latched door halfway down the hall. Lynzie had disappeared upstairs, scouring her room for cards, which I would never play. Thomas, engrossed in his game, wouldn't notice me even if I sprouted horns. Deserted in a hallway that was not familiar, ignored by a family that was not mine, scared of the conversation held behind a closed door, I spun without considering the consequences and chose the only responsible option.

The escape came easy.

With my bag still sitting by the elevator door, and my violin held firm in my grip, I karate-chopped the elevator call button and strolled inside. Proud of my decision, I was halfway there, even though I had no idea how I would get there or where there was.

The doors opened in the lobby. "Can I help you, young lady?"

Ignoring whoever was pretending to help, I marched to the lobby door, and by extension, my freedom, heaving into it with all the backing my pack and violin could offer. Nothing gave. I tried again. Damnit. Frustratingly, I fiddled with the handle until that same voice that offered to help ironically announced the reason for its resistance.

"Sorry, kid, but nobody passes through these doors unless I say it's okay." The doorman, the New York City equivalent to the nosey neighborhood watchdog, had made his presence known. Waving a remote and lightly tapping on a button marked 'lock,' he swaggered over to the door and rattled it to prove what I already knew to be true. Then slipping the remote from his pristine white gloves into the pocket of his double-breasted suit, he reached over my head to pick up the lobby phone.

"Hello Mr. Scott, yes, this is Carson down in the lobby. I believe your young visitor has lost her way."

I faintly heard Jack's terse response.

"Of course, yes sir, I wanted to alert you to the situation."

How nice it must be to stroke the ego of millionaires. I scowled at this doorman as he swung the phone by its cord before setting it back into its cradle.

With my back up against a wall, I slid down and stewed, watching the lighted display above the elevator flash with each floor it passed: seven, six, five, four, three. I closed my eyes. Ding.

"Get up," Jack ordered, clasping his hands to the top of his head, the pressure letting out a sigh.

"I thought—"

"Ryder. Stop. Please, get up and don't talk." Nudging me into the elevator, he saluted Carson then drummed his fingers fast against the closing doors. "Listen to me, everything between us is a private matter. Did you say anything to Carson?"

I traced over the seven ornate buttons, stopping to circle the one lit up at the top. "No. I don't like him."

Jack's glare was a knife.

That wasn't very nice. "I mean, I don't not like him. Should I go apologize?"

A pendulum in motion, his finger swung from the elevator door to his chest and back again. "To him? What about to me, to Sarah?"

"Oh, yeah, no, I mean, yes, I'm sorry, but you were talking with the social worker, and…" My mind was that fly buzzing up against the glass.

The doors opened, and a storm engulfed us. Within seconds, Sarah's hug robbed me of breath until, holding me at arm's length, she forced a gap and scanned me from head to toe. "Don't do that again. You had us worried sick."

Was I even gone five minutes? When she led me to the living room, her hand crushed the circulation in mine.

A click drew my eyes up: Jack had locked the balcony door. The swoosh was imprisonment: he had lowered the balcony blinds. Darker now, it was déjà vu. I checked to make sure there was enough light to see my hand.

"Ryder, sweetheart." Sarah's voice was tranquil and concerned, taking a mere second for guilt to swallow me whole. "Yesterday, you asked us to believe you. Do you remember?"

I nodded yes to what I didn't know.

"Do you trust us?"

Tired of lying, it was a relief to speak the truth. "Not at all."

"Does it help you that we understand?"

Her shoulders relaxed enough for her long brown hair to fall behind. I wanted to run my fingers through it, to bring it back to the front. "Arthur Levinson is our family lawyer." My mother's hair was cut short, like Hermione's when she got older, when she was no longer playing Hermione. "He's unsure about the laws of wayward children, but he's verifying your story so we can make sense of it." I never wanted to run my fingers through my mother's hair, maybe because I knew the feeling would end too quickly: too short in length or too short of patience.

"Ryder?"

Reaching for her hair, I teased out a few strands. She waited, remaining motionless until I had finished looping a thick lock around my finger. "Honey," she said softly, taking hold of my hand. "Come back to me." A few strands of my hair fell next to hers.

"Same color," I said.

"Used to be." A wink morphed into a warmer smile. "Clairol Nice-n-Easy, Dark Mocha Brown. Listen, sweetheart..." she paused, letting my eyes wander to hers. "Are you ready to go on?"

More relaxed, I slouched into the couch, sliding down until my feet reached the bottom shelf of the coffee table. It hit something. I toed it aside. But when Sarah bent to retrieve it, my spine stacked like a lightning rod waiting for its charge. I breathed heavy watching *My Life* binder move into her lap.

"We have to know about the missing information," she said, recklessly changing course. "Your father—"

The serene music playing in my head screeched to a halt. "Does he want me to live with him?"

Instantly, her face melted into a sad confusion.

"I mean, I don't want to live with him. I never want to see him again."

Reenacting the scene from less than twenty-four hours ago, Jack perched himself opposite me. "Ryder, please help us. We need to know about your father."

Wrongfully choreographed, that binder was passed to Jack, freeing Sarah's hands to handcuff mine. They were sweaty, even though the room was cold. Only in her presence for twenty-four hours, I could tell Sarah's body was off. Normal one moment, her face flushed red the next. It wasn't from anger either, but rather a warmth that shed a layer, a bead of sweat that needed a window to crack.

"Is he in Manhattan?" Jack's finger ran down the page. "At 42 W. 171st street?"

Bursting from Sarah's trap, I snatched the binder from Jack, slamming it on his finger. "Don't call that man. Did you call that man? Don't call him."

Massaging his knuckle that had been caught in my rage, it reddened at once.

"I just want to play at Carnegie Hall. Please don't undo that." I wedged the binder under my thigh, under a place where no grown man would dare to touch.

"That may not happen, sweetheart," Sarah cut in.

What? Everything splintered, and time stood still. She did not say that. Jack cruelly nodded. No. The blinds were closed. The city lights couldn't distract. I looked towards Jack, sitting neutral on the edge of the table, to Sarah, heartlessly prying the binder from under my legs.

"Maybe something will work out," she continued. "We need to take it slow and see how things pan out."

No. Who took this slow? If I wanted to play at Carnegie Hall, I made it happen. Maybe my mother hardly ever looked me in the eye like Sarah always did, maybe she didn't let me twirl her hair, or give me time to answer, but she got things done, just like I did! Their kindness was just a hoax, an empty box presented as a prize. Only now, after they unwrapped their gesture, did I see it for what it really was: nothing. Scrub me clean, present me to the authorities, and receive due praise.

"When are they coming?"

"Who?" Jack asked.

"Child Protective Services."

"Nobody is coming for you, Ryder."

"You lie."

"No, we're not, but you are. Where is your father?"

My words slurred so fast that specks of saliva followed. "He doesn't want me. Nobody wants me. I'm fine the way it is. I work hard. I practice. Please, please don't take the orchestra away."

Fists forced against Jack's chin held back the hurtful words that were sure to come. "We're impressed, you know that, don't you?"

With what, my lies like your wife's lies, like when she told Mr. Schroeder I'd be ready for the concert in May? The one you're telling me was never going to happen.

"You play beautifully, and we see what it means to you." The binder opened, and his wounded finger slid over the only important page. "First place." He flipped the pages. "Over and over again. You're not a bad kid. You might have made some lousy decisions, very lousy." He locked onto my eyes. "But you've done well. Did you put this together?"

A question resurrecting the past, which set the spiral to go. I suppose I didn't have the will to stop it, knowing my lies from last night would punish me forever.

The cat jumped to the top shelf, toppling a picture, which Jack rushed over to catch. It was of Sarah and Jack from a time long past, years before Lynzie and Thomas were born, an eternity before a runaway crashed into their lives. That frame preserved a moment they wanted to keep. Maybe it happened just as it appeared, maybe not. Maybe a fight broke out just before the flash, or after. Nobody would know.

The ladder toppled. It was the truth.

"Did you put this together?" Jack repeated.

"I'm sorry; I need to go." Tapping my fingers, I created the diversion to the question arresting a memory I didn't want to preserve. I chose the music that made everything stop: 'Mozart's Sonata, in C major, No. 16.' It was fast, with no rests, no gaps to allow even a single thought. A scale running up the entire octave, another trickling down, my fingers dancing against my thumb at a breakneck pace. "Sorry, we can talk later."

Sarah, lost for how to respond, sat still, completely baffled how this preteen before her went from pensive to agitated in a blink of an eye.

"I'm sorry." I was—for causing them so much trouble, for confusing her, for only knowing one way out. "Just to the back room. I won't run away, I swear. I just really need to practice."

Sarah shook her head, but not to say no.

A sigh filled the room, and Jack, rubbing the corners of his mouth, rose from his seat and walked towards the balcony door.

"Please!" I called after him.

Determined, but guarded, he paced back to the couch and leaned his entire weight on its arm. "Who put the binder together? You answer this, and then you can go play your violin."

"Katherine." I shot to my feet. "She's the social worker who took care of me after my mother died."

He flicked through the binder, air rushing audibly through his nose. Forward, then back, another grown man desecrating my past.

I grabbed it from him, smoothing out the plastic sheaths. "Katherine's not in here, but she put it together." His breathing slowed, and I let him have more. Told them all about this woman who lied better than his wife, who justified evil, who fabricated sympathy for a man who deserved none. "Don't believe a word she says!"

"Ryder, she perjured herself for your own good."

"Oh yeah?" By concocting a story about a man suffering to understand his wife's death, of a man breaking his promise of fatherhood to better himself for *my* future. "Whatever." Protection by way of deceit? "If she had told the truth, then I wouldn't have stolen all that money from the foster family or hung out with the homeless. I wouldn't have lived with a drug dealer!"

Stealing, homeless men, drug dealer—words better left unsaid.

"What's Katherine's last name, and is she in San Francisco?" Jack asked.

"Johannsen and yes."

"And your father?"

"Vegas. Your lawyer can find him slumped over a Blackjack table at the Bellagio."

And with one last sigh, he let me go, but her hand held onto mine until I pulled the tip of my finger away from her grasp.

CHAPTER FOURTEEN

Behind every question, there was always something more complex, vital to the process but hidden from view. Somewhere deep within that interrogation came truth: from Jack, from Sarah, from me. I knew what I withheld and the reasons for doing so. But nothing revealed their game.

Later that night, as carefully as I watched Sarah bread the chicken or Jack reading in his armchair, I remained lost. That brief but expedited release of distrust that unfolded with my escape thinned into a veneer of assimilated norm. Dinner came, dinner went, and nothing more was added to the fray.

Blending into their illusion, we moved to the living room as a family that we weren't, and I edged onto the couch, daring to make myself at home. Slowly, watching them watch me, I curled into a ball that willingly absorbed my fatigue. This day, this second day away from Levi's and into the arms of uncertain comfort, had been a year.

My vision blurred before my head hit the surface, but in a battle to stay awake, both eyes sprang wide when darkness came. I struggled to be a part of their silent circle. To watch Jack read while he ran his fingers through Lynzie's hair, or Thomas smile as he made it to a new level in his game; to listen to Lynzie nibble a biscuit. But most of all, I focused on Sarah. She cared, and I noticed.

At the slightest noise, she would home in ready to fix, eager to please. All around the room, she measured her family's happiness—all eyes, all the time, on them, on me.

"No, I'll get her." Jack's voice merged into my sleep. "Up. Come. Time for bed."

Collapsing into the fold of his arm, he guided me past Thomas with his iPad and Lynzie with her empty biscuit tin. We moved as one down the hall until the gravity of the moment brought alertness to the fore. I stopped to take in this anomaly.

"Do you always do this?" I questioned.

"Do what?"

"That." I outlined the margins of the living room, trapping each one of them in an imaginary lasso.

"We try," he said. Did I sit with my parents in the living room and let my dad run his fingers through my hair? No. Did I ever see my mother pretend to read her book only to catch her eye? Hell no.

"What's wrong?" he asked as I watched Sarah from afar, her three fingers pressed to her lips fanning forward. A kiss flew.

"Nothing."

"Nothing is what you say to somebody when you don't expect to hear anything worthwhile in return," he said, scooching me into my room. He should have ended it there, but he couldn't. No, he made sure I washed my face and then critiqued the time I spent brushing my teeth. Only when I held up my pajamas did he slide the door closed just to inch it open a few moments later. "All good? May I come back in now?"

This was the light flooding their entry all over again, contrasting the past to what stood before me now. So present, too involved. Why not just send me to bed like a normal dad?

"My father left us when I was ten. He found a new wife and a new life, just didn't need us anymore." A single reflection, two acts of past injustice. When he began smoothing out the edge of the carpet with his toe, I joined him. "And it took a while to get over the rejection. I know what you're going through. I know you think I don't, but I do."

For some time, we worked that carpet and its stubborn edge; for longer, I dwelled on his meditative stare, which mirrored my own.

"Absent closure should come from death, not from somebody sitting in the same room," he summarized.

If closure was a painless ending that came with time, then how come this old man standing in front of me seemed to never have reached it?

"I want him dead."

His foot stopped. "No, don't ever say that. There will be times in your life when you forget the bad and remember the good." And then he said the impossible, that one day I'd find it in my heart to forgive him, that people leave for different reasons, and sometimes it wasn't easy—no, it wasn't possible to explain. "They twist their stories into so many different versions, their signals cross, and what they project outwards towards others sometimes reverses the truths they hold inside. Do you understand what I'm saying?"

I shook my head.

"He's too confused within himself to realize how upsetting he is to others. Do not let his demons question your soundness. You have every right to be baffled by that man, but let it be mystifying, not disorienting. He is your father, and it would be nice to understand him, but it may not happen."

Not until the day he didn't show at the airport in San Francisco was I ever baffled. My dad left the house early, worked late, traveled always, and stayed out of my mother's way. Normal.

"Learn from him," he said, "take this lesson and apply it to others. You know how it feels, so you know not to repeat it to others."

How? When all I knew as ordinary; now, because of two days with this man and his family, felt like I had lived a lie. "Jack? Do you have *good* memories of your father?"

"Mixed."

With his eyes trained on the living room, he offered a shy smile, and it was kind of fun. "One time," his voice hushed, "my brother and I stayed overnight, and we could tell he didn't want us." Assuring himself that this mischief remained between us, Jack scooched me further inside the bedroom. "We begged for eggs the next morning, and he was really annoyed. Even more so after he realized we glued them to the bottom of the carton."

I couldn't contain the giggle.

"Yeah, I know, don't tell Sarah." A wink followed, the same as his wife's. "He broke four eggs before he realized what we did. His hands were saturated in goo." Raising one finger to his lips, he sealed our bond. "Shhh, our little secret."

***

Egg whites and goo occupied the first thought of my third morning with the Scotts, if you consider four a.m. morning and not a fading night. Thievery and sacrilege occupied my second. Missing. Stolen. No, parented.

Under my pillow was air, not my mother's iPad I had wedged into the crease between the mattress and the headboard. Only two days with the Scotts, and I finally felt my best friend's daily struggle.

"Spending time on my iPad is not a crime!" she would rant. Every morning as we waited for the school bus in Seattle, she mourned the precious time lost the night before. *Screen time over* was her parent's favorite phrase. Screen time, the way she said it, sounded like time spent behind bars. I laughed at her then. I cried with her now.

Frustrated, with no chance of drifting back to sleep and no internet to distract, boredom hit fast, and the tedium obliterated any hope of embracing the helicopter parent. In retaliation, I set off to explore. If they hadn't taken my iPad, I wouldn't be bored, and if I weren't bored, then I wouldn't have to snoop. They brought this on themselves.

Still dark, I spider-walked my fingers along the hallway walls until my hands fell into the openness. From there, the lights of the balcony led the way. And what was visible became exploitable, because what would never have been tolerated during the day, beckoned at night.

I found my target. Beyond my reach, so high as to require an artful climb, I pulled down a wooden structure that could have been a Lilliputian's saddle. Tossing it back and forth, smelling it as if that would help, I remained at a loss. Once on the floor, I put it on its end, its side, even turning it over and analyzed it from a position I knew was wrong. Something in it sparked an insane curiosity that utterly destroyed my will to sleep. I scurried off in search of my missing iPad.

But Sarah collided with my crusade. "It's a Somali headrest."

Too curious to worry if she saw me climbing like Spiderman across her shelves, I picked it up and cradled my head into its curve.

"Noooo. Like this." And she tugged it from my hands and laid it on the floor. "Grab the other one up there." Apparently, not minding that I used her furniture as a ladder, she pointed to the highest shelf and said, "That one." Then, like a team rescuing a precious gem off a precarious cliff, I gently lowered it to her before she assisted me with my descent. "Don't let Jack see you do that." Egg whites and goo. "Come, bring it over here."

Near the balcony, she placed them side by side. All of me wanted to focus on those dusty wood blocks, to inspect the headrests she took an interest in sharing, but I couldn't. The pull of the city was too intense. So many tall buildings sliced up the sky. Scattered lights mesmerizing me before I had time to blink—total randomness surrounded by perfect order. "It's beautiful," I said.

"Well, not really, I think they're rather dingy looking, but Jack seems to like them, so now we're stuck with 'em. But since he's a he, and not into decorating, I can hide them where they receive the least amount of attention."

"The lights, and look, you can see the New World Trade Center, right? Is that what that is?"

"Oh, you are referring to our view," she said, joining me by my side. "Yes, it is beautiful. It's called the Freedom Tower."

She lost herself in a story, said that she stood right here when the twin towers fell, that Jack couldn't be reached by phone because the networks were jammed, that she panicked as the hours passed and an awful scenario played on repeat in her head. "That night, I knew we had to start a family." She kissed my crown as if I were a part of that start. "But that was many moons ago, and many cycles. Back then, I had them."

"What?"

"Menopause."

I nodded to show I totally knew what she was talking about. I had no idea what she was talking about.

"Come, lie down," she instructed. "They're kind of comfortable, no?"

They were, and I could feel myself melting.

"Jack got them in Somalia."

Staring into the dark and watching the city's reflections dance on their ceiling, she rambled about Somalia, the war, about the decades of instability, terrorists, and chaos, about Jack as a journalist, about Jack and his past. "He covered the Battle of Mogadishu in 1993."

"Was it safe?"

"Noooo, not at all. I hated it when he went to those places, but thankfully 1993 was a long time ago, and he no longer puts himself in danger. I don't do well with worry." Copy that. "Listen, you, tomorrow Jack will drive you to school, and you *will* stay put. Please just agree." Applying a dose of guilt, she went on, "If I come to pick you up, and you're not there, I'll spend the rest of my days looking for you. Don't do that to me, okay?"

"You don't trust me."

"Ryder, let me paint you a picture. First, in the alley behind the restaurant, you tried to run: twice. Second, we left you alone for two minutes in our foyer, and you immediately bolted down to the lobby."

I adjusted the headrest, so my vision traveled away from her eyes. It met her lips. Full, so much more so than my mother's.

"You lasted less than twenty-four hours with that foster family in San Francisco. And right now, we're breaking far too many laws by having you here without notifying the authorities."

I shot upright. "Really, how many?"

"Ryder, you're missing the point. It's not a competition."

I got the point. I just wanted to deviate from it. Sooner rather than later, a knock would come on the door, badges would flash, and I would be taken away. I was not missing *any* point.

Working my way from sitting to standing, she caught my hand halfway and lowered me back to the floor. "Just lie here for a bit with me, okay? You know, this menopause, I just can't sleep."

We lay at peace while our heads rested on slabs of ancient wood, and I liked the closeness. It let my thoughts drift without direction, and I liked that too. So much in the present, I stopped worrying about the Scotts and their leash, school and if I were to get caught, about the orchestra and if I'd lose it. About my mother, my father. Lying there in silence, listening to her breathe, took me to a better place, as it must have for her because when her rhythm slowed, I knew she had fallen asleep.

Patiently, I marked time until it felt okay to rise and safely hover, to analyze her face and scrutinize her motive. Why had she let her husband bring a runaway girl into their lives? Why would she worry about me until the end of her days if I disappeared tomorrow? Why did I matter to her, but to no one else? Why?

Sarah stirred, letting out a hushed groan. Twitching, her right arm moved rhythmically, and by instinct, I grabbed it, but it didn't stop, nor did she fully wake. Perhaps she was there, deep in her slumber, more peaceful and serene than she appeared on the surface. The movement stopped, and quick, her eyes sprang wide. They didn't blink, just passed over me slowly, methodically, questioning who I was.

"Sarah? Are you okay?" I pulled away. The moment lasted too long. But faster than it started, she became herself.

"Oh, sweetheart, sorry, I must have drifted off to sleep. Come, let's get you to bed. We still have about an hour left before we need to start the day." She bounced to her feet but wobbled fast, falling hard against the wall. Jiggling her left foot as if that would make her body respond, she then clapped her hands together before looking at me looking at her. "Right, let's get you into bed."

A mom at her core, putting me to bed was inborn and genuine and totally at odds with my mother, but I didn't want to think about that anymore. I wanted to think about Jack, and how he tucked me in so tight, I could barely move, about how he smiled honestly just like Sarah did now. How describing egg whites and goo seemed to be just as crucial as talking about wooden saddles and 9-11.

All of it somehow worked, even though none of it would last.

CHAPTER FIFTEEN

"Daddy says you're going to work with him today." Lynzie leaped into my bed. "It's totally not fair. I never get to go with him."

Darting upright, not knowing why or how this buoyant little thing landed next to me, I blinked ten times to make the image go away. Lynzie. And she reminded me of her age by hovering over my face closer than I hung over Sarah's the night before. Much closer.

Too tired to care, I collapsed into the sea of pillows, covering my ears to shut out the chaos intensifying in the hall.

"Lynzie, she's not coming to work with me," Jack shouted from the hall. "I'm driving her to school." Bending around the doorframe, Jack poked his head into my room. "It's time to get up, honey."

"Get up, sleepyhead!" Jumping from foot to foot, Lynzie slipped on a pillow, our skulls collided with a thundering crack. A red-hot knot instantly formed. If I pulled the covers over my head and rubbed it really hard, my face would match. I could declare a fever.

"What are you doing?" Sarah arrived with a pile of laundry in one hand and a fork in the other.

"I'm sick, I shouldn't go to school."

Ignoring my well-planned proof, she used the fork as a pick and tossed me the shirt on top, then a pair of jeans. My underwear flew through the air. When she held up my bra, Thomas walked into the

119

room.

"Sarah!" How could she laugh? Out of bed now, I ran to the bathroom to conceal to all what nature had done to me.

A knock on the door and then a rattle of the knob brought with it a sense of déjà vu. "Hey." And the low male voice on the other side only made the memory stick. "Chop, chop, my little violinist, I have to get you to school, so I'm not late for work."

But this time, when I opened the door, no clenched teeth or folded arms were there to greet me. No, this time, a brown reusable bag sailed into my hands, the word *Ryder,* scribbled across the front.

"Alright, hon, get out there and down that cereal." And by out there, Jack meant in the land of unbroken racket.

"Thomas, take the dishes to the sink. Lynzie, what did I tell you about blowing bubbles into your milk?" Sarah commanded through her back, which proved this woman had eyes behind her head.

"But Mom, it's so cool, look!" A froth burst up over the rim and lapped onto the kitchen table.

"Hey!" Thomas whacked me on the forehead with a spoon, and I wondered how many more thumps I would have to endure before I escaped this morning chaos. "Check this out!" He rubbed a spoon on my shirt and stuck it to his nose. *Crash!* "Well, it worked when my friend Aiden did it."

"You're done." Jack whisked my bowl away. "Let's get going." No room for the weary in this house on a weekday morning. He nudged me out of the chair.

"Hey!" A third welt was sure to form. Thomas crouched in close and whispered in my ear. "Listen—" cuffing his hand around his mouth, "if the police come for you at school, just go to the bathroom and climb out the window."

"I can hear you, Thomas, and no, Ryder, you will do no such thing." Jack tugged at my backpack.

In the parking lot, Jack's buffed and beautiful black Tesla sparked to life. Mysteriously I might add as if it knew we were on our way. A second later, the passenger-side door popped opened despite us standing four feet away. When the seat slid itself back, I tensed as if a spider crawled down my spine.

"Climb aboard."

Checking out everything from the supersized iPad sitting in the middle of the dash to the hidden compartments in the center console, it took me a while before I noticed the sunglasses. I blinked slowly, turning my head towards the window only to see a slender brown glove tucked into the door. I opened the glove box.

Empty except for papers, I drifted back to the woman's sunglasses dangling from the visor. Tortoiseshell, Harry Potter-like, boring yet fashionable, they were exactly the same as my mother's. A blindsided punch. I slammed the glove box closed. The car accelerated, and the sunglasses fell into my lap.

"What school does Thomas and Lynzie go to?" I asked briskly.

"Do. What school *do* Thomas and Lynzie go to? The answer is Dalton."

Does was correct. Does, like Thomas does. It was singular, and school is singular, so school goes with does, and he was wrong!

He lifted the center armrest and absentmindedly chucked the glasses in. "Your words reflect your capacity. If you limit them, you limit yourself."

The screen on the dash went black, and I tapped it to keep it alive. "What else *does* that screen *do*?" It powered down was what it did.

"Why is *do* incorrect and *does* correct?" He asked.

I really hated to embarrass him, so I let *Siri* do it for me. "Siri, why is do incorrect and does correct?" Not amused, well kind of amused; he chuckled before confiscating the iPad and instructing Siri to mind her own business.

"You do have confidence, kid. I'll give you that. Today, your mission is to figure out why I am, in fact, correct, and you are, no doubt, incorrect. You may ask your teacher for advice."

My teacher, the same one that had us underlining subjects and circling verbs? "Can I switch to Dalton?"

"May I." And then the tires turned towards the curb. "Ryder, we have to talk."

Shit. Mortified by my assumptions, I reached for my iPhone.

"Stop thinking." He gently lifted that from my hands as well and coupled it to my iPad under his seat. "I'm going to have to insist on that. You've done very well for yourself so far. Just the fact that I'm dropping you off at a school that God only knows how you managed to get yourself into is a feat unto itself. No doubt, you are a capable young lady, and we're trusting you enough to leave you there unsupervised today. But—" he swiveled my head, "look me in the eye and tell me you haven't made some poor choices." His fingers pinched my chin and moved my head up and down. "We're here to help you correct those, and you need to trust us, just like we're trusting you."

I drifted away, locking onto the visor where the sunglasses had been. "I'm sorry I've caused you so much trouble."

"You have nothing to be sorry for except keeping things from us. Don't do that, and we're fine. Okay? Now, let's get you to school."

And after two more lefts, we were idling in front of one of those poor decisions. Gabe, or Gabriel if you wanted to piss him off—which I didn't—noticed us straight off.

"Okay. No monkey business and Sarah will pick you up at 3:15 sharp. If you're not—"

"I'll be here." If for no other reason than to reunite with the two lifelines hidden under his seat. Gabriel stepped closer to the car and, leaving a thick mud-stained streak, slid his slimy hand over the buffed hood of the Tesla.

I gasped. "I forgot my violin. We have to go back."

It started as a smirk but turned into something cruel.

"Why are you laughing at me?"

"I'm not laughing. Is this the boy who owed you money?"

"Please, you won't be that late. I'll run in really quick and get it."

His head shook like it didn't matter. "Ryder, listen to me. Bullying is nothing more than exposed insecurity, and that boy is scared to death to be with himself. You, on the other hand, are a strong young woman. You don't need to hide behind your music."

"I like my music," I said timidly, suddenly embarrassed by being exposed.

"I know you do, kid." In his mind, ruffling my hair must have made this all better. "And let this boy know it too. Your confidence will make him back down. Every time you avoid his eyes, he sees an opportunity because he thinks you're weak. He taps into that to rid himself of his own shortcomings. But you're not, are you?" His head shook. "Not from what I've seen." Two fingers adjusted his glasses, the way only a self-assured man would. "Look him straight in the eye, own the moment, and then just walk away."

"Easier said than done."

"Said the girl who jumped from bus to bus and landed a slot at

Carnegie Hall." The latch released, and the door eased itself open. "We're here for you now if you need us."

I stepped out, and no less than a second passed before Gabriel Jensen attacked. "Whoa. Nice car. Comin up in the world, are you?"

Ignored and regressed, I staved off his stare by doing exactly what I was told not to do. I looked back, choosing instead to take comfort in the head of my new world. *Walk away*, Jack mouthed. And I hated that it took only forty-eight hours for me to need this man.

The stairs were wet with dirty snow. I slipped and fell, the wound on my palm cracked open and bled. Laughter circled, and I clung to my moral support, but when I turned, Jack was gone.

"Hey, Ryder, I guess you didn't hear me. I was complimenting you on your new-found riches." Gabriel used my moment of weakness to cut off my route. "You smell nice today, too. Good to see you finally found a bar of soap."

Oh no, I wasn't *that* kid, the stinky kid in school. Spinning around, flushed with embarrassment, I landed smack-dab against the chest of Gabriel's nefarious friend.

"Seriously, where's the money from?"

"Gabe, I'm just staying with a friend's parent. It's no big deal." I looked again to where Jack and his car once were, to the light blue Honda that had taken its place, to its dented fender, duct tape over the light. "And it's only temporary." Somebody somewhere laid on their horn.

Any more of this, and I would snap. Gabriel and his torment, the fact that all the kids think I smell, Jack, and his 'we have to talk.' How did this end?

I started to think it was on another bus.

***

I walked through those school doors, breathing through my mouth in a failed effort to block the mildew. I headed straight for the bathroom. It stank worse, like toilets flushed a thousand times. I left. Cutting through the cafeteria, where the cutlery reminded me of Thomas and his foiled spoon trick, of Sarah tossing me my clothes. I ran a finger over my raised lump on my brow—and Lynzie. I inhaled the sweetness of morning cinnamon and...

nothing stirred. That was when it hit me.

I wasn't hungry.

When I peeked into my pack and saw that brown, reusable bag with *Ryder* running between the folds, I smiled. I imagined little carrots cut into equal wedges, a homemade sandwich wrapped squarely in clear plastic wrap. Maybe an orange, a bundle of grapes, and of course, a note: *All my love, have a wonderful day!* ☺

I'd always wanted a note like that.

It took everything I had to sit still waiting for the lunch bell to ring. When it finally happened, I bolted to Mr. Meyers' office, knocking over students on my way.

"Well, look at you. No instant noodles today," he beamed as I laid out this testament of affection right there on his desk.

No sir, I had—assembling them neatly in a row: one sandwich, six cut apple slices in some kind of ego-friendly container, four slices of cheese, and a note.

A positive attitude might not be the answer to all your problems, but it will annoy enough people to make it worth the effort! Xoxo

Overtly witty prose from an astute woman married to a grammar-obsessed man. Why was I not surprised? All of her spoke of controlled confidence, and people felt it, like Jack did yesterday, when Sarah touched his arm. It was her touch that converted him, that simple brush, which changed his mind about orchestra practice, allowing me to go. Sarah was a force, for sure. From endorsing a climb over her furniture to confronting my conductor with trickery, Sarah could convince a rabbit to warm to a coyote.

The door opened, and as if leaping from my thoughts, there stood Sarah, right here in the music teacher's office. "You like that quote?" She asked. "I just finished up with the admin office and thought I'd swing by."

Mr. Meyers let out a playful chuckle. "I like it. Did you come up with it?

"Ah, no, some guy named Albright. It's a quote I had taped to my desk when I was working as a political correspondent."

Unwrapping my sandwich, Sarah told him all about it as she popped the eco-container and thrust a fork into my hand.

Forks, for apples?

"Well, some of that," she continued, answering Mr. Meyers

endless questions. "But mostly just covering health-related legislation. I quit after I was promoted to mother."

I slid down the only wall not cluttered with instruments, distancing myself from their conversation by working on with my unfinished essay.

"Well, I'll leave you two be." And this kind music teacher walked out of his own office, leaving the two of us alone.

Not able to slide down the wall as artfully as me, she braced herself against a chair and crumpled to the floor with as much grace as a toddler. "Okay, so let's see what we have here." Skimming, but nowhere near the end of my assignment, she laid it down gently to set the tone for the conversation that followed. "Mr. Meyers knows the truth, and so does the administration."

"So does? Or so do?" Pretending indifference was my new-found skill.

"Does, wait, do is plural, but administration is—" and she stopped, looking to me for clarification— "singular?"

"Yeah, see, it's hard."

"Did you get something wrong on your assignment?"

"No, in the car."

Her one dimple, Thomas' dimple, sank further into her cheek. "Don't let him get under your skin. Jack's words are his life, and he expects as much from his children."

Sure, go ahead, blur those lines.

"Speaking of which, Jack and I are cut from the same cloth." Pointing to sections of my essay, she definitively showed me how. "Consistency is good, but redundancy is bad. You used the verb 'went' six times in one paragraph."

Better than how she started this exchange, I embraced the switch. Correcting my grammar versus dissecting my lies, it wasn't a difficult choice. "I could use 'move' or maybe 'quit.' Does 'left' work?"

"Or died. Can we safely say that nobody knows?" Sarah asked.

I swung my finger from my notebook to her chest.

"Yes, obviously."

And then to her ring.

"Clearly, yes, Jack and I know. Anyone else?" A dip in tone signified a change. "Ryder?"

Mr. Meyers hadn't returned, leaving the room deathly still. I looked at the photos framed on his shelf, the memories he chose to keep: four guys at a baseball game, a dog, an elderly couple. Nobody frames moments that were better off buried.

"Did you talk to CPS?" I diverted.

Mocking my pantomime, Sarah pointed to her watch, the same as Jack's, and Mickey tapped his foot.

"I guess that means the office isn't open yet on the west coast." Mickey disappeared. "I don't understand why you need to contact them because I already told you *everything*. My father said he didn't want me. What's more to know?"

"Physical custody differs from custodial legalities. The right to make decisions for a child's welfare is determined by the courts, whereas the custody, where the child will live…"

Seriously? Worthless information. She just rambled, described my personal predicament as the embodiment of American strife. As if I, and my stranger-than-fiction narrative, represented an integral component of some award-winning human-interest story. Water filled my eyes. The idea of living with them had taken root, and well, when it happened, *if* it happened, I could move on. I could replace the people from my past with people who cared; people who cut apples into slices; who wrapped me like a burrito when they tucked me into bed.

"And first drafts are like one side of a phone conversation. You get the general gist, but the details aren't there to hold the substance together."

"Wait, what?"

"The essay you're writing." She waved my notebook overhead. "Creative writing is a mirror, a way for others to see themselves through your words."

Dumbfounded, I missed the transition from when she switched from destroying my life to building my writing career.

"So, this is good, but tonight, let's work on this some more, okay? Be out front at 3:15."

"Okay." Okay. So, that went well. I think.

CHAPTER SIXTEEN

Conspiracies are peculiar. You never know when you're a part of one until you realize you've become a victim. Life became too ordinary too quick, and even though they gave me no reason or any one thing I could point to, I felt their game, and I would beat them at it even though I didn't know how.

That day, after school, we went to Target because well-adjusted children obeyed their guardian and followed them around regardless of the destination. They didn't remind them they were breaking the law by harboring a runaway child or discuss sending them back to where they knew she didn't wish to go. No, they followed them to Target and listened to her son argue about the cost of a caster board. Because families that lived in a Penthouse in Manhattan quarreled over $59?

"Mom, when I turn ten, do I get a raise?" Thomas begged.

How was $59 a lot if $32,853 was so little?

"Thomas, you don't get a raise simply for getting older. You must earn it. How much do you have saved?" The quibbling persisted until a deal was struck. Told that he must contribute, Thomas accepted the packet of snow peas as a means to an end.

"And Thomas, when you get that wobbly skateboard thing –"

"It's called a caster board, Mom."

"Whatever it's called. You are not to let your father touch it."

"Why?"

"Because he keeps forgetting that he's not twenty, and I don't want to feed him out of a straw for the rest of his life."

That night we ate without the man who forgot he wasn't twenty, just the four of us plowing through a homemade meal of chicken in red sauce with broccoli on the side. It was spicy and tingled my lips, and Lynzie—declaring it unfit—refused it after barely tapping her tongue to the fork.

Jack's absence felt appropriate, familiar even, and I decided his acts of participatory parenting by means of bedtime assistance and approachable dialogue was a façade. Dads didn't act that way.

Wrong. No less than an hour later, when he strode out of the elevator, Lynzie jumped into his arms, and Thomas ran to his side. The head of this house planted a kiss on Sarah's lips and then leaned in to do the same to my crown. A Norman Rockwell picture, this scene framed a plot, a fantasy that no family could possibly uphold.

I vowed not to be complacent. I think. Actually, I always forgot what complacent meant, that and hubris. My mom used those words too many times for me to not know their existence, but I kind of just said them, and nobody ever corrected me. Maybe they didn't know what they meant either. But I knew this: one described excessive pride and the other excessive pleasure. Either way, trouble waited for me if I didn't respect the dangers of becoming too at ease with something I only presumed to deserve.

Jack flicked my forehead. "Thinking again!"

A beer can cracked, and Sarah skidded a plate along the kitchen bar. It had a single breast and enough red sauce to drown a duck. "Thanks, hun," he said, spooning the sauce as if it were a bowl of soup. "Oh, wow!" He swigged his beer, and half the bottle drained in a single sip. "Bit overboard with the chili," he said, panting, which only bolstered Lynzie's stand.

"Dad!" Rushing in to secure the scraps of his father's attention, Thomas ricocheted off that large plate glass wall dividing the living room in two. Sliding next to his dad, he tossed the packet of seeds in front of his plate.

I focused on the glass wall and left Thomas with his needs.

Before me stood an outdoor space inside, a glass enclosure right in the middle of their apartment. An atrium. It was bizarre in that it completely split the living room in two. To the right of it was the area with that fluffy sofa and easy access to the fireplace remote. I called that side A.

The flipside, B I guess, was a different story altogether: rigid chairs, dark tables, cold marble, no doubt inspired by the décor of Downton Abbey. And in between, this oasis of calm, a garden refuge enclosed in glass.

Thomas blurted again, loud enough for all of us to turn. "Dad, I'm going to start growing our own food."

"Oh, really, Thomas. You do know it's forty-two degrees today," his father teased.

Crestfallen—either from not commanding all the attention or realizing it's winter—Thomas walked up to that glass and put his hands flat against it. Blowing, I thought he was going to draw something in the fog, but instead, his tongue plowed into the glass.

"Thomas!"

"Mom, your tongue will freeze onto glass if it's really cold outside. I saw it in *A Christmas Story*. Wait, that was a metal pole. Wait, maybe I need to be outside where it's colder."

Thomas opened the door, and that winter air attacked the room. I immediately tucked into a ball, throwing my hands under my arms. Lynzie pulled a segment of her father's scarf from his neck and slid herself under it. Thomas, clearly on the fence, stood there contemplating if he should test his theory.

Sarah walked straight into the arctic blast.

"Sarah, Jesus, you really need to see your gynecologist," Jack said.

"I'm managing this just fine."

"Hon, look, I'm right there supporting any decision you choose. It's a natural transition, I know. It will pass, I know that too. I hear you, but Sarah, you're miserable." Jack pulled the scarf out from Lynzie's hands and walked outside to talk with his wife. "And isn't forty-eight too young for menopause?" His words that followed were soft and comforting and then gone. The door to the glass enclosure slurped shut, instantly terminating the conversation.

I pressed my ear to the glass.

"You won't hear anything. See, watch this," Thomas said. "Shhhiiiiitttt!"

I clamped my left hand over his mouth, while my right index finger pointed, ready to unload a lecture on this ignorant little boy. Surely, he knew the consequences of swearing in front of his father.

"What are you doing?" Squirming to counter, his arms flailed as he batted mine away. "Shhhiiiiitttt!" He said it again. Louder, more obnoxious, and—with one look through the glass at the couple sitting calmly on a bench—totally unheard. "Look and learn, these walls of glass are *solid*, just make sure the door is closed tight. Lynzie, show her." And she pushed it with every bit of her fifty-pound frame. "If you do that, they can never, ever hear you."

"Huh." Circling all four walls, I worked my way around the glass as if I were a minnow swimming in a pond. Ah, a fishbowl. Got it.

"Ryder?" Lynzie trailed my loop. "What's a gine cyst?"

I stopped, scrunched my brow because that was what you did when people didn't make sense. Thomas, who didn't see Lynzie, collided into her before he clarified. "It's called a genie-collegeist."

"A what?" I peered through the glass to find some help. But they were still engrossed with each other, not hearing any of our chatter. Just a happy couple holding hands. A woman nodding, a man gently caressing her shoulder, I wanted to take a picture, and start a collection. Capture moments to begin anew.

"A genie-collegeist, he helps women, my friend Aiden's mom went to one when she had a baby." Thomas insisted.

"Oh, you mean gynecologist. It's a woman's doctor."

I scrunched my brow again. Did that mean Sarah was sick? I liked her and didn't want her to suffer, but if Jack and Sarah had something worse to worry about, well. Wrong. I was such a bad person

But right. They should focus on each other, on Sarah. And I should blend in, hide the past, stick with the story. Stop struggling to understand what happened and start building a wall.

That was how I would play this game.

***

Now Tuesday, four days with this family felt like an Easter vigil: good at the beginning but soured by the length. It threatened my commitment to faith.

I'd shown them too much: Levi's, the orchestra, the school. Told them too many lies: the Christmas lights, the stairs, the blood. No more. I slammed that door shut, closing off that part of my life forever.

But they knew something was up. Less effort was spent slogging through the cold, hard streets than deciphering their philosophical looks. And it was during that afterschool lull where I found it hardest to keep my mind at rest. Hurtful memories always surfaced, and I found it impossible to stop the bad thoughts from poking through the good.

Sarah plopped down next to me on the couch, trying to look cool but failing. She wanted to talk. I rose to leave.

"Wait. What did you think would happen to the boy?" She asked, and I squinted. "You remember, Werner, the orphan, the blind girl's friend. I think the orphan boy needs the blind girl, so he can learn how to trust."

Again, with that book, *All the Light We Cannot See*. Perhaps she savored my anxiety, used it to fuel her sense of altruism. I hid behind a magazine and pretended to read that instead. *The Mysteries of Menopause*, I flipped a page.

"He learns how to cope with his own disadvantages through empathizing with her disability," she continued.

Really. Why adults found such issues with teens doing nothing, saying nothing, interacting with nothing, was as incomprehensible as it was annoying. In a deliberate act to remind her of my wounds, I dragged the magazine off the table and took it over to the cold, dark, and unfriendly chair in side B.

But Sarah knew mind play like a magician knew his cards. Premeditated, her words intentionally planted a seed for thoughts to grow. That boy, the orphan, I had nothing in common with. Orphans pushed brooms over concrete floors and sang about their hard-knocked life. I was not an orphan. That girl, however, that blind and vulnerable girl, the one who loved her father until the day he disappeared. Well, I could identify with her because I didn't see it coming either. Forget her disability, ignore that she lived in darkness. She put all her trust in a man that became invisible.

I closed my eyes and saw my father. I opened them and saw him still. What did it matter that this girl was blind?

Sarah trailed me to side B. "Close your eyes again. What do you see?"

Nothing: my father was no more. In his place was shade, and light, and energy, and fear. I opened them abruptly.

"Yes, it's scary isn't it, to live in darkness. Isolating? Lonely? *Secret*." The last word turned down because it was there as a statement, not a question to ponder. "Thomas, Lynzie, come in here, please." A pitter-patter answered. "Close your eyes and trace your hands over this table. You too, Ryder."

I moved slowly, scared where this may lead.

"It feels cold." Lynzie played willingly.

Thomas' face was painted with a curious readiness, his hands resting three millimeters above the edge, anticipating a puzzle to solve. "It's not smooth," he said. "Kind of feels like it has goosebumps."

"Ryder?" Sarah asked, and Thomas' right eye opened a sliver.

"Um," I hesitated. "The corners bend around quickly, and my finger picks up speed as it makes the turn, like a rollercoaster rounding a curve."

"Cold, goosebumps, and then a rollercoaster: words play on each other without you even realizing it." Her voice turned to me. "It's nice to have others to help interpret all the things you cannot see, isn't it? To lend control and let somebody else make decisions for you, especially when you're used to making them on your own. It requires a lot of trust, and that's not always easy."

Eyes open now. Before me sat a disciplined tutor, so different from my past. My thoughts ping-ponged from my mother to my father, to anger, then spite. I quickly restacked the bricks of my wall.

"When I was about your age, Ryder, I broke my arm. It was before the days of computers, so I couldn't peck away at my assignments with one hand. I had to write with my left hand, and I failed miserably. My older brother volunteered to transcribe my essays, but he kept adding *his* ideas to *my* paper, insisting that I should trust him."

I rolled that well-formed bulge of tissue inside my lower lip between my teeth.

"And I got an A."

Lynzie's tiny fingers burrowed into her mother's arm, her jaw dropping fast. "But Mommy, you cheated!"

"It wasn't intentional," I was quick to add.

"Right. It was cheating, but there's always some gray between black and white. Like trust, it doesn't just exist. When a relationship develops, connections form, then break, then mend and evolve. Do you see?"

Maybe. I saw curtains bulged in a wave, and the cat finally emerged at the end. Looking alarmed at his new surroundings, he dived back under cover, his bell fading as he scurried away.

"Every life has struggles, sweetheart, some more extreme than others, but what sets us apart is how we react to them. You may think this was the worst thing that could have possibly happened to you, and it may be, but the future is a mystery. Worse than these tragedies from your past would be to discover the memories of your future alone; a support system is your salvation. The center cannot hold."

CHAPTER SEVENTEEN

Centers and trust, futures and support, puzzles and riddles, I was lost for how to respond. Mentally. Physically, I knew. With minors and melancholy, and a vibrato so slow, it pulled me away. I chose a song and hummed it all during school, tapping my foot under my desk to introduce the thud of a drum and force the melody into my mood. My pulse beat fast as the music grew in speed. But no, too much guilt, the fantasy was not enough.

After school, bursting from the elevator doors, I grabbed my violin and ran to my room. Ba-bum-ba-ba-bum-ba-bum-bum. No longer a hum, I slapped my fingers against the board, the bow sliding solidly across the strings. All of me swayed to *Hedwig's Theme* from Harry Potter. Low and dolorous, an ethereal tone swam through the room. Over and again, the same piece, the same intro. When Jack's voice echoed in the living room, I knew hours had passed.

Finally feeling composed, I wouldn't allow him to take it away. I kicked the lock on the door. No more riddles, please. I played harder and faster and let the tempo slow my racing heart. Brave, bold, the music swelled.

A knock.

Leave me be. And then Jack was inside the door with a key held limp in his hand. "Play some more."

Stunned, unsure what was worse, the invasion of my privacy or the breach of peace, I slid the violin back into its case. "I don't like playing for people."

"Ryder? There will be thousands at Carnegie Hall, all watching you."

"Not me, the symphony."

"But it should be you. I'd love to hear you play that solo. And well, then they'd be watching you."

Yes, thousands that caused both fear and serenity in equal measure. And they would vanish, all of them, once that first note sailed off my string. When the melody, the rhythm, and the intensity became a therapy by way of music.

Sarah appeared by his side, her hand bouncing rapidly against her thigh. Jack, the always attentive husband, oblivious to her jitters, casually slipped his over her shoulder. "Thanks for coming home early, Jack. Honey, that was beautiful, truly." She stretched, going for what I thought was a hug, but the half-hearted embrace morphed into a scoot. "Why don't you go help Thomas set the table for dinner?" And her head tilted, but not towards the dining room. "Go on." She did it again, this time adding a look. The one that said a woman who cocked her head towards an empty space was a woman who had something on her mind.

"Guerin's covering for me, reluctantly," Jack said. "I told him you'd make dinner for him on Friday. He's expecting the enchiladas—the chicken ones, not the ones with those white beans."

Guerin, the man with the belt buckle that read GL, the one with the voice that resonated long after he left. He worked with Jack?

Sarah spun and headed for the home office, not interested in hearing more from Jack. We followed her into the hall.

"What? He's a busy man, and this didn't really ease his burden."

"Burden? He's your best friend, and best friends help in times of need."

"What need?"

One of her fingers pointed to me and flicked twice to indicate where I should head, another bumped open the office door. And just like after orchestra on Sunday, I stood abandoned.

Maybe now more familiar with my surroundings, the four days that passed didn't stop the walls from closing in when left alone. I walked away from isolation and headed for the consoling chaos of Thomas' crashes. But there was none of that, only a dutiful son fanning plates around the table.

I scooched silently back towards their chamber of secrets, then scurried back to the kitchen to double-check. Lynzie, now nearby, slid her nail against a napkin's fold, while this rule-deviating boy randomly placed mismatched glasses anywhere around each setting. Wrong, they belonged an inch from the top of each knife.

Back at the office door, a sliver of light escaped, and the pssts of whispers followed. "No!" Jack's voice suddenly boomed. Gasping, he walked further from the door, his words fading with each step he took. "Alone? How?" And then I heard a string of words I didn't want to decipher: "avoidance coping at its best."

Shuffling occurred. Papers ruffled. A footstep came near, and my socks slipped sideways on the polished wood floors as I darted down the hall. The table was set. Thomas had his head inside the fridge, and because he thought he was alone, he closed it and dragged the cookie jar to the edge of the counter. Nobody followed me down the hall.

Back again, peering into the slice of light, Jack and Sarah had changed positions.

"No, Jack, promise me. It's too early. You need to promise." Sarah's words implored. "Even if it takes a year, don't intervene. It must come naturally."

Unexpectedly, and fast, the door opened, and because my hand had been precariously positioned, I fell. "Um, I, um, set the table." Nothing. "I was just coming to tell you that we're ready."

Jaws dropped, eyes bulged, they didn't help me scramble to my feet. "Were you listening?" Jack asked.

I shook my head really, really hard.

"Off you go." And Sarah's finger flicked again.

Walking a good distance ahead of them didn't deaden Jack's parting words. "So much for waiting a year."

I stopped, and finding my inner Jem, the words unleashed. "Um, was that about me?"

Women may tip their heads when they want to talk, men point. "Let's you and I have a little talk, shall we?" In an instant, Sarah had her back to me, muffling words to Jack, more secrets told. She spun around full circle; a grin plastered on her face as fake as the hardened look on mine.

A nudge when we reached the fishbowl directed me to side B, to that cold and heartless chair. "Did you hear what we were discussing?" Jack asked.

"No, I told you already." I traced my finger across my lap, over the arm of the chair, and straight onto the table's edge. It was cold, gave me chills, and when I closed my eyes, my stomach felt like I was in a rollercoaster rounding a bend. "You have nothing to be sorry for except keeping things from us. Don't do that, and we're fine." I lifted my hand away. "You told me that in the car."

A prolonged inhale appeared to quiet his nerves. "I did, yes."

"You don't believe me."

"We believed you, and we still do." He swallowed loudly. "Unless—"

"Dinner's ready." Sarah sprang into the room with that grin still masking the truth. "Sweetheart, we believe you, and you're smart enough to know that we needed to speak with Katherine for legal reasons. For right now, you'll stay with us."

Unless. Unless what, Jack?

"Come, I made dinner, and it's getting cold."

Dinner, just another mask, voices raised up then down with laughter and questions. People talked over each other and not. Time was divided, parceled out to each person at the table. Thomas told about his successful layup in gym; Sarah, some birthday present she bought for her friend. Then to Jack, who rambled about a man who worked at refugee camps in a place called Nauru.

"Lynzie, it's your turn. What did you learn today?"

"My teacher is going to have a baby really, really soon, so I won't have a teacher anymore." A steady stream of nonsense. "She has Play-Doh in her belly, and it forms into the baby. It cooks there and gets hard. She has to stop teaching us so she can cuddle it and make it soft again."

"Really."

"Yeah."

"Yes."

Complacency. I guess it was okay.

***

This all occurred on Wednesday night. In two more nights, this journey as a pseudo-family would total a week. Seven days that could have been a year because every night repeated: biscuit tins and books, dialogue and togetherness. Sarah's mask morphed into an unconvincing confidence. *For now, you'll stay with us.* That was what she said. But *Unless*, that was what he said, and that was the word that echoed the loudest. Unless what, Jack?

Complacency: being smug with one's achievement. I looked it up on my iPad while we sat around our evening circle. How could I become complacent with *unless* hovering over my existence?

"I'm going to go to bed now," I said, too mentally fatigued to watch them any longer.

"Okay, sweetheart, make sure you wash up."

In my room for over an hour, lying on this bed that was too high, kicking my feet against the poles that served no purpose, I wrestled with dueling flashbacks. My mother smiling while tightening my bow, Christmas lights, my first violin with finger tape on the board—flashing red and green—swings in parks, Christmas lights, the paramedic stringing yellow tape across our door.

I slapped my cheek to change the slide: bunnies made of napkins, buckles with GL, Sarah's kiss flying. Frame it. Keep it. So much effort, the strain of it all hung weights from my lids.

Subdued by the drone of the family hum, calmed by the whispers floating towards my door, I slipped into sleep and blended their world to mine. Lynzie laughed. I twitched. Falling again, the shapes took form: dark shadows, flashes of light, images merging without a sequence. Dishes clanked. I twitched again. Back deeper, I saw a blue suit, white shirt, no tie, walking down a wide sidewalk. Sarah's iPad opened. The light was bright, it illuminated her face. The suit crossed the street and kneeled, then sat. His leg stretched and touched mine.

I flung my eyes wide.

Scared of a dream I didn't understand, I slipped from my room and felt my way, creeping like I did just five days before. Hypersensitive to the silence, the darkness spooked until, entering the living room, those reassuring city lights brokered a path between the couch and that fishbowl. Its glass was cold, and I moved my hand towards the handle. I pulled. The slurp of the suction worried me for a time, but when no lights came on, and nothing stirred, I knew I was alone. *They can never, ever hear you,* Thomas' words echoing in my mind. A burst belted from my lips. I waited: nothing. Louder, my squawks became shouts.

Quickly, paddling my way back to my room, I grabbed my violin, then hustled back to this soundproof refuge. Plucking at first, the sharp staccato of the A string was terse, only increasing the tension from the dream. I slid my bow across the string.

Delicate, the sound was steady, strong, as was my intent. My vibrato came slow, wavering, but in a rhythm.

A flash—that blue suit, that leg that stretched and touched.

"Beautiful," said the man not wearing that suit. "Very."

My bow froze mid pull. I looked past him to the door that hadn't slurped.

"I heard you through my bedroom window." Jack pointed towards the opening above us, to the stars in the sky. "Sound travels in open spaces." Jack pulled his robe tighter. "Sarah gets hot at night. You know, menopause."

I nodded, agreeing again to something to which I had no clue.

Gently lifting the violin out of my hands, he strummed the strings as he walked towards the only bench, and like a nervous mother watching a distant uncle with her newborn child, I reached for it.

He grabbed my hand. "You're cold. Come, sit next to me."

I took one step forward.

"Closer."

I took one step back.

"You're scared of me? When did that happen?" The crunch of the garden stones echoed around the chamber as my feet slowly moved towards the glass door. "Do you want to talk to Sarah?" He was standing now. "I can get her if this is important." Unsure of the complex emotions I had laid out for him to guess, Jack opened the door carefully, avoiding my personal space. "Come."

"I'm not scared of you."

"You look scared of me, and I'm not quite sure what I've done to deserve it."

My violin swung at its neck, perilously teetering between his two middle fingers. "You didn't finish your sentence before. But..." It just rocked smoothly, and no harm came. "But... I don't think I want to know why anymore."

He flicked on the kitchen light, and we both squinted to adjust to the brightness. That iPad came into focus first, the one with the red cover, the one with the scuff mark at its edge.

"I had a dream about that."

"This is Sarah's iPad. Why was it in your dream?"

"I have no idea."

"Dreams are like that."

***

"You both look tired." Sarah's vortex doing nothing to lift my sails.

Jack slid his mug my way. And Sarah pushed it back.

"She's too young for coffee." Without pausing, maternal instincts carried on: cutting carrots into wedges, wrapping cheese in plastic. I watched through sleepy eyes as a marker scribbled on napkins and reusable bags. And wondered again why they never got reused.

I lifted a blueberry off Lynzie's plate.

Concentrating hard, the little girl traced her finger through a maze on the back of the Cheerios box until, at a dead-end, her tiny hand stopped to scratch her hair.

A rare peace permeated the morning, and it followed Jack and me to the car, staying even as we hit the open road. Well, not open, this was New York City at seven a.m. But still, when we wedged into traffic, we both accepted the lull in the conversation, making a silent pact to forget last night. I used the time to master the controls of the electronic console on the dash.

"Your grandmother expressed interest in having you live with her," he said, casually breaking the deal. "Your mother's mother, we were a bit shocked as well. Katherine said she attended the funeral but left early."

The console decisively lost all appeal. "She's just feeling guilty for birthin' such a jack—" Wait, my *mother's* mother? The one who held me at arm's length as if I were worthy of review but far too costly to keep. The one who, with as much compassion as Levi, signed me over to Katherine, the social worker, without thinking first to discuss it with me. "Was *that* what you were talking about in the office? Why didn't you just say so? I'm not going to go live with her. I don't even know her."

Jack stayed silent, which only invited dread. I gripped the door handle to stop Katherine from crystallizing in my mind. But it came anyway. Her pink nail polish, next to a delicate silver ring. It led me to the front row in church, introducing me to my mother's mother. She guided my hand towards that strange woman whose smile matched the woman lying in that open box.

I squeezed my eyes hard, trying to force a different image, but it wouldn't come. I loved my mother but dreamt of my dad, and

Sarah but not Jack. Why?

He stopped at a light. "May I ask you what you're thinking about right now?"

"My dream." And worse than my want, when I saw Sarah's face, I hated myself for liking it more.

"All I know of dreams is what not to read into them. Don't create a plot where there isn't one, okay? Your dreams reflect your thoughts, and they come scattered and disconnected for reasons best left misunderstood." The light turned green. "Let me ask you one more question." He pulled to the curb. "No family that you knew of? Nobody came to visit you and your parents on holidays?"

Two questions, one theme. No. Sometimes we had Thanksgiving with our neighbors or went to a hotel for Christmas dinner. Never did my parents talk about their parents. I had no aunts or uncles. "I don't think they got along with their parents. Both my grandfathers are dead. My mother liked things quiet." The car's engine died. "And dark," I added.

"She didn't have many friends?"

"Some, but she played the violin too. I think she liked that more than her friends, more than me."

Probably true because beyond the funeral, nobody stayed. And when that happened, I felt my mother's loneliness in full. It rotted in my stomach, and I couldn't breathe for knowing what I could have done. People showed to say all the right things in all the correct ways, to stroke my hair or pat my shoulder, but never did they trip and get too close. *Later*, they said. *Get her settled over the holidays*, they insisted. *Yes, after Christmas, we'll find her someplace permanent to live. We have a bit too much going on.*

Bit too much? If I were a bit too much then, I would be a bit too much always.

"I'm not staying at my *grandma's!*"

The engine started, and the car pulled from the curb. "Would you rather live with us?" His voice faded as the sentence ended, and I pressed my forehead up against the window to decipher why.

The solid yellow line painted on the road broke in two, then three, and little dashes took over. The car lurched, blurring the lines. Maybe they were solid now, maybe not. And in my stomach, I felt the indifference. "Do you want me to live with you?"

"Tonight," he said, not answering my question. "There will be a woman coming to our house." His eyes fixed on the road ahead, his words paced as if led by a metronome. "She has your file from California, has spoken to your father, and your grandmother, and Sarah met her at her office yesterday afternoon." He pulled into the empty drop off zone at school. Gabriel Jensen was nowhere in sight. "There is a possibility you would be allowed to stay with us, that we could be appointed your temporary guardian. But honey, so much is beyond our control. That was why I hesitated last night."

The wind circled a plastic bag around the deserted schoolyard. It moved purposefully until it got stuck. It rippled then collapsed, an effort not worthy of the risk.

"You're late. Listen, I asked you to trust us, and I know I held back, but I did it to protect you. If somebody had told me that my father wanted me to live with him after my parents divorced, I would have latched on and never let it go. And then, when the dust finally settled, the truth would have been more than I could bear. Sometimes you see better in the dark."

Wrong. A blindfold creates fear. Sarah taught me that.

***

"Is she here yet?" I paced as if my life depended on it. "Is Jack home yet?"

I pictured the flight to California, not at all like Thomas and his first-class ticket when he met the president, where a mis-apportioned button was the only thing worthy of his grief. No, I saw suits: orange jumpsuits. Did they wear those in Juvenile Detention? Maybe this social worker knew I stole the umbrella.

Bing.

Up went my gaze straight to the elevator door. Sarah pulled chocolate chip cookies out of the oven, and I knew I was never going to survive this night.

Thomas thrust me through the glass door to poke at the dirt and wonder, like we did every night, if the ground had thawed enough to plant his seeds.

"Hey!" A millisecond passed before the door slurped open. "Keep your hands out of the dirt. And your feet. And—" Sarah's eyes darted around for something else to include. "Just don't touch anything," she ordered as she went back to the kitchen, to tend to the cookies, the evening, to everything a mom was supposed to do.

Thomas immediately dropped to his knees, scooting around the soil, jamming his index finger two inches beneath the surface. And I watched and thought: *Yep, this is my brother; oh, my brother's such an idiot. My brother got in trouble yesterday. My brother…"* I smiled.

The elevator door opened, and the silent movie rolled. Jack walked in with a young, petite woman who stopped talking long enough to flick her hair over her shoulder and laugh. Sarah, the doting wife, materialized from the kitchen with her hands patting a towel, and Lynzie, feigning a shyness she didn't possess, folded into her legs.

Jack motioned for everyone to make themselves comfortable on the couch, and to us, he beckoned. A gesture to which we responded by turning our backs against the glass.

"So, are you gonna be like my sister now?" Thomas asked.

The suction broke, leaving no time to even consider an answer. "When I ask you kids to do something, I expect that… oh, Thomas, you're filthy." Jack shook his head before eyeing his wife. "Thomas, go wash your hands and then meet us on the couch. You-be-on-your-best-behavior," he said, waving a finger at his son.

Lightly amused by the idea of Thomas getting in trouble, I giggled, then went about surveying this social worker for flaws. Tense, and a bit fidgety, she held a thin binder in her hand. Not even a centimeter thick, she couldn't have much. Or maybe she knew everything about me by heart. Maybe she already made her decision. I widened my eyes before my mouth dropped open.

She held out her hand. "Hello, Ryder, I'm Bailey." She shook mine with the formality of a kindergarten teacher. "Mr. and Ms. Scott tell me you'll be performing at Carnegie Hall next month. That's quite astonishing. And impressive, if I might add."

And like that kindergartener, I skipped her eyes and picked up the cat. "Well, not next month, it's in May."

"Oh, yes, well, I bet you're pretty excited about it." She ruffled the cat's fur. "And it's pretty cool to be living with a celebrity, too, no doubt."

Celebrity? Did Sarah's quirky sayings make her more famous than they should?

"Sorry," she stammered as her eyes followed Jack walking away. "Just a bit star-struck myself. We watch you every night."

I dropped the cat, my mouth hanging three-inches wide. "You're famous?"

"Not famous, well-known and only in certain circles. I'm no

Anderson Cooper." Concluding a conversation that wasn't going to start, his hands folded together. "Please, let's begin, shall we?"

The seriousness in his eyes gave us little choice, and everybody sat as one. Talk commenced about legalities and commissions, about magistrates and jurisdictions; it droned on and on. Questions posed to Jack and Sarah seemed juvenile and pedantic. Still, they sat on the edge of their seat, nodding, giving every morsel of their attention to this woman with that open binder resting in her lap.

She flipped through it, and visions of Rubi, the runaway, sprang to life. Little boxes followed one another down the page, and with each question asked, a box got checked. At first, they were simple, "how were decisions reached in your household?" Then, broadened, "how did you make members of your family feel loved and wanted?" But last, they delved into topics that caused shuffling and stammers. "What are your reasons for adopting a child?"

Adopting?

The pack of snow peas landed in Thomas' hand, and a scooch sent all three of us into the fishbowl. Sealed off from the only question that mattered, I couldn't keep my anxious mind still. Visions of my dad at the Bellagio surfaced, of him sober, regretting what he said, how he acted. I pictured him wandering around, looking for the thirteen-year-old girl who looked like him. I framed that: a memory I wanted to keep.

"Ryder, look on your phone to see how to plant these things?" Thomas asked, pulling me from my thoughts. I couldn't make sense of him crawling around the soil, ramming his elbow deep into the dirt. "The hole has to be wide and deep, I think."

I perched my thumbs an inch above the screen, willing to help Thomas, but desperate to search for the truth. I looked through the glass wall and studied Jack. His hands were nestled together in a studious pose. Attentive, he leaned as if nothing it the world was more important than listening to the woman who controlled my fate.

Who is Jack Scott?" Search.

- Jack Scott (News Anchor, Author) – Wikipedia
- Jack Scott – Monday through Thursdays 5-6 p.m. ET
- Jack Scott – responds to the growing Palestinian threat.
- Jack Scott – on Australian Parliament's decision over Nauruan refugees.

So, Jack had a Wikipedia page, okay, but that didn't make him famous. I might not be the coolest kid in the class, but I knew fame: Miley Cyrus, the Kardashians, Taylor Swift, Ellen—all of them famous. There was no Jack Scott on that list.

Bailey, on the other hand, blinked so much you would have thought she was sitting next to Noah Centineo. I bet she couldn't wait to run home and tell everyone she knew the name of Jack Scott's cat.

The slurp popped our heads.

"Ooohhh, Thom-mas." Sarah's head shook as if a red sock got caught with the whites. "Don't touch a single thing until we can get you into the tub. Okay, now, let's say good-bye to Bailey."

"...that's correct, Jack. Thank you, but clearly, this home visit was a formality. Please prepare yourself. For open and closed cases like these, with signed waivers from living parents, and a home visit cleared on a single inspection, things could move quickly after Monday's visit with the judge."

Signed waivers from living parents.

"Well, Bailey, thank you for coming." Jack shook her hand, then Sarah, then, of course, Thomas. And behind my back, his whispered directive came.

And I shook too.

CHAPTER EIGHTEEN

Always, fantasy worked itself into my waking world. Starring in somebody else's life was a daytime vice that kept me more entertained than gossiping girls and teenaged heartthrobs. Kids at school mocked me for walking the halls with a goofy smile, a remnant of some hilarious imaginary conversation. Everything was real in what was fake. If it were funny, I'd laugh; intense, I'd cringe; sad, I'd start to well. Often, I didn't know if or when my inner monologue crossed the line into the public domain.

But now, that imaginary support, the one I fantasized about while wiping tables at Marco's was suddenly real. Kind of. Because it felt as if everybody was just pretending, not admitting that my future had yet to be declared. That Monday and the indecision surrounding it was as unknown as the existence of life on Mars.

But still, I got dragged into their illusion because—in no uncertain terms—I wanted it. I liked their life, how it contrasted with my old one. I loved their togetherness, that they didn't fight, how they seemed to want to be with each other.

By the time Friday night arrived, when their best friends, Guerin and Evelyn LeBlanc, showed up for chicken enchiladas with white beans on the side, my emotions were so knotted in confusion I chewed a massive welt under my lip.

I agonized because come Monday, it might not matter that Thomas seemed at ease with me becoming his sister, or Lynzie wanted me to teach her the violin. Come Monday, I might be on a plane flying off to live with a wrinkled woman I had met only once, missing the man who wrapped me into a burrito at night.

I might not get a chance to know Jack's oldest friend, this odd and audacious woman, who just walked through the door. And I wanted to. I really wanted to be a part of their life.

Her name was Evelyn LeBlanc, and she and Jack had known each other since primary school. The wife of his best friend,

Guerin, she was so much a part of this family, when she picked up their mail, she chose what they should read. One by one, the junk mail piled into the trash, and I stood in awe, wondering if I would ever feel that at ease.

"Thank God you're here Ryder," she said as if she read my mind. "This family needed a shake-up. Have you noticed how stuffy they are? Even their cat is arrogant. He'd correct my grammar if he could."

I couldn't suppress a smile; my worries instantly put aside.

"Where is that thing?" Her head swiveling, but not really looking, she caught my eye and winked.

"That *thing* is called Charlie, and he's hiding from your sarcasm." Jack deliberately cut off Evelyn's path.

"Ryder, do you like cats or dogs?" Not even completing a breath, she left no space for even a shrug. "Cats are the by-product of their owner's personality."

"Hardly, Evelyn," Jack said, offering her a bundle of grapes only to swing them away before she had a chance to refuse. Seated opposite him at the kitchen table, she reached over and swiped a twig anyway. "It's probably the other way around," he added, snatching the last two grapes out of her hand just as they were about to enter her mouth. "And why are you talking about owners? Cats don't have owners, they have butlers. Speaking of which, where's yours?"

"Guerin's still working hard at the studio, you know, pulling *double* duty and all." Her tone playfully shifting from needling to normal. "He'll be here soon."

Evelyn blended into this family like salt did to water. Their synergy was a game for Jack, where trampling each other's flaws and refusing to acknowledge where they agreed, was all an act to disguise a bond.

"Hey, Evelyn, you're here already. I didn't hear you come in." Sarah stepped in where Jack left off, rambling about a man called Lee, and his upcoming move to Australia. Mila and her new art exhibit on 5th Avenue. And somebody named Hollie whose unfortunate incident on a bicycle landed her in the hospital with fourteen stitches in a place no one should discuss.

Like a tennis match, I watched this exchange unfold, amazed and envious of their easy-going banter.

"Ryder." Unexpectedly, Sarah included me in the conversation, and I leaped to my feet, eager to play a part. "Would you be a doll and take the kids upstairs? Maybe read them a story. And don't stay up too late. Okay? You have orchestra tomorrow."

Oh.

"Yeah, let's read about Bilbo Baggins." Lynzie tugged at my hand before I fully grasped they were shooing me away.

How abruptly can a life change? At this very moment last week, I scurried into Marco's restaurant swallowing air as my only nutrient, desperate to scrape together another week's rent. Now here I was, the leader of a pack. Six years older than Lynzie, three and a half years senior to Thomas, suddenly, I was first to the crown.

"Read, read." Lynzie squealed as she pushed me onto Thomas' bed, thrusting the book into my hands. Her enthusiasm was my catalyst. What a privilege to have a job that made somebody else feel so secure. It *was* an honor, how could my mom not feel that? The book fell against my chest, an uninvited memory flooding in.

"What's wrong, Ryder?"

"Nothing. Just thinking about Bilbo and his adventure. Where were we?"

"He's in the cave with the Goblins. Oh, yeah, and he finds that ring! How cool would that be—to wear a ring that made you invisible?"

By the time I was Thomas' age, I had one just like it welded to my finger, helping me to hide, to live in a world of my own making. Maybe all these lies I told now were no different than the lies I told myself in the past. A different reality for different narrative.

I continued to read, lowering my voice until tiny snores dominated the room. So innocent and loved, I swaddled them in a blanket, staring at their little chests rise and fall. Slowly, I tiptoed to their door, flipped off the light, and worked my way down the hall.

"No, she would need to convert." Huh? "Somebody from her background wouldn't fit in." Evelyn's voice carried up the stairway.

I crouched, compactly wedging between the rails of the staircase, even my breathing turned stealth.

"Japan has something like a five-percent Muslim population." Jack's tone was sharp.

Muslims?

"Five-percent? Really? Try one percent, if even. And most of them are probably immigrants, not ethnic Japanese." Evelyn fought back.

"Okay then, Ms. Know-it-all, how many lesbians are there?"

Her husband, Guerin, said this because their voices I could trace: this conversation, not a chance. Muslims, Lesbians? I didn't know much about Muslims, but I knew a lot about lesbians. I watched Ellen.

Evelyn clipped her words. "Probably more than reported, but that's not the point. The math doesn't work. Follow me: an ethnic Japanese woman has a ninety-nine percent chance of being Buddhist, or whatever, but not Muslim. Okay? Okay. Fine, she's a lesbian. Okay? Okay. Why would she convert to Islam, a religion that forbids her lifestyle?"

"There are Catholic lesbians." In contrast, Sarah's words played, sing-songed like a kid on a swing.

"Yes, but do they convert, or are they born into it? A Japanese Muslim woman would need to convert."

"*Need to*? You're talking out your ass."

Wow. Language Jack.

"Shut up, Jack, finding an ethnic lesbian Japanese Muslim would be like finding a dog that didn't want its bone."

Too amused by both the punch line and the drink, Sarah could have woken the entire house with her laugh. "Fitting analogy. Look or listen or whatever, we already have a Jew, a Greek, an Indian, a Chinese, a Dutch woman, and a purebred Nebraskan All-American."

Jack broke in— "And you, Sarah, the obligatory Irish Catholic."

"And me, yes, married to the self-righteous atheist. Our book club simply wants to upsize our diversity but downsize our membership. We need to fill our ethnic and religious quotas in one person. The Japanese, the Muslim, and lesbian have to be one."

"Well, good luck with that. I think you got yourself a Catch-22. So, how's the kid?"

Wait. What?

Seemingly sobered, Sarah willingly welcomed Guerin's pivot. "Oh, that's another Catch-22." Just like with Bailey, she parceled out my misadventures, as if they were on parade in front of a judge. "This kid should be a mess. I mean she had no rules governing her. Probably not even when she was with her parents, given her propensity for independence."

That was right. My life—the algorithm gone wrong.

"Ah, then that's not a Catch-22," Evelyn clarified. "A Catch-22 is when a person can't win because of a set of contradictory rules. Apparently, your little Ryder won without any rules."

Won?

"Look, at the tender age of thirteen, she actually created a new life."

Did I?

"Could your kids do that? I mean not now, but in three years, could you see Thomas restarting his life successfully after you drop dead?"

"Charming thought, Evelyn."

"I'm serious, Jack. Maybe good parenting means less parenting. Is it the nature or nurture that became Ryder Stephens? Do you think she would be the same person she is today if you raised her from birth? If you answer yes, then you're living a contradiction. Jack, how hands-on are you? Very." Never one to linger, Evelyn's conversation waited for nobody. "When was the last time you, honestly, let Thomas choose his own adventure, independently, without the protection of buffered boundaries?"

This time, amazingly, she paused, but Jack said nothing. He was probably looking to Sarah for advice, but it wouldn't matter because Evelyn pressed on.

"It's a valid question, Jack. Do we need to spend countless hours scolding, creating boundaries, and pushing back against what society tries to make our children become? Or would the nature of the child overrule the nurture we could provide?"

"Well, I'll tell you what. I'll throw her back onto the streets and check back in ten years."

I had to risk it and get a glimpse. With his back pressed solidly against the chair, his arms folded across his chest, my thoughts were Evelyn's.

"Oh Jack, don't get defensive. This is simply an academic discussion. Without a doubt, if she were left alone, penniless, living in a brothel like she was, she would have eventually turned to drugs, and history would declare itself. But we're not talking about that. We're discussing the subtleties of parenting in the middle class. Or worse, the upper class, where we have everything at our disposal."

"I'm providing this kid with the love she justly deserves."

I jolted backward, scared my presence would stop Jack from

declaring more.

"Right, and you will change her—" shifting the needle back to normal— "for the better."

"Ah." Guerin tipped the wine bottle upside down, and two drops dripped into his glass. "This bottle's broken. Parenting's just a Catch-22 anyway, two contradictory rules, and it's just dumb luck if the kid wins." Hun, go fish another red. Right, on to the Middle East..."

More interested in Middle Earth, I left that conversation and then spent the rest of the evening forgetting about it. Bilbo Baggins and his team of trailing dwarves invited me back into their adventure. So much so, come morning, the image of a talking dragon and fire-throwing wizard lingered, and I lay in bed entirely at ease with what must have been the better part of my dream. Bilbo Baggins couldn't win, poor little Hobbit, so out of his element, out there in nature—so many rules to break.

That's a Catch-22.

Waking me outright, middle earth morphed into the middle of last night, and Guerin's voice rattled inside my head. From its better hiding place under my mattress, I reached for my iPad and flipped open the cover. With every intention of tapping on the letter C for Catch to end that mystery here and now, my finger, remembering a more intriguing part of last night, somehow compressed the letter J, for Japanese. And then it spelled out three innocent words: Japanese, lesbian, Muslim. Search.

Ohhhh, Ohhhh. That cover closed faster than my racing heart. Guilty just from peeking at the titles, I should have stopped while I was ahead. Should have. Opened again: *Muslim lesbian porn videos, lesbian Muslim sex free sex videos.* It went on, and so did my curiosity. Too tempting, tapping through the *you must be eighteen to enter this site* nonsense, my finger overrode my inner voice and responded to that big red arrow begging for my attention. Click and regret. "Ohhhh, baby..." moaned the stark-naked woman spread-eagled for all the house to bear witness.

Cover slammed! Well, I guess that answered that question. Apparently, in this world of seven billion, there were plenty of lesbian Muslims. Well, plenty enough to make an adolescent surrender her morals. Mesmerized by a world I seldom entered, I couldn't hold back and peeked again. Consumed by the images floating off my now muted screen, I heard nothing but recognized the stir of an all-too-recent interest.

"Whatcha doin'?" Jack's looming body filled the open door.

And my guilt punished. How do you cover your tracks when wrecked by the forbidden? The iPad flew under the pillow. "Hey, Jack." I scratched my head to look both interested and innocent. "Is there any bacon?"

I didn't wait for an answer. Escaping into the kitchen, Jack followed with just enough lag that I should have seen it coming. But I didn't, and there it was. Over my head and handed straight to Sarah, my iPad now belonged to a higher order.

Shit.

***

I wore the carpet down. I couldn't come to terms with having a coming of age chat with a man who insists on looking you in the eye, and a woman who takes your hand and then does the same.

Even so, Saturday was an okay day, a welcome lull in the emotional rollercoaster that had become my life. Up and down, my confidence was no less stable than a buoy afloat at sea. There were times when I had none, call up Thomas and his *duck to the bathroom and climb out the window* moment, and then there were times where I had a ton. But most times, I sat with my confusion on the edge of a fence, letting words like *unless* compete with so *many things are out of my control.* When all I really wanted to hear was: *He's providing me with the love I so justly deserve.*

"What's your password?" But Sarah's words got me pacing again. "Well?" With her hands glued to the edges of my iPad, thumbs hovering over the screen, neither would move until I gave in.

Seven days ago, I would have run. Four days ago, I would have stewed about why Sarah wanted to be a part of my life. But now, studying this devoted mother, with absolute control over my life, I mimicked Evelyn and flipped through a stack of mail.

"Ya know," she sing-songed, tugging the envelopes form my hand. "Funny thing, if you try and fail to unlock an Apple device ten times, it locks you out forever. Permanently! That would be bad. I'm on my eighth attempt.

Cruel. I spun the fruit bowl in circles, tracing my fingers around the ribbon of cherries, curious why the handle was cracked.

"Where's Jack?"

"He's in the office, writing."

When I spun the porcelain bowl really fast, the red dots blurred into a solid line.

"What's your password?"

"Why did you ask Guerin and Evelyn to my concert?"

"Listening in, were you?"

Let's see: explaining my interest in lesbian love or suffering through a lecture about eavesdropping. "What's a Catch-22?"

"Maybe Monday. Whatever happens on Monday, know that we tried and wanted only the best."

The bowl spun out of control and almost tipped over the edge.

"Oh, Ryder, please be careful, that was a wedding present. Listen, the laws regarding children's guardians are complex and are not always desirable. The State says they want the best for the child, but sometimes it places them right back with the person who hurt them the most." Determined, her fingers punched yet another combination of numbers into my iPad. "That's a Catch-22."

The tear set a course without anything to stop its path.

"No, no, we're not having that." Jack walked past me, then looked at Sarah like she was insane. She looked at him like she knew she messed up. I closed my eyes and saw my mother's face.

"You know what's another Catch-22?" Jack carried on as if my collapse was not on full display. "A person needs the password to unlock an iPad, but if he tries to enter the password, he ends up locking the iPad. So, hun, how many attempts are we up to?" Nobody rushed to hug me. The iPad slid into view. "Punch it in."

Sarah then spent the rest of the day blocking content. That she did so in plain view did not trump the fact that she turned the screen when she created the passcode to set the restrictions. And while she never opened Safari, never touched Google, she knew my password, and was getting savvier about my hiding places. Unless I cleared my history and quick, that recent search would become yet one more conversation I didn't need to have. "Can I have it back now?"

"May you, and yes." She slid it across the table. Yet, determined to violate my privacy, she twisted the knife. "Bear in mind there is now a two-hour time limit. It will— Ryder, stop with that look. It will give you plenty of time to read your books or even watch a show or two. After two hours, it will lock itself. Just ask me for the password to unlock it, and if it seems reasonable, I'll do that for you."

"You're kidding! I have to ask you when I want to use the iPad?"

"No, only when you have been on it for more than two hours. Ryder, I don't want you on that thing all day." She passed it to me as if I just won the lottery. "Here you go. I'm sure you're not surprised that I've restricted the content to your age-group."

This was a crime against humanity. To my best friend in Seattle, please forgive me for not sympathizing.

Foster parent's rights. Search.

Foster parents have, for the most part, rights equal to that of biological parents. They serve to provide guidance for all of the child's needs, which include but are not limited to, behavior issues, after-school events, and punishments.

The state remains the legal custodian of the child.

Legal custodian? Huh?

Kids in Foster care. Search.

Two hours wasn't enough. One link led to another. And after reading about so many kids worse off than me—of cigar burns and basements, lousy schools, and runaways. Of kids dumped into society at age eighteen with nowhere to go and no education to get there, I lowered the ego a notch and took stock in what my life had become.

Sarah was over the sink pushing lettuce up and down in a pool of water. She picked up one piece, inspected it, and put it back. Then another, squinting her eye, then tossed it in the trash. People who pay attention were people who cared.

The screen went black; the time limit was up. I went to the kitchen and flipped over the chicken sizzling in the pan.

CHAPTER NINETEEN

The Internet said that in the United States, on any one day, there were 428,000 children in foster care. Jesus. And these kids weren't babies either. They were not abandoned at birth without memory of their roots. No, they remembered because they were eight, nine, ten, and even thirteen.

And on this last day of January, of my thirteenth year, I was off to see a judge about becoming number 428,001.

As we approached the courthouse, the same one whose columns I counted when we drove home from orchestra practice just eight days ago, I caught our reflection in its glass. A beautiful woman strode next to me on my left, a handsome man on my right: a framed photo of the perfect family. One who walked past those of lesser means, who spent far longer than a week to reach its door. A family that bypassed those who would present their case in an open court, who breezed by security en route to their private and expedited review. Nothing slowed our stride.

Not even the receptionist who stood at attention as soon as she recognized Jack. "Did you need me to pass that to the judge, Ms. Scott?"

As she spoke, the object of her interest moved from Sarah's hand to Jack's. "No, thank you, we'll take it in with us."

If it weren't for the fact I had never seen that folder before or that my name, Ryder, was scribbled on its tab. If it weren't for the knowledge that the writing was neither Jack's nor Sarah's, I could have resisted. I reached.

"Now, Ryder." Jack moved it farther away. "When we go in there, stand up straight and shake his hand, look him straight in the eye, and focus on what he's saying."

"Um, what's in the file? Is that what was in 'My Life' binder?"

"No, it's your entire life, don't worry about it."

"Who gave it to you?" Pulling his arm closer, I ignored his

155

voice, which dropped an octave, and then his hand, which forced me into the hall.

Bending at his waist, he lectured. "Listen to me. Get this out of your head." He waved the folder high. "You walk in there. You shake his hand. You don't say um. You answer honestly. Got it?"

Back in the lobby, the judge's door opened with a sinister creak, a forewarning of what was to come. Tall, robed, and spindly, the judge's face sagged from gravity working with age. He? No, and she looked mean, a female version of Severus Snape.

Within the blink of an eye, Jack and his lecture went the way of the wind, for both of us.

"Hi. I'm Sarah Scott. Thank you for taking the time to meet with us on such short notice." Always ready to diffuse, Sarah thrust her hand between us two idiots dropping our jaws, and the judge who had hers clenched as tight as a vice. Too hard for pleasantries, when the women shook Sarah's hand, our fearless leader didn't hold back the flinch.

"Take a seat. Let's get down to it," the judge ordered as she slowly rolled her sleeves. "This is a big undertaking, Mr. and Ms. Scott. Have you thought this through?"

Jack and Sarah, who had barely settled into their seats, bolted upright.

"Perhaps we could have Ryder wait outside while we unravel the details." It was not a suggestion, and Sarah hurried me to a penalty box reserved for those who did nothing wrong but were meant to feel as if they did. "Don't wander," she added.

Not in body, but surely in mind, and when that too turned bitter, I ignored her instructions and headed towards the hall.

"Um," the receptionist grunted as she removed the bud from her ear. "Where are you going?"

Fairly sure this was an act of duty rather one of concern, I said what she wanted to hear. "The restroom." I could have told her Mars, and it would have produced that same listless nod. She popped the bud back in and turned her attention to her screen, bobbing her head to a silent tune.

All around me people looked as bored as they were anxious, and a snapshot of any one of them, at any moment, would capture their perpetual state of insecurity. Even the policeman leaning against the wall, with his coffee mug suspended inches from his lips seemed troubled. The Asian man looked exhausted, barely holding himself up from his desire to sleep. The black man had to be cold, wearing knee-length shorts wrongfully exposing his scrawny legs. There were babies and teens, mothers and drifters.

The steady beat of a boy's head against the wall drew my focus. Donned in a hoodie, all I saw was the thin white cord snaking from his ears. I moved closer. I froze. Miguel. The boy who looked like a rat and smelled like a skunk, the druggie who offered me a way out by grabbing his groin. I backed away, tripping into the policeman with his cup, hot coffee splashing on my coat.

"Well, well, if it isn't Ryder, the free-rider. Movin' up in the world, I see. Don't you look swag."

"It's not like that."

"Oh, yeah, what it like then, huh? Rich man comes in, pays off Levi, and swoops ya off to the Promised Land. Now, look at ya. Forgotten your roots?"

"I wasn't always like that." As soon as I said it, I regretted every word. Embarrassed, I saw my guilt reflected in this boy's eyes. "Do you need help?"

"What? From you? Ya gonna to buy me off too? Ya know it takes more than money to solve society's problems. Take a look, babe, I'm Mexican! You and your little privileged white ass, you people think racism is only for the movies? Think your big rich daddy would rush in and pay off Levi for me? No." He rammed the earbud back into his ear. "Go fuck yourself."

I opened my mouth, ready to defend, but truth underscores all rants. Miguel, the teenaged Mexican druggie, would have about the same chance of stumbling into a couple willing to help him than I did of being randomly stopped and frisked by Manhattan's Finest.

"Ryder." At the bend of the hall, stood Jack: tailored suit, perfect posture, clean-shaven Jack. The shame from both directions pulled my eyes south.

"You better go. Wouldn't want to work him into a tizzy and throw a hair out of place."

Too slowly for my would-be guardian, I moved away, glancing over my shoulder three then four times before reaching Jack and his tug. I looked back. Miguel flipped me off. "He needs help." Jack pulled my hand. "Really, he does. I know him." And with that fact registering something unknown, his hand fell from mine. "Please," I begged.

"Ryder, what is it you would like me to do? There are a lot of people out there that need help. We can't help everybody."

"You helped me."

"That was different." He knew why. I knew why. The boy knew why. "Ryder, not now! I'm not goi—" His gaze reluctantly made it to the boy.

Running back to Miguel, I thrust him the bill Jack had fished from his wallet.

"I'm not taking your charity." Handing it back, we both noticed its mark.

"Fifty dollars can go a long way. Please do the right thing with it." I spun towards Jack, then back to Miguel. "Do the right thing." I ran to Jack's side, comfortably in angst about why I felt so protected.

Trailing along like a toddler in tow, Jack pressed his hand deep into mine, squeezing out the memories of my first days in New York. Of the wind whipping around my frozen body, General Tso's chicken wedged into broken tiles; of the bus driver returning my fare only because she saw the desperation in my eyes. All of it etched into my conscience. Levi, even Levi, how would I ever forget the nervous reassurance he provided? Stealing was right, even though it was wrong because minimum wage for tipped workers didn't cut it. And public schools, well, they suck.

Jack's hand reached for the doorknob to the Judge's office.

Yeah, that was right. They suck. And Jack and Sarah would take me out of it. I didn't want to go back. Why would I want to wake up and see those porcelain eyes in a flea-infested room?

"You're a good kid," Jack whispered to his feet, like he needed convincing before twisting the handle. "All teenagers do spontaneous things." This time his grey-green eyes tunneled into mine. "And all teenagers learn from their mistakes." He pulled away from the door, from me, from making a concrete decision. An eternity passed before he sank into the couch in reception, sighing like his life depended on the next move he made.

The door creaked open. "Jack, we need you in here to sign the papers," Sarah's voice was sure.

And then I was alone, dissecting his words, his body language, matching it to the relaxed and reassured face belonging to his wife. *All kids learn from their mistakes.* There was no bigger mistake than the one I made on December 21st, the day I should have come home from the park.

Whatever was happening behind the judge's door—the decision of where I would stay and for how long, the papers signed, the guardianship transferred—I knew only this as fact.

Never again would I make the same mistake twice.

PART THREE

CHAPTER TWENTY

It was red.

As we drove away from the courthouse, I focused on that. Not the practiced calm from the man who made his living in front of a camera, nor the nervous chatter from the woman who could use more practice. I zeroed in on the napkin Sarah pulled from her lips, on the white surface sprayed faintly with crimson spots.

Using that as an anchor, I tried to catch hold of Sarah's pendulum. It swung wide, swooping to cover what clothes to buy, which diaries to keep, how to include me in their family traditions. And all the while, Jack said nothing. Feigning a pre-occupation with the road, he steadied his hands on the wheel, mirroring the day we plopped over potholes on the way to the orchestra.

The car dived into the garage, the blue sky replaced by florescent lights, the fake reality of a transient space. Sarah coughed again into the other side of her napkin, and when she pulled it away, it was clean. No speckles, no red, no worries. The blood I saw no more than a figment of my imagination, just as I hoped my anxiety was over Jack.

"I want to show you something," Sarah said. "Now that you're a part of the family."

She didn't wait for my reply or even the elevator to reach the top. Rummaging through her bag, she found the device she took pleasure in controlling and flipped open the cover. I watched in horror as *her* fingerprint unlatched the lock on *my* iPad, barely suppressing the attitude en route to the surface.

Her heel caught between the elevator and the threshold, sending her airborne across our front entry. I laughed. Jack dove. More concerned with protecting the ten inches of glass than the woman sprawled out on the floor. He quickly retrieved the iPad and inspected it as if it were a precious gem.

"Oh, you two, don't worry about me. I'm fine." Crawling on her hands and knees, Sarah toddled over to the couch, and in a position of Islamic prayer, stretched her hand far underneath. "Ah, I've missed you." One blue and white sneaker waved triumphantly in her hand. "Found it."

The lines etched into Jack's brow transferred to the corners of his eyes, where the arc of his smile joined to share the moment. His arms zoomed over my neck and rested solidly against my shoulders. "Ryder, what Sarah wants to show you is the wonderful online tool she's set up for the family. Look at this."

If only for a moment, because finished with self-interest, in came disbelief. Because what was there when I last reached my time limit was now gone. Everything was rearranged. Icons were missing, apps crammed into folders, different apps took over the dock bar. "Where are my books?"

"Ryder, trust me, you're going to love this," Sarah rushed over so excitedly, she dropped the shoe on the cat. A screech came next. I felt his pain.

"Where are my books?"

"Ryder, hush. She pivoted the screen towards her, swiped left, then right. "Oh, here." Her index finger bounced off the glass with an unimpressive thud.

Scattered squares filled the screen with old people's Apps not worthy of the megabytes used. A green elephant with a white square at its core? A big red circle with a white swoosh filling its center? None of them reached an acceptable level of cool.

"Where are my books?"

"Wait." Her finger thunked against that white swoosh, and nothing magical happened. Well, kind of something happened. An array of photos sprinkled across the page: a book cover, a collage of mouth-watering valentine cookies, a bedroom decorated in a musical theme. There was a door painted to look like a keyboard, a coat hook dropping down from a treble clef, pillows with musical notes swirled in a whoosh, and—

Sarah's finger punched it away. Gone were the interests I didn't know I craved, and in rushed a page with my name splashed across the top. "Welcome to the wonderful world of Pinterest!" She beamed.

I squinted to get a better look at the photo squeezed into a circle, the one Sarah took yesterday on side B, in the formal chair, which spoke of class or, so she said. "I thought you took that for court today."

"I did, but it's so beautiful, it needs to be repurposed again and again." She kissed my brow.

This woman deserved so much more than a sassy child amused by her tumble. I mean, here was a woman who *always* kissed her husband goodbye, who laid out cheese and crackers for her kids after school. Who, after measuring the depth with her finger, would put down her car keys to fill the cat's dish with an extra inch of water before she felt comfortable leaving the house.

"Thank you," I said meekly, glancing away.

"You don't even know what it does," she laughed. "Here, come, I'll show you."

I supposed I knew what was to come, that she would lead me by the hand, beckon Jack to join us at her side, and that the gesture would be a relief. Because for the first time since staying in this house, the effort didn't feel forced, or fake, or something that wouldn't last. And it wasn't because of the court order stuffed inside Jack's wallet, with my name printed on top, or that the word guardian doting the page. It was the smell of his spice mixed with her flowers, the scent of home.

"See here. There are three boards in your Pinterest account. This one is mine, that one belongs to the big guy next to you, and that's yours."

One, two, three, I held up two fingers to remind her of the children she forgot. "What about Thomas and Lynzie?"

"Thomas has his own account, and Lynzie's too young."

Before I could absorb the tiny images crammed into the digital box, she tapped her finger, which sprinkled them across the screen. "I've already uploaded a bunch of images to mine. See? All of these photos link to websites."

Now enlarged and definitely inviting, I aimed my finger towards the one with the musical notes twirling over pillows. They looked comfortable and oddly stimulating, and...

Gone. Ousted again by Sarah's twitchy finger

"You asked me about it on Saturday." A website flew open. Oh.

My mother forbid me from reading the book until I was sixteen, so naturally, my friend and I bought a copy when I was fourteen. It's the only story I've ever read where I've laughed and cried all at once...

In life, things aren't perfect. Happiness and sadness are only two shades of a spectrum that holds billions. Catch-22 manages to encase that spectrum; it reminds us that the world isn't black and white and that complication and absurdity are a part of human nature. It's a brilliant story about how reality is just a bridge suspended by the beliefs of those who must traverse it; sometimes people get halfway across and lose sight of the two directions at hand. Sometimes, the only way to find your way again is to let go of what you thought was sane.*

A teenager's review for Catch-22 by Joseph Heller, whose wise and truthful words lent genuine support to my ordeal.

Reality is just a bridge suspended by the beliefs of those who must traverse it.

I believed one life was real, and now I was to trust that another was possible.

Let go of what you thought was sane.

"I thought it might help make sense of things," Sarah said as her fingers swept the hair from my eyes. "Now, to answer your question."

A new world flew open, maybe even—I dare say—a better world? Loaded into digital shelves and filling each row were books. Some old, like *To Kill a Mockingbird*; some new, like *A Man Called Ove*; and one I couldn't wait to read titled *Catch-22*. I hurriedly scrubbed my index finger along the bottom bar until I reached the very last page.

"Noooo."

"I just need to make sure everybody is still okay in the end. You know, so I don't get too attached."

Sarah's cry folded into a reluctant sigh. "Oh, Ryder, I don't know how to respond to that. You shouldn't—"

"Ah!" I slanted the iPad away from Jack, the four-letter words flushing my cheeks before I could stop him from turning it back.

Laughter echoed off the walls, which of course, sounded in my ears like the hypocritical mocking that it was. Last I remembered, even the one with S brought on a scowl, and this word not only began with F, it vividly described its meaning.

"Kiddo, you can read it. It's a part of our life and culture. You just can't repeat it," Jack said, barely containing his grin.

"That makes, like, zero sense."

"Listen." And then came his go-to move: the hand on crown swivel. "It cheapens you to speak vulgarities, but since they surround us, we won't hide them from you. How else will you master the nuance of artful dialogue? Hear all of it, take in the best, and then you'll learn that speaking with knowledge and conviction moves the masses more than filling the pauses with colorful metaphors."

I *paused*. Nope, still BS.

I brought my index finger to my mouth, and when my nail slid off my lower tooth, it made a click I found oddly amusing. So, I did it again and then again until Jack tapped my chin and trapped my finger between my teeth. "Ouch!"

"It doesn't matter that you don't agree. Now, open mine," Jack said.

Sarah's face lit up faster than a firework, her elation so heated it zoomed past me and headed straight to Jack. "Oh, honey, you're playing along."

Wedged in between a bear hug, I tapped on Jack's board, eager to see the images he chose to post. I inhaled fast and forgot to release, too stunned by the picture staring back. A chipmunk, with its eyes guiltier than its smile. A cartoon, which would have been cute if not for it leaning against a door with his hand cupped to his ear. I shook my head spastically to erase the post that would open Pandora's box. I pawed the screen and pinched it closed. The App no more. The image gone.

Jack knew I heard. But I didn't hear. But he thought I heard. But heard what? Unless, Jack said. Unless I wanted to live with my grandmother, he reassured. But that didn't happen, did it?

I focused on the cat sitting next to the leather chair and watched it lick frantically. One leg high in the sky, the other stretched long. His tongue clicked with an audible moistness, and it pleased me to be disgusted with something other than myself.

"Do you think you could play this for me?" Jack's voice was softer than I expected. He reopened his board and pointed to the second of the two images: a big red arrow obscuring a well-known face.

"Hey, that's Itzhak Perlman," I said, my unbolted adolescent mind this time working in my favor.

"It is. And he's playing that solo Mr. Schroeder had you play that day at orchestra practice. Did you know Itzhak Perlman played at Carnegie Hall when he was twenty? You beat him by seven years, kid." The matching number of Jack's fingers waved in the air.

As silly as the comparison was, as broad as my smile grew. "He's my hero."

"And you couldn't have picked a better one. He's disabled, you know, by polio." I nodded. "Of course, you knew. Did you know he was on Ed Sullivan at the age of thirteen?"

I lost myself in the dream of performing at Carnegie, with Itzhak Perlman conducting, this violin virtuoso watching in awe as my fingers danced flawlessly across the strings. He burst with applause.

"You don't know who Ed Sullivan is, do you?"

I scratched my chin to pretend I cared, but inside I only saw Itzhak, his bushy eyebrows, bulging cheeks. I could feel him positioning my violin under my chin, correcting my elbow, toying with my hand to loosen the grip on my bow.

"Sweetheart, will you play it? Jack repeated.

Sarah left us on the couch, returning a moment later with the violin, the case already popped. Her hand reached in, and ever so wrong lifted the instrument out by the strings.

I rushed in a panic. "No, no. No, no. Don't do that, ever."

Both adults shot their hands up in surrender, then settled into the couch to watch a show. It was the moment I both dreaded and summoned. As much as I was honored to capture their interest, I feared disappointment. My nerves swelled and frayed in a single second. "I haven't practiced it since last year."

Yes, this time last year, alone in my room, I had played this piece over and over again, never stopping until I got it right. Until I felt a confidence surge; until I heard my mother pull into the garage. Such selfishness, why wouldn't I let her listen to me play?

"Ryder, if you don't want to play, that's okay." Sarah spoke words I barely heard.

"I don't want to disappoint you."

"You're not, come," she said, drumming the seat next to hers. "Let's finish up with Pinterest. You haven't seen your board yet." She tapped my name, and the board was empty. "That's yours to fill. Whatever you'd like to share with us. Maybe a video you saw at school or with your friends, or an article you stumbled on. Anything you come across on the internet that makes you think of us, just click this button that says *Pin it*, and images from the website will appear. You select one and then choose your board. We're all on the same account, so when we log on, we can see what you posted." She placed her chin on my shoulder. "And don't be shy about posting useful stuff for *that* guy"—pointing accusingly— "like 'how to move your dishes from the sink to the dishwasher in one easy step.'"

---

https://www.commonsensemedia.org/movie-reviews/catch-22/user-reviews/child

CHAPTER TWENTY-ONE

A week had passed since that judge stabilized my life, since Sarah showed me the wonderful world of *Pinterest*. And one thing was for certain, Sarah Scott relished having another child to educate. "Okay, Ryder, now take your belts and loop them over the clothes rail." Rows of leather straps lined the rod in my bedroom closet. "If you use a hanger and stack them one on top of each other, you can't get the bottom one off when you want it."

In the space of the next hour, Sarah moralized on free education, admonished the media—despite her husband making a living from it—and debated the shortfalls of democracy. Listening, kind of, I rearranged five belts in ascending order of thickness, and hung my t-shirts following the colors of gay pride.

"I'm a little bit anal when it comes to organizing," she winked. "Actually, for most things. I'm comfortable with rules, and I know this is a change for you. Your parents weren't wrong in letting you explore on your own. They were just different."

Poof.

The belts, the t-shirts, the order I created faded away, swapped out once again by the outline of my mother's face, a ring of unrest entirely out of my control. It was as if my mother waited for the helicopter to pass before she landed straight back into my thoughts.

This was my new life as a fostered child, no less vexing than peeling a hard-boiled egg. Every now and again, my old life would effortlessly fall away. Like when an entire morning passed without thinking about my mother, or when Jack replaced the sins of my father by genuinely wanting to hear me play.

But then came the rest of the time, when little fragments of my old life stuck. Like when, four days after we walked from that courthouse, I returned home from school with something as innocent as a permission slip. All Sarah had to do was sign. But no,

I cringed as her pen slashed dramatically through the word parent. A wide circle then looped the word guardian, certifying the person for which this document belonged was forever different and from a separate stock.

I handed over that permission slip purposefully folded, its signature hidden from rumor-seeking eyes. Already a self-imposed outcast, with my new clothes too designer, and the violin I carried just as uncool as the songs I hummed. I didn't need any more scrutiny.

If I only had the guts to ask what I really wanted to know. What were their intentions, how long would I stay, would she ever sign anywhere other than guardian? The best time to ask was now, during the after-school lull, after Sarah exhausted her lectures about belts and politics. But when I opened my mouth, Sarah's eyes darted to Thomas and his stencils, to Lynzie with her Barbie, to the children that shared her DNA.

I dragged my iPad off the kitchen table and headed for the couch, so much easier to ask an audience who couldn't look me in the eye.

How do you ask your foster parents about adoption?
Search.

A foster carer should know the boundaries between being a foster parent and a biological/adoptive parent. None of my carers stayed within those boundaries, and it becomes extremely difficult for the person in care. I care about my foster parents deeply, but no one can replace my parents no matter how awful they were*.

Did I feel that way? Was this person saying that foster parents rarely became adoptive parents because of set boundaries? That it was inevitable I would switch carers, that I would want to? These Internet advisors sent my mind reeling; their first foster family was different than their second, which differed from the third. This wouldn't happen, would it?

To Jack and Sarah, I was the ball hit behind home plate. Out of nowhere, I popped into their lives, and they took me home as a souvenir. There was no planning involved, no deliberation about helping a child in need, no application, home visit, or introduction to their new child via a hurried social worker knocking on their door. Sarah spent so much time sweating on the living room sofa from her menopause, having another child was probably the furthest thing from her mind.

Do foster families usually adopt the kids they save? Search.

Unfortunately, less than fifteen percent of fostered children are permanently placed. Adopting a foster child is risky and—

The screen went black. I tapped it twice, three times, pounded mercilessly on the home button. Nothing I could do would extend the two-hour time limit my guardian had set.

Across the room, Sarah leaned towards Thomas, whispering into the ear of the son who shared her genes. I fretted more as they walked into the fishbowl, both actively consumed with watering the plants.

I forced a shift by pulling the audition excerpt I had nearly mastered from my bag, filling my mind with the scribbles in the margins and the fingerings written over the notes. Confident in my progress, there was no rush to practice. I pushed it aside, switching my attention to the sea of colored pencils Thomas had left behind. With fifty colors to choose from, I immediately zeroed in on brown, an odd choice given my mood felt more like gray.

Not nearly as skilled as Thomas, I used his pad to sketch out a mouse, my go-to scribble when bored in class. It had tiny mis-proportioned feet, with a bulging, bushy tail arching over his head to tickle his enormous ears. I held it afar, appraising my mediocre work.

It leaned. Too far. Too familiar.

Without the power to stop it, the mouse transformed, looking less like what I drew and more like what I saw. A chipmunk. Its ears searching for a door—Jack's cryptic photo trapped on his Pinterest board, the one I had yet to click.

Sarah rushed out from the fishbowl just as the timer dinged. "Dinner will be ready in thirty minutes. You should probably start practicing?"

"Um, can, sorry, may I have more time on my iPad?"

"Ryder, no. I know how much you want the solo, and the audition is this Saturday."

"I know, I'll be ready, I just want to check something."

"You know," she said, gaining momentum by spinning her wedding ring loosely around her finger, trying and failing to work it over the knuckle.

Here it came.

"The internet is a gold-mine of information but a pitfall of deception. What you click on squeezes you into a bubble, and that cloud follows you around, hovering over your head everywhere you go. Your digital imprint becomes your world…"

How many times must I hear this? "Never mind." I pulled the sheet music off the table and headed towards my room.

"Wait, please, could you come here for a moment?" The dramatic thud of her collapsing into the couch sounded the alarm. "You know, it's been two months that you've been with us, crazy, huh? And we've never really talked about what happened, how your life has been turned on its head. I don't just mean with your mother's death. But you're living in a new city, studying in a different school. Surely, the way we do some things must bother you."

None of my carers stayed within those boundaries.

"No, I'm good." I diverted by turning my attention to Thomas' artwork proudly hanging on the refrigerator door. The spirals zoomed if I looked at it closely, then tunneled if I stepped back a foot. The boy had talent, for sure.

I opened the fridge, suddenly craving that quiche leftover from this morning. But when I snuck a fork under the plastic wrap, unexpectedly, and for reasons I could never explain, I saw my mother lounging under the sun. A plate in her hand, a fork stilled in mid-air, she looked up and smiled. My father stood behind her, with his beer can raised. Did he even know where I was? Did he care?

"You know, we hadn't thought about having three. I mean, just—"

"My mom is dead. I need another."

It was as if we fell into a pool, neither of us took a breath, every sound muffled, and the eternity that passed wasn't long enough for me to understand why I blurted that out.

Sarah walked over to the window, and I followed her head as it followed a cloud. "I have a cousin." She paused before pressing her hands flat against the glass to support her weight. Both eyes were scrunched, her head tilted—it was the face of a woman ready to unlock a thought.

I tumbled into Thomas' spirals.

A deep sigh renewed her purpose, and she joined me at the refrigerator, prodding me aside to lift the quiche off its shelf. "A tiny snack before dinner," she said, as she sat at the table, the lightness of her words lifting the weight off my chest.

"My cousin, well, I've known her my entire life. We grew up together in New Jersey, climbing trees when we were little, ogling after boys when we were in High School. She was my bridesmaid; I was hers." Her hand patted the seat. "Come sit with me. I've wanted to tell you this story for a while. I think it will help."

I sat, but under the table, my knee trembled. Fully aware of where this conversation might lead, I searched my mind for a different topic. Maybe the endless discussions she had with Jack about the Gynecologist, and her sleepless nights, about the hormones he wanted her to take.

"Let me just start by saying that my cousin is my hero, just like your Itzhak Perlman. That woman creates everything by determination and drive." Sarah stalled, absently running her fingers through her hair. The silenced stretched, and I rose. Ready to join Thomas outside in the atrium poking at his snow peas, or Lynzie galloping her Barbie over the sleeping cat.

Sarah lowered me back into the chair. "It was when we were about thirty-five, maybe thirty-six, a couple of years before Thomas was born. Anyway, we were cutting through Central Park, chatting about nothing in particular, probably our husbands, maybe our jobs when—out of the blue—she vanished. I mean, one moment she was laughing at my joke, the next she was gone. I panicked, for her, but also for me. I rushed over the bridge we just crossed, and there she was peacefully kicking a patch of dirt."

I scooched forward in my seat.

"My cousin, who for all I knew never experienced an ounce of trauma in her life, looked up and said, as calmly as if she was describing the weather: 'I was raped here when I was sixteen.'"

My trembling knee froze.

"I didn't know what to do with the information. I tensed and stammered, but my cousin touched my hand and told me it was okay. This woman who was raped comforted me. Do you know why?"

That knee started to bounce.

"Because enough time had passed. She told me it took two decades for her to come to terms with the wound. Said that when she was younger, in her late teens and twenties, when a trigger would poke the memory, she would run and hide, bury the moment faster than it had time to surface. Often, she'd lie to herself, always to others, make up an alternative reality to prevent her from reliving the pain."

Sarah grabbed my hand.

"At one point, she almost convinced herself it didn't happen, that it was just a dream."

On my feet, I gathered the sheet music quickly. "Sarah, you're right. I should go practice. I'm not ready."

"I know you're not, sweetheart, but when you are, please come to me. I'll always be here for you. Just think about her story, not how she stashed the memory away, but how talking about it set her free." Sarah released her grip, freeing her hand to blow me a kiss. "Honey, you can go practice now. But do me a favor and give me a hug first."

I felt the love in the force of her squeeze and ignored the guilt from not giving her more. Who was I but a girl with a secret that would never cross my lips, no matter how much I matured? Because of this I was sure: nothing would ever set me free.

Hiding in my room, I punched my fingers against the board, grinding my bow into the string. It squeaked and slid—the sound of a novice. My fingers were too tense, my mind too cluttered. Why wasn't the music working?

"Ryder?" The bedroom door opened an inch, and a tiny hand wandered through. "Um, Thomas wanted me to get you. He needs help." Lynzie cradled up to my side, stroking the violin with an innocent freedom I barely remember having. "What is this string called?" She asked.

"An A."

"Like what you get in school when you're good."

I touched my index finger to the E string. "This note is an F. It's what you get in school when you're bad." I plucked, and the high pitch resonated. "But the best thing about music is that there's no good or bad. Everything is perfect."

She smiled, and it melted the tension from this disastrous practice, from the unmistakable message in Sarah's story. We walked as sisters to the fishbowl, where a boy in need kicked his toe into a pile of dirt.

"Ryder, I don't know what went wrong. It's not growing," his small voice sank.

"We'll start over," I said. "Go get the seeds."

Happy to be a solution to a problem instead of a cause. Together we collapsed to our knees and muddied our clothes, whispering encouragements to the little pod buried deep beneath the surface. "Come on, little guy, I know you can make it." We stood as one with both hands on our hips, staring into the dirt, hoping to bypass the present and leap unscathed into the future.

Ding.

Our heads zoomed to the elevator.

"Lynzie, you didn't close the door," Thomas whispered.

True, because when Jack walked off the elevator, we heard his briefcase thud against the floor, his jacket whoosh over the couch. His solid heals clicked rhythmically against the wooden floor as he made his way to his wife.

"Jack? What are you doing here?" Sarah asked, her eyebrows raising as if a monkey just swung into the room.

"Well, for starters, I live here." He pecked her cheek. "Up next, it's Friday. Been doin' it for fifteen years, hun. Show doesn't run on Friday."

"It's Friday? I'm losing it. I thought it was Thursday."

"And Bailey. She's coming over tonight, remember? Monthly social worker review as ordered by the court." Jack reminded.

I gasped, the opened door hurling my shock into their space. With my arms crossed, I shouted as if the door was sealed. "Why does she need to come all the time?"

Their heads turned, registered indifference, then went back to the discussion I didn't want to hear. "And that's about what?" Jack asked.

"Avoidance coping at its best." Lower, but not soundless, she mumbled clearly. "I told her about Cassie." Jack's eyes raised; his brow tented with curiosity. "Not a chance. She ran off to play her violin."

Was it disappointment or disgust? Why did Jack turn his back?

And why was the dinner that followed so silenced and stressed? Or was that just me? Or, I pulled my knife against the steak. It stuck. Harder, I threw my body weight into it. Thomas gnawed and kneaded, his teeth grinding into the rubber he chewed in his mouth.

Lynzie's head turned, her napkin capturing the lump spit from her mouth. Too polite to offend his wife, especially when her cooking usually rocked, Jack pulverized the overcooked meat with a manly chomp, and all the while, Sarah played with the peas.

"Ah, honey, not hungry?" Jack asked.

"No, not really. How is it?" Her head tilted like a dog waiting for a pat. And around the table, eyes met eyes, young mouths started to part.

"It's fine," Jack stopped us all from speaking.

Determined to guide my siblings out of the awkward moment, I announced what we did that we weren't supposed to do, that we ate a box of cookies before dinner, and that we were ashamed. I kicked Thomas under the table. Thomas kicked Lynzie, and the deed was done. We bowed our heads. "Sorry, Sarah," I said, circling my hand over my fellow accomplices. "We're not hungry either."

Thomas hurried the baffled Lynzie to the sink, where he took my dish and scraped the remnants into the disposal. Teamwork continued, a secret shared, all of it validating the fact that some truths were better left blurred.

Buzz.

Not a ding because that would be the elevator. It was a buzz from the lobby, which meant *that* woman was here. Bailey, the nosey social worker, had arrived with the intent to overstay her welcome. Of this, I was sure.

Her first visit, the one before I was documented, was fine. She acted appropriate, professional even, callously referring to me as the case. The next one, though, pushed the boundaries of her role. She strayed off-topic, chatting passionately about Jack's show, about those refugees in Nauru. She touched his knee.

But that last visit, well, that was when I had enough because Bailey McPherson did not have permission to sort through our mail. That type of behavior was reserved for Evelyn LeBlanc, Guerin's wife, Jack's *lifelong* friend. The same woman who Jack insisted I call Aunt. That woman was allowed to steal grapes out of Jack's hand. Bailey, the court-ordered social worker, definitely was *not*.

And tonight, when Bailey McPherson pranced into the foyer, it had become increasingly clear that this cute and affable social worker loved this 'case' more than she should. Maybe even added visits to her log for the sole purpose of gawking at Jack.

Dressed to the nines, her paper-thin dress clung to her curves as if it were painted to her form. Her earrings swirled in a spiral cascading down her neck. She looked cool, for sure, but still.

"Did she just bat her eyes? Did you see that?" I whispered to Thomas, forcing out the disgust by squeezing my arms against my chest.

Clunk.

Thomas, unfazed and oblivious, answered my question by popping the footrest on Jack's leather chair, and tossing his hands behind his head as if he were sunbathing on a beach. "What does it matter that she blinks a lot?"

Jesus. I unfurled myself and bee-lined to Sarah, who stood detached, organizing take away menus at the breakfast bar. "Why are you doing that?"

"I just don't have the energy to cook anymore. I'm stacking the menus in order of regions and ethnicity. The Italians are first, followed by the Indians. The Asians are all lumped together in the back."

Indians were Asian, but whatever. "That's great. Look at that, doesn't it bother you that other women fawn over your husband?"

Contemplating the Lebanese menu, she slid it behind the Japanese. "Are you kidding me? That man is far too much of a homebody to have an affair. Every time he hears about some celebrity sleeping with a nanny, he just shakes his head in total amazement, wondering how they have the energy." She plucked out the Lebanese and put it in front of the Italians. "Trust me, Jack Scott would much rather be at home sunk into that ancient, beat up, leather recliner than flirting with the hottest supermodel on the planet. I've known that man," pointing to him with the help of the Mexicans, "since I was seventeen. No, I'm not remotely worried."

"Or maybe he just loves you a lot."

"Well, of course, that too."

Their relationship baffled me. How odd was it that they battled with sharpened tongues, but that no sparks flew: ever? Still, Sarah clearly had enough, clapping her hands with such force, we all jumped a foot. "Okay, I think we're good."

"Well, actually," Bailey injected. "There is a bit of a hiccup regarding the paperwork. I was wondering if the three of us could speak in private."

It was a moment that reshuffled the deck. No longer just an

annoying hair-thrower, Bailey McPherson was now a hair-thrower with power. Jack nodded. Sarah joined. And the woman who usually chuckled for effect somberly followed them into the office.

Chipmunks and doors and big ears rushed into my head. And I ran to the closed door, soundlessly scooching close without making contact. Nothing. It was as if that door was made of the fishbowl's glass. I searched my hands for a scab to pick, but none were there, time already healing those wounds.

Thomas did something to make Lynzie giggle, their innocence echoing down the hall. I loved them. I would miss them. I didn't want to go.

Crack.

Sarah stepped out first, followed by Jack, who shook his head in disapproval. "Ryder, what did I tell you about eavesdropping?"

Bailey crossed the threshold next and immediately began cooing over the cat. With her smile so full, my mind spun trying to decipher why.

In polar opposite directions, Sarah ushered Bailey to the elevator while Jack targeted that banged-up, beat-up leather chair. Shooing off his son, he assumed the exact same position before burying himself behind his book. The elevator door closed. "See how I suffer for you, Ryder?"

Him? I was the one left in the hall with my ear an inch from door, the one straining to hear a morsel of conversation to know if—or when—I needed to pack my bags.

"Something the matter, kid? Are you bothered by Bailey's visit?" Jack's glasses had slipped down his nose so that he had to tip his head up to see me clearly through the lens.

"I'm always bothered by Bailey's visit. Why does she have to come?"

"She just needs to make sure you're adjusting well." He patted the arm of the chair. "Come on over here., please."

Deliberately drawing my attention, his finger slid instructively over a single sentence in his book. *The deeper sorrow carves into your being, the more joy you can contain.* Twice, his finger tapped the word can.

He spoke aloud now, purposefully pacing his words.

"Your joy is your sorrow unmasked. And the selfsame well from which your laughter rises was oftentime filled with your tears. When you are joyous, look deep into your heart and you shall find it is only that which has given you sorrow that is giving you joy."**

The pages turned in bulk. Sarah returned from the elevator and perched on the other arm.

"Your children are not your children. They are the sons and daughters of Life's longing for itself. They come through you but not from you, and though they are with you yet they belong not to you. You may give them your love but not your thoughts. For they have their own thoughts. You may house their bodies but not their souls. For their souls dwell in the house of tomorrow, which you cannot visit, not even in your dreams. You may strive to be like them, but seek not to make them like you."

He squeezed me tight. "Ryder, stop worrying. The future will take care of itself."

That's exactly what I was worried about.

---

https://www.theguardian.com/commentisfree/2016/feb/12/our-lives-in-foster-care-what-it-feels-like-to-be-given-a-new-family
**The Profit, by Kahill Gibran.*

CHAPTER TWENTY-TWO

The future will take care of itself. Well, Jack, according to your wife's book, the future looked pretty bleak.

Books on menopause scattered the living room. I picked one up and read about the woman who opened a window when it was fifty degrees, who forgot to take the steak out of the oven, who couldn't remember when it was Friday. Mood swings, heat rushes, memory loss, this book nailed each and every one of Sarah's troubles.

Maybe if I learned more, I could steer her into a diversion, get her talking about *her* future, not *my* past. I could remind her that sorrow carves a hole so that joy has someplace to go, that this menopause thing will be her sorrow unmasked.

The book fell open to where a crease had formed. *Just because the flow of blood has stopped coming from your vagina, does not mean that the juice has stopped circulating in your loins.* Loins? Skip. *The menstrual blood does not collect inside your uterus.* Skip. *Blood.* Skip. *Vagina.* Skip. *Clitoris.*

Jesus. What did I get myself into?

I flipped to the last page: *From the time a woman first menstruates, she has the privilege of starting a life.*

Ah. No. Progression into womanhood by way of sullying my wardrobe with uninvited crimson splatter was not my idea of a privilege. Uh-uh. Having just entered the world in which Sarah was leaving, I felt no pity whatsoever. In fact, it was more like a pang of jealousy for her supposed troubles. I abandoned the effort.

Stepping over Lynzie torturing the cat, I stare into the void of the NYC skyline. Life had changed, and in more ways than how my hips had curved. The snow had melted away, bringing in the unpredictable New York City spring. Slanting rain one day transformed into jacket-shedding sunshine the next, and my wardrobe morphed to meet Mother Nature's mood. But on my student ID, on those forms from the family court, my name was always the same: *Stephens*, Ryder *Stephens*. And I had to prepare myself that it would never change to Scott.

"Ouch! Stupid cat." Lynzie rubbed her arm crisscrossed with evidence of mismatched love, and Sarah rushed over to balance the wrong. "Mommy, I was just trying to show her how much I loved her."

"Honey, sometimes just paying attention is the most honest way to love. Give the cat some distance, okay?"

Sarah winked in my direction, then distanced herself by typing on her computer. She chuckled, and a steady hum filled the room. It was a single bar stuck on repeat. Over and over, Sarah couldn't move past the monotonous drone. "Ah, what is that song?"

"Um, Beyoncé?" I picked the only oldest woman I could think of.

Her laugh energized the room. "Noooo. This song is from the eighties, from junior high. Hey, I think I was about your age when it came out." More humming. "Oh, I know what it is! Siri, play *Life in One Day* by Howard Jones."

And magically, her computer sprang to life, instantly transforming the room with an upbeat entrance of a lively high-pitched jingle. Even before the lyrics spoke, I knew that the person who wrote this song wanted you to feel alive, begged you to savor the wealth of life.

Sarah sang as if lecturing the world, tapping the air to emphasize the words, the simplicity of the message impossible to deny.

The old man said to me, don't always take life so seriously. Play the flute and dance and sing your song. Try to enjoy the here and now, the future will take care of itself somehow. The grass is never greener over there.

Lynzie, bouncing her head from side to side, perfectly matched the symmetrical beat. She rose to her feet, skipping around the room, forgetting all about the scratches and tainted love. In her own world, Sarah's smile grew into an infectious joy, that song molding the moment into what life was supposed to be.

Don't try to live your life in one day. Don't go speed your time away. Don't bite off more than you can chew, only so much you can do.

The wonderful world of music and lyrics, doctoring life with the only medicine that healed. I beat my foot, then my knee. Before I knew it, I had Lynzie in my arms twirling circles around the cat. The meaning behind Jack's words last night morphed into something worthy.

Life was fun. Life was good. Life will take care of itself.

Jack paid attention, and attention was love. I was no longer starving on the streets, haven't thought about money since the first time I walked off that elevator. I was going to audition for a solo at Carnegie Hall tomorrow.

Yes, I was. Sarah had injected energy into my veins. I ran to my room and played hard. And powerful. And determined to *dance and sing my song.*

I didn't need Sarah's menopause to create a distraction. I needed what I always needed: music, my violin, a crescendo, and a beat. All of that wore away the storm.

***

And the next day, when I walked into the music hall, the confidence I owned twelve hours before crumbled the moment I saw that first violin. His scales flew up in a dramatic climb, then down with a sinuous flow. Focused and beautiful, Spencer, with his meticulously disheveled hair, executed each note with the impossible combination of precision and grace.

"Hello, Ryder," he said, interrupting his warm-up to thoroughly dismantle my nerves. "Best of luck to you."

I dropped my jaw. Spencer Schrader, this boy who played like a pro but looked like a surfer, just called me by my name.

He pinched his lips together only because I gave him nothing. Not a smile or a shrug. The one kid I've met since moving to this city that I sincerely envied, and I couldn't even manage a wave.

"Well, see you on stage, then," he said, walking away to talk with somebody sane.

He tuned his instrument with the help of the second chair, and the mismatched harmonies clashing with adolescent chatter rattled me further. The noise grew, my nerves twitched, and I couldn't find the switch to turn it off.

Mr. Schroeder banged his baton—I jumped—and bows that dropped away from strings held still in the air. "Okay, my young prodigies, let's begin." Our conductor pointed his baton into the wings, and the lights magically dimmed.

The first candidate emerged, and the lonely spotlight found a bead of sweat. He shook, the stress from the attention ruining his chance for success. The next one followed, and it was more of the same, narrowing the competition still. A third, a fourth, and then came Spencer. Tall for his age, with the posture of a model and lips full enough to remember, he extended his hand to Mr. Schroeder like a man in pursuit of a deal. Confident. Not a drop of sweat anywhere to be seen, nothing in his body quivered. Spencer sat on the edge of the chair poised, executing Vivaldi's Concerto No. 4 in F Minor as if he were Itzhak Perlman himself.

"Okay, Ms. Stephens, you're up." Mr. Schroeder said with a tone suggesting I need not bother, that his decision had just been made.

Ready, no. Nervous, most definitely. I took a deep breath and harnessed the bundle of nerves that sparked the flame, extinguishing those that fanned it out of control. The moment stretched too long, and I forced myself to step inside a bubble. I couldn't let Spencer's confidence override mine.

"We're ready when you are, Ryder."

The neck of the violin was gripped tensely in my hand, and I forced an inhale, willing the muscles to relax. They tightened. I looked through my bubble and saw the few souls sitting, impatiently waiting for the audition to finish. A man standing off to the side moved into the light.

Jack.

He nodded once, and a trusting smile crested.

Your children are not your children. You may give them your love but not your thoughts. For they have their own thoughts.

And their own talents. My bow flew over the strings, syncing to the tempo of the furious beat. In a million-mile sprint, rivulets of sweat ran from my temples. My vibrato escalated until it stalled into a trill. Strong and determined, I burst through my bubble, and on the other side was Jack. His attention moistening my eyes.

With the excerpt finished, fatigue seized my breaths. I wiped my brow with my palm, dragging salt into my eye. It stung. I turned away from the light only to be blinded by Spencer's look. It belonged to a face, which I couldn't read, to a boy who wouldn't forgive.

"Okay, that's all six of you," Mr. Schroeder declared. "We'll take a break for a half-hour, and when we return, I'll announce the selection for the solo."

For thirty minutes, I talked with the cellos, watching YouTube videos of people who were supposed to be cool. Yet all the while, I surveyed the stage, looking for the boy who seemed to be looking for me.

The baton clicked rapidly to cow the crowd, our bracelet wearing hippy losing patience with our adolescent noise. Tap—the wood of his stick banged against the metal stand, but the chatter only swelled. Mr. Schroeder cleared his throat. No response.

Suddenly, a painful shriek pierced the air, and all heads turned to Spencer, to the boy with four fingers angled against his lips. The whistle worked, the children behaved, and Jack's head popped from behind a post.

I smiled.

"Thank you, Mr. Schrader. Well, as disinterested as you all are to learn of this year's selection, it must be announced." Nervous laughter split the air. "This year, that person is..." His baton slowed. "You didn't make it easy for me." The rhythm tapered until a heartbeat filled the space between the clicks. Slower, two pulses, three. Stagnant. Just tell us!

"Ryder Stephens."

I spun to Spencer, his mouth an O. A flush filled my face as his hands slowly raised, ready for what I did not know.

He clapped. Slow at first, the tempo built in speed, until, without animosity or resentment, that O spread wide, and a tender smile arched. Spencer Schrader, this boy who should have won, who transformed his disappointment faster than I had time to process my joy, he glanced at Jack, then whispered to me.

"Look how proud you've made your father."

**

Father.

"Lynzie, go tell your *father* we have to leave for Ryder's concert now if we're going to make our dinner reservations. Oh, and Ryder, *Jack* looked over the essay you wrote for your history class. It's over there on the kitchen table."

Oh, Spencer, if you only knew the conundrum surrounding

your innocent remark.

Lynzie's father responded to Thomas' mother and met his fostered child at the elevator door.

"Are you ready for your big solo tonight, kiddo? I'm so excited for you." He cuffed his hands around his lips. "Sarah, we're at the elevator. Not the one who will make us late," he said, drumming his fingers over the elevator door. "Come on, hun, Ryder's getting nervous."

"I'm not nervous."

"Uh-huh. Did I ever tell you about when I first started on television? I had to bolt mid-interview to vomit." He mocked a gag. "I'll never forget it. But I tell you what, once the blood returned to my head, I was good to go."

"So, I should make myself vomit?"

"I thought you said you weren't nervous?"

"I'm not!" I thrust my rock-steady hand out to prove it, which he seized, then spider-crawled his fingers over the palm, my elbow, working his way under my arm. Every child's nightmare, I almost peed. "Stop it."

"Okay, you two, stop foolin' around. We're meeting Evelyn and Guerin at the restaurant at five, and Ryder's concert starts at seven," Sarah said, swooshing into the room, saving my clothes from an inadvertent splash. "Let's get going!" This was yelled in our direction, even though we had our jackets on, shoes tied, and I had my violin case solidly in hand. "Kids!"

Two sets of pattering feet pounded down the stairs, and the four of us waited at the elevator while Sarah topped up the cat dish, scooped out his litter, checked to make sure the toaster was unplugged, the gas stovetop off, the fishbowl sealed.

"Sarah!" Jack shouted.

"Coming, coming."

The entire taxi ride to the restaurant Jack rambled incessantly, something he never did with an "outsider" present. Perhaps because the taxi driver turned a deaf ear, or didn't care, or was a republican, he didn't even acknowledge Jack.

"I wonder if Itzhak vomited before his first concert. Should we swing by and ask him? I think he lives someplace around here," Jack laughed.

"Jack! For the last time, I'm not nervous!"

"Not even a little, Ryder? You're telling me that once you're on stage—"

Thud.

Stopped at a light, the banging increased in speed, then grew harder and angrier. Through the space between the front two seats, I saw a man's hand pound savagely against the hood of the cab.

"Oh, for Christ's sake!" Jack jumped out of the car just as the cabbie lost his cool. 'Nuanced dialogue' ensued, and hands covered Lynzie's ears.

"Eh, oh, oh, eh, we're walkin' here!"

"Guerin!"

Guerin LeBlanc thought it was hilarious. "Ah, come on, that's what good New Yorkers do. They teach it in pre-school!" I loved this man's voice. Its rhythmic low could both rock you to sleep or smooth over a bitter New York City cabbie. "Sorry about that, my friend," he said, passing the pissed off driver a fifty-dollar bill.

"Teach what? How to incite road rage?" Sarah hopped from the taxi next. "Hi. Evelyn. Can you please control your man?"

"No. Can't. Just ignore him. Where's the little star?" Evelyn dragged me out by the arm, barely giving me time to grab my violin. "There she is, excited? Hey Ryder, fun fact—"

Jack quickly wrestled me out of Evelyn's grasp and sent me flying into Thomas.

"Don't worry, darling." She cupped her hands over her mouth so that all of midtown Manhattan would hear. "We'll talk later. Aunt Evelyn has all the gossip."

Thomas, expressing a sophistication nobody would have guessed, insisted on carrying my violin all the way to the restaurant. "Ryder, she does have good stories. Did you know that Dad and Aunt Evelyn grew up together, like they've known each other since they were six or something? And they went to the same school when they were little. But different high Schools though. Dad thinks it's really funny that they were in the same English class in college. Said so because they hadn't seen each other for like the whole time they were in high school. I don't think that's very funny. Do you, Ryder?"

I glanced back at Jack, to his one arm wrapped around his wife, the other jokingly pushing Evelyn away. "Is that where Jack met Sarah, at Georgetown University?" I asked Thomas.

"Huh? Uh, no. Mom says that when she was homeroom queen in high school, it helped Dad's reputation."

"Homecoming Queen," I corrected, simultaneously taking stock in Sarah's long legs, her soft, sweeping hair, her gentle smile when she locked eyes with Jack as they spoke.

Forty-nine minus, did Sarah say they starting dating at seventeen? That would be nine minus seven equals two; four minus one would be three. Wow! They'd known each other for thirty-two years. Inconceivably long. Spencer and I are thirteen, at forty-nine....

"Hey, you two, you walked right past the restaurant. Hurry up, we don't have too much time before Ryder's needed back on stage."

Evelyn rushed over, filling the space next to me with an invigorating breeze. It was fresh, like a recently vacated shower. "Just enough for one story," she whispered.

"No, Evelyn!" Jack cut between.

"Oh, Jackson, it's innocent. This one time," she began, unfazed by Jack and his obsession with privacy. "Jack and his buddies dragged a keg, in a Radio Flyer wagon, down the Capital Mall. Then, violating all historical decorum, they scaled the Lincoln Memorial and hung a sign around old Abe's neck. It read: 'Beam me up Scotty, there is no sign of intelligent life down here.'"

The adults erupted in laughter.

"See," Thomas murmured. "I don't think that's very funny either, do you, Ryder?"

A point to which I had to agree. A Radio Flyer? And who was this Scotty, and what did she mean by beam? Was that like an Airdrop or something?

"If any of these children did that today, it would have been photo-documented, posted on every social network in existence, and landed them in jail with multiple felony convictions," Sarah concluded, marking each penalty with the end of her fork. "It would brand them for life."

Missing her point by a mile, I disagreed, explaining that it would be videoed, not photographed. Thomas concurred.

The meal unfolded with much of the same: me pretending, Thomas joining my forced laughter, and Lynzie trying and failing to fold a napkin into a bunny.

"Ah, we're late." Jack stole the bill from Guerin's hand and passed it to Sarah, who held just high enough for Evelyn to tease it free.

Out on the street, sandwiched between Guerin and Jack's conflicting advice, the rest of the gang sprinted to catch up. "People, you're going to make her nervous with all your heavy breathing. You should let us professionals rid her of anxiety." Jack said, shielding me in his arms.

"You're a news anchor, not a performer."

"Excuse me, Evelyn, but Guerin and I have to charm the ladies just as much as Tony Stark." Blank looks. "You know, Tony Stark, Iron Man, Robert Downey, Jr."

"Oh, Jesus Jack, you are *not* comparing yourself to the hottest man in Hollywood."

"I sure am." Jack winked, then pulled me into a bear hug that could have suffocated a lion. "We're here. Listen, you go get 'em, kid! And don't forget to wave to your old man in the crowd."

My old man.

***

Backstage, and throughout the entire first act, I methodically searched every row. Even as Mr. Schroeder summoned me to center stage, and the crowd quieted to a lull, I combed through every seat.

"We have a special young woman with us tonight," Mr. Schroeder began.

A child-like whoop came from the ground floor, about twenty rows up and off to the left. Found 'em. All heads swiveled to Thomas, who had his fists high in the air. He sat to the right of the woman suppressing a giggling, and the left of the man wiggling his fingers.

"Fresh to New York, but obviously not to her fans," the maestro said, pausing to sweep his hand over my ardent supporters. "Please help me welcome one of our youngest members, thirteen-year-old Ryder Stephens."

I gazed into the sea of applause. To think what I would have seen two months ago: nothing, nobody, empty eyes vacant of a connection. Guerin broke the wall with a gallant salute. I smiled, shifting my attention to the child-like antics of Thomas, who still had his double thumbs-up piercing the air. Sarah blew me a kiss.

Goosebumps spiked, and taken by surprise, my breathing grew shallow, my palms moist, the confidence I mastered shattered by the attention I didn't expect. The heat from the lights was a fire to my nerves; the hush of the crowd, a match. I licked my lips before I bit down hard.

Jack held his hand out in front. It was steady and calm, and mimed a message from a confident man, reminding me it was only human to be on edge.

I bit harder.

His index finger pointed at me, then the ceiling, looping around until it aimed into his open mouth. A feigned gag came next, his body convulsing to mimic his first time on TV. It lasted too long, drawing the attention of his wife, whose body matched mine as we absorbed our laugh.

I unclenched my teeth from my lip, releasing it from the unjustified nerves. Shifting my bow to free my hand, I did as I was told.

Jack waved back.

My old man.

Mr. Schroeder tapped the stand, and the readying orchestra forced my mind into gear. I closed my eyes and let the darkness play with the shadows splitting the light. All sounds were waves, all movement still. My mind disappeared inside that bubble.

The orchestra began. It was a sturdy march, a measured tempo held at bay by the maestro's baton. I felt its beat in my gut, marching over my chest. I listened, waiting for their argument to transform into a burgeoning dispute, my pulse accelerating with each orchestral stroke. It grew louder and more powerful, increasing in dominance, refusing to yield.

Then, silence. A pin could speak.

I inhaled, let out a fearless smile, and exploded, a burst of rapturous speed that dominated the room. The orchestra stirred, begging for their turn, eager to steal the mood. Slowly, they swelled, prodding the concert hall with a force that competed with mine, backing down only when I broke free from its leash. Me versus them, back then forth we argued, pushing for control, deliberate in our intent. But no one won. United, we owned the moment.

Applause.

Up ahead, that crew of six never shifted their focus. That center, the one unwilling to let me fail, bore its hole. No longer was I that young girl trying to admit and forget her past, or the fighter confused over an ever-changing present. I was what they had created, a young woman: strong and confident, needed, and above all else, loved.

Yes, I did well.

The concert ended, sending a wave of parents backstage in a staggering rush. They picked up their children and smothered them with hugs. Jack parted the curtain, and eyes darted as the whispers came.

"Everybody is staring at you because you're famous," I murmured.

"No, Ryder." He leaned forward to execute his trademark move. With his hand on my crown, he turned my head, but this time he took it one step further and planted a kiss to my brow. "They're staring at you because you've earned it. I love you, kid."

Loved me. Beside me stood a man who had never said that before, who acted as if he were my father. A man who—as much as I wanted for that to be true—wasn't.

I swallowed.

"Come on, everybody's anxious to see you."

We snaked through the cellist and the flutist, past the boy with the triangle, whose parents beamed with pride. Jack finally found the part in the curtain and whipped it open.

"Oh, sorry." Spencer stepped back from a girl, his pinky swinging distractingly close to her thumb.

Jack didn't notice, I looked away. He dragged me across the stage, down the stairs, and up the aisle. A concert hall filled to capacity, I looked back through the crowd to unsee what I saw. Evelyn's unmistakable enthusiasm mercifully changing the scene. She whisked me in a hug before Sarah had a chance to get close. "I want her," Evelyn said. "You guys already have more than enough. Honey, when you get tired of living in that stuffy house, you come live with your favorite aunt."

"Not a chance," Sarah cut in. "This one's mine. I'm so proud to be a part of your life, sweetheart."

A tug-of-war ensued, a clamor broke out, and never in my life had I felt so loved.

"You looked so calm." "Weren't you nervous?" "Can we get some ice cream to celebrate?" "You were great." "Seriously, some ice cream?" Nobody heard a word anybody else said.

Thomas snuck his hand into mine.

And never let it go.

CHAPTER TWENTY-THREE

The strangest thing happened after the concert. I stopped searching the internet. I'd ready my finger to punch Safari or Chrome or Google, to type in *why* or *what* or *how*. But without will or effort, it landed on iMessage, faithfully wandering over to Thomas' name instead.

"What r u doing?" Send.

A nanosecond passed, and my iPad dinged.

"Posting what I want 4 my bday on Pinterest."

Ding. A screenshot of an art set loaded. It had everything from crayons and markers to watercolors and oil pastels. The middle section popped up into teepee, a miniature easel to satiate the dreams of an ambitious boy.

Thomas drew incessantly, everywhere, on the backs of cereal boxes, on envelopes. Every once in a while, a stick figure could be found sketched on the toilet paper roll. And I—wholeheartedly respecting his passion—would place the little white square on the sink, protecting his impromptu masterpiece from mother nature's soil.

Ding. Ding. Ding. He stopped at my bedroom door. Ding. Walked over to my desk. Ding. Nudged me to the edge of my chair. Ding. Ding. Ding.

"Thomas, you don't have to message me if you're practically sitting in my lap."

His nose wrinkled from the chuckle.

"Hey, you two!" Wrath stood at my door, and its nose wrinkled for an entirely different reason. "Not funny!" Sarah's licked her puckered lips to rid away our fun. "Thomas, your father does NOT like practical jokes." The lips tried to stay pursed, to fight against the desire to break face, they failed.

Sarah's good-natured tolerance of our fool-hearty adventures was our permission to continue. This time it was salt in the sugar bowl, next time we plotted to replace Sarah's screensaver with a screenshot of all her apps. We belly-rolled just thinking about how Sarah would punch the mail icon and watch nothing happen. Toggle the iCalendar, nothing. iMessage, Pinterest, a screen frozen because it was only a photo. We were just that cool.

"And Ryder, if Jack knows you taped the toilet seat to the base, you don't want the lecture. Do you hear me?"

I did. You just called the man you married two different names depending on who you were talking to.

"It's time for bed. Both of you, off to your separate and *disconnected* rooms." By the end of her lecture, two iPads, one iPhone, and for some reason, an empty picture frame from the top shelf piled into her arms. "Go to your room, Thomas. Stay in yours, Ryder. Goodnight to you both."

She left only to return in less than a blink. "Sorry, honey, I forgot to kiss you goodnight. Love you."

Jack sauntered in with that egg whites and goo look of pride. He then tucked the sheet, adjusted the pillow, and nestled the comforter under my chin before cocooning me so tight I couldn't move.

He then went about imparting his wisdom, a nighttime ritual I would long for if missed. On Wednesday, it was a one-liner about the inventor of the frozen French Fry—some guy named Simplot. Last night it was all about deciphering anagrams. Listen, if rearranged, was silent; inch was chin; desserts was… He left me hanging, walking out of my room before I could unscramble the letters. I powered my brain until it ran out of gas, never solving the riddle before I slipped into sleep.

Tonight, I got a tickle and a tease. "Figured out the anagram to desserts yet?"

"Ah, I forgot to look it up."

"Not search the internet, search your brain. Work at it to keep that noggin sharp."

Tesserd, serdest, my nose crowded my eyes, trying different

ways to rearrange the letters in desserts.

"Listen," he said, poking me on the nose. "*I'm* okay with practical jokes as long as you keep doing them to your *mom.*" A wink.

I unraveled *desserts* and spelled out *stressed.* Jack's play on words less a teaser about anagrams than a reminder of a palindrome.

Mom.

***

The next morning, that very palindrome rolled out breakfast with detail and care, with bread not from a bag, but from the toaster, and cereal not sitting in a box, but poured into our bowls. Sarah *always* was two steps ahead of our needs. Whether it was basketball shoes for Thomas before he knew he made the team or ballet slippers for Lynzie, Sarah loved her job. A job that started ten years ago today.

"You were such a tiny thing, four weeks early. The doctors wouldn't put you on my chest. They whisked you away, and—"

"Yeah, Mom, you told me. But, I'm big now, double digits!" Thomas loved the fact that his age had two numbers instead of one. "When's Dad coming home from work so I can open my presents?"

"Present, Thomas, singular," she reminded him, a tradition lamer than a millionaire commuting by bus. Why, with so much money, did...

The elevator dinged, and when Jack strolled out, Thomas dived for his present as if it were a football loose in a quarterback's grip. The gift popped free, and an all-out skirmish played out on the living room floor. Lynzie piled on Thomas, who piled on Jack; even the cat got a piece of the bow.

Victorious, Lynzie emerged the proud owner of a battered box.

"Thanks," Thomas said, dusting himself off before casually lifting it from her hands.

I suppose I should have laughed at the playful scene, the one where a child desperately wants a gift more than the love of the parent who bought it. I didn't. I spun my ring, crushing it against my knuckle, forcing a physical pain to help me forget.

Rip.

Wrapping paper flew around the room as if it were confetti shot from a gun.

"Yes!"

Thomas' birthday present was a success if not a given: an art set with an easel. Just like he posted on Sarah's board, on Jack's, like he printed out and taped to the refrigerator, the elevator door, the mirror in the master bathroom.

I had done the same, wanting that ring more than I wanted anything else. I remember changing the screen saver on my mother's computer, so it would be the first thing she saw each day. I begged. She said no. I whined. She told me we couldn't afford it. I told her that a decade living on this earth was worth the price of an opal, and she said she could relate because, at forty, four of them passed for her.

Thomas beelined to the table to set up the easel, and I turned the ring to obscure the opal from view. I didn't want to remember when her secret broke, that unexpected moment sitting in my favorite restaurant when her smile morphed into a playful giggle. I couldn't bear to see the tiny box with a pink bow on top.

I squeezed my fist, and the prongs holding the opal cut into my palm. Harder, I pushed, willing it to crack and break free from its nest, to have it disappear like she did.

"Did I get my other wish," Thomas asked. "It's a wish, Dad, not a present. It won't make me spoiled."

Nervous, Sarah pursed her lip to hide a truth. Jack's head quivered, like the smaller the motion, the less disappointment Thomas would feel. Looks passed between them. "Sorry, son, not this year," Jack murmured.

Why Thomas looked towards me, I couldn't guess. If I had their money, I would buy this burgeoning artist an entire studio.

"Okay." Sarah clapped her hands. "We're out of here. Everyone grab your jacket. We're walking to the restaurant," Sarah's command was urgent.

"It's June, Sarah," Jack injected, happy to steer the conversation away from Thomas and his puppy-dog eyes.

"Oh, yeah, well, I'm cold. Isn't anybody else cold?"

"I thought menopause made you hot. As far as I'm concerned, menopause is just an excuse for you to act weird and get away with it." He insulted her. She laughed. Something was up.

Hustling down the street, my stride fell short of theirs. "Ryder, honey, catch up. Don't leave such a space." Sarah said that because we passed another Miguel, one of the many homeless souls. Every time we did that, she pulled a little tighter and hurried a lot faster. "Ryder, please. Jack, they're everywhere now."

"It's the opioid crisis, it affects every class. The overdoses are hitting record highs."

"Just like the suicides."

"One and the same."

I purposefully slowed, distancing myself from hearing more, scratching my feet against the pavement to cover their words. That boy was harmless, only hurting; maybe his mom regretted the things she'd done. I retreated to his pile of blankets. He smelled, and a line of angry red dots trickled down an overused vein. Reaching into my pocket, I held out a stick of gum.

"Thanks." It sounded flat, like the hunger within drained him of all inflection. Unwrapping it, he swallowed it whole.

I knew his pain and matched it to my own. An uncontrollable urge took hold, and I slid the ring from my finger. "Here," I said, freeing my past from a tangible reminder. "Take it."

The space between Jack and me rapidly closed, and my gift in kind transformed into a gift in cash. "Son, go buy something to eat. Ryder, let's go." Four paces later, the ring passed from Jack's hand to mine. "Your past makes your future. Don't do things that you'll regret. Do you hear me?"

That little lump inside my lip, the one swollen from too many moments like this, received another beating. It bled. I tasted salt. The distraction was just enough to ignore Sarah's raised eyebrow as she held open the restaurant door.

"Cool, isn't it?" Lynzie, noticing nothing odd, tucked her small hand into mine and yanked me through the door. "Come on."

An instantaneous diversion, it was as if I dove into an ocean. In front of me was a sea; literally, shades of blue tiles swirled around each other in a dizzying wave. If I stepped back, it zoomed; away, it tunneled. Now, I understood why Thomas chose this restaurant to celebrate.

A yellow brick walkway started after reception and meandered mysteriously around a bend. I craned my neck to peek just as Thomas catapulted me forward with a shove. We landed at the aquatic version of the Emerald City. Inches from our feet, strands of blown glass whirled. Loops passed under curves, twists reduced to spirals, glass fish, glass seaweed. Wow.

"Makes you forget your troubles, doesn't it?" Jack's hands on my shoulders startled me at first. Then, I took comfort under his arm, entirely at peace in this land of make-believe.

"What's that?" Lynzie, oddly indifferent to the magic in front of us, waved her hands wildly in the air. "I wanna see it." Jumping to reach a large white envelope in Sarah's hand, she missed and fell, crashing against the glass wall blocking the display. "Ouch."

"Follow the waiter, monkey," Sarah prodded.

Monkey, I never understood that nickname. She seemed less like a Monkey than she looked like a Lynzie. I would have called her Button, as in cute as a.

"But what is it?" She jumped in time with her mother lifting it away, an invisible string running between.

"Just follow the waiter."

Reluctantly, she compromised, following the waiter backward down the hall. He led us to a table, which, to my astonishment, matched the walls. A dizzying mosaic of glass tiles splashed across its surface. Thomas, having seen this before, reached for a stack of neon-colored coasters and, positioning it like a paper football, flicked it with his finger.

"Just the family-sized Margarita pizza, thank you," Jack shooed off the waiter. "Thomas, stop that. Lynzie, please pick it up."

The envelope emerged again, and Lynzie, re-surfacing from under the table with the coaster in her grip, immediately let go and dove for the prize hanging from Sarah's hand. The corner tore.

"Stop." Jack batted Lynzie's hands away, then pried Sarah's from its edge. Slowly, he passed it overhead to Thomas who, tracing his fingers around the sunburst chiseled into the table, was the only person not intrigued.

"One last present, son. Or actually, a wish," Jack said, shushing his son with a finger to which Thomas grinned knowingly, unrestrained energy sizzling within.

Thomas' fingers dug into the fold, trying to lift the sealed edge. Rotating it as if it were a Rubik's cube, he attacked the other side. Making little headway, he used his teeth. Finally, teasing out a single sheet, he crinkled his brow, his head tilting to question the content. Swiftly, though, and too quick to be good, he buried his face.

"Well, what is it?" Lynzie bounced with curiosity, oblivious to Sarah's fingers drumming worryingly on the table.

The envelope lowered just enough so I could see Thomas' eyes. They welled. Back up it went, shielding his face. I heard a sniffle, then just as he peeked over the edge, he whispered three words that have stayed with me until this day. "Do you know?"

No. I didn't.

Lynzie and I traded baffled looks because of the five people at this table, only the two of us were at a loss. Thomas' tear tracked down his cheek. Jack sighed with what sounded like relief. And Sarah, tenser than a drum, increased her tapping until it got so loud, I grabbed her hand to keep her still.

She flipped it around and latched onto mine instead. "Oh, sweetheart, I hope that's what you wanted."

I still didn't know.

Sensing that, the paper transferred from Thomas' hands to mine, and it was then that I saw it. My sorrow unmasked. Ryder Scott, no middle name—my new official title.

The weight of their stares penetrated and judged, and I wanted to hide my emotions as much as run from the attention. Something I craved, something I dreaded. Both in equal measure, a fantasy realized too soon. I looked at that paper and my hand holding it, at the opal ring speaking to me from the not too distant past.

A picture frame lowered in front of me, a group selfie Jack snapped the day of my solo. It showed five people leaning against the balcony rail just as the sun came out. The Twin Towers were nowhere in sight because the Freedom Tower had taken its place. I choked back a tear.

"We want you to be a permanent part of our family," Sarah said.

My emotions swallowed my words. And when I cradled my face in my hands, I felt that cold ring press against my cheek, an indestructible reminder of the woman who created my past. I pulled my face away and focused on the people in the photo, my new family sitting at this table, a new beginning for a life that had crumbled away.

No, Thomas, I didn't know. How could I know that your birthday wish matched the only present I absolutely needed, but somehow always feared?

My father really didn't want me.

CHAPTER TWENTY-FOUR

Little things that shouldn't have even been things transformed back to mindless worries that defined adolescence. And for the first time, in a long time, it felt safe to be a kid again.

It was July now, six weeks after the adoption, and with summer here, and that mind-numbing school in my rearview, a new chapter started, or a new book, really. Because unlike every other summer break I'd experienced, rich people didn't let their kids while away the hours in front of the TV. No. They scheduled. Every moment had a purpose because every breath was accounted for. Camps overlapped practices; field trips merged into projects.

Sarah's head spun trying to keep the pace. She took naps, lots of them, and paid less attention to herself. Her zigzagged roots turned grey, the paint on her nails chipped. But even though her fatigue sometimes shortened her fuse, what I respected most about my new mom was that she never said she was too busy. She always made time to a snuggle on the couch.

We'd watch reruns of *Friends*, and I loved how she hit pause to explain stuff. Like why Monica lost it when Rachel misplaced the pen so she could *write* a message, or why, of the six of them, only Chandler had a computer. "You see, Ryder, people didn't need personal computers back then. Chandler's only had twelve megabytes of RAM."

"Only Twelve Gigabytes, you mean?"

"No, Megabytes."

"What? How did he watch a movie?" I'd ask, sending her into hysterics, which left me at a loss, but entirely pleased. I liked seeing her happy because every time I heard her laugh, the tears from my old life dried a little more.

Sarah was my new Mom, Jack, my new Dad. I had a brother and a sister and a cat named Charlie. That opal ring, well, I threw it into the junk drawer, the one where things got lost for years. If I overheard people talking about Las Vegas, I'd hustle to another room. Flashing lights couldn't wake the memory of Christmas bulbs running down the stairs. No. Because if it did, I'd throw on my headphones and blast music into my ears until it hurt. Nothing and nobody would trigger my past. I was not Sarah's cousin.

I was Sarah's daughter, and she *wanted* to be my mom.

I mean, here she was flipping pancakes at seven o'clock in the morning. Who did that? I hoped that when I was old, I wouldn't hastily put a cereal box on the counter. I wanted to care, like her. To be in the moment, like her. I wanted to have the presence of mind to adopt a daughter and then immediately change her Pinterest board.

No longer Sarah, her board read Mom, and I loved opening the App just to read her title. Admittedly, it would have been nice if she kept up the family tradition and posted like she used to. But she was tired and busy. And honestly, as long as she wasn't checking, it gave me a little wiggle room to roam.

You see, I missed a boy. I'm pretty sure he didn't miss me, but I could *not* stop thinking about Spencer Schrader. So, when I saw somebody who reminded me of him, I pinned it. I mean, right, that was the point of Pinterest: to save a reference for something you loved. And I had a serious crush. So, I hopped from one link to another, clicking and pinning any photo of a boy with a smirk and dimple, any boy with meticulously disheveled hair.

"Ryder, who's that you've posted on your board?"

I tensed before looking up to see a woman using the end of a spatula playfully tapping her screen. She chose now to restart the tradition? Slamming mine closed as if that would prevent her from seeing my posts, my cheeks flushed bright. "Ah, Sarah, I mean, Mom"—it still felt weird sometimes. "I'm, um, I was just looking at hairstyles," I hyperventilated a bit, trying to force a thought. "I think Thomas should get this one. It would...It would..." I couldn't hold back the sneeze, or the little bits of saliva that showered the glass.

Such a fortuitous diversion, I sneezed again. Fake, but effective, the dribble from the remnants of last week's cold running from my nose.

"Oh, sweetheart, that cold is getting worse." The pancake sizzling in the pan transferred to my plate, and the end of the spatula emphasized her point. "But you need to cover your mouth when you sneeze. You don't want to be responsible for getting other people sick."

I wiped my nose with the back of my hand, and then looked at the streak perplexed, unsure of the best way to clean it without drawing attention. To my right was a book on menopause. To my left, a magazine on women's health. How did this woman not tire from reading article after article on hot flushes and hormones? Just go to the doctor like Jack kept insisting.

I smeared it against my jeans.

"No, Ryder." My mom threw her hand against my brow, thrusting my head back to swaddle my nose as if I were three. "Blow.".

I sneezed instead. Okay, that one was real, and she received a shower. Maybe I was still sick because when I stood up, black spots floated in front of my eyes. A ringing started, and a tiny man with an icepick stabbed inside my head. I collapsed back to the chair, surprised to be fatigued from the effort. "You know, maybe I don't feel so well."

She pulled my arm, but deciding to milk this for what it was worth—and distract her away from my board—I willingly let my knees buckle. I tumbled to the floor. Marveling at my acting, which by all standards was as convincing as it was authentic, I reached for her shoulder, ready to feign more. But when I met my mother's panicked face, I faltered. "I'm sor—"

Rashly she spun before I could come clean, slamming her toe into a chair, which catapulted her forward. Her head hit the floor, sounding a deafening crack. Jack and the kids flew into the room.

"What happened?"

Sarah's speech ran like a train out of control. "I'll call Alex upstairs and see if she can watch Lynzie. You take Thomas to summer camp. Where's my phone? I need it to find the nearest urgent care." Our mother's reaction didn't compute.

"Hey, hey, calm down, we got it. Thomas can miss out on camp," Jack said, shooting a warning against protest to his wrongly inconvenienced son. "I'll take both of you to the urgent care. Honey, you need to see somebody, and I'm not talking about the menopause, but the egg-sized welt on your forehead. Are you okay?"

"Noooo, I'm sorry," she mumbled, running her hand over the bump. "Why does this keep happening? It's okay, Jack, I'll take

Ryder. I think I need to talk to someone."

Jack's sigh was a well-earned relief.

"I'll just grab my coat." She rubbed her hands together so frantically her wedding ring slipped free and clinked against the tile floor.

We left the penthouse shortly after that. Two people grappling with guilt walking down the streets of Tribeca on a sunny morning. Me in my t-shirt and sandals, my mother wrapped in a raincoat like a homeless woman waiting in line.

The doctor fussed less over me than he did over her, and I let it happen. But this born-to-be-a-mother had none of it. "What's her temperature? Does she need antibiotics? Should I keep her out of music camp?"

The doctor brushed my mother's hair away from her brow and ordered commands: follow my finger, touch your nose, look into this light. "Okay, now try to balance on one leg," he asked politely.

She refused, saying that a scratch on her head was nothing compared to how I fell off the chair.

"Mom, I was exaggerating. Seriously, I just didn't want you looking at my Pinterest posts."

"And I only tripped on the coffee table. Doctor, so, about Ryder…" Sarah wouldn't budge.

When I reminded her that Jack wanted her to ask about hormone replacement, she told me that Jack was now Dad and that Urgent Care clinic didn't address those issues. Then, to my frustration, this doctor not only concurred but let us walk from the building with a bottle of unnecessary antibiotics for me and nothing for her.

She sneezed the next morning, then coughed all during breakfast. Unable to contain her running nose, she popped *my* bottle of antibiotics and slugged back a dose. By dinner, with her voice scratching and squeaking, she only played with her food.

"I think I'll turn in," she said, slowly rising off the chair. Her face was pale, skin pasty, a streak of sweat smeared her hair across her brow.

Nobody commented that it was only seven, or that our father seemed more perturbed than supportive. He shuffled around the kitchen, opening cabinets, chugging a Diet Coke in two swallows before hiding on the balcony. Gone for only a moment, he treaded back inside, stopping a foot short from me.

"Ryder, what did the doctor say, *exactly*."

"That I should keep away from other kids and drink lots of water and orange juice."

"Not you. About Sarah."

When I told him she didn't want to touch her finger to her nose or follow a light with her eyes, my father shot from his seat and clamped his hands to his hips. He left us in the living room, where we listened to bits of an argument penetrate their bedroom door.

And we—left to our resources without instructions or limitations—covered up the noise by watching one YouTube video after another, the horrifying video of a baby turtle tangled in plastic upsetting us more.

***

Morning came, and I couldn't shake the image of the turtle. Trapped and afraid, the poor little guy didn't have a chance. Equally horrified, Lynzie spelled out 'no plastic' with cheerios on the table, and Thomas, more interested in irritating his sister, blew them off.

"Daddy. Make Thomas stop!"

"Keep your voices down. I don't want to upset your mother. She's still sleeping."

"I'm right here," Sarah had trailed Jack into the kitchen.

His touch to his wife's cheek was gentle, as it had been since she had taken ill, but guarded, like a ring of fire circled around her feet. "How are you feeling?"

"I'm fine," she answered falsely, the way Gabriel, the bully said "sorry" when he was forced to after his attacks.

Whispers passed between them, out of earshot at first, then further from our view. They sat together on the formal couch nodding, only occasionally smiling. When the cat jumped into Sarah's lap, she didn't take note.

I helped Lynzie spell the words 'save the earth' with her cheerios, while Thomas contemplated if he could live without his plastic toys.

As stimulating as the biased dispute unfolding between us evolved, when our parents returned, they couldn't be bothered. We were told three things: one, Mom and Dad were "fine;" two, we needed to do *all* the chores so Mom could feel better; and three, we were prisoners until Dad came home from work.

Ergo boredom.

And it hit fast. Never would I tsk-tsk our mother's obsessive scheduling again. I missed my music camp, even longed for the snaking lines at the bank. Any errand would be better than sitting in this stuffy penthouse on a beautiful day, staring at the black screen of the mega-TV because we weren't allowed to turn it on.

"Do you think we can order pizza?" Lynzie asked, and a brilliant question it was.

The clock on the building across the street read 4:07. Dad wouldn't be home for hours. Mom, who hadn't left her room all day, would probably be starving after skipping lunch. "Yeah, Lynzie, let's order pizza."

Ding.

The reflex Pavlovian, our three sets of eyes shot to the elevator door, to the man with two plastic bags swinging from his hands. We all rushed at him, our memory of the suffering turtle fueling our attack.

"Daddy, every piece of plastic made still exists today," Lynzie scolded.

"Yeah, Dad, the ocean is not a recycling center," Thomas educated.

"Where's your mother?" Not only did he not hear us, after he unpacked the groceries, he scrunched up the plastic bags, and then tossed them in the trash. "I said, where's…oh, sorry, Sarah, I didn't see you there."

Bedhead had taken over, matting the hair in the back, fraying it in front. Our dad tucked an errant strand behind her ear, and she recoiled, reaching to pull it back.

"Why are you home so early?" She deliberately circled him to avoid his touch.

"Daddy, can we order pizza?" Lynzie asked.

Joining the three kids at the table, our dad wrapped his hands around the nape of his neck, and many moments passed before Thomas decided to take his silence as a yes. Skidding over to the takeaway drawer, he stopped mid-slide. "Um, Dad, why is Mom sitting by herself in the fishbowl?"

Suddenly, every eye shifted to the disheveled woman imprisoned behind the wall of glass. She shuffled her feet, mouthing words, looking every bit as homeless as I once was.

Too loud to be ignored, the chair legs scraped along the tile floor as Jack Scott drove it a foot away from the table.

"Dad, do you want pepperoni, or ham and pineapple?" Thomas had the phone hanging from his ear.

The answer was a deafening thunk because when Jack lifted himself out of the chair, the force kicked it backward, sending it straight to the ground.

"Ryder? Pepperoni or pineapple?" Thomas' voice was urgent. "Quick, the guy's waiting on the phone."

Who cared when the two steadfast leaders of my new life were now bizarre caricatures of somebody else's? Inside out: roles reversed. Lessons from my past educating my present, never again would I miss a sign.

Our father marched into the fishbowl wearing the face of a man we didn't know. Parking himself on the bench next to my mom, he dug his toes into the gravel and bowed his head. No movement was not good because silence brought uncertainty, and uncertainty brought resentment, and resentment lasted. I knew this much to be true.

I coped by grabbing a magazine and zeroing in on a highlighted passage. *The symptoms of menopause are a direct result of a sudden loss of estrogen. Up to seventy percent of women experience some level of irritability.*

Our mother rose. Our father stayed seated. Then, as if nothing was amiss, Sarah strolled through the glass door and patted me on the cheek. "It's all good, Ryder."

Really. Because last I checked, words replaced emotion only when appearances couldn't.

Jack reluctantly followed her inside.

"Hey, Dad, do you know what I learned today?" Thomas said, oblivious to the tension. "If you keep a goat in a racehorse's stable, the horses stay calm. If somebody sneaks in and steals the goat, the horses get all fussy. They race really bad. So, if you wanted somebody else's horse to do bad, you got their goat. Get it, Dad. It's like you're always saying: 'Get your goat.'"

Our father didn't smile.

I buried again into the magazine. *The irritability can be a point of strain for a relationship or the family.* Got it. Estrogen was the goat, and it left the stable.

"Hey Ryder," Lynzie said as she inched her chair next to mine. "Mommy looks really sad tonight. Maybe she can take pills to make her happy like your mommy did."

Jack's mouth dropped, his eyes squinting before his nose flared. "Sarah!" His voice boomed; my hands trembled. "What were you thinking dragging our first-grade daughter into this?"

"I don't remember telling her that." It came out sad.

"But you did! She didn't' take any pills," I yelled, shooting little dots of saliva across the room. "Never talk about my mother again, ever."

All attempts to bury my past thwarted by a middle-aged woman gossiping with a seven-year-old girl. I spun in circles looking for something to replace the images crashing through my mind. Nothing but the truth appeared. She did take pills. She was sad. Helpless to stop them, I saw my mother's body stretched out and still, her lips a deathly blue. Christmas lights strobed down her body. A trail to an end, the one I should have stopped if I had only come home on time.

"Ryder, I'm sorry, but we need to talk about this."

I threw up my hands, a physical barrier to stall her words

"Ryder, enough." Sarah reached towards me, but I blocked her embrace, choosing instead to beat my fist against her chest. She struggled. I surged. Blue lips. Puffed eyes. Rigid body. I could see nothing else. I gained momentum, and when Sarah opened her mouth again, I shoved her hard.

Smack.

The reverberation of her slap against my cheek echoed. I raised my hand, blocking another assault. Stumbling backward, tripping over Jack's feet, suddenly, I was back inside the bully's lasso. Jack stepped in between. Her push toppling him into me, and me onto Thomas. By the time I looked up, she had gone.

A door slammed.

On high voltage, that unbolted energy surged into the red. "Stay here!" His voice louder than a cannon.

The three of us stilled by fear. Breathing fast, we listened as the emotions escalated behind the bedroom door. From safe to wrecked in the space of seconds. How? We waited. I waited because it only took ten minutes in the fishbowl for the dust to settle. But an hour passed, then another, then I placed the pizza that didn't get eaten in Tupperware and fought back a memory of stacks of them. That day, the 21st of December, offered no warnings. On this day, seven months later, the 23rd of July, sparks flew from the moment he walked through the door.

The yelling stopped, but the bedroom door remained shut, and staring at it for an absurdly long time didn't make it open. Lynzie stayed quiet. Thomas cried. I didn't know what to do. My cadre trailed me into Lynzie's room, and because I was their leader, they crawled under the covers when I lifted them into the air.

***

It took some time to shake off the fog. Why was I in Lynzie's bed? How come I was still wearing my jeans? Why did my cheek throb? Oh. Even from a distance, the mirror answered, and a bluish-purple bruise cresting above my left cheek announced the residual of my mistake. "Get up, Thomas."

"I don't want to go to summer camp today."

Accidentally, or rather, purposely, I tagged him with my foot so hard it jolted him from sleep and then the bed. At the dresser, he shoved me for my sins, and the mirror zoomed closer.

"Dude, she really got you."

And more than just physically. Sarah told Lynzie, which meant she knew more, and not just more; she knew details. The casual conversation about trust, about blindfolds, about the hidden secret of her cousin's rape worried me more than the welt swelling under my eye.

Lynzie squeezed in between us. "I'm going to wake up Mommy."

"No!" Thomas and I latched onto her arm, pulling her apart like a human wishbone.

"Let go! Ooouucch!"

"Lynzie, cut it out. You're going to get us in trouble," I reprimanded.

"*Us*, Ryder? Me and Lynzie didn't do anything. You did. Last night was all *your* fault."

My middle finger was a call to arms.

"Umm, I'm tellin'." And with that, Lynzie broke free, hopping down the stairs and across the kitchen en route to our parent's room. At the living room, she stopped cold, toppling us like dominos in a queue. Our eyes homed in on the lump on the sofa, on the empty beer bottle tipped sideways, the one sock hanging tenuously off the table's edge. A blanket partially covered our father's legs, and Lynzie, acting like the fool, arrowed in and pecked the sleeping lion on the cheek. "Hi, Daddy."

We gasped.

"Oh, good morning, Sweetheart."

And then exhaled.

The master bedroom door creaked, and we all turned as if our heads were pushed through sludge. Our dad grabbed his shoes, hustling as the footsteps grew louder. Heading to the elevator, mumbling something about getting the paper, one blink later, he was gone.

And in the second that followed, our mother stood over the blankets thrown askew on the floor. Lifting them like a magician, she looked baffled. "Where's your father?"

"He went to get the paper," I answered, even though I knew that she knew he read it online.

Bordering on offensive, her eyes were puffy, smeared with makeup; she too had slept in her clothes. "Ryan, go get me some Motrin, will you?"

I knew she meant me, but instead of correcting it, she said it again. This scene was not right; not what I had been adopted into. This, all of this morning, all of last night—confused then distraught mother, disappearing father—it all belonged to my past.

"Some Motrin, Ryan, my head is killing me."

Killing me, killing me: it echoed too loud. *You're killing me, Max, killing me.* In my room, I hid from it always: the fights, the drama, the wishing. *Killing you? I have to live through your crap. We all do. Why don't you just end it for all of us?* I hated that man.

"Ryder, please." Retaking my father's makeshift bed, she curled into the blanket and succeeded in looking wholly defeated.

Everything in front of me was a mirror from my past, and I wouldn't let it happen again. Slamming through cabinets in bathrooms and closets in halls, I failed at everything: to locate the Motrin, to push the memories aside, to make it better. "I can't find any, Mom." I slid her wallet from her bag and five dollars into my back pocket. "I'll go out and get some." Her eyes were closed. I slipped in another ten before disappearing into the elevator.

Carson, the doorman, never failed to comment. "Looking for your dad?"

Our lives were our lives. How many times had I heard that coming out of Jack Scott's mouth? I didn't answer.

"He's at the coffee shop across the street."

Through the glass door, I could see the silhouette of a broken man, his head cradled dejectedly in his hands. I crossed the street with a plan, moving my lips to practice my lines, rehearsing how to stop the conversation before it started. Confident, but intimidated, I stood behind the man who I gladly accepted as the head of my life. "About last night, you see, what happened was—"

"You lost your iPad for a week."

"Huh? No, it's been on my—" Oh. And all that rehearsal was for nought. I stamped my foot. "That's not fair! I didn't do anything wrong."

"I'm the father, you're the daughter, and putting that aside, you know exactly what you did last night. Just because you were as shocked as I was, you were not justified to respond like you did. We've been through this before. When we get home, you hand over all your iDevices: the phone, the tablet, and the computer."

"You're not being fair."

"So, you said."

"You're mad at Mom, and you're taking it out on me."

"Yes, I am, and I think we need to talk." His voice softened, and that scared me more than the anger. "Are you ready?"

Speechless, when the waiter arrived with a pen aimed at his pad, I almost hugged him for the intrusion. "May I see a menu?" Quickly, I regrouped, enlisting him as the grateful diversion. "No, I mean, actually, can you just tell me what type of coffee you have?"

"Since when do you drink coffee?" He pushed his empty mug to the edge of the table. "Just refill my cup, and I'll give it to her."

The waiter, not uttering a single word, left, and my anxious nerves filled the void. Empty except the two of us, the restaurant's quaint wooden tables no longer invited. And that sliding ladder Lynzie always pushed back and forth cast menacing shadows over the discussion to come.

"Last night in the bedroom, it wasn't about you, Ryder." He lied. The waiter was at the coffee pot, waiting for the last drips to fill. "We were working out some promises we made to each other." I grabbed the newspaper from the table behind me and pretended to read. "Tell me." His eyes bore into mine with more glare than a courtroom lawyer. "Has your mother been acting strange while I've been at work?" The gears had shifted long before his hands folded into a scaffolding for his chin; before his narrow gaze signified the only conversation he truly wished to pursue.

I readily embraced the change. "No, not really." He didn't blink. "I mean, she had the flu and has a bad headache right now. That's why I left to get her some Motrin."

He latched onto my hand. "She's allergic to Motrin!" But in the same breath, he abandoned it and threw his hands into the air. "She knows that." Flustered, his fists fell to the table. "Are you sure she said Motrin?" No answer was expected. "Something's wrong. Everything that happened last night was just wrong."

Maybe this wasn't about me after all, but I didn't wait to find out. "Dad, it's the menopause. I've been reading." The restrained courtroom lawyer returned. "A woman feels like she's losing her mind while she's going through it. I read this one story where a woman said she took the same bus to work every day for like twenty years, but one day she couldn't remember which bus to take. It scared her half to death because she thought she had…"

The waiter arrived, poured the coffee, and lingered a bit too long. Our stares forced him away.

Quieter, I resumed, "The woman thought she had Alzheimer's, but it turned out to be a low estrogen level."

"The book said that?"

"No." A puff of air left my lips, silently making a case against confiscating my devices. "An online blog." Reassured by his changed demeanor, I confidently educated this middle-aged man on menopausal women. "See, women have trouble sleeping, and when this happens night after night, they get disoriented." The fragrant coffee further lighted the tension, and to accelerate the effect, I took a sip. "Christ, this is horrible!"

Not even a hint of a smile or a reflexed reprimand, he took the cup back and glued himself to the newspaper in front of him. "No, Dad, listen to me. Mom just needs some estrogen." He flipped the page to prove he, too, could pretend to read. "And some flowers, please don't be mad at her."

"Ryder, it's complicated."

"Fine!" I said as I tore at the paper. "So uncomplicate it. Just buy her flowers and say you're sorry. It doesn't matter that you did nothing wrong." Points scored. "Just fix it. She physically abused me, and I'm not holding a grudge."

His thumb circled my cheek. "You need to put some make-up on that." Yep, *our lives are our lives.*

And Sarah's life was a part of ours. Pushing my chair away from the table, I stood, ready to leave. "We need to go get Sarah some Tylenol."

"Her name is Mom. Why did you just call her Sarah?"

"I don't know. I guess because she's not really acting like a mom."

"You can't pick and choose when somebody's your mom, just like I can't pick and choose to call her my wife. For better or worse, even when worse has completely lost her mind."

***

"Sir, you don't have your cell phone on!" Panic streamed across the doorman's face. "Your kids, they're very upset." He was panting. "They came down looking for you, but I didn't see you across the street. I couldn't get it out of them, and then they ran back upstairs."

Guerin LeBlanc threw open the lobby door with a crash, winded from rushing across the street. "What's going on? Thomas called and said he was scared, that I needed to come over right away."

Shocked. Confused. Now, worried. Hitting the elevator call button repeatedly didn't make it come any quicker. The two men almost took to the stairs when the door slid open, and my dad worked his way into the gap. The ride up was a mile. Doors opened. We poured out.

And nothing.

Thomas had his feet casually crossed on the coffee table. Lynzie cradled herself under her mother's arm. Our mouths hung wide as we listened to my brother calmly read aloud a passage from *Harry Potter and the Sorcerer's Stone.*

"I'm going to fucking kill that doorman." Neither my dad nor Guerin corrected my absolutely appropriate language.

In fact, Guerin added to it. "Fucking idiot!"

"Hi, Uncle Guerin, I couldn't wake my mom, and I got scared, but it turned out she was just sleeping really hard. Sorry," Thomas offered as if that explanation was enough.

Guerin turned his back to the couch, his eyes lifting to question his best friend. "Would you like me to tell the studio you'll be running late this morning?" Guerin spun back around, punctuating his question with a loud clap. "Well, I'm off. Sarah, are you sure you're okay?"

She waved him adieu and pointed to Thomas' book, urging him to continue.

"We bought some Tylenol. Ryder said you asked for Motrin. You know you're allergic." It was an accusation, and I was ticked. This wasn't uncomplicating things. He needed to put makeup on his own wounds.

"I meant Tylenol, thank you."

"...Harry Potter crossed his fingers under the table and a second later the hat had shouted GRYFFINDOR!"

I snatched the book from Thomas' grip. "Mom, is your headache gone?"

Rubbing her forehead as if she couldn't remember whether she had one, she stopped when her husband handed her a glass of water and two white tablets.

He elbowed me forward.

The nudge shook off the dust. Sarah had a problem to solve, a crisis to manage. I plotted, eager to usurp the topic from last night, and make her issue the *only* issue. "Did you sleep well, Mom? Maybe that's why you forgot my name this morning."

Bulldozing, my dad pushed me aside, seizing the moment I had teed up for him to play. "Sarah, you forgot her name?"

"Noooo. I misspoke, called her Ryan."

A hush pulsed through the room before her husband, who finally decided to make an effort, sat by her side. He toyed with her wedding ring, rocking it back and forth. It spun freely and slipped. He caught it before it fell onto the floor.

"Honey, you're losing weight."

I scanned her from head to toe because I noticed too. At dinners, she pushed her food around like a toddler, fed the cat off her plate. She made sure Thomas got more so she could serve herself less.

"Jack, my belt loop is at the same hole as it's always been. It's just water weight," she said, defending her words by lifting her shirt and tapping the well-used hole.

That was true! I read it. Female hormones made you bloat. That was why clothes "shrunk" at that time of the month and expanded as soon as it passed. My mother had *no* estrogen, so, by the associative property—I think—she would shrink, ergo, her ring would slip.

"Please, Sarah," Jack inhaled, suspending the moment. "I don't ask much. Just chat with the doctor about options, make sure all of this is normal: the headaches, insomnia, the loss of appetite, the weight loss."

"Water weight."

The air passing through his pursed lips was no less strained than a leaking pipe before it burst.

"Okay. Jack. I'll make an appointment. First thing in the morning, I'll call."

CHAPTER TWENTY-FIVE

All hail to the gynecologist.

For a woman so reluctant to see a doctor just forty-eight hours ago, those pills must have been magic to get her this excited. My father would have readily bought stock in the drug that saved his marriage right then and there, and she agreed, said it was a miracle, the type that kept Sarah Palin out of the White House.

"The doctor said that most times women don't need to take hormones, but for those who have a clear disruption in their life, using them for as little as six months will make a world of difference." My mother stabbed the chicken with her fork, then pointed it at my dad. "And that difference happens within a few days of replacing the hormone. It's not like birth control pills, which can take months to override circulating hormones; ya know, the ones wreaking havoc on your cycle." She finally put the piece into her mouth. "Remember when that happened, Jack?"

A smirk concealed the grin of a man caught between yippee, and I told you so.

"You see," she continued. "In menopause, the ovaries stop producing estrogen, there's nothing left to override. Taking hormones simply replaces what's no longer there. This doctor uses hormones for symptomatic relief as well as a diagnostic test. If a woman is in menopause, and her symptoms are from estrogen deficiency, those symptoms resolve immediately once replaced. If the symptoms persist, well, then they're from something else. When he sees the patient back, if her issues have resolved, he advises her to taper the medications at the time of her choosing."

"So, Sarah, when are you seeing him again?"

"I'm not."

He stopped chewing.

"Jack, he said to go back if my symptoms persist. Did I not sleep through the night? Have you seen a hot flash lately?"

"You still grabbed your back when you rolled out of bed, whimpered as you walked to the bathroom."

"You do too. We're forty-eight, Jack. And besides, the doctor recommended yoga or pilates or something to stretch and strengthen. I took my first class today, even bought a book. Where's my iPad, I'll show you."

"Sarah, we're eating, remember, no using electronics at the dinner table, or I'll put yours in the penalty box with Ryder's."

My fork crashed against the plate. "Hey! When do I get my iDevices back? If Mom felt better in two days, then my punishment should match. What if something bad happens to me? How will you find me? You can't call or text or use Find my iPhone. I might be lost forever. Then, how would you feel?"

My dad shoveled the last of his chicken into his mouth. My mother laughed. So, pleased to see them getting along.

After dinner, I stewed. This one week ban on electronics was pointless. I picked up magazines and dropped them, opened the fridge and closed it, looked at the cat with absolute wonder at how it could stand its cordless existence.

"Ryder, why don't you go practice. By the time you get two minutes into it, you'll forget all about your iPad," my dad advised, my mom concurred, and I stamped my foot even though they were right.

I scratched my neck, stretching it long to strengthen the plot building in my mind. I could play the violin. I mean, when the bow slid across the string, Steve Jobs and his inventions would be a world away. But no. That would convey the wrong message, that life could exist without the internet, which was absurd. So, I sat on the couch all night in a dead heat with stubbornness, vowing not to budge until I got my way.

Still, somehow, I woke the next morning in my bed wrapped like a burrito, suffering the joy and consequences of a caring and disciplined father. Already off to work, I missed my opportunity to beg, so I lay in bed, devoting myself to Plan B.

Loading my words as weapons, I found my target pecking away on her computer, the tympanic sounds of plastic keys in a race against time.

"Mom, I wanted to explain how—"

The clicking stopped so she could spin her screen, crumbling my offensive in a single move. In front of me was a picture of a bottle tipped on its side, pills trickling over a table. I moved my focus to the blurred image of the woman behind, to her hand covering her eyes, the tear tracking down her cheek. In real life, I'd seen that image before.

Sarah Scott's call to arms. Three days had passed since Lynzie's words uncorked all I bottled, and this is how she chose to bring it up.

"Ryder, I'd like to speak with you about what happened the other night. About what I told Lynzie. Please believe me. I do not remember discussing your situation. My mind is…just…"

I shoveled smoke, pulling the two-day-old guacamole from the fridge, declaring it obscene, then flicking on the disposal even though it was far past the need to pulverize. "We don't need to talk about this." The running water adding to my cover. "I forgive you."

"Turn that off, please." Her hand came from my periphery to flip the switch, and the sudden silence hurt. "We need to talk."

Her fingers brushed my fringe away, as mine traced the crack in the fruit bowl, the fractured edge poking my skin. "How did this break?" I asked.

"It's not important."

It was. "I think if you fill it with Elmer's glue, the crack will smooth out, so it won't hurt anybody." I rubbed my finger. "Do you ever wonder who Elmer was? And why his name stuck?"

"Very clever play on words." She let my ramble lead us away from her intentions. So much so, that the plastic keys clicked again, replacing the image of pills, with a Wikipedia page. "Huh, interesting, Elmer wasn't a man, but a symbol, the name of the bull. It's a marketing logo."

We both read in silence about the glue made from casein, which was a byproduct of milk, which was created in 1920, which—

"Ryder." She closed the laptop. "Hun, I understand. You're not ready to talk, and I don't blame you. I wouldn't want to either. And I know it's easier to read about Elmer the bull than to rehash memories that hurt, but I think you should talk to somebody. If not me, a professional maybe."

I shook my head. The grain of the table creating a trail to follow, which the wooden floor picked up when the table ended. A soothing antidote to this turbulent conversation, I got up, walking toe to heal until I reached the yoga mat sprawled on the floor. It was smooth and soft and about an inch thick. "So, this is where you do your yoga?"

She nodded.

"I bet it's like playing my violin."

"I bet it is." The laptop opened, the plastic keys clicked, and up popped her new passion: *Using Yoga to Transform the Old You.*

I had to chuckle. Another book. Sarah Scott was a woman who attacked a foe at full speed and full read. This book on yoga had no doubt replaced the collection on menopause, which surely replaced the ones about child-rearing.

"This yoga stuff's amazing. Would you like to come to class with me?"

I crept my hands closer to the disposal's switch.

"Don't be like that. It's helping, and you should be happy for me."

The image on her screen changed once more, to a photo of a woman so contorted, she could have been Houdini's double. "Let's try this one."

As grateful that I was she allowed Elmer and a yoga mat to buy me time, the woman posing in that picture was just wrong. A backbend not even a pretzel could master, how did that not hurt?

"Okay, ready?"

No.

"Position yourself on the floor, like this." She closed her eyes.

No choice, either I squatted on the floor like a clam, or that smothered topic would rekindle like a neglected fire.

"Inhale."

I didn't.

"Firmly, press the base of your foot into your palm." Dedicated and committed, her face pinched with pain, the effort to heal trumping all. "Exhale. Plant your hand behind, wait, in front of, wait." She opened her eyes. "Why are you just sitting there? I'd thought you'd want to play along. Well, can you hold my arm back so I can reach my leg around my shoulder?" As instructed... "Wait, wait, wait, oh, shit, STOP!"

"What?"

"Let go. Fuck, fuck, fuck, fuck, fuck."

Not once had I ever heard her swear: never. "What's wrong?"

As if lightning hit, anguish contorted her face into a tormented expression. To touch her would be wrong, to move her couldn't be right, so I just stayed still, waiting for her shallow breaths to settle.

"I really pulled something."

"Do you want me to call Dad at work?"

"No, no. Just let me lie here, please."

And just like I did oh so many months ago, back when I first noticed the lights of their balcony, when I first hovered over her sleeping body to figure out why this strange woman cared so much, I just watched: wondered, and watched. A small tear welled at the base of her eye. It filled, then crested at the lid, sitting there as if deciding what to do. I followed that tear, focused on it. It rolled down her jaw and disappeared. Without it, I had nothing.

"Okay, okay." At half-mast, her lids fluttered, then shut again.

"I think I should call Dad. It's Friday, he doesn't air his show today. He can come home early."

"No, no. This will pass. It always does."

This happened before? When?

"And besides, he's the guest on some show tonight."

Adamantly refusing my pleas to call anybody, insisting it was just a pulled muscle, that a massage would do far more than having people crowd around. I waited until she offered me a hand. Then slowly, as if lifting a baby from a crib, I helped her to her feet. She stumbled, then let out a moan.

An hour passed, and the limp improved. Back at her computer, the tympanic taps started again. Rapid then a pause, she picked up her phone.

"Okay, I got an emergency appointment at the spa." Only somebody in lower Manhattan could get away with a statement like that. "My cell phone's on, keep the balcony doors closed, so the bugs don't get in." She checked the latch on its door. "And no snacking. You hear me? I'll be home by six."

"Mom, don't worry so much. I'm just happy you're feeling better."

"Don't be smart!"

I counted to five before I summoned the two tattletales, luring them to the TV with a bottle of coke and a bucket of chips. Turning up the volume to distract them further, I set out on a mission. I mean, really, how did this punishment fit my crime? I *needed* my iPad.

Flat on my belly, I checked under every couch and cabinet. I ruffled the curtains, even climbed a few bookcases. Nada. Where was this penalty box anyway, under an invisibility cloak? Defeated then bored then curious, I rolled around on my parent's bedroom floor, swirling my fingers around knots in the pine until...

Oh! I speed-crawled under the bed until only my legs were sticking out. Found it! Something flat, something rectangular, wrapped in layers of towels, I ripped them off and exhaled one last time before, what? *Lady's Home Journal?* Who hid a magazine like that? I mean, you hid magazines like...

Driven by this sudden want, my curiosity to find what I was not supposed to find cast aside my need to locate what had been taken away. To the office, I went, and on the closet's top shelf, posing no challenge at all, a row of Macy's boxes spread from wall to wall. Heavy, the first one thumped just right, so I lowered it to the ground, slowly opening it to preserve the moment. Magazines, yes; magazines, no, wrong ones.

But wait, was that? Noooo, so young, *Jack Scott, Man on the Move.* Jet black hair? One lock of it curled in front of his left eye. And his hand, what was that all about? Halfway inside his pocket, it looked like he was trying to be the next James Bond. Whatever.

Next.

Learn the backstory of the man behind the stories. GQ? Really. Next, Vanity Fair, I knew that one. Rolling Stone? You must be kidding me?

Buried in the weathered copy of GQ, I stumbled backward until his desk chair willed me to sit, and there I read and learned and shook my head in disbelief. This article made him sound like a man who would say *Yeaahhh,* baby, not yes, with an s. Were they sure they interviewed my dad?

I scanned his office. Jack Theodore Scott was one anal man. Very. Papers stacked seamlessly sat parallel to pens, which paralleled the keyboard, which paralleled a mouse. All white, all cordless, all as if on display in an Apple store. I slid open the top drawer and go figure: a ruler. No doubt, a contributor to this immaculate display. On a role, I toed open the filing cabinet, chuckling how each tab stacked behind the other like a battalion in a field. I toggled through the folders stopping by instinct at the letter R. One folder filled its sleeve. I hesitated. It was the exact one my dad passed to my mom six months ago when they were still just Jack and Sarah.

Far off down the hall, I heard Thomas laugh, then Lynzie. I slid the folder out of its sleeve.

Page one:

The said, Maximilian Ethan Stephens, does hereby in writing expressly consent and agree to the termination of his/her—someone circled his—*parental rights concerning the above-said child.*

That my consent is permanent and cannot be revoked, that I irrevocably waive any hearing regarding termination. That when the court terminates the parent-child relationship, the child's adoption is not required. That all rights, powers…

The shaking paper in my hand was a battered flag fighting a storm. I skimmed to the bottom, circling his signature ten times with my eyes. Termination, parental rights, permanent, how many times would I need to read this for the meaning to change.

"Ahem."

A low voice at the doorway cleared his throat. My father was home. Did I care that I was caught? Would he reject me too for violating the sanctity of his office, for finding the magazines, disrupting the order? I glanced at my watch; three hours had passed since my mother left. He beat her home. I glanced at the magazines: *Jack Scott, man on the move.*

"Hey, Dad," I mumbled, still staring at the paper, "Mom said you were coming home late tonight, that you were on some talk show."

"Well, your father is coming home late, but not because of a show."

Low, southern, a voice that was not my father's, I surged to my feet, arms out in front, feet spread.

"Whoa there, Jackie Chan," said a towering black man filling the door frame. He threw his hands in the air. "You must be Ryder." His chuckle moved his belly. "I come in peace. Hungry?"

The paper in my hand slipped through my fingers, and as I watched it sail peacefully to the floor, I thought: a stranger in my father's office, his hands up in the air as if at gunpoint, asking me if I were hungry. The window behind me, the walls closing in, my heart beat fast trying to make sense of the moment.

Thomas darted between his legs. "He's the producer on Dad's show. Ben. He's really cool, and he brought us pizza!" Looking beyond his massive frame, I waited for heavier footsteps, but only little ones came. Lynzie squeezed into the opening.

"Um, where's my dad?" I asked.

"After your mom got her massage, your father decided to take her to dinner. He said it was your idea, that you told him to 'fix it.'" He winked. "Anyway, he asked me to bring over some pizza."

The smell of tomato sauce and mozzarella interfered with me chewing the welt growing under my lip.

Adamant, that was how my mother acted when I suggested calling my dad. But, wait, he called her. "But." I glanced at the magazines, at the man who adopted me, the man who always fulfilled his obligations. "He was supposed to be on some show."

"Oh, that's been taken care of."

No phone call, no text message, no hint this morning when he left.

"So, the rumor is true. You do overthink. Come to the kitchen, my friend, I see your nose sniffing. Wouldn't you rather worry about getting your fair share of the pizza than deciphering your parents' love life?"

He disappeared, and by the time I shook off the image of my parents pawing each other over a romantic dinner, when I entered the kitchen, Thomas was on his third slice. I slip-slided over the floor to secure my stake.

Strands of cheese clung to the box as Ben lifted a piece onto an empty plate. Lynzie rushed in to slice the threads in half. "Here ya go, Kiddo."

Kiddo. A fake name that useless men use to forge relationships that will never happen. My father used it.

That my consent is permanent. I irrevocably waive any hearing regarding termination.

I plopped my piece on Thomas' plate, an even exchange for the use of his phone. I guided his thumb to unlock it, forgetting that he already told me the password. I pulled up my real father, the one who loved me, who called me hun.

Snatch! Out of thin air, Ben's hand swiped the phone, decentering me on the chair, and sending me straight to ground. "Your mom and pop had a big night planned, romantic if you know what I mean. Best to hang low." Another wink, no less fake than his last. "Ryder, listen, they just don't want to be bothered."

"We're not a bother," I said, rubbing my arm, which took the brunt of the fall.

"Of course not, but your pop brought me up to speed on the fight and on *your* recommendations: the date, flowers, about doing something nice." He raised his Pepsi into the air. "Get it, kid? You done good. Let's give them their night, okay?"

A great night for them maybe, a shit one for me. A sizeable knot grew under my elbow where I hit the floor. *My consent to the child's adoption is not required.*

"I'm going out to get some dessert."

"Ryder, clearly, you're upset over something, but let me remind you that *your* father passed me specific instructions and disobeying them would not be in your best interest."

"Um, Ben, she doesn't mean it." Thomas picked up his fourth slice, waving it back and forth to tease, then taunt. "She's just going through a phase."

We heard that on TV last night, which opened the usual floodgates: what was a phase, how did you spell it, was it someplace you go, was it fun? I told him it was a temporary time that passes the moment you wish for something else.

"Ryder, I wish for some java chocolate chip ice cream when you're in the new phase, okay? Me and Mom like it," he said, with a mouth full, cheese dangling from his chin, the tip of the pizza positioned overhead waiting for the swallow. A warmth passed through me as he finally lowered it into his mouth.

I left the apartment restored by Thomas' trust, only to be thwarted by Carson's meddling. Our too involved doorman assaulted me the moment my foot hit the lobby floor.

"Hey, kiddo." I cringed. "Why wasn't your father on air tonight? He was plugged for a special about the refugee crisis, but they filled his seat with that doofus from CBS."

And how did this overdressed doorman know that if he was on duty? I should turn him in, especially since he was not hip enough to watch something other than *Inside Government with Jack Scott.* I mean, really, so dry, with boring battles over stock prices, and useless banter about that leader with the pudgy cheeks and the funny haircut. If my father would only learn from Ellen, he would be so much more relatable.

"He's on a date with my Mom," I mumbled. Carson's suspicious look suddenly hitting home.

***

"He's still here!" Thomas shook me from a coma. "Get up! Go talk to him!" He yanked the covers completely off the bed. "And Mom and Dad aren't here, and nobody slept in their bed. And that man is on *our* couch, sleeping!"

Thomas didn't wait. Choosing irrational panic over foolish calm, he rushed to the coffee table and swiped his phone. But Ben, the provider turned intruder, bolted upright in confusion, reflexively clamping Thomas' wrist. "Whoa, buddy, where's the fire, little man?"

"Where's my mom?" Thomas shouted.

Ben's palms faced down, attempting to quiet the little man, and we three crossed our arms, trying to intimidate the big one. We waited, not the least bit patiently, for the truth to emerge.

"Okay, here goes."

Apparently, my father chose to make more than a night of it. He put champagne on ice, reserved a suite at the Waldorf, and wooed our mother with room service, a mini-bar, and a night filled with romance.

Arms still crossed, I added a scowl for many reasons, the least of which was because I didn't understand what he meant by wooed. Or maybe I did. Oh, Ugh.

"You know, maybe I'll just get your father on the phone. How's that?" Why would he go into the bathroom to make the call, and why when the door finally opened, did I not hear a flush? He passed the phone to Thomas, to which I rightfully intervened.

"No." Ben pushing my hands aside was an invisible blow. "Your father prefers to speak with his son."

What? I managed my siblings. If some message needed to be passed down the chain, it started at the oldest link.

"Okay...yeah...no, we're fine...bed on time...yes...love you, too." Thomas hung up.

I grabbed the phone from his hands, incredulously staring at the black screen. "Thomas, did he want to speak to me?"

"No. He said he's coming home tomorrow."

Even Lynzie's mouth dropped in shock.

"Listen Kids, Guerin LeBlanc, will be coming to stay with you until Sunday night." One hand pocketing his phone, the other held up to stop my protest, Ben, the intruder turned collaborator, exercised undeserved authority. "Do not call your parents. They earned some time for themselves." And then he poured salt into the wound: "Ryder, since you've been with them, how many nights have they not been at your beck and call?"

I stapled my lips closed with guilt.

Within the hour, Guerin arrived, adding to it. Explaining that before I came into their lives, they always had a babysitter every Saturday night. That from the beginning, they promised each other that having children would not ebb away at their marriage. "It's been a whirlwind since you arrived, hun: the social worker's visits, the court appearance, your violin lessons, the concert."

I needed to apologize to them, and the tremor building inside told me to do it now, before the guilt rotted, and the blame spiraled. Before—I looked at Guerin, his thumbs on his phone pounding ferociously as if in a war with time.

Jack and Sarah left us alone, and it was all my fault. Everything, always my fault. *Are you happy now, Ryder?* Memories of my mother flashed by: a smile on her face, a box of Christmas lights in her hands. *We won't have to have a Christmas without lights now. Come help me hang them.* Why. Why. Why didn't I stay? *No, Mom, I want to go to the park.*

I broke into a cold sweat. Yes. I had to apologize. Now! Before something bad happened, and I would never have a chance. I teased Thomas' phone over the table's edge, letting it fall soundlessly into my waiting palm. I glanced at Lynzie playing with the cat, at Thomas standing obediently at Guerin's side, at Guerin, his thumbs hovering, then pounding again.

Thomas' phone buzzed in my hand.

"Ryder," Guerin said. "That call's for you."

"Um, hello?"

All him, none of me. My father paced his words, not forcing them with anxiety nor pausing in deliberation. Relaxed and smooth, his inflection varied enough, but not too much; the man was not at all upset. And then he told me to be the same. "I didn't mean to upset you, Ryder. I'm sorry, very. This is the type of weekend we needed. You'll understand when you're older." He paused. "But I hope you'll forgive me today. I love ya, kid, okay?"

"Yeah."

No 'yes' to correct. And then I remembered the magazines. Covers, window-dressing—*Yeahhh baby*—not just anybody could pull off the perfect false front.

CHAPTER TWENTY-SIX

Always look for a better story. Each of life's moments were building blocks that could either lead to something grand or be taken apart and then restored. Life was just an illusion, wasn't it? Our interpretation of events, how we judge or were judged—all of it depended on our will to find comfort. If we needed it, the right words would swell like a magnifying glass running over a page. If we needed it, we'd find them, those words that made us safe.

I needed them.

Because when Jack, the performer, stepped from the elevator, his script fell apart the moment he opened his mouth. A slurry of nonsense, and then, *ah, wonderful weekend.* A blank look in the direction of nothing, and then *just what we needed.* A comparison to fool, *like when you all sleep over at your best friend's house.* Never did he look me in the eye.

With each act of bravado, his shoulders dropped an inch. And by the time he made it to the living room sofa, his forged words saddled him with guilt. He confessed.

Thomas marched to his father, stopping inches from his face. Breathing heavy with the heartache of a boy wounded by betrayal, he whispered. "You weren't at the hotel? You were in a hospital? All weekend?" The cleansing of our father's inner voice met the judgment of his only son. "You lied to us?"

"I'm sorry." It came out flat and without diction, like he'd forgotten to practice that line.

Stumbling over words, as though our father were unsure if he should apologize, explain or defend, every few seconds his eyes darted elsewhere. Eventually, he spoke, pulling his words through a pinhole. "She's sick." His chin quivered. "Doctors take a long time...it's the weekend... short of staff...no answers." That magnifying glass ballooned over the filtered words my dad wanted to hear. "But." His spine went straight, and the performer returned.

"The doctors are positive she will be released tomorrow, and boy is she excited to see you all."

A better story.

A contest of stares followed until Guerin walked between us, sweeping his hand over the top of our heads. He emphasized how important we were; how we needed to help our mother, not argue, and give her time to heal.

"Yes." Our father interrupted, taking back the reins. "Each and every one of you needs to be your happy selves as much as possible, and that will help her out as much as possible. I know you all can do that..." Those shifting eyes found my mother's sneakers peeking from under the couch. He mumbled. "As much as possible." Our father, the talking head, the man who interviewed the powerful and spoke flawlessly in front of a camera, rambled.

"Okay, Dad." Thomas' betrayal bested by childhood naivety, he turned on the TV. Lynzie asked what we were having for dinner. Later in life they would learn how far you fall when you surrender this easily to trust.

"Dad?" I asked.

A series of crackles let loose as he bent to tie the laces of those sneakers. He slid them under the couch, and for too long, his eyes lingered on the indent left behind. He picked at the fibers, flicking each thread with the tip of his finger. When the last one rose, he closed his eyes.

"Dad?"

"Ryder, I can't deal with you now." And the man I had waited forty-eight hours to hug, the man who knew all the answers, who could walk gracefully through quicksand. That man turned his back and walked away.

A vice clamped down on my chest, stealing breaths that left me gasping. My fault. My mother was sick. My fault. My mother was dead. I saw lights, flashing, alternating from red to blue, horizontally bouncing above the car. Voices echoed, falling over each other. *What time did I come home? Was she alone when you left for the park? Where was my father?*

Nowhere.

He walked away.

***

Be back with Mom by nine a.m. Ryder, set out breakfast for Thomas and Lynzie.

Between that note and last night, our father had been a ghost. Guerin had left sometime during the night.

The house hummed with the mystery of an elusive dream, one that left you questioning then concerned. But neither won because when our mother passed through those elevator doors, a different truth emerged. Not one hair was out of place, and every stroke of her makeup was perfect. The energetic woman that sauntered into the living room was as far away from death as I was to the sun.

"Tell me all about your weekend. I missed you all so much."

"Mommy, you're going to be okay, right?"

"Of course, I am Lynzie. Just like when your Aunt Evelyn needed surgery. Remember, she was in the hospital for three days." Blank looks. She chuckled, and naturally too. "Oh, I guess you were too young. She's fine now, right? Same thing for me."

The backside of her hand brushed my cheek, and my mouth opened ready to tell her that I was sorry, that I would talk, that I wouldn't ignore her questions about my mother ever again.

"Maybe we'll lay off the yoga for now, huh?" Then laughing quickly and hard, she lifted Lynzie as if she were a feather, spinning her around until the breakfast bar blocked her path. "Ryder, I'm fine."

To my surprise, she continued, waltzing over to the balcony, delighting in the late summer morning. She eyed the kids in the park kicking balls, the women ogling over displays, men in ties with jackets thrown over their shoulder. "Look at life."

I looked at my dad, at the film covering his eyes, at the forced happiness he reluctantly displayed.

"Jack, I'm fine."

A kiss sealed the charade because his nostrils flared when a smile came, a nod agreed as his body shrank: happy and pleasant, and yet entirely ill at ease.

My mother set Lynzie down on the couch and announced her plans to catch up where she left off. To sort through her scrapbook and vow not to miss a moment, swipe through Pinterest until she found just the right theme for Lynzie's birthday. To stop worrying about her ills and her aches and smother us with attention whether we liked it or not. "Who wants to help?"

"I do," said Lynzie. "I do," dittoed Thomas. And they left,

bouncing their way upstairs with the urgency of a kitten in pursuit of a string.

Left alone with my father, we stayed fixed on life seven floors down. On the man in jeans swapping taxis with the woman in a dress. "Dad, are you going to work today?"

He pressed his forehead against the glass.

"Are you going to talk to me today?"

"I asked you to make things happy for your mother." Harsh and bitter and dissociated from the moment before, his breath left a cloud on the glass. "Challenging me works against that. Do not make things difficult for her."

Difficult. My fault. I brought home the flu; I eavesdropped; I turned on the disposal.

He turned, ramming his foot into my violin case I forgot to put away. Cursing under his breath, his shape diminished in size as the distance grew. At the office door, he paused, sinking his hand into the knob.

"Dad."

Nothing.

"Dad."

His head banged into the door, the thud echoing down the hall. "Jack!" I shouted, jarring him and his hand away from the knob.

"Picking and choosing, are you?" Every muscle in his face tensed.

"No, Dad, I just wanted your attention."

"You and everybody else." The office door's slam was a bullet.

I stood on that spot, unable to move, watching the cat weave between my legs in a confusing pattern of trust and restraint. I picked him up, willing his purr to create a calm, to reassure me that I wasn't alone, wasn't at fault. But I was.

I left.

Outside, the humidity and heat suffocated, and my clothes clung to my body. All of it adding a burden for which I couldn't cope. Spinning in circles, trying to locate an escape, the world blurred into streaks and streams, smearing together in a mishmash of color. The cool breeze of the air-conditioned bakery drew me to a stop. I took one step in its direction; I took one step back. Guerin LeBlanc, the best friend of the man who broke my heart, walked out its door. Aborting, I spun again and headed for the stairs.

And the morning commute took me away. Each subway stop

piled one suit on top of the other until I was trapped in a circle of ties and necklaces. At the Wall Street Station, they filed out, but in their wake, I saw her: dirty clothes, greasy hair, bitten nails, a kid that used to be me. I batted down my pockets, looking for anything to ease her pain. I had nothing but Thomas' phone.

The doors opened, inviting the masses to enter, and when I returned to that homeless girl, she was gone.

Yes, that girl was gone, and in her place, a new person came. One who distanced herself from her old life to embrace another, who clung to her saviors so fast she forgot only a tenuous bond had formed. What she did and said mattered because she didn't have years of good memories to offset her faults.

Aimlessly—or maybe out of need—I exited at Harlem. I walked past the black men in long shorts loitering in front of the McDonalds, under the yellow police tape blocking the sidewalk, past the trash and the filth. I pushed through it all until I found the place I vowed never to return.

"Well, well, well." I think I wanted to see him. "You look like shit."

"It's been a hard weekend, Levi."

"Fuck! First-class problems." Nothing had changed for him; everything had for me.

"Don't be givin' my girl a hard time now. Ya missed me, huh? How ya doin', little lady? Tell Simon what ya been up to."

Simon. That was his name, and I learned this only now, why?

His bright smile was as welcome as his gentle hug. This homeless man, the same one who taught me how to survive, who provided shelter over my head, he dutifully escorted me to a bench. "Go ahead, spill it. Somethin' definitely on your mind."

A torrent unleashed. I told him what I allowed myself to admit: my mother's death, the string of lights, how I never stopped feeling the guilt. I told him how Sarah wanted to talk, but I didn't. How I thought if she stayed sick with the menopause, she would stop asking me questions. But now she was really sick, and my dad wouldn't tell me with what because he was mad and tired and because I made it difficult.

"I hate him."

"Ya know, it sound to me like you purposefully focusin' on this five-minute conversation with your new dad to stop thinking about your new mom." He paused to throw his arms over the back of the bench. "Ya know the best way to deal with the unknown?"

My next breath would come only after I heard his answer.

"Ya don't. It's unknown, and it needs to run its course."

"That's your advice?"

"And it's excellent advice. So, they shuttin' ya out. Somethin' happened this weekend that, for whatever reason, they wanna keep to themselves, and instead of acceptin' that, yous yanked up the anxiety and turned against this guy." He gave me a shove as if to get me on my way. "Go home, my friend. Hug your mother."

"I hugged the cat." He raised his brow. "If I hug my mother, she won't tell me the truth."

"So, what? Why do you need to know?"

"Because I love them."

"And there ya have it." His warm smile told me to agree. "Go home and hug your mother and aks for nothin' in return."

Standing now, he unwrapped a stick of gum, split it in half, and handed me the bigger end. "Kid, I like ya a lot, but you don't belong here. You never have, and you never will. And, that ain't no rejection. It's a promotion. You a good kid, and just the fact that you come back after being swept away into the good life says a hell of a lot. I respect that. Don't you ever lose sight of it. Got it?"

Got it.

"It don't matter how rich you are, or how famous, adversity will find you, in different forms, but it will come. And just like all of us down here in the ghetto, you—" stabbing me in the chest with his finger— "will survive. Just pace yourself. Got it?"

Got it.

"Now, go hug your mother."

My mother was sick; my father couldn't cope. She was in denial; he was in full retreat, and my homeless friend told me to just wait.

Thomas' phone buzzed in my pocket. *Where are you?* Buzz. *You're scaring me, where are you?* Guerin must have set off the alarm after he saw me on the street. A long delay, but the telltale three dots of an evolving text pulsed.

What are you doing in Harlem? Stay there, I'm coming to get you.
No. Mom, I just boarded the subway. I'll be home in twenty minutes.
You are now speaking with your father. Get home right this instant!
Shit.
And when you get home, every word out of your mouth will be a truthful one.

Same to you!!! I powered down the phone, and an eternity passed before I reached my stop.

I stormed into the lobby only to be met by a penetrating stare. "Upstairs," my father barked. "And head straight into the office."

"No side B?"

"No backtalk." Lips pursed; his mouth barely moved.

Fuming by the time I crossed the office threshold, it took only one shallow breath to regret all that I had done.

"Sweetheart, Harlem?"

"Mom, what's going on?" My voice cracked, and everything Simon said went out the window. "I know you're not telling me the truth, and I can't take it." I even forgot to give her a hug. "I need to know."

She motioned to Jack, choosing to comfort her husband instead of me. "Honey, I'm going to beat this thing. We tell Ryder, and Ryder will keep it between us," she said, kissing him gently. She turned. "Ryder, everything we say cannot be repeated to Thomas or Lynzie. I can beat this." My heart skipped a beat, and the vacant space filled with dread. "Words are scary, Ryder, so don't focus on those."

No, I focused on Jack, and the pain etched across his face.

"Not all words mean the same—like the word 'went', remember that from way back when I was helping you with your paper? Diseases are the same. When somebody has a heart attack, they might go home with medications. Right? But someone else could need tests, still others have surgery: one disease, many different outcomes."

Right, illness as a thesaurus: no. My father's lips were tense, his hands squeezed tight between his knees.

"We caught it early. I only stayed in the hospital for two nights so they could run all the tests they needed and start the medication to help me heal." Her voice was fast then slow, the cadence was wrong. "I can beat this."

People fight infections. They opt for surgery. They recover from injury. They beat—

"Cancer, Mom?"

"Words, sweetheart, only words." She explained fast, adding far too much detail. She said it was straightforward, that it had been done by millions of survivors before her, that she would start chemotherapy, and my dad would take time off to help.

"I can help."

"I know you can, sweetheart. But you don't have a license, a credit card, or a car." She laughed.

He didn't. "What were you doing in Harlem?"

I avoided his eyes by examining my fingernails. They were dirty, filled with the lingering residue from the long weekend that passed. I dug beneath them slowly, my meticulous strokes stretching time.

"I find you there again, you will *never* forget the punishment. Are we clear?" His voice stayed somber. "Give me Thomas' phone."

I wheeled the chair back a foot. "I'll give it back to him!"

"Hand it over." He pressed the side and waited for the black Apple logo to fill the screen. "This stays on at all times. This—" his fingers flew quickly through the settings until he reached the iCloud server— "never gets turned off. You disconnected in the middle of our text message, and we had no way to tell where you were."

He freed his hand from his wife's and tapped on a panel at the base of the side table. A pop came, and a hidden drawer sprang open: the penalty box revealed. "This iPad and phone are not an invitation to start Googling about your mother's condition." He meant to look stern, to exercise authority, but his hand shook. His wife stilled it. "We are going to live in the moment, not by what somebody wrote on their blog or by the Mayo Clinic's definition of disease and treatment. Do you understand?" I nodded. He handed over the tablet and phone.

They were sending a message to themselves.

***

Keeping secrets had a cost, and my body reacted to it as if sprayed with a slow-acting poison. All my defenses returned: I picked, resumed muted obedience, obsessively practiced my violin.

Day in day out, for the weeks that passed since learning the diagnosis, I played the melodies that matched my lonely mood: ballads, serenades, songs that yanked your heart to pull it low. Nobody else wanted to hear it: not Thomas, not Lynzie, even the neighbor had commented to my dad. But there was no other way because I only knew one outlet.

Schindler's List played on repeat, the soundtrack to a past war masking the present. Upsetting and dissonant, I heard the death in the hollow chords, saw a ghetto emptied, people deserted. I wept from the beauty of the music, for a tragedy worse than mine.

I saw the movie on a plane. My mother asleep, my father God knows where, I sat mesmerized, disturbed by the story, the music, by that little girl in the red dress walking alone against a tide of hate.

How could I think about Sarah when that little girl suffered? She had no one. I had a family. She would die. I would live.

I played the piece over and over again, falling into an alternative world. Nothing could touch me inside that bubble. My bedroom door creaked open, and I played. My mother moved towards me, and I played. She grabbed my bow.

"Ryder. No more."

The melancholic tunes clinging to my core tried to make sense of the serene expression lining her face.

"No more ballads, okay?" She kissed my forehead, and the scent that lingered was a paradox: not fresh or clean, but sterile, a hospital's residue. When she pulled away, humming that funereal tune, a patch of her eyebrow was gone.

"Mom? I'm sorry."

For everything: for not talking when she wanted, for not listening when she talked, for making her sway to the music that made the whole world sad. I cleared my throat, ready to unleash the burden trapped by guilt, but I couldn't because my words were not just words.

"You have nothing to be sorry for, sweetheart."

But I did. I just couldn't tell her because I had become my father, a man hiding behind an invisible shield, a hermit crouched behind an impenetrable wall.

"Your father and I are heading back to speak with the doctor."

I grabbed her arm. "Why?"

She laughed at me, at my concern. And then, she casually ordered papers in her hand, dog-earring one, tossing another in the bin. "It's a routine appointment, Ryder," she chuckled, bouncing her keys in her palm. "Nothing to play sad songs over. Keep it positive, all right? And keep an eye on your brother and sister. It's just down the block, so we won't be too long."

She left, and the little girl in the red dress snuck behind my lids once more, her stride in sync with the sad music swelling between my ears. She walked past German guards and harmless Jews, past mothers with babies, and fathers with sons. A bullet went through the back of an innocent man's head. And still, she walked on. The tragedy of war, the innocence lost, it was better for me when all of them hurt.

I supposed, thinking those thoughts, I deserved to be where my wandering feet took me, in front of a file cabinet reading what I knew would hurt. I toggled my fingers through the alphabet, pulling out that folder starting with R. Already knowing the pain from seeing my father's signature, I went searching for more.

Family and Children's Services
City and County of San Francisco
Katherine Johannsen M.S.W.

> *Ryder Stephens, thirteen-year-old female, abandoned by her father by choice and orphaned by her mother by death, had become a challenge. The accepting family lodged a complaint after learning Ryder's religion. They accepted her for the Christmas holidays, but efforts were underway to place her in an alternative setting. She disappeared before a home was secured.*

> *Her father contacted social work denouncing our work as sloppy when she had arrived in Las Vegas unannounced, undesired, and unwanted. The whereabouts of Ryder Stephens remained unknown until New York City Child Protective Services informed us she had been living with Mr. and Mrs. Jack and Sarah Scott of Manhattan, New York.*

> *Sincerely,*
> *Katherine Johannsen M.S.W*

Disruptive. Undesired. Unwanted. I closed my eyes to see that German soldier march through the snow with a force of a bull, pulverizing it with a vulgar scrunch. His pistol swung by his side. The long, narrow muzzle took aim.

I chewed mercilessly on a small tag hanging from my cuticle, the salty skin giving way to the metallic taste of blood. I peeled the tag away. Little specks of blood dotted the page.

"Sweetheart! What are you doing?"

"Mom." My voice pitched high. I didn't care that I was caught. "How could you want me with a letter like this?"

"Words, just words, honey, like I told you. We looked beyond them and saw who you really were. You came to us, and we saw a child deserving much more than what life had offered." She took the letter and folded it in half. "We didn't feel worthy of you, and you have not disappointed. Well—" squeezing playfully— "you took ten dollars out of my wallet."

I pulled away.

"Oh, sweetheart, I see everything. All the time, I watch all my children. Someday, when you're a mother, you'll understand."

"My mother didn't love me."

"Oh, you don't know that. In fact, I know you're wrong. Your mother didn't love herself. What happened to her had nothing to do with you." She hugged me tight. "I know, honey."

She knew.

I opened my mouth to spill the truth she deserved to learn, but I wasn't ready to hear the words describing the image I saw. "Um, Mom…"

"Yes."

"Can I come with you next time when you have your chemo?"

My dad stepped under the door frame, his head shaking from side to side.

"No, sweetheart, that time is for your dad and me."

"You're going to be okay, right?" I pleaded with my eyes.

"As long as I have all of you, I'm going to be just fine."

That wasn't an answer.

CHAPTER TWENTY-SEVEN

Avoidance coping was our new norm.

"I'm not talking to you, Sarah. You're putting ketchup in my soup." My dad smirked as he said it, adding a chuckle when the plastic jar burped after his wife continued to squeeze. "Don't laugh, you disrespectful wife, it's the ultimate insult to a chef, adding ketchup to anything." He winked and chortled again.

All the world's a stage. It was now August; cycles of chemo had come and gone. "Mom's right, Dad, this soup needs more salt. Can you pass me the ketchup?" Thomas asked. *And all the men and women merely players.*

"No!" He passed his son the salt. "*This*—" waving the shaker— "is acceptable to draw out the flavors. *This*—" he rose from the table with the bottle of ketchup and tossed it in the trash— "smothers them." The schoolboy gasped. "It was almost empty. I'll pick up another one tomorrow." Another wink and a laugh and Thomas mimicked the sound of the air escaping with the squeeze.

None of this worked for me.

No, Thomas, I did not want any salt. No, Dad, I won't stop biting my nails. I tolerated this deception as much as I welcomed another lie. She wasn't getting better. Her clothes hung too loose; her eyes sunk. "May I go to my room? Please," I added only to play along with a promise I found increasingly impossible to keep.

"Have fun sulking in your room."

Oh, Thomas, if you only knew.

Jovial chatter continued. For Thomas and Lynzie, the world still spun in the same direction. Unfair. And sealing myself behind the bedroom door and listening to their laughs only added to the injustice. I flung the door open and marched into the living room. "I need the cat."

"It doesn't look like it needs you."

"Shut up, Thomas."

"Watch it, young lady," both liars said as one.

I hugged the squirming cat who, sensing my mood, flailed his paws and scratched at my skin. Blood oozed from one of his many efforts. He needed to purr, damn it, to console me. I tossed him into the bedroom and closed the door behind us.

I yanked my desk drawers open, and the cleaning began in earnest. Rustling through papers occupied my mind. I found post-it notes with doodles and the ten dollars I stole. Digging deeper, there were earrings and tissues, wrappers with used gum waded inside. In rapid succession, everything landed in the trash.

The cat scratched at the door.

I took the entire bin and dumped it into a plastic bag. Shaking the remnants so violently much of it missed the bag and landed on the floor, giving us both something else to do. I picked up an old napkin and winced.

A positive attitude won't solve all of your problems, but it will annoy enough people to make it worth the effort.

I showed the once-loved napkin to the cat. "Doesn't seem worth it to me, Charlie." He scratched the door again, wanting to be with the woman who wrote those lies. "No." His punishment for his loyalty to them was to remain trapped inside with me. "Come here, you unfaithful thing. You don't deserve this, but I'll let you play with it anyway."

From my own designated penalty box, I retrieved my iPad, the one returned to me the night of the diagnosis, the one I promised not to search. And I hadn't. Because as much as I resented being forced to lie to my siblings, I made a promise.

"Come here, Charlie. It's a game for cats."

I flipped the cover, and it refreshed to the last App opened: *USA Today.*

The lead story took up half the screen, and I found myself tunneling into the eyes of the man who just lectured his son about ketchup, into those of a woman too sick to tell her kids. Dazzling and looking surreal, my dad wore a tailored black tuxedo, my mom a beautiful pastel pink gown. Plucked from a time gone by, they stood together arm in arm.

Sarah Scott, Wife of Jack Scott, Diagnosed with Stage Four Cancer.

I tilted my head and read it again. The newspaper knew, but my

brother and sister didn't?
Click.

Jack Scott: journalist, author, and chief anchor, who has been on temporary sabbatical for over a month, has officially announced his leave of absence. This is Mr. Scott's first prolonged departure in thirteen years. The network confirmed that his wife of twenty years has recently been diagnosed with Stage IV Malignant Melanoma. The family has asked the media to respect their privacy.

The article continued with irrelevant things from the past, nothing to help me predict the future.

What is malignant melanoma?
Click. I skimmed, looking for a simple heading. Click.

Melanoma is the most dangerous form of skin cancer. The disease arises from abnormal melanocytes and often resembles moles.

I toggled through each stage, not caring until I reached Stage 4.

Stage 4 melanoma means cancer has spread to other parts of the body…it's difficult to cure… the five-year survival rate is low.

Click *What is a survival rate?* Click.

The percentage of people in a study who are alive after a given period of time after a diagnosis.

Click. *What is the survival rate for Stage 4 malignant melanoma?* Click.
No definition, just blog headings: *My mother was diagnosed and given 6-12 months to live. My father was given 2-6 months. Don't wait to do things with your sister, this cancer moves fast.*
I clicked. I read. And with each blog finished, my breathing grew heavy. I slammed the cover and kicked the iPad under the bed. Months? Months to live? Everything spun: my thoughts, my stomach, the room. I stood up too fast, and immediately regretted it for the nausea it caused, so I sat back down. Then up, forgetting why I sat down. Everything moved in slow motion around me. I reached for the dresser; it moved. I stretched further, closing my

eyes when the ringing started. I tried to steady myself by taking deep breaths, but that made it worse. That ringing, and then darkness came.

When I came to, the house creaked as if the ghosts had already arrived. Running my fingers along my lower lip, I felt nothing, only numbness. I folded it out and squatted beside the mirror, my teeth had embedded themselves into the tissue as if it were a plastered mold. How long had I been out? Long, but not long enough to deny what I read. Not telling me was deliberate.

My father, I needed to talk to him. I picked up the phone, fully aware that he was in the next room, and then dropped it. Only now, with my stomach in knots and my hands tingling from shortened breaths, did I understand why he couldn't call that first night, why he left it to Saturday. How it was easier for him to speak *to* Thomas than *with* me.

Recent memories took on new meaning. With Mom at his side, he calmed. Alone, he stared blankly, unaware of his surroundings, unwilling to engage. I saw the death of a woman I knew for thirteen years. My father knew and loved this woman for thirty.

This wasn't deliberate; this was denial.

And it was my turn to add to it. Where was the evidence? Tell me that! My mother just put ketchup in her tomato and basil soup and then threw her head back to laugh. Dying people didn't do that. No, they were Steve Jobs, walking skeletons with sunken eyes and shrinking frames. When I hugged my mother, I felt... I traced my ribs. When I hugged my mother, I felt bones, bones that weren't there before.

The cat jumped and dislodged the handle, pawing open a small slit in the door, letting in sounds that added to my denial. All of life kept going despite the reality of the written word. I closed my eyes to force a different existence, to see the life in her eyes, to unlearn my mistake. But nothing came. I opened the door, and the cat darted to freedom, sliding into the wall before taking off down the hall. I followed it, creeping along the margin until the edge of the kitchen came into view.

Carefree and buoyant, my mother was stacking the dishes. "Sweetheart, there you are. Do you want some ice cream?"

What an odd question to ask at a time like this.

"Oh, we're out. Do you want to go get some?" She moved willingly, as free as a woman unshackled by a fatal disease. "You okay?"

My tongue felt heavy, too dry to respond. I nodded instead.

"Do you still have that ten you took from me?"

Thunder cracked against the open sky. And when she reached around to dig into my back pocket, I saw the first drops of rain slant into the balcony glass.

"Ah, there it is." Dark shadows extending from the bridge of her nose circled under her eyes. Her cheekbone jutted out from her face. A mark of death.

"I like the Java chip, the one with the little chocolate chips mixed in." She tucked a collapsible umbrella under my arm. "Don't be too long. I think it might pour."

Carson met me in the lobby, and I opened my mouth, desperate to hear the truth.

"You okay, hun?"

I bit my lip. *Our lives are our lives.*

"Watch your bag, the zipper's open."

When I opened the door, the wind whipped my hair across my face, and a drop of rain fell against my nose. I let it roam the bridge until it reached the apex. It stayed, oddly tethered. Another drop splattered the sidewalk inches from my feet; a third landed on my crown. The air was stale, filled with the smell of trash, of life wasted, of a city that didn't care. The drop fell from my nose, maybe, because tears came from my eyes.

Water everywhere. A little girl with red galoshes passed by. I watched her stroll through the pouring rain, unbothered by the wind billowing her jacket. She found a puddle and stopped.

Jump, I urged. Play. But she just stood there.

"Don't scream." An object was at my back: sharp, pointed, and I didn't care. "Take it," I said. I had neither the strength nor conviction for this thief and his want.

The girl circled the puddle twice. The object moved away from my back, as I collapsed my shoulders to let my bag with my phone go free. The girl jumped, and her smile was as wide as the sea. Footsteps ran away.

What did a phone mean to me if my mother was dying?

CHAPTER TWENTY-EIGHT

Above all, don't lie to yourself. The man who lies to himself and listens to his own lie comes to a point that he cannot distinguish the truth within him, or around him, and so loses all respect for himself and for others. And having no respect, he ceases to love. *

My mother, Samantha Stephens, read that to me when I was eleven. Just like she did with excerpts from *Brave New World*, *Catcher in the Rye*, *East of Eden*, and so many others. Never the story, only passages of meaning that illustrated the struggles within.

She read it to me because I broke a glass table that didn't belong to me. And since I didn't own it, I didn't care. There was a kid around to take the blame, a seven-year-old named Jordan, whose family was rich enough to buy a replacement and then ten more. But Jordan's parents were cheap, which was why they hired an eleven-year-old to babysit in the first place, and they were adamant, which is how my mother got involved.

"Did you do it?" she asked.

Arms crossed, mine, not hers, I rolled my eyes to communicate what was already known: she was an idiot. That night, she read me the passage. *...a man who lies... cannot distinguish the truth... loses respect... ceases to love.*

And here I was two years later, sitting in my adopted family's formal living room, Googling that very same passage. I *pinned* an image of it to Pinterest, the one with an old man in the corner, with a candle illuminating his face. It seemed serene, something my mother, Samantha, would like. But the cat jumped into my lap, meowing with that curious urgency, and my senses reset. If I *pinned* this, Sarah would see it, Jack would react to it, and they would hurt. Delete.

Why did I have more nerve to reminisce about the dead than I did to speak with the dying?

"Ryder!" My father bolted through the elevator. "Where's your iPhone?" His clipped words sprung the cat from my lap. "I called. You didn't pick up. A recording said it was no longer in service."

"Where's Mom?" My voice barely raised above the cat's meow.

Now at my side, hovering with a look that might as well have been a slap, he scowled, "She's at the hospital. Your phone, where is it?" Still sweaty from the outdoor swelter, he crawled out from under his leather messenger bag, leaving a two-inch sweat stain splashed across his chest.

The iPad fell to my lap. "Why didn't she come home with you after chemo?" I inched forward so my feet could touch the ground.

"She's dehydrated. They wouldn't let her leave." He moved closer, and I couldn't decide if it was the body odor or the denial that bothered me more.

"I asked you where your phone was."

I pushed back, letting my feet and the explanation dangle. "Stolen."

"And you were going to tell me this when?"

Never. I had committed to that. Texting could happen through my iPad, which, if he weren't so clueless, he would have figured out on his own.

His phone rang, of course, because old people were inefficient.

"Hello." Gruff and annoyed and blunt: his way with me extended to others. He bullied the poor recipient with chopped questions and curt replies. "No comment, goodbye."

A flurry of activity followed as he dug through his messenger bag to retrieve his MacBook. Juggling it with one hand, he ran through the commands until he turned off the program that he forbade me to touch. "Ryder, Thomas." His tone accentuated the summons. "Go get your devices and turn off the iCloud server." Always eager to please their dad, the two kids bolted into the formal room, and being such a good boy, Thomas extended his iPad in full cooperation.

"You said never to—"

"We've been hacked!"

The phone rang again. "I asked you not to call!" He switched ears. "Oh, sorry, Guerin, some guy just rang and asked for comments on photos." His fingers ran frantically through his hair. "Yes, yes, exactly the same thing. He has your number too? Where? Did you read it?" The phone was placed on speaker, freeing his hands to dance through commands and land on that dreaded *USA Today*. A slideshow flashed by of pictures I knew too well: of Thomas, Guerin, and my dad in a lightsaber battle, of me at Carnegie Hall, of all of us squeezed together on a couch. Shit.

My screensaver.

"Thanks, Guerin, I'll take care of this." A storm brewed. "All of your devices, now." My iPad hung tenuously off the table, and he grabbed it before my reflexes could kick in. "Why is there no password on this?" The vortex was about to land. "Did you remove it?" The calm before the storm. "Did your *stolen* iPhone have a password?" I bit my lip, sealing in my mistake. "Answer me!"

"You already knew the passwords, and it got annoying entering it, so I turned it off."

"What the hell is wrong with you?" He yelled, louder, scarier, and unlike the man we knew as our father. "That password was not to protect your information from us, but ours from *them!*" Thomas and Lynzie dived to safety behind my chair.

His eyebrows converged until they touched, storm clouds culled. A step forward brought his hands to his hips, and his anger surged. Anger like we had never seen it, that ceased love. Anger that he took on alone because his companion of thirty years lay suffering in a hospital bed.

Impulsively, I reached for his hand.

"No. Never." He pushed me away, soft but hard. I fell against the wall.

No. Never? What did that mean? He marched down the hall in a rage that punctuated with the slamming of the office door.

Lynzie began to cry.

"Thomas, no, don't follow him." I clung to his arm with all my strength; he would see the bruise for days to come. "Thomas, please, please don't go in his office." I didn't know what to do, but I knew one thing above all else: The man behind that door fell hard for his lies.

Thomas yanked himself free and cradled Lynzie in his arms, acting in a way that his loving parents taught.

"I want Mommy," Lynzie whimpered.

I wanted out. My anxieties multiplied and tangled all synapses, making it impossible to stop one thought before the next began. I couldn't dissect the moment. "I'll go get her." I abandoned them, carelessly leaving them to fend for themselves.

Spilling into the chaos of strangers, people were everywhere, conforming, bouncing between the boundaries of normal. A stable society. A functional order. How could that be when my life was in full collapse?

I planted my feet firmly on the gum-stained sidewalk. The sky was a cloudless blue. All of it wrong. A shadow of myself crawled inside my brain and curled into a ball. I focused on the traffic. A man crossed the street and slammed the hood of a taxi with his fist. A flash: Guerin LeBlanc did the same on the day of my solo. A horn blew; a finger came out; the subway took me away.

I didn't have the stamina to push towards Harlem, nor did I have the will. I got off at 47th Street, directing myself towards Rockefeller Center, where the man who slammed the hood of a taxi would calm and reassure and pull me into a hug.

A guard's arm swung in front of my chest. "Sorry little lady, you can't go in there: restricted. Need one of these." His finger pointed to his badge, a gesture I hastily matched with my summer camp ID. "No, my friend," he said, chuckling in a way that belittled. "Slow down. You need one that allows access to *this* building." And that finger swung to the gold-embossed plaque on the wall, *Home of ABC studios.*

A beep sounded as a man exited, and I pushed harder on the metal bar separating me from them.

He lifted my ID from my hand. "The Summer Youth Art series, my nephew did that," he said, flipping it over, "Ryder Scott. Any relation to Jack?"

"He's my father."

His face dropped, and the bend came away from his body, his chuckling grinding to a halt. "You know he's not here now." Everybody knew.

"I need to speak with Mr. LeBlanc."

"Okay, hun, you come sit over here," he said, masking his pity by walking over to the opposite end of the counter. He picked up a phone.

Hurried people scurried by en route to an agenda. A man in a suit greeted a woman in a dress. They kissed, they hugged, they could have been Jack and Sarah. I wanted my life back. I earned it.

Guerin LeBlanc pushed through the metal bar. "Uncle Guerin, it's not fair!" All of him smothered me in a hug, and his cologne, same as my father's, circled.

Once inside his office, the lingering scent brought me back to a time when Jack's secret message ended with a kiss on my brow instead of a slam against a wall. "It wasn't my fault. I couldn't tell him. I didn't want to hurt my mom. I know he's scared. But she'll come home tomorrow. He's only okay when she's around, and now she's gone. What if she's gone forever? I need to tell her the truth."

Slow, maybe afraid, Guerin sank into a chair, the color draining from his face. "Sarah's in the hospital again?" A slow breath exited.

"Guerin?" Cruel, but I needed to know. "Is she dying? *USA Today* says she is."

Rubbing his face as if that would wipe away all that was wrong, the color returned.

"He won't speak to me. I know he's hurting, but Guerin, Thomas and Lynzie don't even know she has—" my eyes found a picture framed on a shelf— "it."

With his eyes closed, he spoke with the cadence of a consoling pastor. "You know, Ryder, I have known your parents for a long time." Open now, he paced his sermon. "At times, I've idolized your father. He was always one step ahead of me. Mr. Composed, continually prepared for any situation. When you came along, I knew they would adopt you. That's what they do, see? Because no challenge is too large. For Jack and Sarah Scott, everything can be fixed, and if it can't, well, then it's just not a problem worth fixing, is it? But now, Jack has a problem that needs a cure, but he can't find one, and he can't let it go because that problem, his wife, is now, and has always been, the most important part of his life. He has no control over the speed of this cancer, the seriousness of the diagnosis, or the timeline the doctors gave them. It terrifies him, hun."

It meant something to hear a calm voice work through a process honestly. "Guerin—"

"Have you ever heard of Elisabeth Kubler-Ross?" But he didn't want a dialogue. He wanted to talk—about butterflies carved into walls at Nazi Concentration camps, about how this woman Kubler-Ross was bothered by them, about prisoners and stages. He wanted to tell me about insects and how they helped us to understand the process of dying.

Irrelevant trivia.

"Please, Guerin, I just want my dad to talk to me." So, I could find out when he would stop yelling. I wanted to go back to a time when he would pull to the curb and trick me into accepting his advice; when he would take my iPad away because he cared. But Guerin kept talking about grief and stages and how Jack has passed through the first one, about how I should know because I had entered it too.

I shook my head.

"Yes, you have. It flowed from your lips as soon as you saw me. You said it wasn't fair. Anger replaces denial, and it reveals itself in many different ways. Whatever happened today with the hacked iCloud account—"

"It wasn't my fault."

"What-ev-er happened," he said, outstretching his hand to halt further protest. "That outburst was much more about Sarah's disease than anything else. Do you know how this ends?"

"At a funeral."

"Acceptance." He didn't say no. "Think about your mother."

I bit down hard on my lip.

"Are you remembering how you denied it at first, maybe thought she had just passed out, that you imagined it. Are you remembering how angry you got, thought she was selfish for leaving you alone? Did you bargain? Maybe if you did everything right: got into school, and the orchestra, got selected for the solo, then all the hurt would stop. But when it didn't, you got sad, right? Yes. All that, my friend, comes before acceptance."

"That was different."

"No, honey, it isn't."

Battle-worn on two sides, Sarah's cancer and Jack's withdrawal, when my mother died, I felt more in control. And I told Guerin that, but he said I just forgot, that it was the power of the process.

"This isn't helping, Guerin. I'm sorry. I really need to speak with my father." Freely. "He needs to talk to Thomas and Lynzie too. I can't keep this up. If he is angry, he needs to get over his denial before he starts shouting. He *needs* to talk to me. I *need* to know what happened. I *need* answers!" My voice rose with each burst. "I *need* to know what is going to happen and when!" On my feet now, he rose and placed his hands firmly on my shoulders.

"Stop, stop, okay, listen to me. Yes? Then, listen to yourself."

I didn't want to hear him anymore or think about me and my process. As much as I thought I wanted to talk to anybody, I really only wanted to speak with my dad. But the only thing I learned from this man was that it was never going to happen.

"Stay here." He opened the door, left, and then returned to retrieve his phone. "Don't leave. I know you. Don't leave."

I rose to leave, my hand resting on the knob. *Think about your mother.* Why? The power of the process, triumph over will, I tried so hard to forget. Ryder *Stephens* closed her eyes and saw the ladder and Christmas lights and the reason for her mother's end. She heard screams: hers.

Ryder *Scott* opened them and saw papers scattered over Guerin's desk, used gym clothes tossed into a corner, coffee mugs, stained and unwashed stacked on shelves. She saw a framed picture of Guerin and Jack arm in arm.

In one body, I lived two lives, and single-handedly, I was to blame for the demise of both. Six months ago, Ryder Stephens sat on a couch and lied to a woman who was going to die. Seven months ago, a woman died, and Ryder Scott has yet to tell anyone what really happened.

The knob spun under my hand. The door opened, and before me stood a man as disheveled as he was composed, missed as he was loathed. I ran into his arms. "Dad."

"Ryder, I'm sorry."

"You looked for me."

"No, honey, I didn't even know you were gone. Guerin called before he went to get you in the lobby."

All hope tumbled away.

***

"It all started at the spa." He spoke slowly and without a prompt. "That Friday night was the worst night of my life."

Face down on the massage table, Sarah Scott had a seizure, and a frantic staff scrambled. An ambulance was called, a gurney took her away, and nobody thought to call her husband. Because by the time they reached the hospital, everything calmed. She spoke clearly and coherently and talked to her personal physician by phone. Monday, they would meet to discuss it in his office.

Nobody expected to see froth come from her mouth as she crashed to the ground right outside the hospital doors. She had another seizure, and then another. They called my dad.

And they never made it home. Perhaps because he was Jack Scott, or possibly because of his sudden recollection of all that had been wrong, the CT scan happened within the hour. And it was then that everybody saw the little white ovals peppering her brain. A full-body scan followed, which brought with it only one diagnosis. Somewhere in Sarah Scott's body, a cancer had started.

It didn't stop.

They found a spot in her lungs, which they biopsied, and the preliminary results tried to tell my dad the truth. But well, if he waited until Sunday, then the final results would prove them wrong. He was so convinced of their error, when he called home on Saturday, his optimism was real.

"But it was true," he told me now. The lung biopsy showed melanocytes, just like the internet said.

"No, Dad, they're wrong. Melanoma is a skin cancer, and her skin is fine. I looked at her when she was sleeping. I—"

His hand blocked my veto, but I pushed it away.

"And what about the menopause? She got better with the hormones, remember? She can't have two things happen to her at the same time. It's a mistake."

"No, Ryder, no mistake. I had reached those same conclusions."

Illogically calm, the whole time he spoke, he fidgeted, and I found myself focused on his ring. That silver band with two hands clutching a heart. It spun around and around, the heart disappearing, then appearing.

"Melanoma starts from a mole," he continued.

"She has no moles."

"Ryder, please, let me finish." It was an exasperated plea, and I wondered how many times he had told this story.

It was called an ungula melanoma, an ugly name for a mole found under the nail. They weren't irregular like a worrisome lesion, but straight and orderly, as if drawn with a marker. These moles weren't just rare, they were defiantly ambiguous to the untrained eye. Aggressive and definitive, they were the most lethal form of the disease.

"If she—"

"I'm not going there, Ryder. It was hidden from view by the nail polish."

And we both knew that even if she looked, she would have dismissed it as a bruise, said she stubbed her toe, that it takes a while for the nail to grow out. Why would Sarah Scott bother with her health, when everyone else's was so much more important?

"It happened, and we must live with it," my father ended it.

We, as it meant to include Sarah, and *live* as though she would go on despite the careless delay.

"The menopause, though," I asked.

"Yes, that confused the issue. Menopause caused a dizzying array of symptoms, which were immediately relieved by the hormones. Why would we suspect something else? But signs from the melanoma, even at the advanced stage, were minimal and often intermittent. The joint aches were caused by lesions in her bones, the headaches and confusion were from the tumors in her brain, the fatigue from cancer everywhere else."

"Dad? What happened that night she hit me, when you got into the fight in the bedroom?"

Hesitant, fidgeting again, a hanging cuticle had all his attention. He picked at it with one fingernail, but it wouldn't budge. Then, between two nails, still, he couldn't get a grip. Bringing it to his mouth, he chewed repetitively until it finally fell away.

"I never saw her that way in all of our years together." He said she hit him, multiple times, demanded that he leave, insisting that the couch wasn't far enough away. "Menopause, brain metastasis, God only knows what caused it, but it wasn't her. What Thomas saw the next morning when we were out getting Tylenol is something that we both missed. I think she had a seizure."

He took hold of my arm. "Do *not* ask him."

I flew my head back to swallow that bitter pill.

"The seizures are under control with the medication, and he won't see it again. Ryder, they can't know all this. It's too detailed, even for you."

But it wasn't; it was helping. I felt good. Good? He just confirmed that Sarah Scott had cancer racing through her body, and that helped? Jesus. The devil in one ear, the angel in the other, regaining my father's attention trumped accepting my mother's illness. Guilt rained down on my head.

"I won't tell them."

***

Oh, to have been a fly on the LeBlancs' wall.

The next morning, while in the process of deciding how to not approach my siblings, Aunt Evelyn trooped from our elevator battle-ready. But there would be no carnage, no eggshells to walk over, a friendship that dated back almost forty years did not bother with excuses. She had that over my dad.

"Evelyn, we're fine," he sighed as she circled.

And we were. Once we left Guerin's office yesterday, his catharsis stopped, and that wishful dialogue with Thomas and Lynzie I had longed for never happened. But his kiss on the brow lasted a little longer; his hugs were a bit tighter; he looked us in the eye. And that, I accepted as enough.

He cracked open the balcony window, and the September wind howled sweetly as if even Mother Nature had noticed the change. "Evelyn, what are you doing?" he asked.

"Making Get Well cards." With crayons fanned out in front of her, Evelyn picked up one at a time and examined it for character.

My coffee mug hung from my bottom lip, expecting something comical to follow. It didn't. Thomas nudged me, and tea spilled over the brim. I watched as his mouth slowly parted, working its way to form a question I wasn't allowed to answer. I took a long pull of my tea, the bitter moment pursing my lips.

Evelyn held two crayons in the air: one red, one pink.

"Red!" Lynzie ran to her aid. And together, they assembled a house with pink walls, a green roof, and a bright red door. Thomas inched to the table and rolled the dark blue crayon under his thumb.

"Nice choice, Thomas. That was your father's favorite color when he was your age."

"Dad, was it?"

"I don't remember."

"Yes, he does."

A shy smile. I hadn't seen a real one in weeks. Evelyn finished drawing a house and added a mailbox in front. When she used the crayon in Thomas' hand to write out the number twelve, a crease started at the edge of my father's eyes.

"Because he wanted to grow up to be Roger Staubach of the Dallas Cowboys." Her left hand covered my dad's. "Thomas, your father was obsessed with that man. Number twelve, all over the brown paper bags covering our books, remember?"

Her oldest friend chuckled.

"Brown paper bags, it was an art form and a canvas. And that little boy," pointing to the grown man with her crayon, "scribbled every football statistic imaginable from edge to edge." She shadowed the border between the one and the two. "But he always saved the center for that holy number twelve." A wink and then she smiled. "Thomas, he wanted to become a Navy officer."

"You did, Dad?"

"Only because his idol went to the US. Naval Academy."

My dad laughed, not a lot, but just enough.

There was no script for unexpected emotions, but sometimes the tiniest trigger steered the moment in the right direction. Who knew what ran through his mind as he added petals to Lynzie's flowers, or what would happen when he left to pick up his dying wife from the hospital? But I knew this: with his past by his side, the man I loved smiled.

Nobody should suffer alone.

But some did because as much as Evelyn brought relief to my father, nothing changed for Thomas. Throughout that entire exchange—from the moment Evelyn picked up her first crayon to the time she hugged us goodbye—Thomas lingered by my father's side waiting and wanting. His face painted with worry; the fear of decision fixed in his eyes. I knew he had too many questions perched on the edge of his lips. Why was his mother shrinking; how come dark patches circled her eyes; why in the days following chemo, did she collapse, but then never fully rebound?

Seeing our mother go through chemo was like watching an airshow. My mother was the plane, and at its controls, the cancer. Hovering high above us, that awesome bird would mesmerize us with its mystique. It was strong and resolute. But the pilot was cruel, dipping down to scare the crowd only to recover just in time. Each time he teased us by coming close; each time he rose back into the sky, opposing nature. Nobody expected the plane to crash.

Even if given free rein to tell, I wouldn't because a part of me saw that plane land safely. It had to. It was indestructible. So many times, I saw a strength in her that surprised me, which made me question what I'd been told.

Just two nights ago, she was sitting cross-legged on the kitchen floor, picking through a carton of ice cream as if she were a small child discovering the grown-up world.

I wanted to frame the moment.

"Mom?" I spoke softly. "What are you doing?"

"Picking out the chocolate chips." A spoon came at me, and at its tip lay a single, miniature, perfectly shaped chip. "It's the *best* part." She giggled, her sheepish smile shining brighter than the flickering light in her eyes.

Best. Light. Smile. This woman was here to live, to be a part of the world that she never took for granted. She chose life, wanted to celebrate, but she was not given that option.

"Take it," she said. "Put the chip in your mouth and let it play around." Her tongue rolled over her lower lip. "What do you taste?"

"Chocolate." The wrong answer, I knew. I reached for that invisible blindfold, the one she handed me when my hands traced the edge of the coffee table how many months ago. "It's complex." I brought the spoon close to my nose. "It smells nutty." Not enough. "It's smooth, no a bit grainy. It takes a while for the flavor to come. It disappears too quick."

"Promise me you'll never stop doing that." The light in her eye pleaded. "Promise."

---

* Fyodor Dostoyevsky, *The Brothers Karamazov.*

CHAPTER TWENTY-NINE

Guerin forgot to mention it: regret.

"Mom, remember my basketball game starts at three? It's at the school gymnasium, and it's all decked out for Halloween." Thomas said.

"Oh, I'm sorry, sweetheart, I need to stay away from the germs."

"Oh, okay."

But it wasn't okay, I knew, because he just stood there, staring, totally perplexed about how to respond. "Mom." He would turn away, stop, then turn back. "Mom." She didn't make it easy for him. "Never mind." Abort.

Each time I saw this lonely debate, I watched my past crawl into his future. He would regret that he didn't ask. Once he recovered from his anger, he would regret.

"Mom?" I should know because I had something to say as well.

"I love that I'm your mom now," she said as she caressed my cheek, smiling so peacefully that my courage met defeat.

With her last round of chemo, that plane skidded along the ground, and it stayed there for far too many days. It tried to hold steady, to be brave, but the man at the controls wouldn't let the plane fight against its power. And Thomas' response to it was as predictable as the weather it tried to beat. Calm one moment, furious the next, this volatile little boy was left to lick his own wounds in a desert without any shelter.

He kept his dilemma to himself, but his rage spilled over the edge, and it fought against her every whim. With all her effort to keep things normal, she didn't recognize the boy we saw. She wanted him to sing his camp song, he rebelled; to draw a knight on a horse, he stomped his foot.

"Oh, I know, Thomas, let's start a book club for you and your friends."

"That's a stupid idea, Mom!"

No, Thomas, don't say that. I silently pleaded.

"Boys don't have book clubs. That's for girls. Set up one for Ryder. You like her better anyway!"

With that last attack, the hurt ran from her eyes and into mine. This couldn't happen. I wanted him to embrace her, to stock up piles of good thoughts so that when the bad thoughts came, they couldn't compete. I wanted him to sit still while she talked about their time in California years before we were born. To hear her describe the little square house with the gate that squeaked, to see the restaurant at the end of the pier that she cried over when it burned to the ground.

When she watched YouTube clips, I wanted to know why she liked them. I craved to see her eyes widen from memories she shared with my father. She had roommates like the women in *Friends*. He had a neighbor like the guy in *Seinfeld*. These shows meant nothing to me, but everything to her because a smile would come, and a quest for more would follow, and that made her happy.

"Thomas, we could call it the BBC, like the radio station—you know, for Boys Book Club."

"Mom, I said it was a stupid idea, just like the news show. You and Dad have stupid jobs!"

As angry as he appeared on the surface, an undercurrent of confusion rushed beneath. How could it not? Because when the effects of the chemo wore off, and the plane flew back into the air, Thomas' head bobbed up and down. Confused and alone, he couldn't help but wonder if she would fall.

I couldn't watch. "Thomas, let's go for a walk."

Without a peep, he lifted his windbreaker from the hook, picked up an umbrella, and stood rod-straight in the elevator waiting.

His reaction caught me by surprise and left me no time to prepare my lines. Standing in the elevator beside him, I rehearsed, stacking a mental penny with each attempt to clear my conscience. But proficiency never came. Because just as with practicing the violin, I knocked the pile away each time I did something wrong or said something hurtful. Each time I made it worse.

"Where are we going?" He asked.

"Central Park."

"Why?"

Why. Because it was far away, far enough that after I told him, he could have time to vent. Far enough that if he wanted to cry, he could, and nobody would know. Far enough that maybe I would know what to do.

The leaves had started to change, not a lot, but some. I picked up the prettiest one and brought it close to my nose. Shaped like a maple leaf, maybe it smelled the same.

"You look like Mom when you do that."

The stem had three colors, and each of them blended over the other. I twirled it in my fingers, faster and faster until I lost control and it flew from my hand. Running after it, I competed with the autumn wind, and then with Thomas as he gave a little smirk and took off in a sprint to catch it. Tackling him from behind, we tumbled around each other until the leaf landed back in my hand.

"We should press this in a book," I said.

"Why? It's broken."

"Broken, yes, but still beautiful. Thomas, I want to—"

"Mom is really sick." Lying on his back, with his hands nestled under his head, he effortlessly stacked that first penny for me. "That medicine she's taking is making her worse." Two pennies. "I get really scared when she leaves for the hospital because I know what she'll look like when she comes home." Three. "I can't ask her. Dad scares me. Evelyn always changes the topic. Lynzie, I can't talk to her." Four. Five. Six. Seven.

I could do the rest. "She has cancer."

"That means she's dying, right?"

Had he already worked through his own stages? "Thomas?" He lay still, staring into the sky. "Do you remember when Lynzie asked me about how my mother was sad?" No answer. "I yelled and said I wanted that topic dead and buried. I wanted my past to go away so I wouldn't hurt anymore."

"You're hurting?"

Yes. All this with Sarah had reopened wounds too freshly healed. What gave my mother the right to die when others had no choice and wanted so much to live?

He moved closer, tucking himself under my arm. "Your heart is racing so fast, Ryder." He leaned over me. "It's going to be okay."

How can this small boy handle this so well? "I regret so much, Thomas. I don't want that for you." Every drop that left my eye was another memory left unresolved. "My mother never told me she was sad."

"Maybe she didn't know how. Just like my mother doesn't know how to tell me she has cancer." He lay once more on his back, trying to make sense of the clouds streaming fast above. "I didn't understand what was happening," he admitted.

His sniffles picked up speed until his mouth had to shoulder the load. Broken breaths scattering in my ear, and I rushed to protect him. Pulling him close, I used the stem of the leaf to stop a tear, but it only split in two. "I'm sorry, Thomas, I tried." A tiny arm crossed over his swollen eyes, and a burning heat rose in my chest. My extra three years did nothing to help. All my experience and knowledge only layered on top of itself like bricks in a wall. "I failed you. I'm so sorry."

"No." His head shook. "Thank you for talking to me, Ryder." Staggered gasps rose from his chest. "I'm really glad you're my sister."

Concretely, he absorbed this conversation, processing it far better than me, much more efficiently than Jack. He wiped his last tear away and no more came. I envied him for not being there yet, for climbing over that wall, and waiting for what the next second would bring. I wanted to be him, or maybe her, to regress and sit on the kitchen floor, cross-legged. I wanted to pick chocolate chips out of coffee-flavored ice cream.

"Ryder, do you miss your mother?"

"Sometimes. Mostly, I feel guilty."

The early evening air brought with it a chill. He sheltered again under my arm, and the wind blew around us, billowing our jackets. That beautiful leaf I had wanted to press in a book took off again. We let it go.

"Should we go home, Ryder?"

"No, not yet."

Immature minds tackling complex issues. "Ryder? Don't tell Mom that you only sometimes miss your mother."

Perhaps he understood after all.

CHAPTER THIRTY

Gutsy people make eye contact; genuine people connect through the heart.

Never give yourself to somebody unless you are sure they are willing to give everything back to you in return. A running appeal, Sarah repeated this, and that, and everything that would have stayed behind a shield if not for the evils of time.

"Look at this." Every day something new: boxes unearthed from dust-filled closets, yellowed letters marked with dates which preceded our birth by decades, books margined with notes in her familiar slanted script. Yesterday, she showed us a picture frame her best friend gave her after she published her first article; today, a locket.

"Look, kids, it's real silver, see how the edges are worn?"

I ran my finger over the side. It was rough and ruined as if it has been dragged mercilessly across the pavement.

Its latch was a simple snap, one that a toddler could open. She struggled. It shook in her hands. Her thin skin peeled away. There was blood. Thomas' glance worried me more, so I freed it from her hands, gently and smoothly as to not further the damage already done by this relentless foe.

"My fingers don't work very well anymore. Thank you, Ryder."

I swallowed.

Inside the locket, a tiny white stone with blue flakes burrowed itself beneath the rim; nothing made it special. This was a pebble, just the same as all the others scattered over every inch of the playground. "He gave it to me," she said.

"Who, Dad?"

"I was just a girl, your age, Ryder." Outside, the lights were on, but inside she had disappeared yet again.

"Mom?"

"Promise me, kids, that you will never take something like this for granted."

Beyond our balcony, I could make out the tiny flakes of snow, visible one moment, gone the next, just like my mother.

"Ryder."

"Yes, Mom?"

"A boy gave me this in the seventh grade, just like you are in now."

"I'm in the eighth grade now, Mom."

"Oh yes, of course, you are. Do you like your new school?"

Would she know if I didn't respond?

Gradual then sudden, like a windstorm entering a tunnel. Yesterday, she sat at this table with five of her closest friends, understanding the need for honesty, owning up to the last CT scan. She admitted that Lynzie must be told. Today, she wandered back in time, finding comfort in a seventh-grade crush instead of her eighth-grade daughter.

"Did you see what I put on your Pinterest page, Lynzie?"

Thomas and I swapped looks of concern, unsure if or how to explain. "Lynzie doesn't have a Pinterest account, only Ryder and I do," Thomas replied.

And why bother with it? For weeks nothing landed on our pages. Not from her, not from our dad, and we knew because we looked. Thomas clicked on his all the time. For him, if she had the strength to link something to his board, she had the power to go on. But when the posts stopped, so did his battle. More and more, he retreated to the recesses of his mind and into the corners of this house. Nobody could pull him from his anger.

Except, of course, the source. "Did you put something in my Pinterest account, Mom?" Spinning to capture any device in sight, Thomas found none. How this house had changed in the last four months since that diagnosis arrived.

"Here, Thomas!" Lynzie ran from the back room and handed him our mother's iPad.

Nobody knew what to do with little Lynzie.

Yesterday, Mom's book club offered advice only because nobody else would. "Don't tell her you may fall asleep," one of them said.

Up until that point, I savored my mother's friends. They infused life into the house, and into her. Gathering around the table to talk politics and travel and books credited existence. This did not.

"Lynzie will take it literally and think she can wake you with a shake."

Mindlessly, her friends dissected Lynzie's possible responses as if it were a puzzle instead of a child, and didactically my mother followed suit.

"Jack and I left a dollar under her pillow last night for the tooth fairy. Monsters still lurk in her closet. She's not ready." Sarah's voice didn't shake.

But my mind trembled. Escaping into the first room I saw, knowing that words not heard were outcomes not seen, I burrowed down then ran headfirst into my dad.

"Shhh," he whispered, "come with me." Tugging me aside, he wanted to eavesdrop, needed to absorb the wisdom of her friends. "Shhh." Because in the end, Lynzie would ask him, and only him. "Why, Daddy?" He pulled me halfway up the stairs, out of view, and lowered me onto a step. He slid down from the one above, cushioning me between his knees. "Shhh," he repeated.

"Sarah, does Thomas know?" asked a voice I knew only as Beth.

"Ryder told him."

I went rigid.

"It's okay," he whispered. Maybe he wished I hadn't stopped there.

"They're not giving me much longer."

My father squeezed me tight. So tight that the effect lingered into today, to when I watched my mother's bleeding fingertip move from the locket to the iPad. Yesterday, my father gave me strength, but today he wasn't here. There would be no hug to distract me from the sight of the woman I saw deteriorating before my eyes.

And I needed it because when she typed the wrong password into the iPad over and over and over again. And when I told her to stop, reminding her of the penalty for failing ten times, she laughed. "Oh, Ryder. Who told you that?"

I wanted to cry.

Thomas didn't. Far too consumed with viewing the post that would make everything better, Thomas went searching. "Here, Mom, I found my iPad." Effortlessly and with such contrast to his mother's labors, Thomas logged on and reached his destination faster than my mother could process the change. His brow grew slack and released the worried lines forever etched into his face. "Mom, I love it!"

Thomas had learned how to dam regret.

Her three posts: a book title, a hairstyle, and a jacket were nothing noteworthy and void of any meaning, but they were something, and something was everything. Relevance be gone, Sarah Scott had reached out, genuinely, and from the heart.

The posts that followed represented an internal monologue she was too fatigued to speak. Every day, there was more, burning behind my lids each time I drifted or slept or blinked. Random thoughts, random images: guitars, a puppy, the sunset, a wave cresting over a white sand beach, a family, Kramer.

From my dad—nothing. Just vacant eyes losing connections as each day passed. That leather chair, the one he used to read in, laugh in, to be a part of the family in, stayed empty. He couldn't fill it because he was too busy pacing. Or staring. Or opening the balcony, walking out, looking at nothing, turning, and walking back in.

That plane circled overhead. Its engine roared as it grew closer and louder, and upsetting and alarming. Some days, I swear I could feel a gush of air sweep across my face. It was going to crash. I knew. Because the Pinterest posts stopped, and the parade began. Evelyn and Guerin, Sarah's mother and father, uncles and cousins, brothers, friends, everyone. Their words blended over their hugs and their silence masked their tears. The moments twisted time back on itself, and the infinity of it drove me mad.

The guilt of it did far worse. I cried. Not for her, but for the images, real experiences overpowering her digital imprint. Never having left, I saw a chestnut casket, with billowed silk sheets, and brass handles hanging from its sides. I saw hands folded peacefully over a white dress. Red lipstick. I cried. Out on the balcony, in my room, inside the fishbowl, but they always found me.

"Sarah knows you're hurting, and she needs for you to be strong."

"I know. I understand." I lied. But I didn't understand because life was cruel, because I would have to do this twice, because it had only been *ten* months since I met Sarah. "I'll be strong," I said it out loud for them, for Thomas, for Lynzie, for the man who brought me here, who gave me a second chance, who didn't know how awful it was going to be.

"Ryder." My father's hand on my shoulder felt comforting. Like when he met me for the first time on those library steps. Nothing bad would happen as long as I had his touch. "Ryder, your mother would like to speak with you."

It scared me to look at her. Not because of the grey veins snaking beneath her translucent skin, or because she lay in that bed and couldn't get up, not because of her. But because of me and my mother, Samantha Stephens.

"Ryder, it'll be okay," my father reassured.

"I have a cough." I couldn't separate it all. "I'm sick." I couldn't tell him why. "The germs, they're bad for her." He needed to understand. "I don't want to make her die."

"Ryder, you are not going to make her die."

Hearing those words, I could see that plane rise higher into the sky. I could hear the noise of the engine fall away. It gave me strength. I could do what he asked.

"Ryder, you need to go in and say goodbye."

The pressure lessened on my shoulder, his hand drifting away. I shook my head. How could he begin with 'not' and 'die' but end with 'goodbye?' He nudged me forward then backed away, blending into the blur of people representing Sarah's past, a past I only briefly knew. I shook my head harder still. I was to be a part of her future, and futures didn't start with goodbye.

I walked into her room dazed, scared that nobody followed. Gutless to meet her eye, I watched her lips move honestly, naturally, openly. "Only when you're ready," she said. It was distorted by her quivering voice, blurred by my dry eyes, which should have had tears. More words came. I would not remember.

I could hear nothing else.

***

That night, I dreamed. There was background music by Vivaldi, the same piece I played for my solo. Fragmented and surreal, I saw the Lincoln Memorial, and a young Evelyn hanging a sign around his neck. I saw my dad with grey hair, in a blue suit, a bare foot on the statue's pedestal. Miles away on the Capital Mall, his wife lay on the grass, her head resting on a piece of ancient wood. Sitting vigil, she watched my father, protecting him. He turned: smiled. He loved this woman for everything she made him become.

"She's gone."

It blended into my dream, but it was the truth. I knew that from the crack in his voice, from the weight of his hand. It sank into me. I cried hard and long for the unfairness of it all. My mind was a mishmash of seasons, a dreamlike state where images didn't end but blurred forward merging into a pointless sequence.

I fell asleep.

I woke to the sight of a single cookie resting on a plate teetering off my nightstand. My dad was gone. The chocolate chips reminded me of my mother. The house was silent. Out in the living room, another plate of cookies was missing only a few. My family was entwined on the couch. The three of them alone. No other soul stood guard.

The scene cleared. That couch was where this all started. I spun. The kitchen was where she told me about her cousin. A satellite view, I hovered over this space, and details crystallized. The table that I ran my hands over, the pizza, me playing my violin in the fishbowl. I heard the music I played for my parents before they were my parents. I saw the balcony and the lights and felt my mother's knee against mine. I went back ten months.

These three people nestled together on the couch, their memories spanned years, decades, a lifetime.

So unfair.

PART FOUR

CHAPTER THIRTY-ONE

The oboe cried.

First slow, with a modest crescendo, building into an accentuating trill. His entire body turned towards the music, his mouth gaping, those burdened eyes never breaking away from the show. Everything about it hijacked his being. No longer able to withdraw into painful reflections, the beauty of the music substituted awe for grief.

If only for a moment. The oboe faded, and those green-grey eyes darted from the orchestra to me to the conductor, searching for where his solace went. But suddenly it returned, climbing upward in scale, increasing in speed until, at its peak, it slid sideways into the long piercing note of Gershwin's *Rhapsody in Blue*.

The symphony had called him back. Resurging, defending, dominating, the oboe harnessed his pain and unmasked his sorrow. It invited him to stay and to be a part of the process.

I lingered on him, watching from the stage as he sat midway up the theater. His shoulders relaxed; his presence opened for the first time since the funeral three weeks ago. From heart, I played my part, splitting my attention between the conductor and this man, a different man, a man attempting to return. My strokes intensified to let the music heal, to swallow him and replace the pain that broke this once self-assured man.

A young boy's fingers danced over the piano keys in an acute and delicate bravado, whisking the moment into a fantasy where music nurtured resilience. This changed man leaned, falling into the chair in front of him, and it seemed that if he succeeded and dissolved into the music, it would make him whole.

Lynzie touched his elbow, passing her smile to him. I closed my eyes to etch it into my world. If I opened them, I might see him once again sullen, unable, or unwilling to respond.

Backstage, I waited, but he didn't show; nobody did. I walked out into the hall, into a rambling crowd abuzz with energy. There they were, a stable nucleus in this veil of current. An illusion. They were not stable. My family was barely surviving.

I approached with measured steps, unsure of what level of emotion to show.

"Absolutely fantastic." My father's hands clapped together in a nostalgic approval. His liberated eyes lit up the smile that filled his whiskered face. "Thank you, Ryder," he said comfortably, and with a casual effort of somebody unburdened by grief.

"Daddy?"

Yes Lynzie, this was your Daddy, the one you used to know. The same man, not the different man, the man who just returned.

"It was good, wasn't it? I want to play in the symphony. Maybe the cello, or the tuba, or that big drum. Maybe we could ask Santa."

Thomas and I watched him intently, waiting for his hand to drop away from Lynzie's, for his eyes to glaze over or wander off. The mention of Christmas would make this so.

"I think those may be too big for the chimney, sweetheart, and two weeks isn't enough time to build a bigger one. Think of the poor reindeer, lugging a tuba." The laugh that left his lips brought with it a wave of memories. Of him being alive, joking with Sarah, teasing her. "Let's be kind to Santa, Lynzie, okay? And ask for something a bit smaller, and maybe a little less noisy."

I tried to catch Thomas' eye to see what he thought of this exchange, but he was too busy bouncing his foot off a chair. That was the new Thomas: always busy. Busy hiding under sketches and drawings, holding himself captive to alternate worlds. How could I fault him when I did the same, filling the emptiness left by death with a pain far worse than loss. I ran, willfully struggled. I turned my back on the Golden Gate bridge only to open my eyes to the Statue of Liberty. Who was I to judge?

"Can we go now?" Thomas' nostrils flared.

This little boy had turned hostile. Tiny things would tip him over the edge. A compliment could incite rage, a habit even. Last week when Lynzie added ketchup to the shopping list, he snatched the pen out of her hand, and using it as a weapon, tore the paper as he scratched the words away. Ketchup was wrong because salt added flavor. His dad teased him about this because they used to have fun. His mother laughed because she used to be alive. He never wanted to see ketchup again.

At every turn, this battered boy seethed. "I want to go! Now!"

"Okay, son," said his father. No words of comfort followed, no hug or reassurance, only a hand that cupped the base of his son's neck.

I scoffed. Right here in this auditorium, almost eleven months ago, a man named Jack, a stranger I barely knew, did the same to me. He placed his hand behind my head and asked me to trust. But it wasn't him who made it all okay. It was his wife. The mother who always stepped in to take control.

I squeezed my eyes tight to force her image away, but they popped open fast when my father's other hand dropped onto my shoulder.

"It seems like you've grown a foot in a year." Thomas shook free, and our father let him go. "I tell you what, Lynzie, on the way home, I'll swing by the mall, and you can talk to Santa."

Shocked, he went on, talking about decorations and lights, of carols and sleds. Explaining how when she asked Santa for her presents, she should speak loudly so—he bent to whisper in my ear. So, I could hear.

That other shoe dropped. He wouldn't come to the mall, refused to see the lights. I was to report back to him. Maybe it would trigger too much, force him to run and hide, to bury the moment faster than it had time to surface.

Maybe that was why I was doing okay. Because for me, this Christmas was a first: the cast had changed, snow had fallen, the tree was real. Seattle, with its rain-soaked streets, could never be New York.

But for him, this Christmas was just like the last: the same house, same decorations, the same mall. Same, same, but altogether different. Maybe that was why today he shed a little bit of his burden; why he engaged with us and held Lynzie's hand. Because my holiday concert was a first and there was nothing to compare. It was the alternate reality he needed to stop the pain.

Jack Scott had veered away from us even before Sarah died. He spiraled downward into an isolated existence, and nobody could pull him from his hole. But now, because of this concert, because of Santa and the mall, I saw the writing on the wall: keep the comparisons away.

Do that, and he would heal. And if he would heal, we would heal. Not even a second passed before I understood what needed to be done: I had to find that box. Because just like the library steps would always remind me of Samantha Stephens, that empty box would forever remind him of his wife.

Noooo! Just thinking about it, I heard Sarah's playful reprimand. *Noooo. You can't use that box.* It echoed in my head as clearly as if it just occurred. Our father would hear it too if he found it first. He would crush that box against his chest, willing away the flashbacks that refused to yield.

I knew, I'd been there.

He would remember the first Christmas present he ever gave her, the one that came wrapped in that box. Then he would cover his face thinking that would help. It wouldn't because every year that box alternated from his hands to hers, hers to his.

Lynzie and I had used it to pack cookies for a bake sale at school.

"Noooo, not that box," our father had mimicked his wife as he yanked it from our grip, flying it high over our heads until it hid behind his back. "This year your mother has to fill it for me."

Never could I allow Jack Scott to find that box, noooo.

That same man squeezed my neck tighter as if he heard my thoughts. "Whatever Lynzie asks Santa for, put it on the Pinterest board, okay?" My hair stood on end faster than Thomas' eyes bulged.

What? This unraveled all that I just worked through.

Maybe it was me that would never heal.

***

In the days that followed, as much as I wanted to obey, to do as he asked and post Lynzie's list on Pinterest, I couldn't.

Pinterest was a sacred site, our mother's site, the ultimate trigger. Untouched by him since months before she died, nothing in his expression the other day registered the painful association the rest of us connected with that sight.

How could he not appreciate how much it would set him back. Or that he would hear her voice when he saw those photos, that each one would correspond to a detailed conversation, to a laugh, a *promise.*

Two months before her death, she pinned twenty-eight images. Three weeks later, in a painful hoax that trapped our optimism, that number surged to thirty-nine, stopping only when the illness won. Lemon poppy seed cake, the last of her posts. She wanted to try it because it used almond flour as a base. I made it for her, and it tasted great. I haven't ordered a poppy seed muffin since.

I opened my new MacBook and clicked on the App, the three boards immediately popping into view. I circled my mouse around her board, the curser transitioning from arrow to hand, hand to arrow. Faster and faster I swirled, blurring the images trapped on her board. I didn't want to slow down, wasn't ready to see the photos sprinkle over the screen.

I cast the MacBook aside and dumped the basket of laundry on the table.

"Ryder, what did Lynzie ask Santa for? Did you buy it?"

My father asked this from his leather chair, a place he rarely left. Did he forget about asking me to pin it? Maybe his lifted mood the other day had nothing to do with comparison. Maybe it was just another false front.

I glanced back to the Pinterest page, to the thumbnail images on her leader board. Wait. I bent closer to the screen to get a better view. How did I miss that? It changed. When? Too busy circling my mouse, I hadn't noticed she'd added another photo. A fortieth. Lemon poppy seed cake wasn't the last of her posts. There was another.

I rolled my eyes up to my father, expecting his stare to force me into a discussion. But he drifted away again, mindlessly flipping through pages in his book.

"Dad?"

He stopped reading, marked his place with his finger, closed it, and looked to the balcony, to the piles of snow mounded by the wind.

"Maybe it's a good idea for Santa to bring Lynzie an instrument," I offered.

The wind bounced off the doors, shaking them, responding to

my question with a clanking and then a calm. Returning to his book, his finger tapped twice, and then slid slowly down the margin. A page turned, and then another, too fast to be honest. I waited until a fifth went by.

"Dad? What instrument would you like to give her?"

Arching his back, hope peaked as I imagined him crossing the room to sit with me at the table, to be by my side so we could work through this problem together.

"Use this," he said, and from his wallet came a Gold MasterCard. It flew before crashing at my feet. Another page flipped.

"Dad, no, I have school and my grades." They had fallen considerably. Never would I be admitted to LaGuardia School of the Arts if my performance during eighth grade had any bearing. "Ms. Ackermann said you could call her." An email had been sent, but my teacher needn't have warned me; I was the one who provided my father's address.

His legs uncrossed, and I waited, yearning for the old Jack to appear. He leaned, shifting his weight forward as if that howling wind had lifted his sails. "You'll be fine. Tell her to find you a tutor." The lanyard snapped; the sails collapsed, and his finger ran down another unread page.

Find you a tutor?! Tell a woman I barely knew, and a woman he'd never met, to be my mother. Denial had passed, as did the anger; bargaining was failing, and now, with his indifference, my patience was a weathered cord.

"Dad!" I stopped folding the laundry and threw Thomas' basketball shirt at him. Missing, it flew over the chair and landed on the cat. My voice shook; the cat screeched; we finally had his attention. "You need to go back to work!"

Leaning over the chair's edge to reach the collar, he flicked it with his finger until, after too much time, he captured it. He traced his thumb over the number twelve, and an illogical jealousy surfaced.

"He has a game this afternoon!" My voice was insolent. "You know that, don't you?"

He reversed the shirt, rightly flipping it outside out and, choosing a calming tone to conflict with mine, he adjusted his apathy just enough to pass himself off as a father. "Lower your voice, Ryder. I'm right here in front of you."

"No, you're not, Dad, you're off in your own world. You're not hearing a single thing I'm saying."

The minutes elapsed having reached the time limit he allowed for our debate, the book cover slipped into the page where the corner was already bent. He stroked the cat. "What time is the game?"

"The cat doesn't know, Dad. Why won't you look at me?" Scared of the answer he might be cruel enough to give, I sucked my lip between my teeth. Harder, I chewed, increasing the pain.

The reading glasses came off. His volume increased. "What do you *want* from me, Ryder?"

"Nothing." I ran my tongue over the welt. Because nothing was what you say to someone when you don't expect anything in return. I let my toe play with the edge of the carpet, a tangible reminder of a time long passed.

He scooched farther back into his chair. "Listen, Ryder," he scolded, pointing his glasses in my direction.

I waited, anxiously counting on a lecture. One second passed, two, a rush of air passed between his lips. He hugged the cat: not me. "I'm not like you. Look at what you're doing right now."

Having folded a shirt over and over, reducing it to a size fit for a napkin holder, a perfect square rested compactly in my hand.

"It's your nature. And, you're stewing, no worrying, about what I meant by that." His chuckle hurt. "You know, the first time I saw you on those library steps, you ran down them, turned around, and then ran back up. Four or five times, two steps down, three steps up. You moved like a kid who had something on her mind."

"I did?"

"Yes, you did. When you started speaking to yourself, I found a crack and let myself in. Honey, I get it. You're worried about me, about Thomas; you're worried about the laundry. We will all be fine. You need to stop worrying. Move if you must, if that helps you heal, but keep it in mind that other people have different ways."

He mouthed those familiar words, "stop worrying," and suddenly, I saw my father in a different space. At a time when I watched the traffic pass as we sat idle at the curb. When I clenched the doorframe, fretting over a blond, blue-eyed bully. I went back to a time where his words healed my many wounds. "Not going back to work then?"

"Not going back to work. Besides, who would supervise you doing the laundry?" He turned the basketball shirt inside out, crumpled it, and tossed it back into the basket. "Need to keep you busy so you'll survive."

And need to keep him still so he would too? "Are you going to call my teacher?"

"Ryder, I have no doubt you are capable of doing well in school, and I don't need a stranger to tell me otherwise. Whatever this woman said wouldn't change what you need to do: focus." Done with this virtuous yet ineffective burst of parenting, his book once more became his shield.

Cut off, I absorbed the title: *Plainsong*, a word so infused with independence and clarity, it made no sense to have a presence in this room.

Phit, phit, phit, the turning pages competed with the clanking wind. A chunk of ice broke away in a thundering crash. It redirected my focus. Overtaking the balcony, the snow was inches from the icicles hanging from the rail.

"It must be warming up outside," he said.

How would he know? We hadn't left the house in days. I shoved the laundry to the center of the table and studied him and his book and its senseless title. Lynzie's t-shirt laid open atop the pile: a magic carpet holding a genie, who held a monkey, who held a lamp. I threw a penny down a well and made a wish. The wind slammed harder, helping me to shake this room. It didn't come true. I made another.

I forced myself into his world, grabbing my MacBook, and flipping through commands. iBooks. Search. *Plainsong*. Buy. I scrolled along the bottom bar, and not wanting to upset the ghost flying above, I stopped midway before reaching the end. I read about two young boys Thomas' age baking cookies with an old lady who could not rise from a chair without their help. I scrubbed the page bar further and found two old men shopping for a baby crib. Backward, a pregnant teenager begged a middle-aged woman to help her talk to the two old men who would later be looking for a crib.

The genie spoke. A middle-aged woman could tell me what to do.

***

Evelyn LeBlanc's voice was strong and resilient—decisive actually, even though I had yet to ask a question. "Ryder, why are you whispering?"

"Because I don't want my dad to know I'm calling you." I cracked the door to the bathroom to peek at my dad before an earned catharsis released. Choosing words over breaths, near the end of my purge, I felt a bit lightheaded and gasped for air, crumbling against the wall to land between the toilet paper roll and the fake flowered plant.

"Alright, got it," Evelyn interrupted.

God save me from Evelyn and her hard-nosed decisiveness.

"For Christmas dinner, we'll just show up. What could go wrong?"

I bolted upright, bringing with me the sole flower in the make-believe plant. What could go wrong? In her make-believe world, nothing. In my reality—everything. I had seen Guerin's office, stepped over the gym clothes thrown in a towering clump. Shook my head at the newspapers everywhere, the books piled high enough to double for a maze. The ordered and anal life of the family Scott versus the chaos and spontaneity of the LeBlancs'. No. These two worlds should not collide unannounced.

"Nonsense."

How was she this comfortable with distorting reality?

"I know your father. Holding a grudge is something he only does for twenty-four hours max. I can wait it out." She hung up before I had time to decide if I knew what that meant.

The bathroom door flew open. "Why are you crouched on the toilet?"

How odd it must have seemed to my dad to see me with my iPhone in one hand and a plastic flower in the other. I pulled my legs tighter against my chest. "Reading."

"Fine, I have to use this room for its intended purpose. Out you go." No comment on the title, which I had forced in front of his face.

Alone in the living room, I flopped into his leather chair and picked up his paperback. I read about a baffled doctor, who just received an entire steer as a thank you for delivering the teenager's baby.

I called Evelyn back. "Um, I don't think that's a good idea, you all coming over for Christmas without talking to my father first. He made it really clear he wanted to spend it just with us."

"Ryder, please, we spent this one Christmas in Austria. Let's see, it must have been just under twenty years ago now."

This chair smelled fresh, like musk and earth. Across the room, I squinted to get a better look at the pictures on the shelf. Every child had a frame, the family together filled another. I wandered my eyes up. Two wooden saddles flooded my mind with dialogues from the past.

"…White Alba truffles. Jack literally moaned about flying off to Europe, staying in a swank hotel, and gorging on Beef Wellington."

"Um, sorry, what?" I had no idea what she was talking about. Lesson learned about conversations with Evelyn, don't let your mind wander for a second, even if it was for something important.

"Why would he do something adventurous like that if he could just sit on the couch and watch football while the women got dinner ready?" She meant leather chair. "But after all that, surprise, surprise, he talks about that trip all the time."

Back in the game, I got the gist. Jack Scott did something with Sarah Scott, and he would want to talk about it over and over again. "He won't anymore."

"He will. Trust me."

"He won't. Trust me."

The phone shifted, probably to the other ear, giving her ample time to gear up for a lecture about age and years and wisdom and experience. "Ryder, by this time next year, he'll be talking about eating Beef Wellington in Vienna."

Doubt it. "Evelyn? What was I doing this time last year?"

"I don't know."

"That's right, and you won't because I don't want to talk about it."

Another long breath came. "Okay, listen, everything happens for a reason, and your presence in Jack's life is well-timed. Ryder, if you want to talk—"

"Yeah."

"Okay, well, we're doing Christmas, and I'll take care of everything. All I ask of you is to keep it from Jack. Trust me. I know you do."

I didn't, but that was irrelevant. Age built a wall between reality and emotion. Wanting to sympathize and having a reason to empathize were not two sides of the same coin, but the older people got, the more they thought they had the right to claim insight. I hung up.

My father exited the bathroom and tugged the book from my grip. Shooing me from the chair, I noticed the clock hanging from the building across the street. 3:28. I had thirty-two minutes to force-feed Lynzie and Thomas a snack before heading out for his game.

I confirmed the time by verifying it with Apple, only to be ambushed by the date. Saturday, 17 December. I covered my mouth when I should have shielded my eyes because the memory rushed.

"Dad!"

Startled, he dropped his book.

"We have to leave for Thomas' game in thirty-one minutes." My chest tightened; my palms went clammy. I wiped them against my shirt and felt my heart beating hard to escape.

"Why are you shouting?"

Because three hundred and sixty-five days ago today, two-thirds of my family joked in a taxi on the way to the airport. Because we had packed two smoked salmons in our luggage to surprise my dad. Because we tore them out as soon as we got to the curb and held them like waiters at a ball and waited for fifteen minutes, thirty, for an hour. I shouted because I watched my mom frantically call and text and panic and pace.

My father never showed.

"He's okay," my mom said, her face awash with pain and peace. "Just got held up in Las Vegas. They comped him a room at the Bellagio." She pretended it was okay, that she understood. "Let's cook the salmon ourselves and christen our new life together."

I didn't want to. I went to check out the park.

"Ryder!" I jumped. Thomas had barged into the room. "I need to eat before my game!"

I rushed to the kitchen to escape this angry boy, my mother's face, to erase the guilt. The package of instant noodles I pulled from the cupboard took the brunt of my wrath. Pounding hard, the bag exploded with a pop, sending bits of dry noodles in every direction.

"Hey, take it easy there, kid." My father's reading glasses were off now, and I waited for nothing to follow.

"Where's my shoes? Ryder, where did you put my shoes?"

"Where *are* my shoes, and I didn't put them anywhere, Thomas. Look for yourself."

Our father turned another page. Any novice knew the trick: put your headphones on, bury yourself in a book, and nobody will ask you for directions, the time, or how to control your son.

At 4:30 p.m., four people went to a basketball game where three people watched, the son threw a punch that got him ejected from the game, and the father said nothing.

***

"I have three children to raise!" My father's tone cut.

Christmas dinner had arrived, and the outcome was everything but a mystery. No sooner did we pull out the chairs and tuck in our napkins did tempers flare beyond even my ominous expectations.

"How can I go back to work with the hours: the stress? My priorities are my children. They need me to be present in their lives!" Our father's glare accused, tunneling his anger towards Evelyn. The subsequent pause felt right. Let him vent.

"It may come as a surprise." Still, Evelyn couldn't hold back the sermon. "But many successful, caring, and capable people in this world were raised by single working parents. May I remind you that *you* were raised by a single working parent?"

A fork crashed onto the plate. "I do not need *you* lecturing me about how to raise *my* kids. My show begins at five, Evelyn, begins! You're married to a carbon copy of me. Do I need to tell you what time I'll be home? No, I don't. It's after the dishes are loaded into the dishwasher, just before the bedtime stories are read. How will my children eat?" His clipped and hostile words sent specks of saliva flying across the table.

Shaking then breaking, his voice escalated. "What? Ryder? You're suggesting I let a thirteen-year-old child raise my children."

"I'm fourteen."

"I did not say that," Evelyn said calmly.

A deep sigh, and then it got worse. "No!" With teeth clenched, his eyes wandered across the table to where Guerin sat in Sarah's seat. Moisture filled his eyes. "Well." He laid the fork down with such grace a fool might think the scene a hoax. "As you can see, I'm not ready to be back in front of a camera." He clung to his knees, while the rest of us held our breath. He marched down the hall.

"His anger will pass," Guerin said. "It's part of the process, a necessary part. He'll be back."

"How wrong would I be if I suggested he hire a nanny instead of that part-time maid?" Instead of helping to cut the cord, Evelyn twisted the tension more.

"A lot. Let it be, Evelyn," Guerin said. "A nanny is part of the final plan but let him get there first."

"No, Nanny!" I broke in. "No third mom!" Jack's love life was over. I saw *The Sound of Music*.

"My family will not be raised by a nanny," said our father as he settled back into his seat. God bless him. Despite all that had been thrown at him since the LeBlancs burst through our doors, my father knew when he had gone too far.

"The scent of pine." Guerin segued rapidly, and everyone's face scrunched to decipher the outburst. "Some people like it; some people don't. And pinecones that scatter the dining room table for artistic effect would seem as harmless as a fly."

With a wink and a smile, Evelyn stashed her ax and granted her husband permission to go on.

"Out of nowhere, those pinecones were chucked off the table by Evelyn's father. And amused only by their cat—"

"Cuddles," Evelyn added.

"Yes, little Cuddles, grateful for the gift, she batted each one across the living room like a hockey puck sent down from heaven." The soft lullaby of Guerin's voice dropped our shoulders, and our spines curved against the cradle of our seats. "The rest of us just took it in and waited for Evelyn's father to calm. But the more drinks he downed, the more Christmas spirit he lost, and his hangover the next day fueled the bulk of the fallout."

Guerin's diversion in full gear, Thomas perched his elbows on the table, cradling his fist against his chin. Lynzie's mouth hung.

"That was when he barged into the living room to announce that Christmas was officially over. Then, with as much accuracy as a two-year-old on a golf course, he kicked at the fallen pinecones scattered around the tree. We all left him to it. Returning, of course, only when we smelled the smoke."

"We did get new drapes out of the ordeal," Evelyn laughed.

"And a new sofa, new armchair, even a better coffee table."

Guerin raised a finger with each item acquired.

"The TV was spared."

Evelyn's father expedited the removal of the holiday décor by feeding the Christmas tree into the fireplace from tip to trunk. And surprising nobody with a fifth-grade education or above, within a half a foot, the under-watered needles burst into flames and took half the living room with it.

"That didn't really happen," I blurted.

"It did. The man was a genius. One time—" he paused to build a suspense that made Evelyn and her ax forever disappear. "He was so tired of seeing the oil light on in the car, he put a piece of duct tape over it so he wouldn't have to deal with the distraction."

"No way!"

"Yes way, and you know that was a pretty good Oldsmobile before the engine melted away." Guerin's hands detonated above his plate.

Evelyn slapped her husband on the shoulder, consummating a shift that we all had made. All, that was, except the one that couldn't. Throughout that entire exchange, our father pushed a pea into a mound of potatoes, burying it once with a spoon, then twice. Only once did he lift his head to Guerin and the chair in which he sat. A tortured soul wishing to be left in his hole, it didn't matter how many times Guerin threw the rope, our dad tossed it back.

When dinner finished, Evelyn bundled into her jacket, but her husband retreated to my father's side. "One last drink in the man cave, shall we?"

The answer was yes, and we all took a moment to pray. Because in Guerin's hand, he held a bag, and in that bag, there was a box.

A very old and very special red and gold striped box.

They stayed in that office for a long, long time.

CHAPTER THIRTY-TWO

Strange, isn't it? Each man's life touches so many other lives. When he isn't around, he leaves an awful hole, doesn't he?

Some old man in a black and white film spoke those words, and my dad, slipping between Thomas and myself, watched intently.

"You know this movie, Dad? What's it about?"

"It's a classic, son." Our father muted the sound. "See, that's Jimmy Stewart. He plays a man named George Bailey." He trickled his words into an indecipherable mumble, a flood of memories dammed. He cleared his throat.

"And, well, ol' George had a bad day—lost his savings, yelled at his family, ran his car into a tree. He threw a few punches in a bar." Thomas' head dropped beneath his pride. "It happens, son, but we find another way, okay?" Thomas nodded. "And then, well, George found the nearest bridge and jumped off."

Lynzie bolted upright, the bowl of popcorn scattering like birdseed across the room.

A suicide.

Locked with mine, my father's eyes penetrated and searched for morsels of truth.

He would never find them. I replaced each piece of popcorn slowly into the bowl.

"Who's that old man chasing George through the cemetery?" Thomas' finger invited us to change course, and I willingly followed it to the screen.

An older man, homelier than George, stood at peace with his hands in his pockets, while George ran frantically darting from place to place. Yelling. Begging. He appeared to pray. Broken one moment, happy the next, something converted George's torment to tolerance.

I reached for the remote to unmute the words coming from George's mouth, but my dad batted my hand away.

"Just watch; you don't need the sound," he said.

George thrust open the door to a house, to a family who raced in with hugs. More people came, flooding the space around him. Happy. They tossed money onto a table. The pile grew high.

Maybe my mother didn't have money.

"He didn't kill himself that day," our father continued. "An angel saved him, reminded him how important he was to those around him. How life would have been completely different if he was never born."

A single piece of popcorn had found itself far away from the others, hiding behind a pile of books where only time would make it known. I crushed it beneath my thumb.

"What's that say, Daddy, the words written in that book?"

"It says: *Dear George – Remember no man is a failure who has friends. Thanks for the wings!*"

Exchanging the remote for his phone, it took only seconds before Evelyn LeBlanc's name flashed on the screen. He hit call, then rose from the couch to talk privately with his oldest friend.

Friends. Failure. Russian roulette to my ears. Why did I go to the park? What friends did my mother have? My heart pounded in my chest. None. She had me and look what I did. I left her alone to pace the walls of a deserted apartment, to mourn the life made possible by the husband who abandoned her, by the daughter who couldn't be bothered. Who would she have called when the sadness came, when she looked around and saw her new life empty; when nobody raced in to give her a hug?

My father paced the floor, opening cabinets, looking at nothing. Chatting with a woman he had known his entire life. She offered him a sense of peace.

The thump in my heart grew louder as my mother's pained face crystallized. I grabbed the remote and cranked the volume.

"Hey, turn it down, okay?" Jack said, pulling the phone away from his mouth.

I jumped from the couch, bursting into the kitchen with an illogical urgency. "Aren't you finished yet!" I needed him by my side now! To pull me close and squeeze out what my thumping heart had forced me to see. Panicked, he didn't notice it; I didn't understand it. Why now? After all this time, why did I see her again as I saw her last? I spun, searching for answers.

"Dad, let's go! Come on, let's watch the movie!" I tugged at his shirt.

"Okay, always, yes, you are forever the thorn in my side, Evelyn."

How could he laugh now? When all that I had worked so hard to block loomed this large in front of my eyes. I tugged harder; he kept talking. I spun in circles, searching for the mother who replaced the other. She was dead. He was on the mend. Who could I worry about so I could make it stop?

The phone now away from his ear, I rushed into his arms, forcing them to lasso me tight, to smother all these memories I couldn't bear to see.

"Your Aunt Evelyn begged for mercy." He didn't notice the strength of my hold. "Said to tell you she's sorry." Playfully, he lifted me off my feet. "Said—"

"Dad? I —"

Holding me at arm's length, his tensed muscles preserving yesterday's anger released, and his grey-green eyes replaced the unsettling image responsible for this unbearable collapse.

"Don't let her upset you, Ryder. She means well." My breathing slowed to match his as he crushed me tighter. He never needed to know what I saw.

A memory forced into exile, I wiped it off the slate and sank into our couch, protecting myself by crawling under my father's arm. Thomas slid under his other arm, and Lynzie crawled into his lap. We watched the movie at full volume, and all that useless noise went the way it always had—slipped under a rock, buried far beneath the soil. It was only my family and I now. Nothing else mattered. His love had made it gone.

Thomas hit pause at the scene we had reached before, and nobody bothered to turn it off. Frozen, that note burned into the pixels of that 55-inch screen. It remained there during dinner, after clean up, throughout the time we all stayed in that space but went our separate ways. *No man is a failure who has friends.* The panic now locked into a concealed vault. Composed, I reread it from a different perspective.

No…friends.

I scrolled through my phone, looking for names I could call a thorn in my side, for a confidant to help me regain the lost progress I made since Sarah's death. I saw names, random identities—not one person with whom I would confide.

Always be true to your friends, Sarah said to me once. *Promise me,* she asked of me always.

I missed her, that woman named Sarah Scott, who loved me like a daughter from the moment I entered her life. She always cared, right up until her last breath. *Only when you're ready.*

I opened my iPad, and this time, I didn't hesitate.

Filling the space where the lemon poppy seed cake once stood was that photo weathered by the harshness of time. Cracked and etched at the margins, a stoic young woman sat erect. She had one arm draped over a table, the other cradled in her lap. Staring straight through me with Mona Lisa's eyes, I tried to look away, but she followed. Sarah's message hidden beneath her gaze.

I shook my head. No. I waited too long. What if I already did something that defied the lesson Sarah wanted me to learn? What if clicking on that Pinterest post evoked so much emotion I broke down? Right here, in the living room, with Thomas sprawled on the carpet, charcoaling the wings onto the backside of a dragon, with Lynzie curled up asleep on the couch, and my father—

I felt his breath on the back of my neck and soundlessly clicked off my device.

"Doesn't it bother you?" I whispered.

"To look at her Pinterest page?" He leaned a bit closer. "Of course, but no more than turning over in our bed and finding nothing or walking into our closet and having her perfume recreate an evening." He circled around the couch and pointed to his youngest child. "Or looking at her."

A carbon copy of the woman we missed let out a moan. And we both watched in silence as Lynzie drew in her legs, squeezing them tight to her chest.

"I should put her to bed." He bent down to scoop her up. "Come on, son, time for you too." With his daughter cradled into his arms and Thomas tucked by his side, he tapped the cover of my iPad. "I'll leave you alone."

The screen light blinded, introducing another stress. With my sudden tailspin and its haunting visions, this night had already been too much. I opened Sarah's Pinterest board and stared at the woman, who stared at me. Both of us tasked to be a part of a dialogue. Trembling, I couldn't bring myself to press.

"Go ahead, hun." My father stood midway up the stairs, a guardian to my fear.

I tapped. A poem.

Tell all the Truth but tell it slant
Success in Circuit lies
Too bright for our infirm Delight
The Truth's superb surprise
As Lightning to the Children eased
With explanation kind
The Truth must dazzle gradually
Or every man be blind

I didn't understand, but the magnifying glass swelled over words with meaning: truth, lies, gradually, blind. I still didn't understand.

Earlier in the evening, Lynzie had lit a candle and placed it at the center of the table. I held an unlit match to the flame. Urgently, it burst, the blaze consuming its tiny head, phosphorus mixing with potassium chlorate. How come I knew that but couldn't understand the poem or the panic or why my father was getting better while I was getting worse? The match now upside down, the flames crept closer and warmer until my fingers hurt. I tossed it into the lid of the candle. It felt right. I did it again.

The burn of the smoke circled the air, shrouding the screen in front of me: *No man is a failure who has friends.* Returning from being a father, he paused only for a moment before clicking the remote and making those words disappear.

"Would you like to talk?"

I lit another match.

***

The school year began just two days after the New Year, and the first thing I did to undo what the holidays had done was Google how to make sense of the mess cluttering my mind.

The secret to making a meaningful friend: Search.

The Life Coach said to open my heart, to share the woes that filled my days with all the people who filled this world. Ah, no. *The Tiny Buddha* asked of me to look for a bond, to be with people who would support all that made me weird. Uh-huh. In the eighth grade? Right. *Look for people who are the brother or sister to your soul.* I paused. I'd throw myself directly in front of a bus to save Thomas or Lynzie, my father, too. I just couldn't talk to them, not about the truth.

I spun my finger through the search results and watched the useless titles blur by. Faster, then slower; crawling, then stopping, the roulette wheel landed on a list: thirty-six questions to bring you closer together.

I could work with lists.

1. *Given the choice of anyone in the world, whom would you want as a dinner guest?*
2. *When did you last sing to someone else?*
3. *Before making a phone call, do you ever rehearse what you're going to say?*

"Is this seat taken?"

Spencer Schrader, the first chair in the symphony. The boy whom I fantasized about all summer, whose twin I posted on Pinterest, who by luck attended the same school I transferred into. That boy ran his fingers through his sandy blond hair and didn't wait for an answer. He pulled out a chair and sat.

"I wanted to tell you how sorry I was to hear about your mother."

I stiffened; he hesitated. Nobody at school openly spoke those words, choosing instead to dart their eyes to school election posters or cafeteria rules plastered on the walls.

He quickly rose. "I'm sorry. I didn't mean to upset you," he said, softly smiling, that solitary dimple sinking deeper into his cheek.

"No, sorry. Please, stay. You just caught me off guard. I was studying."

"On the first day of school?"

"Well, I wasn't studying school stuff."

A mischievous smirk aligned with the tilt of his head. The life coach told me to open up, the Buddha said to ask him what he felt about my approach. Spencer's smirk turned smug. No, not yet, not him. "Do you have a sister named Siobhan?" I diverted.

He shook his head, and a lock of hair fell just above his dimple. Well, okay, maybe him. "Cousin?"

His one eyebrow lifted. "Why?"

"Because I once stole an ID from a girl named Siobhan Schrader and used it to get a job busing tables at a restaurant."

"Really? Brazen. I swiped my older brother's ID to buy cigarettes even though I don't smoke. I just wanted to see if I could get away with it."

A school bus emptied, and a swarm of first graders burst through the door, rushing past us into their building. One stopped in front of our table and stared. "What's your name, little guy?" Spencer asked.

"Thom-as." The kid swayed as if pushed by opposing winds, then scurried off. More interested in the rambunctious ramble of the second bus unloading than finishing off a conversation with a boy twice his age.

I glanced at my iPad, at the questions crisscrossing the screen, considering the first one topping the list. *Given the choice of anyone in the world, whom would you want as a dinner guest?* I found that first-grade boy in a corner huddling with his friend, scribbling on the back of a flyer. It could have been *my* Thomas, a boy I could eat with every day for the rest of my life.

No. Maybe Lynzie. Wait. My dad. "It's a hard question." I blurted without a context.

Spencer's eyes scrunched the way Lynzie's did when she scrutinized the maze on the cereal box. His fingers mindfully scratched his chin. In front of any other boy, I could recover, just show him the webpage and move on. But my breathing increased, bringing with it a dryness caking my throat. A buzzing rippled through my fingers. A bead of sweat collected on my brow.

He turned the iPad.

"Huh. Interesting. Anyone in the world?" His blush came first, then his lip curled under his teeth. "My guest wouldn't be a celebrity, and I know that makes me kind of like not cool."

His mother. That was his answer. Said he loved her dearly and given a choice, he would have dinner with her every night of the week. For him, nobody had the power to right wrongs like his mother did, and that was why he needed me to understand that he understood.

"Ask me another."

I did. And another, and another, and then we raised our voice to compete with the ringing of the bell.

"Give me one that I can think about when I'm in class."

"You're supposed to be thinking about what the teacher says in class."

Those fingers ran through his thick hair once more, leaving it shaggy and a bit unkempt.

"Okay." I skimmed the list for something not too intimate but still personal enough. "If you were going to become a close friend with your partner, please share what would be important for him or her to know."

"Hmm. Okay. Alright, let's meet at lunch, and I'll tell you my answer."

This did not help my grades at all. Everything Mr. Fischer said in Spanish sounded like a muted trombone. In Social Studies, Mr. Lopez's speech on the limits of censor rang in my ears as Spencer, Spencer, Spencer. By Algebra, I calculated the minutes before I would see his locks of hair fall over his freckled face. And don't ask me what I thought about in Biology. Just don't.

"Okay, Ryder, I'll tell you my secret if you tell me yours."

Tucked against the back wall in the crowded, noisy, hormone-filled cafeteria, my heart raced with anticipation, even excitement. I scrutinized every line in Spencer's face, searching for a reason to hold back. But there were none. Before me sat a boy with a placid composure, a caring soul with his hands resting on the table as if he were sitting in confession. Finally, I had the guts to come clean.

"Okay, I'll start," he said. "My brother, he's older, well, he uses a lot of drugs. One time, he emptied my mother's jewelry box and sold it all. Things aren't so good at home right now. My parents are stressed." Without hesitation, his story unfolded as if he were reading an essay in front of class. He had told this before. "Sometimes, I can't concentrate because of the chaos, but my sister has it worse. She sees a psychiatrist and takes these pills that help her focus." Now, his head turned away, that lip curled under his tooth. A secret was breaking.

"I took one once," he murmured, his eyes zeroing in on a teacher pacing the room. "I mean, I feel bad, but ya know what, Ryder?" He looked straight through me. "It really worked. I didn't just have to rely on my violin to block the nonsense, the pill stopped it too."

I leaned forward, suddenly desperate to hear his words. My body tensed, fighting the urge to throw my hands around his neck. To embrace him for having been there.

"I totally hide behind my violin," I admitted.

"To-tal-ly."

We waited through the silence, and the lull felt right.

"Okay. Now it's your turn."

I ran my tongue over my lips, chewing the chapped skin between my teeth. "My mother—" The plastic glass in front of me sweat from the heat circulating the room. I caught a drop rolling down the side with my pinkie. I cleared my throat. "My mother was not the only mother I've had." I grabbed the glass with two hands, strangling it before I gulped the liquid inside.

A burst of laughter came from the seventh-grade section, drawing both our heads as if pulled by a string. Spencer cracked his knuckles. Pop. He twisted his neck. Pop. Pop. Back at his hands. Pop. Pop. Pop. Like a base drum segueing to another stanza, the story shifted. His eyes drooped. Engaged, but ready to jump should a different drum beat. Pop, his knuckle spoke again.

I exhaled. *Tell all the Truth but tell it slant.*

"My mother fell down some stairs and broke her neck. My next mother got cancer and died too soon." Wrong. Why, when I had this chance to tell somebody who genuinely connected, did I continue with my ways?

His eyes sprung wide, shocked by the confession, "Gosh, I'm so sorry, Ryder." He didn't blink.

The Truth must dazzle gradually, or every man be blind.

"Don't be, please. I don't want people to feel sorry for me. I just want somebody to talk to without judging me."

"How could I judge you? I feel foolish now with my confession. It was so trivial compared to yours."

The bell rang, and he still had my hand in his. It felt warm, and when it squeezed ever so much, a fluttering churned my stomach. My cheeks flushed, and my palms sweat. I completely lost my appetite. *Success in Circuit lies.* The acceptance of deception was necessary because *reality was just a bridge suspended by the beliefs of those who must traverse it.*

After school, I waited for my father at the curb. It was just before a snowstorm, and the air outside was filled with still and calm. The clouds rushed together in a row above my head. The first flake landed on my navy-blue sailor's coat. The next on my tongue.

"How does it taste?" My father, as always, snuck up from behind.

"It comes too quick, ends too fast. There is no answer."

"Feeling loquacious, are you?"

Still looking at the sky and the jewels that lived within it, I spoke the truth. "Just feeling a lot of Mom today."

My phone buzzed. *Ask me another of those thirty-six questions?*

As we drove, I scrolled.

- What are you grateful for...

- If you had a crystal ball...

- If you were to die this evening with no opportunity to communicate with anyone, what would you most regret not having told someone? Why haven't you told them yet?

Oh.

I scrolled my finger down the list until I found another. "Dad? If your house caught fire, and you already saved all the people and animals. If you have time to save one last thing, what would it be?"

"Is this what the boy asked you?"

"No. What boy? How did you know it was a boy? It wasn't a boy. I mean, it was." His crow's feet fanned out across his temple. "No, stop, I'm asking *you*."

"Alright. Time to save one last thing," he mumbled. The crow's feet faded. A block passed, then another, and as he turned into our parking garage, the hamster spun. The obvious answer was your phone. "Only you three kids matter to me. Everything else could go up in flames."

"Maybe—" the engine died— "it would be for the best."

***

Over my shoulder, the warmth of my father's breath passed through me, and goosebumps sprouted. He was reading what I read, an eight-line poem pinned to the internet by a woman who was no more.

I slid my fingers to the back arrow, readily jumping over to my father's postings. To a board that hadn't changed since July, the day before an emergency appointment was made at a spa. Uncomplicated and fun, I replayed the video of a cat spastically jumping into the air, terrified of a cucumber placed near his side. A chuckle came from behind me, and then footsteps walked away. I refreshed my mother's board.

As lightning to the Children eased, with explanation kind.

Was I seven or eight when the thunder roared because the lightning cracked, when an electric whip shot through the sky? I had buried under the sheets, shaking, probably crying. But my mother was there, telling me about God rearranging the furniture. Crack. "See, He just pushed a dresser against a wall." I laughed. The lightning flashed. "That's Him taking a selfie to send to his son."

The lie worked, it calmed. Was that so wrong?

The truth must dazzle gradually, or every man be blind.

Lightning and the electricity it released caused thunder. Am I worse off because I learned that in school four years later? For knowing my mother lied?

When was the right time to tell the truth?

Reaching for my violin, I picked it up, put it down, turned, walked back to the TV. No. I stared at the shelves, to the wooden headrest. I sat and lit a match, as I had done a thousand times since Lynzie put that candle in view. The flame was white and cupped like a teardrop. It floated on a pillow of blue. Each time, the glow crept closer to my finger; each time, its flickering flame danced.

"Ryder, please come here," sounded the dominant voice of a man in charge.

I blew on the match, and the smoke curled, racing urgently above.

In my father's hand was an iPad, its cover adorned with stickers defining my life. "This—" he tapped his finger at its center— "will stay with me." I rolled my eyes and focused on the insightful slogan of the most prominent sticker: *Raise your voice, not the Sea Level; Keep calm and always recycle.* "And the phone, it's mine." He pointed the screen in my direction, showing me an email sent from my teacher.

"Oh, that," I shrugged. "It was a hard test, Dad."

"Especially when you don't study."

"So, what?"

His eyes, large then sinking, wandered over to the kitchen table, to the chair that used to be hers. In another time, she would have had an answer. I lit another match.

"Enough."

"Why?"

One breath, then another, by the time a third one came, the conflict was mine. I proudly walked towards my room with the violin case tucked under my arm.

"Ryder." Unable to let it go, he stood rod straight at my door, unexpectantly filling the space with authority and charge. "Put the violin away." His expression turned serious before it went stern.

I had watched his show only once, and he wore then the exact same scrutiny as he did now. I remembered how fixed he was on his guest, how he patiently waited. How, when she said something that aligned with his beliefs, he took hold and wedged himself under her skin. But when she attacked, he never said a word, choosing instead to let the woman's words tumble then stumble then fail.

"I said, put it away."

At all times, his relaxed hands stayed motionless on his studio desk, arched in the middle, with the tips of his fingers barely making contact. That moment with his guest was shared whether she appreciated it or not. "Listen to your facts, not whispers," he said then.

I never knew what that meant.

I handed over to him what he asked, leaving me without a vice.

CHAPTER THIRTY-THREE

"What is it?" Said the sad little boy leaning against my bed frame.

Thomas had been a shadow, hiding behind charcoals and sketchbooks, and easels and doors. The death of his mother had transformed this playful child into a somber youth resigned to tackle all of life's problems with a shrug.

"I'm not sure," I said, sharing in Thomas' confusion. "Spencer just said it would help."

Once a slot machine ready to unload a flurry of untethered chaos, I could have counted on him to shoot me some nonsense that followed neither logic nor reason. Instead, he just tilted his head and sighed. "You know, I should try it too. Maybe it will make Dad happy if I do better in school."

He sauntered away, crawling up the supports of that too high bed, Spencer's gift rolling between his fingers. Scrunching his eyes, he held it up to the light to make out the tiny writing etched onto its surface. "Dad just stares off into nothing. When I say something, it always feels wrong."

The boy had found that brick wall, and it struck me as unlikely that he would mount it any time soon.

"Maybe Dad should take it too, can you get more?"

"Take what?"

Stealth again, I didn't see him until after Thomas raised his palm off the bed, offering to our father my one-month anniversary present from Spencer.

"What is th—"

A squeal drifted down the hall from the living room, followed by giggling and rapturous applause: excitement this house had not heard in months. It reverberated and intensified. No doubt, Lynzie was roused.

Our dad marched towards it, followed by Thomas. I joined them only after I heard my dad shout. "A dog?"

I ran down the hall, my socks skidding on the wood floor to end my sprint. Guerin and Evelyn's faces beamed with pride. It was beautiful: all black, with a bushy tail, crest-white teeth, and a tail that wagged so fast Lynzie couldn't catch it between her hands.

"A dog?" Repeating it twice, I thought I missed the second dog. By the third time, it seemed the idea of a dog did not please our dad as much as it did us, or him. Or was it a her? I quickly ducked my head under her belly. A her, I had another sister. I reached to smother her in a hug, but this spirited mutt of an animal excitedly took off, running circles around Thomas and then myself. A dizzying figure-of-eight, which kept us entertained until, sliding headfirst into the coat rack, it noticed the cat.

"She was just drifting around the kennel and looked like she needed a good home," Evelyn explained.

Crouching low and brushing the floor with her tail, a piece of Lynzie's Lego scratched back and forth against the tile. A grating scrape, which only goaded our father more. "Evelyn, you've got to be kidding me."

Lynzie ran to Aunt Evelyn and thrust her arms across her waist. Clinging to her leg, Evelyn arched it wide to accommodate the weight as she moved to pet this beautiful, black mutt of a dog. "My dear friend, everybody needs a furry friend."

"We already have one."

And on cue, the dog took that as a rebel yell, leaping the couch to chase the cat behind the curtains. Puzzled as she exited the drapes, the dog looped the fishbowl twice before bouncing off the refrigerator. Thomas' sketch dislodged and sailed free, the dumb dog following it as if it were a kite that lost its wind.

"Hey!" Thomas darted between the hissing ball of anger and this drooling fool of a dog before dragging a chair from the table. He pinned his prized artwork as high on the fridge as he could reach, and we all took a moment to marvel at his medieval knight poised upon its horse.

"Young lady," Guerin said. "Would you do me the honor of giving this to the drifter?" He handed Lynzie a bone.

"Come here, Drifter." And out of thin air, a dog was named.

With the bone in tow, Drifter let the cat be. Who, seizing the opportunity, scurried from the floor to the counter to the top of the refrigerator, which, regrettably, knocked loose the shining knight on his rebellious horse.

"Hey!" Thomas' expression matched his father.

"Any advice from the one who caused this commotion in my otherwise tranquil home?"

"Dogs are not that hard to take care of," Aunt Evelyn lectured. "Just make sure they don't wander off. They're not like cats. They're too stupid to find their way back home. You lost that puppy of yours that way, remember, Jack? What were we in? Fourth-grade?"

"Remember what, Evelyn? That dog jumped out the window of my dad's car while he drove us to school. Remember? He couldn't be bothered to go back and get it."

"No!"

"Evelyn, you cried for weeks, wouldn't even look at my dad. You threw a tantrum whenever he came over to pick me up for those weekend visits. Don't you remember when you tore the ears off that stuffed animal he gave me?"

"What are you talking about?" Her face was scrunched into a sad confusion.

"You were a mess, plotting all sorts of ways to get back at him." My father laughed as if her past pains were not her present.

Our favorite aunt drifted into the kitchen to tunnel into the dog's eyes. Squatting, with her knees cracking as old people's knees do, she scratched her head. "Your dog jumped out the window? And he didn't go back to get it?" She stroked the dog's coat gently as if would make up for all of life's sins. "How horrible. No wonder I stashed that away."

"Then, this one time—"

"Dad, she doesn't remember!" Heat rushed my face faster than a match could strike. The amnesia of trauma, how lucky for her to forget something as trivial as his dad killing a dog. "Don't push her! It's fine." I shouted it—loud and clear—drawing the attention of every person in the room.

Guerin cleared his throat. "Ah, Jack, what's that in your hand?"

Ryder Stephens

It took two long breaths before my dad fished his reading glasses out of his pocket. The arms blocked his vision, so he shook them loose, moving the lenses over his nose like the slide of a trombone. "Thomas, what does this say?"

"A-d-d, you can't see that, Dad?"

"It's like size six font!" Our dad squinted harder to see if he could do this without losing face. "Why is it that for the important things in life, like knowing what goes into your body, they use the smallest font possible. But for something as innocuous as trans fats, they zoom it up to size forty?" He thrust the pill to his youngest daughter, who rushed over, ready and eager to show off her intellectual clout. "Lynzie, A-d-d, what?"

"e, r, a, l, l."

Every adult stiffened. The pill was elevated to eye level for Evelyn to judge, but all she did was shake her head. "Tell me again how you don't need help."

I froze between the lasers shooting from my father's eyes.

"Who gave you this?" he asked, flaring his nostrils with every intention to strike.

He stepped towards me, and I knew what I needed to do. Stay silent. Protect Spencer. Because this wasn't *his* fault, it was my dad's. He was the one who took my violin away, who left me without a vice.

"Ryder," he bellowed.

Spencer had looked me straight in the eye, which meant he was sincere. "This will help you concentrate. It works. Trust me," he said.

"Did you take this?"

In my father's hand was a legally prescribed pill, from a doctor, who would never harm a child, just like Spencer would never hurt me.

"It's to help me remember." I spun around, then whirled back quicker. "I mean with school. I remember everything else."

I snatched the pill from my dad's hand and tossed it into my mouth. Within seconds, Guerin had one hand on my brow, the other thrusting my chin, while my dad manically drove his finger around my mouth. It swept from side to side.

"Don't swallow."

I swallowed.

Guerin relaxed his grip. My father pulled his hands from my

293

mouth. Deflated and wilting into the adjacent armchair, the muffled words slipping through his fists barely made it to my ears. "I think we need to talk about what you remember."

All of me turned clammy, my pulse raced, and I begged my body to make this a reaction to the medication instead of the fear of a conversation I might have forced.

Sitting still on the couch, my father lightly tapped his teeth together. "Not now, Ryder, but later. We're going to have that talk." Grabbing the box of matches off the coffee table, he struck it with such force, it smothered fast. He lit another, and the six of us watched as it slowly burned.

There was an image tucked inside my mind for times like this. Of me coming home from the park in San Francisco and finding the house decorated with Christmas lights. Of them blinking, cresting like a wave around the room faster and faster until I was so wild chasing them, I passed out from the dizziness, and never woke up. I never saw what I saw.

But I did.

I found myself studying Thomas, who mirrored our dad. Fingers intertwined and resting four inches from his chest, his nostrils rising with every exaggerated breath.

"I think... I don't want to talk to you." The words fell from my lips despite lingering on my tongue for ages. For longer, I recalled the expression I had hoped those words would evoke. Of a man who would nod, only once, supporting my decision. A man who agreed it was okay to replace facts with illusions, who approved of those blinking lights cresting around the room.

***

It took a week.

Through the balcony window, the sky was a dark abyss. I worried because I was the reason my father didn't come home for dinner. Why he stayed silent in the nights after the episode with the pill. Why he withdrew again into a shell.

The elevator opened, and out he strolled, hours after he usually came home, his boots stamping the mat so hard little clumps of snow fell onto the floor. Jack Scott stared at it perplexed, and the chill that followed him in, ran down my spine.

Rustling his coat, he tossed it over a hook already piled too high with clothes. He scanned the room, taking note of the fire we built. His focus shifted back to the snow, patiently waiting for it to melt.

Puddles formed where the snow had been, and he tapped his toe in twice, silently chuckling as the ripples formed. An emotion impossible to decode, it all seemed odd until noticing the dog dish still crusted with the morning meal, he frowned. I supposed he would scold any one of us, list off arguments against the dog. But he didn't.

He hummed.

"No more pizza," he said, a declaration so out of sync with the scene, only he could make sense of that statement. But he didn't do that either. He lifted the last slice above his open mouth and, ever so gently, lowered it in. "After this one last slice, no more."

His jacket slid from the hook and crashed to the floor.

I twitched.

His whistling resumed, and as he passed behind me, I slapped my laptop closed.

"Keeping secrets?" He patted my crown. "I understand." Sinking into the nearest chair, his laptop creaked open, its light illuminating the features of an unburdened man.

I picked up one piece of popcorn from the bowl separating us, nibbling it slowly. Because, and this I knew as an absolute truth: when Jack Scott reappeared into your life, you never opened a door; never gave him a place to find a crack. Because he would. I moved to the chair opposite him and eased mine open again.

Write five hundred words about the following Mr. Rogers quote: (25 points)

> *Take a silent minute to think about those who have helped you become who you are today. If they've loved you, and encouraged you, and wanted what was best in life for you, devote some thought to them.*
>
> *Whomever you've been thinking about, imagine how grateful they must be, that during your silent times, you remember how important they are to you.*

My cursor flashed that vertical line punishing the unformed thoughts still milling around my mind. Pulsing, in a slow adagio of a beat, it matched the rhythm of the song my dad left stranded in my head.

"Ryder, you look concerned."

I popped a handful of popcorn into my mouth.

"Is that for school? Would you like me to take a look?"

I was savvy enough to avert the question, to start typing before time allowed for another question to form. Acting without thinking, words that popped into my head ran to my fingers: *My father has always cared.* The cursor flashed, and my arms created a pyramid for my chin to rest. I read the assignment through again. *Whomever you've been thinking about, imagine how grateful they must be.* Grateful, no, if the woman who gave me life were grateful, she wouldn't be dead.

"Ryder?" My computer swirled 180 degrees before I could uncouple my hands to make it stop. "Huh. Okay." It spun back to me unscathed.

Across the room, a video game announced the advancement into the next stage of Thomas' virtual life, and I pretended to type.

"Keep it down over there, Ryder's writing some insightful prose." He grinned.

I typed some more. Nonsense, gibberish: *my sister is cuddling a dog, and my brother is hugging a game.* And this I also knew about the rules of make-believe: always do something to make it real. The verb was changed, the nouns switched, a semi-colon became a colon, which became a comma, which all got deleted. The page was blank. I glanced back at my screen, at Mr. Rogers smiling, his red cardigan zippered. That tiger puppet, Daniel, slid over his hand. I typed again: *My father has always cared.*

"I could laugh and cry with my fingers, and nobody would know how I felt." Words not typed by me but flowing from my father's lips. He made no sense, just as before. "Mr. Roger's said that—said that as a child, only his piano knew how to play out his emotions; said he didn't have another way."

I tapped hard against the keyboard, in my own land of make-believe.

"I think a lot of people are like that, don't you? Finding alternative avenues to release life's tensions, be it through music or writing or sport or art." He jerked his head in the direction of his son.

Two faces at peace, Mr. Rogers' and my father's; I only understood why for one. The other started to sing.

Gracias a la vida que me ha dado tanto
Me ha dado la risa y me ha dado el llanto
Así yo distingo dicha de quebranto
los dos materiales que forman mi canto

It was the song he'd been humming, and as he translated it, the candle on the table flickered, swaying to the soft sounds of my father's voice.

Thank you to life, which has given me so much.
It gave me laughter, and it gave me tears.
With them, I distinguish happiness from pain,
the two elements that make up my song.

His laptop closed, and I scanned my eyes over a man who, despite walking through hell in the last few months, looked as though he found his way back.

"That's why I was late. I had a hard day today, honey." A slower cadence came: a somber one, a serious one. One that wasn't from the man who stomped snow from his boots and lowered pizza into his open mouth. But one that came from a father who was ready to talk. "A very hard day."

I shifted in my seat.

"After you all left for school, and for no reason that makes sense, everything rushed at me. Every thought. All I had been avoiding; it just hit me with a wave as painful as if it were an arc of arrows." He paused to tunnel into my eyes. "You've been there, kid, haven't you?"

A lump formed deep in my throat.

"I couldn't rub two thoughts together, couldn't breathe. I just got up and left. Just couldn't be here anymore, not with everything around me. I walked right out our door and didn't stop."

Swirling my glass, the ice cubes whizzed around, creating a barrier that masked his deep and staggered breaths. I put the glass down, right on top of the ring of water that marked it last. And when I lifted it again, a tiny suction pulled.

"First, it was just our neighborhood. But then I found myself studying the arch in Washington Square Park, trying to make sense of the cascading scenes exhausting my mind. Billy Crystal walked under it in *When Harry met Sally*. Your mother loved...."

He pulled away, changing the movie in my head. When his throat cleared, it cracked.

"I moved on. Walking without thinking, shifting all my energy to plant one foot in front of another. Soon enough, I was watching ice skaters circle around Rockefeller Center." His fingers tapped against the wooden table, its tempo still matching that song. "I saw some kids hunched in a corner, passing around what looked like pills."

Not a muscle in my body moved.

"And do you know what I thought?" He chuckled. "I thought, you know, maybe that would help." He paced his words. "Maybe that would force me to concentrate on the moment instead of these memories taking me down."

I felt my mouth slowly hang.

"I understand, hun. We're both not going to do that, but I understand."

He continued with his story, telling me how he knew to keep moving. To wander and find solitude; be someplace where no other soul would follow.

"And there I was cold and alone in Central Park, knowing it would do me harm. But still, I went deeper." He stopped speaking, his baton and its cadence held still in the air. "I crossed over a bridge."

I picked up another piece of popcorn and twirled it between my fingers.

"That same bridge Sarah mentioned when she told you about her cousin, about the rape that happened when she was sixteen. The one she kept to herself until she was thirty-five."

I inched back: stunned enough to not look away, worried enough to be afraid.

"You know why Sarah told you about her cousin." His head tilted, this time forcing a memory to surface. "More than anything, she would have wanted to finish that conversation with you."

He sighed, then focused on an invisible spot four inches away.

"But she knew it was too early." His voice quivered. "I've hated myself for not having the courage to finish what she started. For not being a better father, for having you think that a pill would be easier to swallow than a conversation with your dad."

His pause was long, and although it was wrong, I rose.

"Gracias a la vida que me ha dado tanto—thank you to life,

which has given me so much." He grabbed my hand and lowered me back into the chair. "When I got to the other side of the bridge, I heard a man singing that song. It was so peaceful, the lyrics too much a part of Sarah; it opened a vault I had worked so hard to seal."

A quick gasp ended in a sniffle.

I couldn't look at him.

"It's okay, honey, keep your eyes closed. Just listen. Do that for me." He waited. I nodded. "It was as if she was the one singing, translating those words into a wisdom that made sense of these suffocating demands on my life."

Behind my lids, his words shaped an image of a woman dancing over the snow, with a white dress billowing around her legs, of the Sarah I wanted to remember.

He took a deep breath and held it. "But then the music stopped too fast, too soon." His exhale finally rushed, broken by the heartache of a desperate want. "She left me again."

But not me. I could see her spinning in circles, blowing me a kiss, a vision I strained to keep, a memory I needed to have.

"She left me," he said again. "But the song wouldn't; its message couldn't. Be grateful, she urged. Honor me, she pleaded."

My father's baton slowed until his breaths returned to normal, and when his hand brushed against mine, a silent tear tracked down my cheek.

"And for the first time in what seems like forever, I felt aware of the present. Oh, sweetheart, there are so many things I've wanted to say to you, but I waited for you to come around, for Sarah to get better, for time to pass, for one excuse after another. I just didn't have the courage. I failed you, and I'm sorry."

I opened my eyes, aiming them towards the slanting grain in the table, which took its time to blur into focus. It followed no pattern: one band arched up, the other down, light against dark, patches next to ribbons. I shifted to see my screen. *My father has always cared.* "You didn't fail me, Dad."

"I did. I am. The strength in this family was, and will always be, Sarah. She found the right words at the right time for every moment."

All too suddenly, I saw all that was good in Sarah: the blindfolds and chocolate chips, the hugs and—I couldn't remember more.

"We need to talk about why she told you about her cousin,

about why she suppressed the tragedy."

Of wooden saddles. No, headrests, and 9-11 and yoga and books.

He moved a bit closer.

Of menopause and estrogen and Tylenol, not Motrin. I heaved my chest higher and faster with each added distraction. My body tensing to remember more.

"It's okay, honey. I'll stop. It's okay."

I focused on Lynzie, who was lying side by side with the dog, arms and paws united in an innocence a million miles away. She giggled. The joy from this moment, she would never have cause to relive.

"Do you remember the reason why my father left me when I was ten?" My breathing too rapid; I couldn't follow the tangent. "Look at me. This is about my father, not yours. Honey, why did my father leave?"

Slower, steadier, maybe ready, I swallowed. "You never told me why."

"I know." He paused. "That is where I failed. It never mattered until now because my wife always rescued me—us—she saved everyone. Honey, I'm great at sharing facts. Every day, on-air, I shout them to the world and make them heard, but I only whisper the meaning behind them. Too scared, I think, of sharing an emotion I might not be able to control."

Copy that. I nodded to seal a pact, both of us committing someday to be ready.

"The woman who wrote that song, *Gracias a la Vida, Thank You to Life,* her named was Violeta Parra. She wrote that song one year, and then she committed suicide the next."

I gasped.

A log tumbled in the fireplace, rattling the screen, flames climbing high between the two freed logs. A loud pop came. I jumped. Lynzie giggled. I couldn't make sense of the two.

"Thanks to life, which has given me so much. It gave me laughter, and it gave me tears. With them, I distinguish happiness from pain, the two elements that make up my song."

He spoke the words to this song slowly, deliberately, its meaning swallowing the air around us.

The second log cracked in two.

"To me, I hear one message: find gratitude, and the anger and sadness will leave. For Violeta Parra, what did she hear, Ryder?"

A held breath slowly left when my answer refused to come.

"When I lost Sarah, I thought everything in my life disappeared." His eyes glazed as he watched his youngest daughter use the light from the fire to make shadows on the wall. "But it hadn't. All of her is right here in front of me."

"She built this family." His hand moved to cover his mouth. "I will never understand why she's gone, but I know that I'm grateful." Shaking his head, his eyes never moved off Lynzie. "And if I stop myself from trying, from facing the life, which she took so much pleasure in, which she never took for granted, I'm neglecting her, and all that she gave." That hand swept against his nose.

"Tell all the Truth but tell it slant. Violeta Parra said it slant. Or said a lie. She held things back and hid things from others. Who knew that life troubled her so? What was she thinking, Ryder?" His finger turned my chin. "Why would she take her life if she knew that on the other side of sorrow was peace?"

I stayed motionless, too nervous to even shrug.

"You don't know. Her family doesn't. And nobody ever will. I see you, sweetheart. I hear your silence. Your mother, Samantha, is always with you, and I understand that now. Not a moment passes where I don't think of Sarah—what I forgot to tell her, how I could have made her life better."

His face tightened and flushed with emotion.

"And I knew what was going to happen." The redness from his nose spread to cover his face.

"You didn't, and that wasn't fair. You never had the chance to ask your mother why she was unhappy, why her life was so bad she chose to leave it. You never had the chance to say goodbye. Anger turned to guilt, and I know it's never left you, sweetheart. I see it every time you worry about me, about Thomas. Samantha Stephens, like Violeta Parra, held secrets. Her own. Honey, you didn't miss any signs from your mother."

"I did." The memories clung to my tears, and no matter how many fell, new ones followed.

"No, you didn't. I don't know why your mother did it. I never will, and neither will you. Two separate women, my wife, and your mother, they left this life and abandoned us, but look what we have now.

"In song, Violeta Parra asked us to be grateful. In her death, we should remember only that, not how she left. Her reasons are her own. Your mother's motives were her own, not yours. Look back to times of peace and fun. To times when you saw her being the best that she was. They're there. Find them and hold tight. Life is something to appreciate, and I am so grateful that you're a part of mine. For better and worse, your mother gave me that, and I thank her for her sacrifice.

"You need to forgive her."

CHAPTER THIRTY-FOUR

The next morning, I woke from a dream. I was a mother with three children. Jack Scott was gone. They asked me about their grandfather, about his heritage, if they could go to Scotland to see where they were from.

They didn't understand why I said no.

Not fully awake, I dangled my feet over the side of the bed, pointing my toes toward the carpet, stretching my ankles as far as they would go. They would never reach. One of the shortest kids in my class, Thomas, the tallest. I touched my nose. Arched down and round, not the nose of a Scott.

A knock on the bedroom door had to be my father, nobody else in this house would bother.

"Ryder? Are you okay?" He sat next to me on the bed with his bare feet planted firmly on the carpet, its long fibers hiding his toes. "I've been invited to lecture at Georgetown University in Washington D. C. this weekend." The big toe popped up, and as if disappointed by its view, quickly burrowed and disappeared again. "I'd like you to join me. Just the two of us. We can take in the sites on Friday, and then visit the University on Saturday. Evelyn and Guerin will watch the kids."

"Why?"

He kicked my hanging toes. "Because. I like you."

We left at seven, Friday morning, driving the four-hour trip in five. Billboards shouted from the roadside, and the radio blared from the speakers. A steady stream of noise muffling everything subject to its power. I nodded when he spoke, not hearing the words randomly spilling from his mouth. The exits passed in blurs, while other cars sped by with a whoosh. And up ahead, the Lincoln Memorial impressed.

Ten, eleven, twelve. Twelve gothic columns rose so tall the people beneath seemed like ants. The magnificent structure stole my breath and replaced it with a smile, a memory of a time when seven people sat around a table listening to an old friend tell a story. "You hung a sign around Lincoln's neck," I mumbled.

"You remember that?"

Of course. That story unfolded on the first truly happy day after my mother died. My concert, where everybody stood watch.

The wheels slowed, turning into a curb, and his hand adjusted my crown. "It's over a few blocks. We'll need to walk a bit. I hope you like what I've picked out for us to see."

The air was musky and fresh, the smell of earth on sea. It would storm soon. I kicked the loose pebbles casually toppling the sidewalk. A drop of water hit my navy-blue sailor's coat. The next landed on my tongue. It tasted fresh, then salty. It disappeared too quick.

"We're here," he said.

Not the Capital, nor a memorial. It was a museum, a haunting building towering without décor, a crematorium sprouting ominously from the ground. The doors swung open, and the aura chilled, the sign above announcing to all that work will make you free.

Arbeit Macht Frei. "Dad, why are we here?"

"Because this is your ancestry: half a Stephens, half a Freiberg."

I took one step back to put distance between me and the past he wanted me to embrace.

"And you will forever be a Scott."

The Holocaust Memorial lived in a tomb where nobody spoke, where tourists shuffled their feet over concrete floors. We crossed through iron gates, past piles of confiscated goods, swept our eyes over human hair shaved from the prisoners' scalps. We saw clusters of clothes heaped into a corner as if an orphanage emptied its shelves. A faded red dress stretched peacefully across the top. And in my head, Itzhak Perlman played the song that made the whole world sad.

Round and round, we spiraled down the four stories of grief, through the rooms of exposed brick and steel. The evils of humanity. The tragedy of war. The innocence lost. The cold and emotionless walls crowding my thoughts. It was better for me when all of them hurt.

Trapped but free, I clung to my dad's hand as we read each line of every exhibit. He whispered truths in my ear, not scared to unearth their meaning. Words. About death and remorse, and life and resilience, I saw photos of the survivors going on to lead prosperous lives. I smiled for the optimism it promised, their sorrow unmasked.

Closing in on the exit, the lights brightened, and the crowd came alive. A giggle pierced the air, and kids scurried over the tiled floor. A journey through pain to the other side of sorrow. *Gracias a la vida.* Thank you to life.

Comfortable enough to drop my father's hand, we walked through the final show, the Nuremberg trials. The closure absent from the floors above.

A rope.

Long and braided. It was motionless, hanging as straight as a rod, an oblong circle closing its end. Meant for a head, I froze, retreating, heading towards the solace in the horrors of the scenes before. My father held my shoulders. I pushed back. "Don't look," he said.

But I did.

I raced outside, my long hair whipping across my face like a battered flag in a fight with the wind. I saw it. All of it. My body shook, and he pulled me close. Tears came, and he hurried me to a bench far from tourists' eyes. "Only when you're ready," he said.

She said those words too, Sarah Scott. The last I ever heard. *She would have wanted to finish the conversation with you.* So cruel and kind, so wrong and right, so much hurt and so much healing.

The lights of the Capital flickered in the distance, as a faint echo of laughter traveled across the pond. I stacked a penny: all I needed to do was to forgive myself. Two pennies: just look my father in the eye. Three: with an open heart, an open mind, a willingness to let him share my past, a recognition that I owed it to him to help me heal. Four, five, six.

The wind was a persuasive goad, his hug that followed a mandatory catalyst. A lonely leaf fell off a tree.

The pressure from a tear welling inside broke through. I wiped it away, then looked at my dad, at his knowing calm, his persistent attention. I opened my mouth, fighting every urge to reverse. I couldn't.

"I hear it. Dad." Those words trapped inside. "All the time. Dad, it never stops."

Please, Mamaaaa.

I squeezed my hands over my ears, the memory of the scream too loud to bear. A heat welled inside, surging too fast to contain my thoughts. I gasped for breath, scratching at my neck, trying to loosen the vice clamping down.

"I hear it every day."

Please Mamaaaa! Come down!

I squeezed harder, forcing out the crash of my knees slamming into the bathroom tile, the pounding of my fists against the wall. It circled in my head, repeating, echoing. It was the voice that blamed me for not being present, for not being a better daughter.

My father pulled my hands away, freeing my ears to hear his whispered words. Facts that absolved my guilt.

No.

He squeezed me tight, burying my head into his chest. Wanting to break free, not wanting to. I pushed away, clenching my legs as I had clamped onto hers.

"I tried to pull her down."

My body tingled from the suffocating thoughts. The ringing started. Nausea came, a shadow of myself crawled inside my brain. The full-length mirror had revealed only half her body, her legs dangling above my head. I saw my reflection crumbled at her feet.

"Her shoe came off. I hit her. Dad, I didn't know what to do."

A river flowed from my eyes.

"It wasn't your fault."

Her lips were blue. Her neck wrong. The cord of the Christmas lights tapped against my head.

Please Mamaaaa. Noooo.

A torment like no other. I followed it up, the lights flashing red and green. They circled her neck. I made her buy them. "Why did I go to the park? Dad, why? She would be alive if I stayed."

"No, honey, she wouldn't."

"She would. It haunts me, Dad. Every day, it haunts me still."

That scream that followed me to Las Vegas, to the casino, to the bus that took me to New York. My scream. I couldn't handle it. I picked at my hand, making blood ooze, slept under awnings, froze. I did everything to create a different reason to scream. I ran up stairs; ran down them. I played my music to cover it all: the slam of my knees, the flashing lights, the shoe dropping two feet onto the ground.

Tears soaked my shirt. *Noooo.* It became a whimper. *I'll be better,*

Mama. You can't leave. Not like this. You can't leave.

My father stayed quiet, waiting for my halted breaths to calm. We sat on that bench watching the stillness of the frozen lake. This yearlong sentence coming to a close. Only when the tears dried, did we walk silently to the car. And knowing exactly what to do, he asked no more and respected my confession by kissing my brow and tucking me into bed.

He whispered in my ear.

Your joy is your sorrow unmasked. And the selfsame well from which your laughter rises was oftentime filled with your tears. Look deep into your heart and you shall find it is only that which has given you sorrow that is giving you joy.*

That night, I slept at peace, the release of my burden finally outweighing the pain of holding it inside.

A father's purpose: to make us safe.

Thank you, Dad, for waiting.

**The Profit, by Kahill Gibran.*

CHAPTER THIRTY-FIVE

Over and over, that moment with my father played in my head. At times, it was loud, demanding, and hard to confront. At times, not. Because like me, he was a man freed from the punishment of grief. He set goals, reached them. He made a new friend. Back at work and home at 6:30, by design, he had his show moved to match his changing needs. And when he walked through those elevator doors, his hand always patted the back of Sarah's chair, his way to give thanks.

His message spoke of acceptance, resilience, and gratitude—not in isolation, but collectively. The path to a happy life was circular, and it spiraled around people. Silence and retreat veered off that path, and until that day in D.C., I walked towards the shelter and limits of an isolated life. But now, after the season had changed, when spring melted into summer, I found the loop and never let it go. I didn't master closure, but with his help, every day, I tried.

A man could do no better than to show his children how to try.

I needed that lesson because I had lost a friend, a boy that I had willed myself to trust. Spencer never understood why I voluntarily discussed that pill or why I readily accepted my father's argument. He told his friends, who told their friends, which forced a retreat down those familiar steps towards isolation. But my center held. My support system pushed me back on track, and I circled right back to my family's arms.

"Ryder, now you know," my father said. "Never give yourself to anybody unless they give everything back to you." He ruffled my hair until I laughed.

"Mom said I would know what those words meant when the time came. She made me promise, but I didn't understand."

"She did. I know. She told me. She made me promise things too."

"Do you know she has a locket from the first boy she kissed?"

"I do. It has a stone in it." He winked. "Do you want to put a pill in a locket, so you can tell your daughter about your first crush?"

I loved my dad.

"How do you know when they'll give you everything back?"

"It becomes clear with time."

"Just tell me, so I won't make the same mistake."

"It doesn't work that way. Love is hard, and the only way to know you've found it is to know when you haven't."

My new dad, the same as the old.

Maybe even better.

Ryder Stephens Scott

ABOUT THE AUTHOR

Veronica Ventura is an American Gynecologist and a global public health practitioner. She has worked in remote places such as Somali refugee camps, Ebola Treatment Centers, and villages in Timor Leste, Ladakh, India, and Cambodia. As an author, she attributes her success in character development to the diverse experiences in her medical career.

Dr. Ventura is a graduate of the University of California at Davis, Tulane University School of Medicine, and the Harvard T.H. Chan School of Public Health. She lives in Singapore with her husband, four cats, and two dogs: Ryder and Samantha.